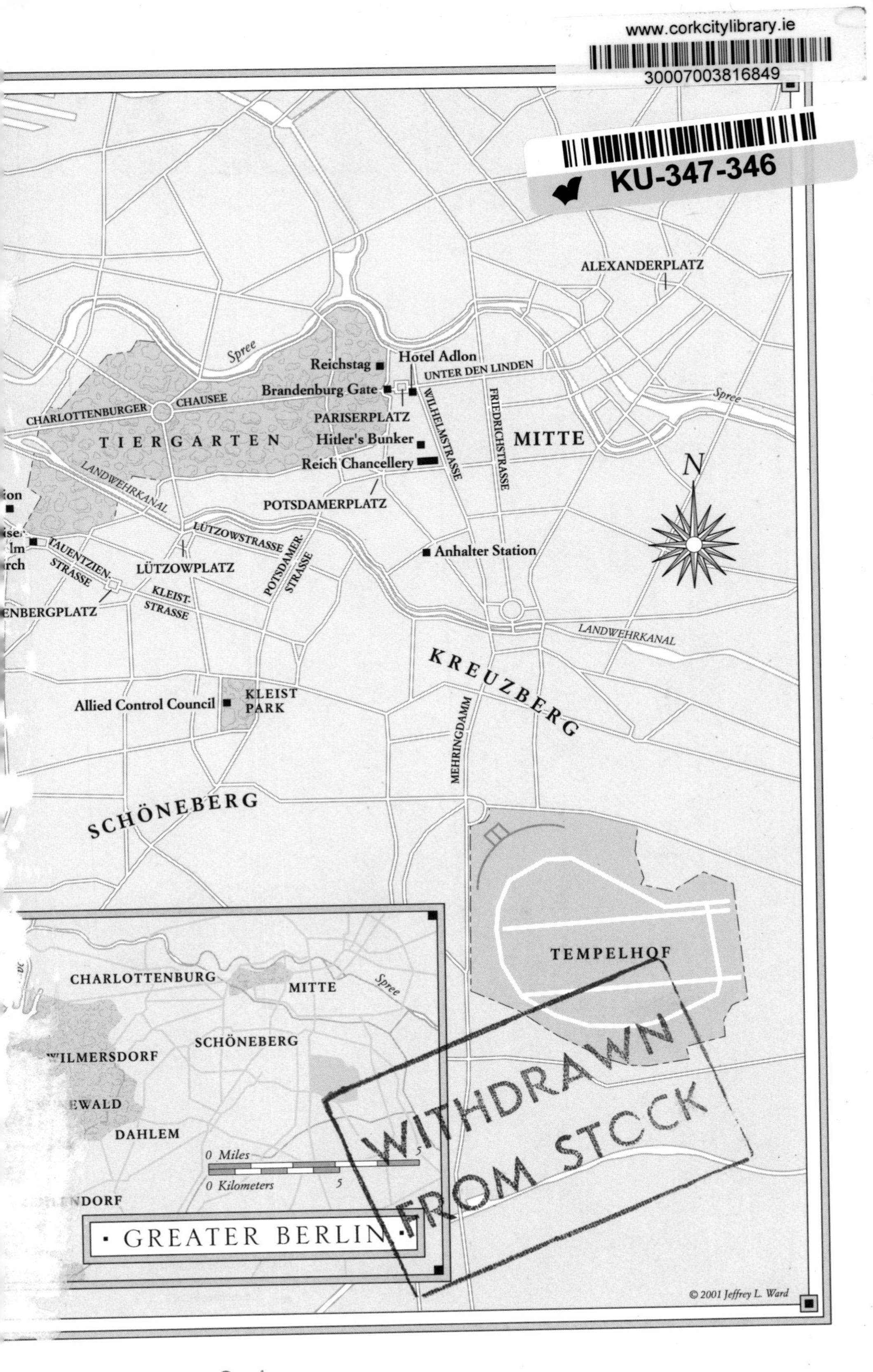
ALEXANDERPLATZ
Spree
Hotel Adlon
Reichstag
UNTER DEN LINDEN
Brandenburg Gate
CHARLOTTENBURGER
CHAUSEE
PARISERPLATZ
WILHELMSTRASSE
FRIEDRICHSTRASSE
Spree
TIERGARTEN
Hitler's Bunker
MITTE
Reich Chancellery
N
LANDWEHRKANAL
POTSDAMERPLATZ
LÜTZOWSTRASSE
TAUENTZIEN-STRASSE
POTSDAMER-STRASSE
Anhalter Station
LÜTZOWPLATZ
KLEIST-STRASSE
LANDWEHRKANAL
KREUZBERG
KLEIST PARK
Allied Control Council
MEHRINGDAMM
SCHÖNEBERG
TEMPELHOF
CHARLOTTENBURG
MITTE
Spree
SCHÖNEBERG
WILMERSDORF
DAHLEM
0 Miles 5
0 Kilometers 5
GREATER BERLIN
© 2001 Jeffrey L. Ward

THE GOOD GERMAN

ALSO BY JOSEPH KANON

Los Alamos
The Prodigal Spy

THE GOOD GERMAN

A NOVEL

JOSEPH KANON

LITTLE, BROWN

A *Little, Brown* Book

First published in the United States in 2001
by Henry Holt and Company, LLC

First published in Great Britain in 2001
by Little, Brown

*All characters in this publication are fictitious
and any resemblance to real persons, living or dead,
is purely coincidental.*

A CIP catalogue record for this book
is available from the British Library.

ISBN 0 316 85196 5

Printed and bound in Great Britain
by Clays Ltd, St Ives plc

Little, Brown
An imprint of
Time Warner Books UK
Brettenham House
Lancaster Place
London WC2E 7EN

www.TimeWarnerBooks.co.uk

For my mother

Author's Note

The Good German takes place in Berlin in July and August of 1945. Any story set in the past runs the inevitable risk of error. This is particularly true of Berlin, whose map has been changed by history several times this past century, and certainly of the chaotic first few months of the Allied occupation, when events happened in such rapid succession that their chronology is often confused even in contemporary accounts, not to mention faulty memory. The alert reader, however, is entitled to know when deliberate liberties have been taken for narrative convenience. The Allies did indeed capture vast quantities of Nazi documents, but it was nearly a year before the Document Center in Wasserkäfersteig, described here, was fully operational. The Allied victory parade actually took place on September 7 and not, as here, three weeks earlier. Readers familiar with the period will know the American occupation authority as OMGUS (Office of Military Government, United States), but this designation was not official until October 1945, so an easier form, MG, is used here rather than the more unwieldy but correct USGCC (United States Group, Control Council). Any other errors, alas, are unintentional.

I

Ruins

CHAPTER ONE

THE WAR HAD made him famous. Not as famous as Murrow, the voice of London, and not as famous as Quent Reynolds, now the voice of the documentaries, but famous enough to get a promise from *Collier's* ("four pieces, if you can get there") and then the press pass to Berlin. In the end, it was Hal Reidy who'd made the difference, juggling the press slots like seating arrangements, UP next to Scripps-Howard, down the table from Hearst, who'd assigned too many people anyway.

"I can't get you out till Monday, though. They won't give us another plane, not with the conference on. Unless you've got some pull."

"Only you."

Hal grinned. "You're in worse shape than I thought. Say hello to Nanny Wendt for me, the prick." Their censor from the old days, before the war, when they'd both been with Columbia, a nervous little man, prim as a governess, who liked to run a pen through their copy just before they went on the air. "The Ministry of Propaganda *and*

Public Enlightenment," Hal said, the way he always did. "I wonder what happened to him. Goebbels poisoned his own kids, I hear."

"No. Magda," Jake said. "The *gnädige frau.* In chocolates."

"Yeah, sweets to the sweet. Nice people." He handed Jake the traveling orders. "Have a good time."

"You should come too. It's a historic occasion."

"So's this," Hal said, pointing to another set of orders. "Two more weeks and I'm home. Berlin. Christ. I couldn't wait to get out. And you want to go back?"

Jake shrugged. "It's the last big story of the war."

"Sitting around a table, divvying up the pot."

"No. What happens when it's over."

"What happens is, you go home."

"Not yet."

Hal glanced up. "You think she's still there," he said flatly.

Jake put the orders in his pocket, not answering.

"It's been a while, you know. Things happen."

Jake nodded. "She'll be there. Thanks for this. I owe you one."

"More than one," Hal said, letting it go. "Just write pretty. And don't miss the plane."

But the plane was hours late getting into Frankfurt, then hours on the ground unloading and turning around, so it was midafternoon before they took off. The C-47 was a drafty military transport fitted out with benches along the sides, and the passengers, a spillover of journalists who, like Jake, hadn't made the earlier flights, had to shout over the engines. After a while Jake gave up and sat back with his eyes closed, feeling queasy as the plane bumped its way east. There had been drinks while they waited, and Brian Stanley, the *Daily Express* man who had somehow attached himself to the American group, was already eloquently drunk, with most of the others not far behind. Belser from Gannett, and Cowley, who'd kept tabs on the SHAEF press office from a bar stool at the Scribe, and Gimbel, who had traveled with Jake following Patton into Germany. They had all been at war forever, in their khakis with the round correspondent patch, even Liz Yeager, the photographer, wearing a heavy pistol on her hip, cowgirl style.

He'd known all of them one way or another, their faces like pins in his own war map. London, where he'd finally left Columbia in '42 because he wanted to see the fighting war. North Africa, where he saw it and caught a piece of shrapnel. Cairo, where he recovered and drank the nights away with Brian Stanley. Sicily, missing Palermo but managing, improbably, to get on with Patton, so that later, after France, he joined him again for the race east. Across Hesse and Thuringia, everything accelerated, the stop-and-go days of fitful waiting over, finally a war of clear, running adrenaline. Weimar. Then, finally, up to Nordhausen, and Camp Dora, where everything stopped. Two days of staring, not even able to talk. He wrote down numbers—two hundred a day—and then stopped that too. A newsreel camera filmed the stacks of bodies, jutting bones and floppy genitals. The living, with their striped rags and shaved heads, had no sex.

On the second day, at one of the slave labor camps, a skeleton took his hand and kissed it, then held on to it, an obscene gratitude, gibbering something in Slavic—Polish? Russian?—and Jake froze, trying not to smell, feeling his hand buckle under the weight of the fierce grip. "I'm not a soldier," he said, wanting to run but unable to take his hand away, ashamed, caught now too. The story they'd all missed, the hand you couldn't shake off.

"Old home week for you, boyo, isn't it?" Brian said, cupping his hands to be heard.

"You've been before?" Liz said, curious.

"Lived here. One of Ed's boys, darling, didn't you know?" Brian said. "Till the jerries chucked him out. Of course, they chucked everybody out. Had to, really. Considering."

"So you speak German?" Liz said. "Thank god somebody does."

"Berliner *deutsch,*" Brian answered for him, a tease.

"I don't care what kind of *deutsch* it is," she said, "as long as it's *deutsch.*" She patted Jake's knees. "You stick with me, Jackson," she said, like Phil Harris on the radio. Then, "What was it like?"

Well, what was it like? A vise slowly closing. In the beginning, the parties and the hot days on the lakes and the fascination of events. He had come to cover the Olympics in '36 and his mother knew somebody who knew the Dodds, so there were embassy cocktails and a special seat in their box at the stadium. Goebbels' big party on the Pfaueninsel, the trees decked out in thousands of lights shaped like butterflies, officers swaggering along the footpaths, drunk on champagne and importance, throwing up in the bushes. The Dodds were appalled. He stayed. The Nazis supplied the headlines, and even a stringer could live on the rumors, watching the war come day by day. By the time he signed on with Columbia, the vise had shut, rumors now just little gasps for air. The city contracted around him, so that at the end it was a closed circle: the Foreign Press Club in Potsdamerplatz, up the gloomy Wilhelmstrasse to the ministry for the twice-daily briefings, on up to the Adlon, where Columbia kept a room for Shirer and they gathered at the raised bar, comparing notes and watching the SS lounging around the fountain below, their shiny boots on the rim while the bronze frog statues spouted jets of water toward the skylight. Then out the East-West Axis to the broadcasting station on Adolf Hitler Platz and the endless wrangling with Nanny Wendt, then a taxi home to the tapped telephone and the watchful eye of Herr Lechter, the *blockleiter* who lived in the apartment down the hall, snapped up from some hapless Jews. No air. But that had been at the end.

"It was like Chicago," he said. Blunt and gritty and full of itself, a new city trying to be old. Clumsy Wilhelmine palaces that always looked like banks, but also jokes with an edge and the smell of spilled beer. Sharp midwestern air.

"Chicago? It won't look like Chicago now." This, surprisingly, from the bulky civilian in a business suit, introduced at the airport as a congressman from upstate New York.

"No, indeed," Brian said, mischievous. "All banged about now. Still, what isn't? Whole bloody country's one big bomb site. Do you mind my asking? I've never known. What does one call a congressman? I mean, are you The Honorable?"

"Technically. That's what it says on the envelopes, anyway. But we just use Congressman—or Mister."

"Mister. Very democratic."

"Yes, it is," the congressman said, humorless.

"You with the conference or have you just come for a look-in?" Brian said, playing with him.

"I'm not attending the conference, no."

"Just come to see the raj, then."

"Meaning?"

"Oh, no offense. It's very like, though, wouldn't you say? Military Government. Pukkah sahibs, really."

"I don't know what you're talking about."

"Well, neither do I, half the time," Brian said pleasantly. "Just a little conceit of mine. Never mind. Here, have a drink," he said, taking another, his forehead sweaty.

The congressman ignored him, turning instead to the young soldier wedged next to him, a last-minute arrival, no duffel, maybe a courier. He was wearing a pair of high riding boots, and his hands were gripping the bench like reins, his face white under a sprinkling of freckles.

"First time in Berlin?" the congressman said.

The soldier nodded, holding his seat even tighter as the plane bounced.

"Got a name, son?" Making conversation.

"Lieutenant Tully," he said, then gulped, covering his mouth.

"You all right?" Liz said to him.

The soldier took off his hat. His red hair was damp.

"Here, just in case," she said, handing him a paper bag.

"How much longer?" he said, almost a moan, holding the bag to his chest with one hand.

The congressman looked at him and involuntarily moved his leg in the tight space, out of harm's way, turning his body slightly so that he was forced to face Brian again.

"You're from New York, you said?"

"Utica, New York."

"Utica," Brian said, making a show of trying to place it. "Breweries, yes?" Jake smiled. In fact, Brian knew the States well. "Fair number of Germans there, if I'm not mistaken."

The congressman looked at him in distaste. "My district is one hundred percent American."

But Brian was bored now. "I daresay," he said, looking away.

"How did you get on this plane anyway? I understood it was for American press."

"Well, there's Allied feeling for you," Brian said to Jake.

The plane dropped slightly, not much more than a dip in a road, but evidently enough for the soldier, who groaned.

"I'm going to be sick," he said, barely opening the bag in time.

"Careful," the congressman said, trapped.

"Just get it out," Liz said to the soldier, a big-sister voice. "That's it. You'll be all right."

"Sorry," he said, half choking, clearly embarrassed, looking suddenly no older than a teenager.

Liz turned away from the boy. "Did you ever meet Hitler?" she asked Jake, the question bringing the others with her, as if she were drawing a privacy curtain in place for the soldier.

"Meet, no. Saw, yes," Jake said. "Lots of times."

"Up close, I mean."

"Once," he said.

A sultry early evening, coming up from the Press Club, the street almost in shadow, but the new Chancellery still catching the last of the light. Prussian *moderne,* the broad steps leading down to the waiting car. Just an aide and two guards, curiously unprotected. On his way to the Sportpalast, probably, for another harangue against the devious Poles. He stopped for a second near the bottom stairs, looking down the empty street at Jake. I could reach into my pocket now, Jake had thought. One shot, put an end to all of it, that easy. Why hadn't anyone done it? Then, as if the thought had carried like a scent, Hitler raised his head and sniffed, anxious as prey, and looked back at Jake. One shot. He held the look for a second, assessing, then smiled, just a twitch of the mustache, lifted his hand in a languid *heil* of dismissal, and headed toward the car. Gloating. There was no gun, and he had things to do.

"They say the eyes were hypnotic," Liz said.

"I don't know. I never got that close," Jake said, shutting his own, making the rest of the plane go away.

Not long now. He'd go to Pariserstrasse first. He saw the door, the heavy sandstone caryatids holding up the balcony over the entrance. What would she say? Four years. But maybe she'd moved. No, she'd be there. A few more hours. A drink at the café down the street in Olivaerplatz, catching up, years of stories. Unless they stayed in.

"Pleasant dreams?" Liz said, and he realized he was smiling, already there. Berlin. Not long now.

"We're coming in," Brian said, his face at the little window. "God. Come have a look."

Jake opened his eyes and jumped up, a kid. They crowded around the window, the congressman at their side.

"My god," Brian said again, almost in a hush, silenced by the view. "Bloody Carthage."

Jake looked down at the ground, his stomach suddenly dropping, all his excitement draining away like blood. Why hadn't anyone told him? He had seen bombed cities before—on the ground in London, ripped-up terrace houses and streets of glass, then Cologne and Frankfurt from the air, with their deep craters and damaged churches—but nothing on this scale. Carthage, a destruction out of the ancient world. Below them there seemed to be no movement. Shells of houses, empty as ransacked tombs, miles and miles of them, whole pulverized stretches where there were not even walls. They had come in from the west, over the lakes, so he knew it must be Lichterfelde, then Steglitz, the approach to Tempelhof, but landmarks had disappeared under shifting dunes of rubble. As they dropped lower, scattered buildings took shape, smashed but there, a few chimneys sticking up, even a steeple. Some kind of life must still be going on. A beige cloud hung over everything—not smoke, a thick haze of soot and plaster dust, as if the houses could not quite bring themselves to leave. But Berlin was gone. The Big Three were coming to divide up ruins.

"Well, they got what they deserved," the congressman said suddenly, a jarring American voice. Jake looked at him. A politician at a wake. "Didn't they?" he said, a little defiantly.

Brian turned slowly from the window, his eyes filled with scorn. "Boyo, we all get what we deserve. In the end."

Tempelhof was a mess around the edges, but the field had been cleared and the terminal itself was still there. After the tomb city they'd seen from the air, the airport seemed dizzy with life, swarming with uniformed ground crews and greeters. A young lieutenant, full of hair and chewing gum, was waiting at the foot of the stairs, picking out faces as they disembarked. The sick soldier had staggered down first, running off, Jake guessed, for the men's room.

"Geismar?" The lieutenant stuck out his hand. "Ron Erlich, press office. I've got you and Miss Yeager. She on board?"

Jake nodded. "With these," he said, indicating the cases he'd been lugging off the plane. "Want to give me a hand?"

"What's she got in there, her trousseau?"

"Equipment," Liz said behind him. "You going to make cracks or give the man a hand?"

Ron took in the uniform, with its unexpected curves, and smiled. "Yes, sir," he said, giving a mock salute, then picked up the cases in one easy movement, impressing a date. "This way." He led them toward the building. "Colonel Howley sends his regards," he said to Liz. "Says he remembers you from his days in the ad business."

Liz grinned. "Don't worry. I'll take his picture."

Ron grinned back. "You remember him too, I guess."

"Vividly. Hey, careful with that. Lenses."

They went up the gate stairs behind the congressman, who seemed to have acquired an entourage, and into the waiting hall, the same tawny marble walls and soaring space as before, when flying had been a romance. People had come to the restaurant here, just to watch the planes. Jake hurried to keep up. Ron moved the way he talked, breezing a path through the gangs of waiting servicemen.

"You missed the president," he said. "Went into town after lunch. Had the whole Second Armored lined up on the Avus. Quite a picture. Sorry your plane was so late, that's probably it for town shots."

"Wasn't he at the conference?" Liz said.

"Hasn't started yet. Uncle Joe's late. They say he has a cold."

"A cold?" Jake said.

"Hard to imagine, isn't it? Truman's pissed, I hear." He glanced at Jake. "That's off the record, by the way."

"What's on?"

"Not much. I've got some handouts for you, but you'll probably throw them away. Everybody else does. There's nothing to say till they sit down, anyway. We have a briefing schedule set up at the press camp."

"Which is where?"

"Down the road from MG headquarters. Argentinischeallee," he said, rolling it out, a joke name.

"Out in Dahlem?" Jake said, placing it.

"Everything's out in Dahlem."

"Why not somewhere nearer the center?"

Ron looked at him. "There is no center."

They were climbing the big flight of stairs to the main entrance doors.

"As I say, the camp's right by MG headquarters, so that's easy. Your billet too. We found a nice place for you," he said to Liz, almost courtly. "Photo schedule's different, but at least you'll get out there. Potsdam, I mean."

"But not press?" Jake said.

Ron shook his head. "They want a closed session. No press. I'm telling you this now so I don't have to hear you squawk later, like the rest of them. I don't make the rules, so if you want to complain, go right over my head, I don't care. We'll do the best we can at the camp. Everything you need. You can send from there, but your stuff goes through me, you might as well know."

Jake looked at him, forced to smile. A new Nanny Wendt, this time with gum and get-up-and-go.

"Whatever happened to freedom of the press?"

"Don't worry. You'll get plenty of copy. We'll have a briefing after every session. Besides, everybody talks."

"And what do we do between briefings?"

"Drink, mostly. At least that's what they've been doing." He turned to Jake. "It's not as if Stalin gives interviews, you know. Here we go," he said, swinging through the doors. "I'll get you out to your billet. You probably want to clean up."

"Hot water?" Liz said.

"Sure. All the comforts of home."

In the driveway the congressman was being bundled into a requisitioned Horch with an American flag painted on the side, the others into open jeeps. Beyond them, at the end of the drive, were the first houses, not one of them intact. Jake stared, everything emptying out again. Not an aerial glimpse anymore; worse. A few standing walls, pitted by artillery shells. Mounds of debris, broken concrete and plumbing fixtures. One building had been sliced through, a strip of wallpaper hanging off an exposed room, scorch marks around the window holes. How would he ever find her in this? The same dust he'd seen from the plane, suspended in the air, making the afternoon light dull. And now the smell, sour wet masonry and open earth, like a raw building site, and something else, which he assumed was bodies, still lying somewhere under the rubble.

"Welcome to Berlin," Ron said.

"Is it all like this?" Liz said quietly.

"Most of it. If the roof's gone, it was bombs. Otherwise, the Russians. They say the shelling was worse. Just blew it all to hell." He threw the bags into the jeep. "Hop in."

"You two go on ahead," Jake said, still looking at the street. "Something I want to do first."

"Hop in," Ron said, an order. "What do you think you're going to do, get a taxi?"

Liz looked at Jake's face, then turned to Ron and smiled. "What's the rush? Take him where he wants to go. You can give me a tour on the way." She patted the camera slung around her neck, then put it up to her eye, crouching down. "Smile." She snapped his picture, busy Tempelhof behind.

Ron glanced at his watch, pretending not to pose. "We don't have a lot of time."

"A little tour," Liz said, wheedling, snapping a few more. "Isn't that part of the service?"

He sighed. "I suppose you want to see the bunker. Everyone wants to see the bunker, and there's nothing to see. The Russians don't let you in anyway, say it's flooded. Maybe Adolf's floating around down there, who knows? But it's their sector and they can do what they want." He smiled back at Liz. "You can get the Reichstag, though. Everybody wants a picture of that and the Russians don't care."

"You're on," she said, lowering the camera.

"If I can get us there. I know the way from Dahlem, but—"

Liz jerked her thumb toward Jake. "He used to live here."

"You navigate then," Ron said, shrugging, and motioned Liz into the jeep. "You can ride up front." Another grin.

"Lucky me. Just keep your hands on the wheel. The whole U.S. Army's got this problem with their hands."

Jake paid no attention, the flirting a harmless buzz beside him. Some people had emerged from one of the piles of rubble, two women, and he watched them pick their way carefully over the bricks, listless, as if they were still shell-shocked. In the July heat they were wearing overcoats, afraid to leave them home in the basement of the ruined house, where everything, maybe even themselves, must be open for the taking. What had it been like these last few months? Carthage. Maybe she was like these two, burrowed in somewhere. But where? He realized for the first time, looking at the women, that he might not find her at all, that the bombs must have scattered people too, like bricks. But maybe not. He turned to the jeep, suddenly anxious to get there, a pointless urgency, as if everything that could have happened to her had not already happened.

He lifted himself into the back, next to Liz's cases.

"Where first, the bunker?" Ron said to Liz, who nodded. He turned to Jake. "Which way?"

Not where he wanted to go, but stuck with it now, a favor to Liz. "Turn right at the end."

Ron let out the clutch. "Don't bother taking notes. Everybody says the same thing anyway. Lunar landscape. That's the big one. And teeth. Rows of decayed teeth. AP had rotting *molars*. But maybe you'll come up with something original. Be nice, something new."

"How would you describe it?"

"Can't," Ron said, no longer flip. "Maybe nobody can. It's—well, see for yourself."

Jake headed them north on the Mehringdamm, but they were forced to detour east and in minutes were lost, streets blocked off or impassable, the whole map redrawn by debris. Five minutes back and already lost. They threaded their way through the ruins, Ron glancing back at him as if he were a broken compass until, luckily, another detour put them on the Mehringdamm again. A cleared stretch this time, which would get them to the Landwehrkanal, an easier route to follow than the unpredictable roads. Only the major streets had passable lanes, the others reduced to winding footpaths, when they were visible at all. Berlin, a flat city, finally had contours, new hills of brick. There was no life. Once he spotted children skittering over the rubble like crickets, and a working detail of women reclaiming bricks, their heads wrapped in kerchiefs against the dust, but otherwise the streets were quiet. The silence unnerved him. Berlin had always been a noisy city, the elevated S-bahn trains roaring across their trestle bridges, radios crackling in the apartment block courtyards, cars screeching at red lights, drunks arguing. Now he could hear the motor of the jeep and the eerie creaking of a single bicycle ahead of them, nothing else. A cemetery quiet. At night it would be pitch dark, the other side of the moon. Ron had been right—the unavoidable cliché.

At the Landwehrkanal there was more activity, but the smell was worse, raw sewage and corpses still floating on the water. The Russians had been here two months; had there been so many to fish out? But there they were, bodies stuck on the piles of the wrecked bridges or just suspended face down in the middle of the canal, held in place by nothing but the stagnant water. Liz had dropped her camera to hold a handkerchief over her mouth against the smell. No one said a word. Across the water, Hallesches Tor was gone.

They followed the canal toward the Potsdamer bridge, which took traffic. At one of the footbridges he saw his first men, shuffling across in gray Wehrmacht uniforms, still in retreat. He thought, inevitably, of the night he'd seen the transports set out for Poland, a big public display down the Linden, square-jawed faces out of a newsreel. These were blank and unshaven and almost invisible; women simply walked around them, not looking up.

There were landmarks now—the Reichstag in the far distance, and here in Potsdamerplatz the jagged remains of the department stores. Wertheim's gone. A burned-out truck had been pushed to the side, but there was no traffic to block, just a few bicycles and some Russian soldiers leading a horse-drawn wagon. The old crowded intersection now had the feel of a silent movie, without the jerky rhythm. Instead, everything passed by in slow motion, even the bicycles, wary of punctures, and the wagon, plodding down a street as empty as the steppes. How many nights of bombing had it taken? Near the truck, a family sat on suitcases, staring into the street. Maybe just arrived at Anhalter Station, waiting for a phantom bus, or too tired and disoriented to go on.

"You have to feel sorry for the poor bastards," Ron said, "you really do."

"Who, the Germans?" Liz said.

"Yeah, I know. Still."

They turned up the Wilhelmstrasse. Goering's new Air Ministry, or its shell, had survived, but the rest of the street, the long line of pompous government buildings, lay in sooty heaps, their bricks spilling into the street like running sores. Where it had all started.

There was a crowd near the Chancellery, an unexpected popping of flashbulbs. Scattered applause.

"Look, it's Churchill," Liz said, grabbing her camera. "Pull over."

"Guess they all want the tour," Ron said, pretending to be bored but staring nevertheless at the stairs, starstruck.

Jake got out. Just where Hitler had stood smiling. Now it was Churchill, in a light summer uniform, cigar clenched in his teeth, surrounded by reporters. Brian next to him. How did he get here so fast?

But Brian's corklike ability to bob up everywhere was legendary. Churchill was stopping on the stairs, disconcerted by the applause. He raised his fingers in a V sign, a reflex, then dropped them, confused, aware suddenly of where he was. Jake glanced at the crowd. It was British soldiers who were applauding. The Germans stood silently, then moved away, embarrassed perhaps by their own curiosity, like people at an accident. Churchill frowned and hurried to the car.

"Let's take a look," Jake said.

"You out of your mind? And leave a jeep full of cameras?" Churchill's car was pulling away, the crowd following. Ron lit a cigarette and sat back. "Go ahead. I'll hold the fort. Bring me a souvenir, if there's anything left."

There were Russian guards at the entrance, squat Mongols armed with rifles, but they seemed to be no more than a show of force, since people went in and out at will and there was, in any case, nothing to guard. Jake led Liz past the entrance hall with its gaping roof, then down the long reception gallery. Soldiers roamed through the building, sifting through the wreckage for medals, something to carry away. The huge chandeliers lay in the middle of the floor, one of them still suspended a few feet above the litter. Nothing had been cleared away. It was somehow more shocking than the bomb damage outside, the visible fury of the final assault, a destructive madness. Furniture smashed to pieces, its upholstery ripped open by bayonets; paintings slashed. Drawers looted and then flung aside. In Hitler's office, the giant marble desktop was overturned, its edges chipped away for keepsake fragments. Papers everywhere, stamped with muddy boot marks. All the disturbing evidence of a rampage. The Mongolian horde. He imagined the guards outside shouting as they raced through the halls, ripping and grabbing.

"What do you think these are?" Liz said, holding up a fistful of cards, blank pieces of stationery edged in gold, the Nazi eagle and swastika engraved at the top.

"Invitations." He fingered one. The Führer requests your presence. Tea. Boxes of them. Enough to last a thousand years.

"Just like Mrs. Astor," Liz said, stuffing a few in her pocket. "That's something, isn't it?"

"Let's go," he said, unsettled by the mess.

"Just let me get a few shots," she said, taking a picture of the room.

Two GIs, hearing English, came over to her and handed her a camera.

"Hey, how about it? Do you mind?"

Liz grinned. "Sure. Over there by the desk?"

"Can you get the swastika in?"

A massive ornamental swastika, lying face down on the floor. They each planted a leg on it, one slinging his arm over the other's shoulders, and grinned at the camera. Kids.

"One more," Liz said. "The light's bad." She clicked, then looked at their camera. "Where'd you get this, anyway? Haven't seen one of these since the war."

"You kidding? They're practically giving them away. Try over by the Reichstag. Couple of bottles of Canadian Club should do it. You just got in, huh?"

"Just."

"How about I buy you a drink? I could show you around."

"Now, what would your mother say?"

"Hey."

"Easy," she said, smiling, then nodded toward Jake. "Besides, he gets mean."

The GI glanced at Jake, then winked at her. "Maybe next time then, babe. Thanks for the picture."

"There's one for the books," she said to Jake as the GIs moved away. "I never thought I'd get picked up in Hitler's office."

Jake looked at her, surprised. He had never thought of her being picked up at all. Now he saw that, scrubbed of combat dirt and bluff, she was attractive. "Babe," he said, amused.

"Where's the bunker?"

"There, I guess." He pointed through the window to the back courtyard, where a group of Russian soldiers stood guard. A small concrete blockhouse, a scarred, empty patch of ground. The two GIs were being turned away but offered cigarettes around until the guards stepped aside to let them take a picture. Jake thought of Egypt, the valley of bunkers where the pharaohs had gone to ground, in love with death. But even they hadn't taken their city with them.

"They say he married her at the end," Liz said.

While the Russians ran wild overhead, the very last hour.

"Let's hope it meant something to her."

"It always does," she said lightly, then glanced at him. "I'll come back. I can see you're not in the mood."

Everybody wants to see the bunker, Ron had said. The last act, right down to the ghoulish wedding and finally, too late, the one shot. Now a story for the magazines. Did Eva have flowers? A champagne toast, before they put the dog down and Magda murdered her children.

"It's not a shrine," Jake said, still looking out the window. "They should bulldoze it over."

"After I get my picture," Liz said.

They moved back into the gloom of the long gallery. There were the broken-up chairs again, stuffing bursting out of the bayonet slashes. Why had the Russians left it like this? Some kind of barbarous lesson? But who was here to learn it? GIs were taking pictures by the fallen chandeliers, oblivious tourists. Near the wall was a heap of medals, thrown out of drawers. Iron Crosses. When Jake bent over to pick one up, a souvenir for Ron, he felt like a gravedigger scavenging through remains.

The uneasy mood followed him up the street, the mountains of rubble no longer an impersonal landscape but the Berlin he'd known, a part of his life knocked out too. At the corner, Unter den Linden was gray with ash. Even the Adlon had been bombed.

"No," Ron corrected him. "The Russians burned it, after the battle. No one knows why. Drunk, probably."

He looked away. But what was a building, compared to the rest of it? The hands you couldn't shake off. Across the square, the Brandenburg Gate was standing, but the Quadriga had skidded off its mount, like a chariot overturned in a race. Red flags and posters of Lenin were draped on the columns, hiding some of the shell holes. As they passed into the Tiergarten he could see a large crowd milling in front of the Reichstag, GIs exchanging their bottles of Canadian Club, Russian soldiers examining wristwatches. Some of the Germans, like the two women near Tempelhof, wore overcoats in the hot afternoon, presumably to hide whatever they'd brought to sell. Cigarettes, tins of food, antique porcelain clocks. The new Wertheim's. A few young girls in summer dresses were hanging on to soldiers' arms. In front of the Reichstag, its charred walls covered with Cyrillic graffiti, soldiers were posing for pictures, another stop on the new tourist circuit.

At the park he hit bottom. Buildings, like soldiers, were expected casualties of war. But the trees were gone too, all of them. The dense forest of the Tiergarten, all the winding paths and silly, tucked-away statues, had burned down to a vast open field littered with dark charcoal stumps and the twisted metal of streetlamps. The jeep was heading west along the Axis, and in the far distance, over Charlottenburg, the last of the sun had turned the sky red, so that for a moment Jake could imagine the fires still burning, glowing all night to guide the bombers. A fragment of one had fallen, and a single propeller stuck up out of the ground, a surreal piece of junk, like those old refrigerators and rusting tractor parts you sometimes saw on the front yards of poor farms.

"Jesus H. Christ," Liz said, "look at them."

A landscape full of people, moving slowly all around them. Suitcases. Clothes tied up in bundles. A few handcarts and baby carriages. The movement of exhaustion, one step at a time. Old people, and families with no bags at all. Displaced Persons, the new euphemism. No one begged or called out, just trudged past. Going where? Relatives in a cellar? A new camp, delousing and a bowl of soup and no further address? Stunned to find, in the heart of the city, a wasteland worse than the one they had left. Yet they were moving somewhere, a survivors' trek, just like the ones in the old engravings, wandering through the burned landscape of the Thirty Years' War.

It wasn't supposed to end this way, Jake thought. But how else? Parades? Berlin as vibrant as ever, with the Nazis taken away? How else? The odd thing was, he'd never imagined it ending. There'd been no life outside the war, just one story that led to the next and then another. And now the last one, what happens when it's over. You go home, Hal had said. Where he hadn't been in ten years. So he'd come back to Berlin, another DP in the Tiergarten. Except he was in a jeep, flying past the stragglers, with a sassy girl taking pictures and a driver lighting another cigarette worth a meal. The people on foot merely glanced at them without expression, then kept going. He realized, with an unexpected lurch, that what they saw was a conqueror, one of the priapic teenagers and souvenir hunters, not a homecoming Berliner. That delusion was gone now too, with everything else.

But something must be left. Years of his life. People survived, even this. He ordered Ron to turn at the Victory Column and aimed them down toward the flak towers at the Zoo, his eyes still cataloguing the missing. The Kaiser Wilhelm Church, its steeple blown away. Kranzler's in bits. More people now. The Kurfürstendamm smashed but recognizable. No glass in the storefronts or the display boxes along the sidewalks, but occasional buildings, roulette winners in the bombing. Left down the Fasanenstrasse.

"This is out of our way," Ron said.

"I know. I want to see something," Jake said, his voice edgy, expectant.

A right past the Ludwigkirche, a route he could follow blindfolded, after all the nights in the blackout. The chestnut trees were gone, so that the street seemed in a kind of unnatural glare, clear all the way to Olivaerplatz.

"Stop here," he said suddenly. They had overshot it, because there was nothing there. For a moment he simply stared, then got out of the jeep and walked slowly over to the pile of rubble. Nothing. Five stories, collapsed, the light brown façade lying now in slabs. Even the heavy wrought-iron-and-glass door had been blasted away. Crazily, he looked around for the caryatids. Gone. A washbasin perched on one of the mounds of broken plaster.

"Is this where you lived?" Liz said, her voice loud in the deserted street. He heard a camera click.

"No," Jake said. "Someone else."

They'd only come here a few times, when Emil was away. Afternoons, the leafy branches outside making patterns on the drawn shades. Sheets damp with sweat. Teasing her because she covered up afterward, pulling the sheet over her breasts, even as her hair lay tangled and moist on the pillow, as illicit as the warm afternoon, the room where they shouldn't be, their time together.

"You didn't mind before."

"That was before. I can't help it. I'm modest." She met his eyes, then started to laugh, a bed laugh, intimate as touch. She turned on her side. "How can you joke?"

He fell down next to her. "It's supposed to be fun."

She put her hand along the side of his face. "Fun for you," she said, but smiling because the sex was playful, part of their other excitement, getting away with something.

The early days, before the guilt.

He walked toward a small pathway in the debris. Maybe someone was still living in the cellar. But the path led nowhere. There was nothing but rubble and the cloying smell. Whose body? A stick with a piece of paper was wedged in the broken bits of plaster like a grave marker. He bent down to read it. Frau Dzuris, the fat woman on the ground floor, evidently still alive, had moved. A street he didn't recognize in Wilmersdorf. *Frau Dzuris is now residing*—the quaint, formal language of a receiving card. He took out his notebook and jotted down the address. A nice woman, fond of poppyseed cakes, whose son worked at Siemens and came to lunch every Sunday. The things you remember. He turned back to the jeep.

"Nobody home?" Ron said.

Jake stopped, then let it go and shook his head. "Not here, anyway." But somewhere. "How do they find anybody? With all this?"

Ron shrugged. "Bush telegraph. Ask the neighbors." Jake looked at the empty street. "Or message boards. You see them at the corners. 'Request information on the whereabouts of'—you know, like a Miss Lonelyhearts club." He caught Jake's expression. "I don't know," he said, still airy. "They do, though, somehow. If they're alive."

An awkward silence. Liz, who'd been watching Jake, turned to Ron. "Your mother raise you or did you just get this way by yourself?"

"Sorry," he said to Jake. "I didn't mean—"

"Skip it," Jake said wearily.

"Is this what you wanted to see? It's getting late."

"Yes, this was it," Jake said, climbing back into the jeep.

"Okay, Dahlem," Ron said.

Jake took a last look at the rubble. Why had he expected anything to be here? A cemetery. "Is there really hot water? I could use a bath."

"That's what everybody says," Ron said, cheerful again. "After. It's all the dust."

Their billet was a large villa in Gelferstrasse, a suburban street behind the Luftwaffe headquarters on Kronprinzenallee that now housed the Military Government. The Luftwaffe buildings were in the same style as Goering's ministry, gray streamlined masonry, here with decorative eagles jutting out of the cornices, poised for flight, but the compound bristled with American flags, flapping on the roofs and the aerials of cars lining the driveway. There was damage here too, burned-out patches where houses had been, but nothing like what they had just seen, and Gelferstrasse itself was in fairly good shape, almost peaceful, some of it still shaded by trees.

Jake had never spent much time in Dahlem, whose quiet streets, away from the center, reminded him of Hampstead, but the relief of seeing houses standing, with their traditional tile roofs and brass knockers, made it seem more familiar than it was. Most of the windowpanes were still missing, but the street had been swept free of glass, tidied up, and the smell that had followed them through the city was finally gone, the bodies swept away too in the general housecleaning.

The villa was a three-story pile of pale yellow stucco, not as lavish as the millionaire mansions up in Grunewald but substantial, the home probably of a professor from the Kaiser Wilhelm Institute a few streets away.

"I had to give the congressman the master bedroom," Ron said, an innkeeper leading them up the stairs, "but at least you won't have to double up. I can switch you later," he said to Liz. "He's only here a few days."

"Hit and run, huh?" Liz said.

"Nobody stays for long, except the MG personnel. They're all on the second floor. One more flight. Dinner's at seven, by the way."

"Where do the enlisted men stay?"

"All over. Mostly barracks down in the old Telefunken factory. Some over by Onkel Toms Hütte," he said, pronouncing it in English.

"Uncle Tom's Hut?" Liz said, amused. "Since when?"

"Since always. Their name. They like the book, I guess."

Jake's room must have belonged to the daughter of the house. There was a single bed with a pink chenille spread, floral wallpaper, and a vanity with a round mirror and pink ruffled skirt. Even the blackout drapes had been backed with pink fabric.

"Sweet."

"Yeah, well," Ron said. "Like I said, we can switch around in a few days."

"Never mind. I'll just think virginal thoughts."

Ron grinned. "That's one thing you won't have to worry about in

Berlin." He turned to the door. "Just leave any laundry on the chair. They'll pick it up later." And then, with a click, he was gone, taking his breeze with him.

Jake stared at the frilly room. *They* who? A house staff to fetch and carry, one of the spoils of victory. What had happened to the girl, requisitioned out of her pink cocoon? He walked over to the glass-topped vanity. A trace of powder, but otherwise cleared off, all the jars and tubes swept into some case on the way out. Idly he opened the drawers, empty except for a few publicity stills of Viktor Staal with pinholes in the corners, presumably no longer her dreamboat. But at least she'd had a room to leave. What about Lena? Did she pack her perfume bottles and compacts and get out in time, lucky, or linger until the roof caved in?

He lit a cigarette and walked over to the window, unbuttoning his shirt. The yard below had been dug up to make a vegetable garden, but the rows had become a muddy tangle, tramped over, he supposed, by the Russians foraging for food. Still, you could breathe here. The wounded city, just a few miles away, had already begun to fade, hidden by the trees and suburban houses, the way an anesthetic blotted up pain. He should have taken notes. But what was there to say? The story had already happened. From the looks of it, building by building, old men and teenagers sniping from doorways. Why had they held out? Waiting for the Americans, he'd heard. Anyone but the Russians. *The peace will be worse*—Goebbels' last warning, the only one that came true. So, the final madness. Whole streets on fire. There'd been roving packs of SS, hanging boys from lampposts as deserters. To make an example. In the camps they'd killed people right up to the last hour. Here they'd even turned on their own. Not war anymore, a bloodlust.

Jake hadn't filed a real story in two months, not since the camps; he had been waiting for Berlin. Now he felt that Berlin would defeat him too, that all the copy would end in Ron's lunar landscapes and decayed teeth, inadequate attempts at scale. He had run out of words. Personalize it. Not the thousands, just one. She'd be here. It wasn't too much to hope for, one survivor. He looked again at the garden. Near a shed in the back, a gray-haired woman was hanging wet clothes over an improvised line of rope. A *hausfrau*.

"But what are you going to do?" he'd said. "Come with me. I'll arrange it. I'll get you out."

"Out," she said, dismissing it, the word itself improbable. Then she shook her head. "No, it's better." She'd been sitting at her dressing table, still in her slip, perfectly made-up again, her nails red. "I'll be a *hausfrau,*" she'd said almost casually, putting on lipstick. "A good German *hausfrau.*" She lowered her eyes. "Not this, all the lies."

"They're not lies," he'd said, putting his hands on her shoulders.

She looked up at his face in the mirror. "The lies to him."

Down below, the gray-haired woman had spotted him in the window. She hesitated, then nodded in a servant's bow and picked up the wicker basket. He watched her cross the muddy yard. Personalize it. What had her war been like? Maybe she'd been one of the faithful, shouting her lungs out at the Sportpalast, now doing laundry for the enemy. Or maybe just a *hausfrau,* lucky to be alive. He crossed over to the bed, dropping his shirt. What did it matter either way? Losers' stories. Back home they'd want the glamour of the conference, Truman horse-trading with Stalin, the great world they'd won, not the rubble and the people in the Tiergarten with the future knocked out of them.

He took off the rest of his clothes and wrapped a towel around his waist. The bathroom was at the end of the hall, and he opened the door to a rush of steam and a surprised yelp.

"Oh."

Liz was in the tub, her breasts barely clearing the soapy water, wet hair swept back from her face.

"Don't you knock?"

"Sorry, I—" he said, but he didn't move, watching her slide down into the tub, covering herself, her flesh as pink as the vanity ruffle.

"Have a good look?"

"Sorry," he said again, embarrassed. A soft woman's body, without the uniform and gun holster, now hanging on a peg.

"Never mind," she said, smiling, a veteran of shared tents and field latrines. "Just keep your towel on. I'll be out in a sec."

She plunged her head into the water to rinse, then smoothed her hair back and reached for a towel.

"You going to turn around, or do you want the floor show too?"

He turned his back to her as she stepped out. A splash of water and a rustling of cloth, the sounds themselves intimate.

"I suppose I should take it as a compliment," she said, wrapping herself in a robe. "You never noticed before."

"Sure I did," he said, his back to her.

"Uh-huh." He could hear the water running down the drain in gulps. "Okay, decent."

She was in a silk wrapper, toweling her hair. He looked at her, then cocked his head like the young GI at the Chancellery.

"How about I buy you a drink later?"

"With my clothes on? Can't. I'm busy."

"That was fast. Not young Ron?"

She grinned. "I wouldn't have the strength." She fixed the towel around her head in a turban. "Just business. Have to see a man about a duck. I'll take a rain check, though." She nodded at the tub. "Better run your water. It takes a while." She gathered her things slowly from the stool, then sat down.

"Are you staying?"

"Jake? Tell me something. That business this afternoon—who was she?"

"Why a she?"

"Because it was. What's the story? You know I'll get it out of you eventually."

"No story," he said, turning on the taps. "She went back to her husband."

"Oh," she said, "that kind of story. She left you?"

"I left Berlin. Dr. Goebbels' request. There was an attitude problem."

"I'll bet. When was this?"

"'Forty-one. Did me a favor, I suppose. A few months later and I'd have been stuck." He waved his hand to take in the city. "In all this."

"So only she got stuck."

He looked at her for a moment, then went back to adjusting the taps.

"She stayed with her husband," he said flatly.

"I wouldn't have," she said, trying to be casual, a light apology. "Who was he? One of the master race?"

He smiled to himself. "Not too masterful. He was a teacher, actually. A professor."

"Of what?"

"Liz, what is all this?"

"Just making conversation. I don't often get you at a disadvantage. The only time a man will talk is when he has his pants off."

"Is that a fact." He paused. "Mathematics, since you ask."

"Math?" she said, laughing slightly, genuinely surprised. "An egghead? Not very sexy."

"It must have been. She married him."

"And slept with you. Mathematics. I mean, a ski instructor or something I could understand—"

"He did ski, as a matter of fact. That's how they met."

"See," she said, playing, "I knew it. Where was this?"

He glanced at her, annoyed. Another woman's magazine piece, the encounter on the slopes, as wistful as Eva Braun's last glass of champagne.

"I don't know, Liz. Does it matter? I don't know anything about their marriage. How would I? She stayed, that's all. Maybe she thought they'd win the war." The last thing she thought. Why say it? He turned off the taps, annoyed now with himself. "My bath's ready."

"Were you in love with her?"

"That's not a reporter's question."

She looked at him and nodded, then stood up. "That's some answer."

"This towel is coming off in two seconds. You're welcome to stay—"

"Okay, okay, I'm going." She smiled. "I like to leave a little something to the imagination." She gathered up her things, slinging the holster belt on her shoulder, and went to the door.

"Don't forget the rain check," he said.

She turned to him. "By the way, a piece of advice? Next time you ask a girl for a drink, don't tell her about the other one. Even if she asks." She opened the door. "See you around the campus."

CHAPTER TWO

DINNER WAS SURPRISINGLY formal, served by the gray-haired woman and a man Jake took to be her husband in a large corner room on the ground floor. A starched white tablecloth was set with china and wine goblets, and even the food—standard B rations of pea soup, stewed meat, and canned pears—seemed dressed up for the occasion, ladled out of a porcelain tureen with ceremony and garnished with a sprig of parsley, the first green Jake had seen in weeks. He imagined the woman snipping off pieces in the muddy garden, determined even now to keep a good table. The company, all men, was a mix of visiting journalists and MG officers, who sat at one end with their own whiskey bottles, like regulars in a western boardinghouse. Jake arrived just as the soup was being served.

"Well, here's a sorry sight." Tommy Ottinger, from Mutual, extended his hand. "When did you blow in?"

"Hey, Tommy." Even balder than before, as if all his hair had migrated down to the trademark bushy mustache.

"I didn't know you were here. You back with Murrow?"

Jake sat down, nodding hello across the table to the congressman, sitting between Ron, clearly on caretaking duty, and a middle-aged MG officer who looked exactly like Lewis Stone as Judge Hardy.

"No broadcasting, Tommy. Just a hack."

"Yeah? Whose nickel?"

"Collier's."

"Oh," Tommy said, drawling it, pretending to be impressed, "in *depth.* Good luck. You see the agenda? Reparations. You could nod off just thinking about it. So what do you know?"

"Not much. I just got in. Took a ride through the city, that's all."

"You see Truman? He went in this afternoon."

"No. I saw Churchill, though."

"I can't use Churchill. They want Truman—how's he doing? I mean, how the fuck do I know? He hasn't done anything yet."

Jake grinned at him. "Make something up. It wouldn't be the first time."

The serving man placed the soup in front of him, looking surprised when Jake thanked him in German.

"You know what he said today? In Berlin? 'This is what happens when a man overreaches himself.'"

Jake thought of the miles of debris, reduced to the lesson for the day. "Who's your source? Jimmy Byrnes?"

"Sounds just like Truman, don't you think?"

"It will, if you use it."

"Got to fill the air somehow. You remember."

"The old graveyard shift." The 2 A.M. broadcasts, timed for the evening news back home.

"Worse. They kept Berlin on Russian time, so it's even later." He took a drink, shaking his head. "The Russians—" He turned to Jake, suddenly earnest, as if he were confiding a secret. "They just went all to hell here. Raped everything that moved. Old women. Children. You wouldn't believe the stories."

"No," Jake said, thinking of the bayoneted chairs.

"Now they want reparations," Tommy said, rolling his deep radio voice. "I don't know what they think's left. They've already grabbed everything that wasn't nailed down. Took it all apart and shipped it home. Everything—factories, pipes, toilets, for Christ's sake. Of course, once they got it there they didn't know how to put it back together, so I hear it's all sitting on the trains, going to rust. Useless."

"There's your story."

"They don't want that either. Let's not make fun of the Russians. We have to get along with them. You know. They're touchy bastards."

"So what do they want?"

"Truman. The poker game. Who's a better player, him or Uncle Joe? Potsdam poker," he said, trying it. "That's not bad."

"And we're holding the cards."

Tommy shrugged. "We want to go home and they want to stay. That's a pretty good card."

The serving man, hovering in a frayed suit, replaced the soup with a gray stew. Salty, probably lamb.

Tommy picked at it, then pushed it away and took another drink. "So what are you going to do?"

"I don't know yet. I thought I'd look up some people I used to know, see what happened to them."

"Hearts-and-flowers stuff."

Jake spread his hands, not wanting to be drawn in. "The poker game then, I guess."

"In other words, sit around with the rest of us and do what Ron here says," he said, raising his voice. "Right?"

"If you say so, Tommy," Ron said, shooting him a wary look across the table.

"Handouts. We can't even get near the place. Stalin's afraid somebody's going to take a potshot at him. That it, Ron?"

"I'd say he's more afraid of being quoted out of context."

"Now, who'd do a thing like that? Would you do that, Jake?"

"Never."

"I can't say I blame him," the congressman said, smiling. "I've had a little experience in that department myself." His manner was looser now, a campaign geniality, and Jake wondered for a second if the stiffness on the plane had been nothing more than fear of flying, better hidden than the young soldier's. His wide tie, a dizzying paisley, was like a flash of neon at the uniformed table.

"You're Alan Breimer, aren't you?" Tommy said.

"That's right," he said, nodding, pleased to be recognized.

"War Production Board," Tommy said, a memory display. "We met when I covered the trust hearings in 'thirty-eight."

"Oh yes," said Breimer, who clearly didn't remember.

"What brings you to Berlin?" Tommy said, so smoothly that Jake saw he was working, the line to Ron only a way of reeling Breimer in.

"Just a little fact-finding for my committee."

"In Berlin?"

"The congressman's been looking at conditions all over the zone," Ron said, stepping in. "Technically, that includes us too."

"Why not Berlin?" Breimer said to Tommy, curious.

"Well, industrial capacity's your field. Not much of that left here."

"Not much of that anywhere in our zone," Breimer said, trying for a backroom heartiness. "You know what they say—the Russians got the food, the British got the factories, and we got the scenery. I suppose we have Yalta to thank for that too." He looked at Tommy, expecting a response, then switched gears. "Anyway, I'm not here to see factories, just our MG officials. We've got General Clay tomorrow, right, lieutenant?"

"Bright and early," Ron said.

"You'll want to see Blaustein over in Economics," Tommy said, as if he were helping to fill the schedule. "Remember him? He was the lawyer from Justice at the trust hearing."

"I remember Mr. Blaustein."

"On the other hand, you weren't exactly best friends."

"He had his ideas, I had mine," Breimer said easily. "What is he doing here?"

"Same idea. Decartelization. One of the four Ds."

"Four Ds?" Jake said.

"Military Government policy for Germany," Ron said in his briefing voice. "Demilitarization, de-Nazification, decartelization, and democracy."

"And the least of these shall be decartelization. Isn't that right, congressman?" Tommy said.

"I'm not sure I know what you mean."

"American Dye and Chemical's in your district. I seem to remember they held the North American Farben patents. I thought maybe you'd come over to see—"

He waited for Breimer to take the bait, but the congressman just sighed. "You're barking up the wrong tree. Same one Mr. Blaustein kept barking up." He shook his head. "The more successful a business became, the more he wanted to tear it down. I never did understand that." He looked straight at Tommy. "American Dye's just one business in the district, just one."

"But the only one with a German partner."

"That was before the war, Mr. —? Who did you say you were with?"

"Tom Ottinger. Mutual. Don't worry, we're off the record."

"We can be on the record for all I care. I'm not here for American Dye or anyone else. Just the American people."

Tommy grinned. "Now that makes me homesick. You forget people talk like that in Washington."

"I'm glad you find us so funny." He turned to Ron. "Well, I can see I'm not winning any votes here," he said, an unexpectedly graceful exit. Then, unable to resist, he turned back to Tommy. "You know, it's easy to attack business. I've heard it all my life, usually from people who don't know the first thing about it. Maybe we ought to keep in mind that those companies, the ones you want to break up, won the war for us."

"They almost won it here too. Now they're war criminals. I wonder where the boys at American Dye would be if things had gone the other way."

"That's a hell of a thing for an American to say."

Tommy raised his glass. "But you'd defend to your death my right to say it." He took in Breimer's blank expression. "Oliver Wendell Holmes. Another troublemaker in the Justice Department."

"No, Voltaire," the Judge Hardy lookalike said mildly, the first time he'd spoken. "If he said it. He was probably misquoted too." A sly smile at Tommy.

"Well, somebody said it," Tommy said. "Anyway, it's the right idea. Don't you think?" he said to Breimer, his glass still raised.

Breimer stared at him for a moment, a politician assessing a heckler, then lifted his glass with a forced smile. "I certainly do. To the Justice Department. And to the gentlemen of the press."

"Bless their little hearts," Ron said.

They drank, then Breimer turned back to Ron, placing his fleshy hand on a paper on the table. "But Clay's a direct report to Ike," he said, as if they had never been interrupted.

"That's right," Ron said quickly, before Tommy could jump in again. "The army's here as support, but Military Government reports in to Ike. Technically, to the Allied Control Council. That's Ike, Ismay, and Zhukov. We're USGCC, U.S. Group Control Council."

He was drawing boxes on the paper, an organization chart.

"Control Council's the final authority for the country, at least for the sign-off, but the real work's here, in the Coordinating Committee. That's Clay, as Ike's deputy, and the other Allied deputies. Under Clay you've got your executive staff line, like Colonel Muller here," he said, turning to Judge Hardy, who nodded.

"Nice to put a face on a box," Breimer said eagerly, but Ron was already moving down the sheet.

"Then the functional offices—Political Affairs, Intelligence, Information Control, and so on."

Jake watched the lines and boxes spread across the bottom of the page, a kind of bureaucratic family tree.

"The functional divisions down here are the ones that work with the Germans—Transport, Manpower, Legal, and so on."

Breimer was studying the chart with care, familiar with the world as a pyramid of boxes. "Where does Frankfurt come in?"

"Well, that's USFET, G-five, civil affairs."

"USFET. The army's got more damned alphabet soup than the New Deal," Breimer said, evidently his idea of a joke, because he looked up.

Ron smiled obligingly.

"In other words, overlap," Breimer said.

Ron smiled again. "That I couldn't say."

"No, you don't have to." He shook his head. "If we ran a business this way, we'd never make any money."

"We're not here to make money," Muller said quietly.

"No, to spend it," Breimer said, but pleasantly. "From the looks of things, we've got a whole country on relief and the American taxpayer footing the bill. Some peace."

"We can't let them starve."

"Nobody's starving that I can see."

Muller turned to face him, his expression grave and kindly, Judge Hardy lecturing Andy. "The official ration is fifteen hundred calories a day. In practice, it's closer to twelve hundred, sometimes lower. That's only a little better than the camps. They're starving." His voice, as precise and rational as one of Ron's boxes, stopped Breimer short. "Unless they work for us," he went on calmly. "Then they get a hot meal every day and all the cigarette butts they can scrounge." He paused. "They're the ones you see."

Jake glanced over at the serving man, quietly removing plates, and noticed for the first time his thin neck bobbing in its oversized collar.

"Nobody wants anybody to starve," Breimer said. "I'm not a hard peace man. That's that nut Morgenthau in Treasury." He glanced over at Tommy. "One of your trust-busters, by the way. Wants to make 'em all farmers, take the whole damn thing apart. Dumbest thing I ever heard. Of course, those people have their own agenda."

"What people?" Tommy said, but Breimer ignored him, sweeping along.

"I'm a realist. What we need to do is get this country back on its feet again, not put 'em on relief. Now, I'm not saying you people aren't doing a fine job here." This to Muller, who nodded dutifully. "I've been in Germany two weeks and I can tell you I've never been prouder to be an American. The things I've seen— But hell, look at this." He pointed to the chart. "You can't do much when you're spread this thin on the ground. One group here, another in Frankfurt—"

"I believe it's General Clay's intention to combine the organizations," Ron said.

"Good," Breimer said, annoyed at being interrupted. "That's a start. And here's a whole other group just for Berlin."

"Well, you know, the city's jointly administered, so there's no way around that," Ron said, still on his chart. "The Coordinating Committee set up the Kommandatura to deal with Berlin. That's Howley—we see him tomorrow after Clay."

"Kommandatura," Breimer said. "That the Russian name?"

"More international than Russian, I think," Ron said, evading. "Everyone agreed to it."

Breimer snorted. "The Russians. I'll tell you one thing. We don't get these people back on their feet, the Russians'll come in, that's for sure."

"Well, that's one way to stop the drain on the American taxpayer," Tommy said. "Let Ivan pick up the tab."

Breimer glowered at him. "That's not all he'll pick up. Well, have your fun, have your fun," he said, sitting back. "I suppose I'm making speeches again and ruining the party. My wife's always telling me I don't know when to stop." He gave a calculated smile, meant to disarm. "It's just, you know, I hate to see waste. That's one thing you learn in business." He glanced again at Tommy. "To be a realist." He shook his head. "Four Ds. We ought to be putting these people to work, not giving them handouts and breaking up their companies and wasting our time looking for Nazis under every bed."

A plate crashed, like a punctuation mark, and everyone turned to the door. The old man, distraught, was looking at the floor, held at the elbow by the short, wiry American who had just bumped into him. For a second no one moved, suspended in a stopped piece of film, then the reel caught again and they tumbled forward into a kind of slapstick, the gray-haired woman rushing out, hands to her cheeks, the old man moaning, the American apologizing in German. When he bent down to help with the pieces, the files under his arm slid onto the floor in a heap of papers and broken crockery. More excited German, a fuss too elaborate, Jake thought, to be about a plate—the fear, perhaps, of losing a job with its one hot meal a day. Finally the woman shooed both men away from the china and, with a bow, pulled back a chair for the late arrival.

"Sorry, gentlemen," he said to the quiet room, busy stacking files on the table. He had a terrier's sharp nose and nervous energy, his face covered with a dark five-o'clock shadow he hadn't had time to shave. Even the air around him seemed to be running late, his tie loosened from its open collar by the same hurried gust.

"Congressman, your three o'clock tomorrow," Ron said wryly. "Captain Teitel, Public Safety Division. Bernie, Congressman Breimer."

"Pleased to meet you," Teitel said quickly, extending his hand and almost colliding again with a plate of stew the serving man had brought. Jake watched, amused, as the old man hesitated behind him, waiting for a safe opening.

"Public Safety," Breimer said. "That's police?"

"Among other things. I'm de-Nazification—the guy wasting our time looking under the beds," Teitel said.

"Ah," Breimer said, unsure how to proceed. Then he stood.

"No, don't get up."

Breimer smiled, pointing to the tall soldier standing at the door. "My ride."

But Bernie wasn't ready to let go. "Frankfurt tells me you have a problem with the program," he said, lowering his head as if preparing to ram.

Breimer looked down at him, ready for another heckler, but Tommy had wearied him. "No problem," he said, mollifying. "Just a few questions. I'm sure you're all doing a fine job."

"We'd be doing a better one if we had more staff."

Breimer smiled. "That seems to be the general complaint here. Everybody I meet wants another secretary."

"I don't mean secretaries. Trained investigators."

The old man now slid the plate between them onto the table and backed away, as if sensing that they were squaring off.

"Well, we'll talk about that tomorrow," Breimer said, preparing to go. "I'm here to learn. Afraid I can't do anything about personnel, though—that's up to MG."

"I thought you were writing some kind of report."

Breimer held up a wait-a-second finger to his driver. "No. Just making sure we're keeping our priorities straight."

"This is a priority."

Breimer smiled again, back on familiar ground. "Well, that's what every department says. But you know, we can't do everything." He indicated the organization chart. "Sometimes I think we let our good intentions run away with us." He put his hand on Bernie's shoulder, an uncle giving advice. "We can't put a whole country on trial."

"No, just the guilty ones," Bernie said, looking at him steadily.

Breimer dropped his hand, the easy get-away lost. "That's right, just the guilty ones." He looked back at Bernie. "We don't want to start some kind of inquisition over here. The American people don't want that."

"Really? What do we want?" Bernie said, using the pronoun as a jab.

Breimer stepped back. "I think we all want the same thing," he said evenly. "To get this country going again. That's the important thing now. You can't do that by locking everybody up. The worst cases, yes. Get the big boys and put them on trial—I'm all for it. But then we've got to move on, not chase all the small fry." He paused, avuncular again. "We don't want people to think a minority is using this program to get revenge." He shook his head. "We don't want that."

The voice of the Kiwanis Club lunch, bland and sure of itself. In the awkward silence, Jake could feel Tommy shift in his chair, leaning forward to see Bernie's response.

"We're an even smaller minority here," Bernie said calmly. "Most of us are dead."

"I didn't mean you personally, of course."

"Just all the other Jews in the program. But we speak the language, some of us—one of life's little ironies—so you're stuck with us. I was born here. If my parents hadn't left in 'thirty-three, I'd be dead too. Personally. So I think this is a priority." He touched the pile of papers on the table. "I'm sorry if it interferes with economic recovery. As far as I'm concerned, you can file that under T for 'too bad.' I'm a DA back home, that's why they tapped me for this. DAs don't get revenge. Half the time, we're lucky to get a little justice."

Breimer, who had turned red during this, sputtered, "I didn't mean—"

"Save it. I know what you mean. I don't want to join your country club anyway. Just send me more staff and we'll call it quits." He pulled the chair beneath him and sat down, cocking his head toward the door. "I think your driver's waiting."

Breimer stood still for a moment, furious, then visibly collected himself and nodded to the quiet table. "Gentlemen." He looked down at Bernie. "We'll talk tomorrow, captain. I hope I'll be better understood."

The entire table watched him go. Jake looked around, waiting for someone to speak, feeling the room grow warmer, as if the quiet were letting in the sticky night air. Finally Muller, staring at his glass, said dryly, "He's here to learn."

Tommy smiled at him and lit a cigarette. "I wonder what he's really doing here. Guy doesn't take a leak unless American Dye tells him to go to the bathroom."

"Hey, Tommy," Ron said, "do me a favor. Lay off. I'm the one who gets the complaints."

"What'll you do for me?"

But the earlier mood was gone, replaced by something uncomfortable, and even Ron no longer wanted to play.

"Well, that was nice," he said to Bernie. "We have to live with this guy, you know."

Bernie looked up from his stew. "Sorry," he said, still on edge.

Ron took a drink, looking at Tommy. "He seems to bring out the best in everybody."

"Small fry," Bernie said, imitating Breimer's voice. "Whoever that is."

"Anybody but Goering," Tommy said.

"Small fry," Bernie said again. "Here's one." He reached into the pile and pulled out a few buff-colored sheets. "Otto Klopfer. Wants to drive for us. Experienced. Says he drove a truck during the war. He just didn't say what kind. One of the mobile units, it turns out. The exhaust pipe ran back into the van. They'd load about fifty, sixty people in there, and old Otto would just keep the motor running until they died. We found out because he wrote a letter to his CO." He held up a sheet. "The exhaust was taking too long. Recommended they seal the pipes so it would work faster. The people were panicking, trying to get out. He was afraid they'd damage the truck."

Another silence, this time so still that even the air around Bernie seemed to stop. He looked down at the food and pushed it away. "Fuck," he said, embarrassed, then stood up, gathering his files, and left the room.

Jake stared at the white tablecloth. He heard the old man quietly clearing the plates, then the muffled scrape of chairs as Muller and the MG end of the table got up to leave. Tommy ground his cigarette into the ashtray.

"Well, I've got a poker hand waiting," he said, subdued now. "You coming, Jake? Everybody'll be there."

The floating game of the war, still going on, press tents filled with smoke and battered typewriters and the steady slap of cards.

"Not tonight," Jake said, looking at the table.

"Let's go, Ron. Bring your money." He stood up, then turned to Jake. "Take a gun if you go out. The Russians are still all over the place. Once they get liquored up, it's like Dodge City out there."

But they'd be rowdy, roving the streets in packs, their good time its own warning. It was the others, the shadows gliding through the rubble, who'd pounce in the dark.

"Where was Breimer going?" he said to Ron.

"No idea. I'm the day shift. Let's hope he gets laid."

"Talk about punishing the Germans," Tommy said, and then they were gone too and Jake was alone in the quiet room. He poured some more wine. The old man returned and after a quizzical look at Jake began emptying the ashtrays, carefully straightening the butts and putting them on a separate plate. Occupation currency.

"Would you like anything else?" he said in German, brushing the tablecloth.

"No. I'll just finish this."

"Bitte," he said, as polite as a waiter at the Adlon, and left.

Jake lit a cigarette. Had Otto Klopfer smoked in the cab while he ran the motor, listening to the thumps behind him? There must have been screaming, a furious pounding on the van. And he'd sat there, foot on the pedal. How could they do it? All the questions came back to that. He'd seen it on the faces of the GIs, who'd hated France and then, confused, felt at home in Germany. The plumbing, the wide roads, the blond children grateful for candy, their mothers tirelessly sweeping up the mess. Clean. Hardworking. Just like us. Then they'd seen the camps, or at least the newsreels. How could they do it? The answer, the only one that made sense to them, was that they hadn't—somebody else had. But there wasn't anybody else. So they stopped asking. Unless, like Teitel, the hook had gone in too deep.

Jake looked around the empty room, still feeling the disturbance. Once, in Chicago, he'd worked the crime desk and the rooms had felt like this, the uneasy quiet that follows murder—the body covered but everything else disordered. He remembered the indifferent photographers, the policemen picking through the room dusting for prints, the numbed faces of the others, who didn't look back at you but sat staring at the tagged gun in a daze, as if it had gone off by itself, and he realized suddenly that he had seen it all again today, that what the city had really become was not a bomb site but a vast scene of the crime. Shaken, waiting for someone to bring the stretcher and erase the chalk marks and put the furniture back. Except this crime wouldn't go away, even then. There would always be a body in the middle of the floor. How could they do it? Sealing pipes, locking doors, ignoring the screams? It was the only question. But who could answer it? Not a reporter with four pieces in *Collier's.* The story was beyond that, a twisted parody of Goebbels' big lie—if you made the crime big enough, nobody did it. All the pieces he might do, full of local color and war stories and Truman's horse-trading, were not even notes for the police blotter.

He got up from the table, his head thick with drink and the humid air. In the hall, the old man was standing in front of an open door, listening to the piano. Soft music, barely louder than the clock. When he saw Jake, he moved away, a concertgoer giving up his seat. Jake stood for a moment, trying to place the music—delicate, slightly melancholy, something nineteenth-century, like the house, a graceful world away from the abrasive dinner. When he looked through the door, he saw Bernie bent over the keys in a pool of dim light, his tight wavy hair just visible across the well of the piano. At this distance his body was foreshortened, and for a second Jake saw the boy he must have been, a diligent practicer, his mother eavesdropping down the hall. It's something you'll have all your life, she would have said. A nice boy, not gifted, who kept his eye on the keys. Not yet a terrier, ready to take offense. But perhaps it was only the room, the first real Berlin room Jake had seen, with its tall stove in the corner, the piano near the window to catch the light. In the old days, there would have been cake with coffee.

Bernie kept his head down after he was finished, so that Jake was at the piano when he looked up.

"What was it?" Jake asked.

"Mendelssohn. One of the *Songs Without Words.*"

"Beautiful."

Bernie nodded. "Also illegal, until a few months ago. So I like playing it. Rusty, though."

"Your audience enjoyed it," Jake said, nodding to the hall where the old man had been.

Bernie smiled. "He's just keeping an eye on the piano. It's their house. They live in the basement."

Jake took this in. "So that's why the plate."

"It's all they have left. They hid it, I guess. The Russians took everything else." He waved his hand at the room, which Jake saw now had been stripped of knickknacks, the afternoons of coffee cakes just his imagination. He looked down at the piano, covered in cigarette burns and water rings from wet glasses of vodka.

"We haven't met. I'm Jake Geismar." He held out his hand.

"The writer?"

"Unless there's another one," Jake said, pleased in spite of himself.

"You wrote the piece about Nordhausen. Camp Dora," Bernie said. "Jacob. As in Jewish?"

Jake smiled. "No, as in the Bible. My brother got Ezra."

Bernie shrugged. "Bernie Teitel," he said, finally shaking Jake's hand.

"So I heard."

Bernie looked at him, puzzled, until Jake cocked his head toward the dining room. "Oh, that." He looked away. "Bastard."

"You really don't want to join his country club, you know."

Bernie grinned. "No. I just want to pee in his pool." He stood up and closed the piano lid. "So what are you doing in Berlin?"

"The conference. Looking for a story, like everybody else."

"I don't suppose I could interest you in the program? We could use some press. *Life* was here. They just wanted to know how our boys were doing."

"How are they doing?"

"Oh, fine, fine. Nobody fraternizes, so nobody gets the syph. Nobody loots. Nobody's making a dime on the black market. Just handing out Hershey bars and keeping their noses clean. Any mother would be proud. According to *Life*." He picked up his files to go.

Jake lit a cigarette and looked at him carefully through the smoke. A DA, not a boy playing Mendelssohn.

"What's going to happen to Otto Klopfer?"

Bernie stopped. "Otto? Summary court. He's not big enough for the Nuremberg team. Three to five, probably. Then he'll be back driving a truck. But not for us."

"But I thought you said—"

"We can't prove the actual killing. No witnesses in the van. If he hadn't sent the letter, we couldn't prove anything. We're sticklers for the law here. We don't want to start an inquisition," he said, back in his dining room voice. "We'd rather cut the Nazis a little slack."

"Summary court—that's you?"

Bernie shook his head. "We try to keep the foreign-born minorities out of court. In case they're not—impartial. I'm just the hound. Right now I'm on the *fragebogen.*" He touched the files. "Questionnaires," he translated. "'Were you a member of the party? BDM?' Like that. They have to fill one out if they want a job, a ration card."

"Don't they lie?"

"Sure. But we have the party records, so we check. Wonderful people for keeping records."

Jake stared at the bulky files, like a hundred message sticks in the rubble.

"Could you locate somebody with those?"

Bernie looked at him. "Maybe. If they're in the American zone," he said, a question.

"I don't know."

"The British files would take a while. The Russians—" He let it dangle, then said gently, "A relative?"

"Somebody I used to know."

Bernie took out a pen and scribbled on a piece of paper. "I'll see what I have," he said, handing him an office number. "Come by tomorrow. I have a feeling my three o'clock will be canceled." He left the piano, then turned back to Jake. "They'd have to be alive, you know."

"Yes. Thanks." He pocketed the address. "Can I buy you a drink?"

Bernie shook his head. "Have to get back to work." He shifted the files under his arm, running late again.

"You can't get them all," Jake said, smiling a little.

Bernie's face went hard. "No. Just one at a time. The way they did it. One at a time."

It took over an hour the next morning to find Frau Dzuris, in one of the crumbled streets not far from the British headquarters in Fehrbelliner Platz. Plaster had fallen off the front of the building, leaving patches of exposed brick, and the staircase smelled of mildew and slop buckets, the signs of a broken water line. He was shown to the second floor by a neighbor, who lingered in the hall in case there was trouble. Inside, the sounds of children, immediately silent after the knock on the door. When Frau Dzuris opened it, looking frightened, there was the faint odor of boiling potatoes. She recognized him, her hands fluttering to smooth her hair and drawing him in, but the welcome was nervous, and Jake saw on the children's faces that it was the uniform. Not sure what to do, she insisted on introducing everybody—a daughter-in-law, three children—and sat him at the table. In the other room, two mattresses had been pushed together.

"I saw your notice in Pariserstrasse," he began in German.

"For my son. He doesn't know we're here. They took him to work in the east. A few weeks they said, and now look—"

"You were bombed out?"

"Oh, it was terrible. The British at night, the Amis in the day—" A quick glance, to see if she had offended him. "Why did they want to bomb everything? Did they think we were Hitler? The building was hit twice. The second time—"

The daughter-in-law offered him water and sat down. In the other room, the children watched through the door.

"Was Lena there?"

"No, at the hospital."

"The hospital?"

"Not hurt. She worked there. The Elisabeth. You know the one, in Lützowstrasse. I said it was God protecting her for her good works. You know, the others, in the basement, didn't make it. Herr Bloch, his Greta, everybody. They killed them all." Another glance. "Herr Bloch wouldn't go to the public shelter. Not him. But I never trusted the cellar. It's not deep enough, I said, and you see it wasn't." She had begun to wring her hands, and Jake saw the flesh of her upper arms hanging in folds, like strips of dough. "So many dead. Terrible, you can't imagine, all night—"

"But Lena, she was all right?"

She nodded. "She came back. But of course we had to move."

"Where did she go?"

"She had a friend from the hospital. After that, I don't know. It was hit too, I heard. A hospital. They bombed even the sick." She shook her head.

"But she didn't leave an address?"

"With me? I was already gone. You know, there wasn't time for addresses. You found whatever you could. Perhaps she had relatives, I don't know. She never said. You can't imagine what it was like. The *noise.* But do you know the strange thing? The telephones worked right to the end. That's the thing I remember about Pariserstrasse. The bombs and everybody running and there was a telephone ringing. Even then."

"And her husband?"

"Away somewhere. In the war." She waved her hand. "They left the women for the Russians. Oh, that was terrible. Thank God I—" She glanced toward her daughter-in-law. "I was lucky."

"But she must be somewhere," Jake said.

"I don't know. I told your friend."

"What friend?"

"The soldier yesterday. I didn't know what to think. Now I see. You didn't want to come yourself, that explains it. You were always careful, I remember. In case Emil—" She leaned forward and put her hand on his arm, an unexpected confidante. "But you know, none of that matters anymore. So many years."

"I didn't send anybody here."

She withdrew her hand. "No? Well, then, I don't know."

"Who was he?"

She shrugged. "He didn't say. They don't, you know. Just, how many are living here? Do you have milk cards for the children? Where did you work in the war? It's worse than the Nazis. Maybe he was counting the dead. They do that, so you can't use the name for the ration cards."

"What did he say?"

"Did I know where she was living, had I seen Emil, that's all. Like you." She looked at him. "Is something wrong? We're good people here. I have children to—"

"No, no. Nothing. I'm not here for the police. I just want to find Lena. We were friends."

She smiled faintly. "Yes. I always thought so. Not a word from *her,*" she said, as if she still hoped for a chat over coffee. "So proper, always. Well, what does it matter now? I'm sorry I can't help. Perhaps the hospital would know."

He took out his notepad and wrote down the Gelferstrasse address. "If you do hear from her—"

"Of course. It's not likely, you know. Many people left Berlin before the end. Many people. It was hard to find a place. Even like this. You see how we live now."

Jake looked around the shabby room, then stood. "I didn't know about the children. I would have brought some chocolate. Perhaps you can use these?" He offered her a pack of cigarettes.

She widened her eyes, then grabbed his hand and shook it with both of hers. "Thank you. You see," she said to her daughter-in-law, "I always said it wasn't the Amis. You can see how kind they are. It's the British who wanted the bombing. That Churchill." She turned back to Jake. "I remember you were always polite. I wish we were back in the American zone, not here with the British."

Jake headed for the door, then turned. "The soldier yesterday—he was British?"

"No, American."

He stood for a second, puzzled. Not an official, then.

"If he comes back, you will let me know?"

She nodded, clutching the cigarettes, nervous again. "You're sure there's nothing wrong?"

Jake shook his head. "Maybe just another old friend. He might know something."

"No," she said, answering something else. "There was only you."

A hospital would have records, Jake thought, but when he got there he saw that a fire had swept through that stretch of Lützowstrasse, taking the Elisabeth and all its paper with it. Only a few walls were left, black and open to the sky, one of Ron's decayed molars. A work brigade of women was clearing the site, handing pails of bricks along a line that snaked over the heaps of fallen beams and charred bed-frames. The breeze that had come up during the night was now a steady hot wind, blowing ashes, so that the women had had to cover their mouths with kerchiefs, like bandits. Jake stood for a while watching, trying not to notice the heavy stench that hung in the street. How long before one didn't smell it anymore?

He wondered what she'd done here. Emil hadn't wanted her to work, a traditional husband, so she'd left Columbia for idle afternoons at home. They'd had to take on Hannelore instead, a thick girl with inadequate English and, Jake assumed, a direct line to Nanny Wendt. But Lena still came to parties, until it became awkward to see foreigners and Emil asked her to stop, and then she only saw Jake. Had he ever suspected? Frau Dzuris didn't seem to think so, but how could she know? There'd only been a few times in Pariserstrasse, when they couldn't go to his place because Hal was there. Always careful, alert even to the flick of a curtain at a neighbor's window. But Frau Dzuris had known somehow, maybe just from the look on their faces.

Emil, surprisingly, had been at the Anhalter when they'd all come to see Jake off, a defiantly raucous party, Hal and the rest of the gang guzzling champagne while Emil looked uneasily at the platform guards. Lena had given him flowers, the respectable send-off for an old boss, never meeting his eye until one of the party became sick and in the confusion of hustling him to the men's room they'd finally had a moment together.

"Why did you bring him?" Jake said.

"He was there when they called from the office. I couldn't come alone. How would it look?" She paused, looking down. "He wanted to come. He likes you."

"Lena," he said, reaching for her.

"No. No scenes. I want him to see me drink champagne and wave, like the others. Then we'll take a taxi home and that's the end."

"I'll come back," he said, hurrying, hearing the loud bursts of English near the men's room.

"No, you won't. Not now," she said simply, nodding toward all the uniforms on the platform.

"I'll come back for you," he said, looking at her until she raised her eyes again, her face softening, no longer public.

She shook her head slowly, glancing to see if the others were still away, then put her hand up to his cheek and held it there for a moment, her eyes on him, as if she were trying to memorize his face. "No. But think of me sometimes," she said.

He stood there, just looking. "Lena," he said, moving his face against her hand, but then she dropped it, a quick graze as she looked over his shoulder.

"My god, it's Renate," she said, pulling away. "They called her too? She's crazy—it's not safe for her." He heard the platform noises again, the private second gone. When he turned, he saw Renate's knowing sharp eyes, which had taken in Lena's hand, the way they noticed everything. His best tipster, off the books because you couldn't hire Jews. But she just smiled, pretending not to have seen.

"Hello, Joe, what do you know?" she said, American slang an endless joke.

"Hey, it's Renate!" The boys back on the platform, surrounding them, Berlin closing in again. He tried to catch Lena's eye, but she avoided him, hanging back with Emil, helping Hal pour champagne into cups. More drinks and jokes, Renate brazenly cadging a cigarette from a passing policeman with a flirtatious thank-you. Just to prove she could do it, while Hal looked on, appalled. With the train whistle, there was a final round of hugs, crushing the flowers. Emil shook Jake's hand, looking relieved that the party was coming to an end.

"Any news on the visa?" Jake said to Renate, embracing her.

She shook her head. "Soon," she said, not meaning it. Bright eyes, a head full of dark curls. The train attendant was closing doors.

"Jacob." Lena's voice, then her face next to his, a formal kiss on each side, light, leaving only the smell of her skin.

He looked at her, but there was nothing to say, not even her name, and the hands at his back were pushing him onto the train. He stood on the stairs as the train began to move, waving, hearing drunken *auf wiedersehens*, and when she took a step forward he thought for a second, wildly, that she would do it, run after the train and come with him, but it was only a step, a push from the crowd, so that the last thing he saw in Berlin was her standing still on the platform with Emil's arm around her shoulder.

The rubble women had stopped moving their pails, scrambling over the bricks to the middle of the building. One of them shouted down to the street, where another group picked up a stretcher from a cart and followed. Jake watched them lift a body out of the debris, turning their faces away from the smell, and swing it onto the stretcher as indifferently as if it were another load of bricks. The stretcher team plodded back, stumbling under the weight, then overturned it into a cart. A woman, her hair singed away. Where did they take the bodies? Some big potter's field in the Brandenburg marshes? More likely a furnace to finish the burning. Renate would have died like that, her sharp eyes finally dulled. Unless she had somehow survived, become one of the living skeletons he'd seen in the camp, their eyes dull too, half alive. The crime so big that no one did it. But they'd kept records in the camps, the long roll calls. It was only here, under the bricks, that a numberless body could vanish without a trace.

He ran over to the cart and looked down. A stocky, faceless body; not Lena, not anybody. He turned away. This was as pointless as Frau Dzuris. The living didn't vanish. Emil had been at the KWI—they'd know something. Army records, if he'd been in the war. POW lists. All it took was time. She'd be somewhere, not on a cart. Maybe even waiting for him in one of Bernie's questionnaires.

Bernie, however, was out, called to an unexpected meeting, according to the message tacked on his office door, so Jake walked over to the press camp instead. Everyone was there, drinking beer and looking bored, the typing tables littered with Ron's bland releases. Stalin had arrived. Churchill had called on Truman. The first plenary session would start at five. A reception had been arranged by the Russians.

"Not much, is it, boyo?" Brian Stanley said, a full whiskey glass in his hand.

"What are you doing here? Coming over to the other side?"

"Better booze," he said, sipping. "I had hoped for a little information, but as you can see—" He let one of the releases fall to the bar.

"I saw you with Churchill. He say anything?"

"'Course not. But at least he said it to me. Special to the *Express.* Very nice."

"But not so nice for the others."

Brian smiled. "Mad as hornets, they are. So I thought I'd poke around here for a bit. Stay out of harm's way." He took another sip. "There's no story, you know. Can't even get *Eden.* We ought to just pack it in, and instead there's tomorrow to worry about. Want to see what our lot's handing out?" He reached into his pocket and passed over another release.

"Three thousand linen sheets, five hundred ashtrays—what's this?"

"Preparation for the conference. Last blowout of the war, by the size of it. Try getting a story out of that."

"Three thousand rolls of toilet paper," Jake said.

"All from London. Now, where've they been hiding it, you wonder. Haven't seen decent loo paper in years." He took back the sheet, shaking his head. "Here's the one, a hundred and fifty bottles of button polish. Broke, but still gleaming."

"You're not going to print this?"

He shrugged. "What about you? Anything?"

"Not today. I went into town. They're still digging up bodies."

Brian made a face. "I haven't the stomach, I really haven't."

"You're getting soft. It never bothered you in Africa."

"Well, that was the war. I don't know what this is." He took a sip from his glass, brooding. "Lovely to be back in Cairo, wouldn't it? Sit on the terrace and watch the boats. Just the thing after this."

Drifting feluccas, white triangles waiting for a hint of a breeze, a million miles away.

"You'd be in London in a week."

"I don't think so, you know," Brian said seriously. "It's the boats for me now."

"That's the whiskey talking. When a man's tired of London—" Jake quoted.

Brian looked at the glass. "That's when we were on the way up. I don't want to see us go down. Bit by bit. It's finished there too. Just the Russians now. There's your story. And you're welcome to it. I haven't got the stomach anymore. Awful people."

"And there's us."

Brian sighed. "The lucky Americans. You don't need to count the loo paper, do you? Just streams out. What will you do, I wonder."

"Go home."

"No, you'll stay. You'll want to put things right. That's your particular bit of foolishness. You'll want to put things right."

"Somebody has to."

"Do they? Well, then, I anoint you, why not?" He put his hand on Jake's head. "Good luck and God bless. I'm for the boats."

"Don't you guys ever work?" A voice coming up from behind.

"Liz, my darling," Brian said, instantly hearty. "The lady with the lens. Come have a drink. I hear Miss Bourke-White's on her way."

"Up yours too."

Brian laughed. "Ooo." He got up from his stool. "Here, darling, have a seat. I'd better push off. Go polish my buttons. Probably the last time we get to sit at the high table, so we like to look our best."

"What's he talking about?" she said, watching him walk away.

"He's just being Brian. Here." Jake took out a match to light her cigarette.

"What have you been doing?" she said, inhaling. "Holding up the bar?"

"No, I went into town."

"God, why?"

"Look at the message boards." Charred bodies.

"Oh." She glanced up at him. "Any luck?"

He shook his head and handed her a release. "The Russians are giving a banquet tonight."

"I know. They're also posing." She looked at her watch. "In about an hour."

"In Potsdam? Take me with you."

"Can't. They'd have my head. No press, remember?"

"I'll carry your camera."

"You'd never get through. Special pass," she said, showing hers.

"Yes, I would. Just bat your baby blues. The Russians can't read anyway. Come on, Liz."

"She won't be in Potsdam, Jake," she said, looking at him.

"I can't sit around here. It just makes it worse. Anyway, I still need to file something."

"We're taking pictures, that's all."

"But I'd be there. See it, at least. Anything's better than this," he said, picking up the release. "Come on. I'll buy you that drink later."

"I've had better offers."

"How do you know?"

She laughed and got up from the stool. "Meet me outside in five. If there's any trouble, I don't know you. Understood? I don't know how you got in the jeep. Serve you right if they hauled you away."

"You're a pal."

"Yeah." She handed him a camera. "They're brown, by the way, not blue. In case you haven't noticed."

Another photographer was at the wheel, so Jake crammed in the back with the equipment, watching Liz's hair flying in the wind next to the aerial flag. They drove south toward Babelsberg, the old route to the film studios, and met the first Russian sentry on the Lange Brücke. He looked at the driver's pass, pretending to understand English, and waved them through with a machine gun.

The entire town had been cordoned off, lines of Russian soldiers posted at regular intervals up to Wilhelmplatz, which seemed to have got the worst of the bomb damage. They swung behind the square and then out the designated route along the Neuer Garten, the large villas facing the park wall looking empty but intact, lucky survivors. After Berlin, it was a haven, somewhere out of the war. Jake almost expected to see the usual old ladies in hats walking their dogs on the formal paths. Instead there were more Russians with machine guns, stretched along the lakeshore as if they were expecting an amphibious assault.

The Cecilienhof was at the end of the park, a big heap of stockbroker Tudor with brick chimneys and leaded windows, an unexpected piece of Surrey on the edge of the Jungfernsee. Ther were guards posted at the park gates, more menacingly correct but no more thorough than the first set on the bridge, then a long gravel drive to the palace forecourt, where MPs and British soldiers mingled with their Russian hosts. They parked near a row of official black cars. Through the opening to the inner courtyard they could see hundreds of red geraniums planted in the shape of a huge Red star, an ostentatious display of property rights, but before Liz could photograph it a liaison officer directed them around the building to the lawn that fronted the lake. Here, on the terrace next to a small topiary garden, three wicker chairs had been set out for the picture session. A small army of photographers and newsreel cameramen were already in place, smoking and setting up tripods and shooting uneasy glances toward the patrolling guards.

"As long as you're here, you might as well be useful," Liz said, handing Jake two cameras while she loaded a third. One of the guards came by to inspect the cases.

"So where are they?"

"Probably having a last-minute comb," Liz said.

He imagined Stalin in front of a mirror, smoothing back the sides of his hair for history.

Then there was nothing to do but wait. He studied the building for details—the double-height bay windows with their view of the lake, presumably the conference room, the chimneys of patterned brick too numerous to count. But there was no story in any of it, just architecture. The lawn had been mowed, the hedges trimmed, everything as tidy as a set shipped down the road from the soundstages in Babelsberg. A few miles away, the rubble women were dumping bodies in a cart. Here a breeze was blowing in from the lake, the waves flashing in the sun like tiny reflectors. The view was lovely. He wondered if Crown Prince Wilhelm used to walk across the lawn, towel in hand, for a morning dip, but the past seemed as unlikely as Stalin's comb. No sailboats now, just the Russian sentries standing back from the water, hands resting on their guns.

Churchill was first. He came onto the terrace in his khaki uniform, holding a cigar and talking to a group of aides. Then Truman, jaunty in a gray double-breasted suit, trading jokes with Byrnes and Admiral Leahy. Finally Stalin, in a dazzling white tunic, his short frame dwarfed by a circle of guards. There were a few informal shots as they shook hands, then a flurry of taking seats, aides crowding around to settle them in. Churchill handed a soldier his cigar. Truman tugged at his jacket so it wouldn't ride up as he sat. Had the places been decided beforehand? Truman was in the middle, his wire-rimmed glasses catching the light each time he turned his head from one to the other. Everyone smiling, casual, as if they were posing for a group shot at a class reunion. Truman crossed his legs, revealing a pair of ribbed silk socks. The cameras clicked.

Jake turned when he heard the shout. Sharp, in Russian. Now what? A soldier at the lake's edge was calling out, pointing at something in the water. Surprisingly, he waded in, wetting his boots, shouting again for help. On the terrace, some of the aides glanced toward the water, then turned back to the photographers, frowning at the interruption. Jake watched, fascinated, as the Russian soldiers began pulling a body to the shore. Another floater, like one of the bodies in the Landwehrkanal. But this one in uniform, indefinable at this distance. Still, more interesting than chimneys. He started down the lawn.

No one stopped him. The other guards had left their posts and were running toward the body, confused, looking toward the palace for instructions. The first soldier, wet now to the knees, was pulling the body up on the mud. He dropped the lifeless arm, then grabbed the belt for better leverage and yanked, a final heave to the grass. Suddenly the belt gave way, and Jake saw that it was a kind of pouch, ripped now and spilling open, the wind from the lake catching bits of paper and blowing them over the grass. Jake stopped. Not paper, money, bills whirling up then floating in the air like hundreds of little kites. The sky, a surreal moment, filled with money.

The Russians stood still for a second, amazed, then lunged for the bills, grabbing them out of the air. Another gust sent them higher so the guards now had to leap up, no longer soldiers but astonished children snatching candy. Everyone on the terrace stood to watch, and a few of the Russian officers ran down to restore order, brushing past bills scattering across the lawn. They shouted to the guards, but no one listened, yelling instead to each other as they chased the flying paper, stamping the ground to hold down the bills, and stuffing them into their pockets. So much money, blowing like confetti. Jake picked one up. Occupation marks. Hundreds, maybe thousands of them. So much money.

Now the photographers began to break ranks and head for the lake too, until the Russian officers turned on them, holding them back with pointed guns. But Jake was already there. He went over to the body. An American uniform, the torn money belt lying in the mud, some of the notes drifting back into the water. But what was he doing here? Floating in the Russian zone to the most heavily guarded lawn in Berlin. Jake knelt down to the body. A face sickly white and puffy from the water, the tag chain at his neck hanging to the side. He reached for the tags, then stopped, thrown. No need. Not just any soldier. The shock of a corpse you knew. The boy on the flight from Frankfurt, white-knuckled, clasping the bench in fear, his fingers outstretched now, shriveled.

It was then, stupefied, that Jake noticed the bullet hole, the dark matted fabric where the blood had been. Behind him men were still shouting in Russian, but suddenly he was back in one of those Chicago rooms, everything disrupted. The eyes were open. Only one riding boot; the other pulled away by the water. How long had he been dead? He felt the jaw, clenched tight. But there was no coroner to turn to, nobody dusting for prints. He felt the blunt tip of a gun in his back.

"*Snell,*" the Russian commanded, evidently his one word of German.

Jake looked up. Another soldier, pointing a gun, was waving him away. As he stood, the other grabbed the camera, saying something in Russian. The first soldier poked the gun again until Jake raised his hands and turned around. On the terrace the Big Three were being hustled into the house, only Stalin still rooted to the spot, assessing, an anxious look like the one from the Chancellery steps. A sharp crack of rifle fire startled the air. A few birds bolted up out of the reeds. The men on the terrace froze, then hurried quickly into the building.

Jake looked toward the sound of the shot. A Russian officer, firing into the air to stop the riot. In the silence that followed, the guards stood still, watching the rest of the money blow toward the Neuer Garten, sheepish now, afraid of what would follow, their perfectly arranged afternoon turned squalid, an embarrassment. The officers ordered them into line and took back the notes. Jake's Russian pointed again to the house. Lieutenant Tully, who was afraid of flying. Four Russians were picking him up, flinging the money belt onto his chest as if it were evidence. But of what? So much money.

"Can I have my camera back?" Jake said, but the Russian yelled at him and pushed him forward with the gun, back to the photographers. The lawn was swarming with aides now, directing everyone back to the cars like tour leaders. Apologies for the disruption, as if Tully were a drunk who'd spoiled the party. The Russian guards watched, sullen, their one piece of luck blown away.

"Sorry," Jake said to Liz. "They took the camera."

"You're lucky you didn't get shot. What were you *doing* down there?"

"It was the guy from the plane."

"What guy?"

"Tully. The kid with the boots."

"But how—?"

"Let's go, let's go." A brusque MP. "Fun's over."

They were herded behind the others to the car park. Before they reached the gravel, Jake turned, looking back toward the lake.

"What the hell was he doing in Potsdam?" he said to himself.

"Maybe he's with the delegation."

Jake shook his head.

"Does it matter? Maybe he fell in the lake."

He turned to her. "He was shot."

Liz looked at him, then nervously back to the cars. "Come on, Jake. Let's get out of here."

"But why Potsdam?" In the park, a few of the bills still bounced along the grass, like leaves waiting to be raked. "With all that money."

"Did you get any?"

He uncrumpled the salvaged note in his hand.

"A hundred marks," Liz said. "Lucky you. Ten whole dollars."

But there'd been more. Thousands more. And a man with a bullet in his chest.

"Come on, the others have gone," Liz said.

Back to the press camp to drink beer. Jake smiled to himself, his mind racing, no longer walking dazed through ruins. A crime. The way in. His Berlin story.

II

Occupation

CHAPTER THREE

WORD HAD ALREADY gotten around the press camp by the time Jake got back.

"Just the man I'm looking for," Tommy Ottinger said, looming over the typewriter Jake was using to peck out some notes. "First thing that's happened all week and there you are, right on the spot. How, by the way?"

Jake smiled. "Just taking some pictures."

"And?"

"And nothing. Dead soldier washed up in the lake."

"Come on, I've got to go on tonight. You can take your own sweet time with *Collier's.* Who was he?"

"How would I know?"

"Well, you might have checked his tags," Tommy said, waiting.

"I wish I'd thought of that."

Tommy stared at him.

"Really," Jake said.

"Some reporter."

"What does Ron say?"

"A John Doe. No tags."

Jake looked at him for a second, thinking. "So why did you ask me?"

" 'Cause I don't trust Ron. I trust you."

"Look, Tommy, here's what I know. A stiff washes up. Dead about a day, I'd say. He had some money on him, which got the Russians all excited. The Big Three left in a hurry. I'll give you my notes. Use whatever you want. Stalin's face—it's a nice touch." He stopped, meeting Tommy's stare. "He had tags. I just didn't look. So why would Ron—?"

Tommy smiled and took a chair. "Because that's what Ron does. Covers ass. His own. The army's. We don't want to embarrass the army. Especially in front of the Russians."

"Why would they be embarrassed?"

"They don't know what they have yet. Except a soldier in Potsdam."

"And that's embarrassing?"

"It might be," Tommy said, lighting a cigarette. "Potsdam's the biggest black market center in Berlin."

"I thought the Reichstag."

"The Reichstag, Zoo Station. But Potsdam's the biggest."

"Why?"

"Because it's in the Russian zone," Tommy said simply, surprised at the question. "No MPs. The Russians don't care. They *are* the black market. They'll buy anything. The others—the MPs'll make a sweep every once in a while, arrest a few Germans just to keep up appearances. Not that it matters. The Russians don't even bother. Every day's Saturday on Main Street in Potsdam."

Jake smiled. "So he wasn't attending the conference."

"Not a chance."

"And Ron doesn't want his mother to read about her boy in the papers."

"Not that way." Tommy looked behind Jake. "Do you, Ron?"

"I want to talk to you," Ron said to Jake, visibly annoyed. "Where'd you get the pass?"

"I didn't. Nobody asked," Jake said.

"You know, we've got a waiting list for press credentials here. I could free up a slot any time I want."

"Relax. I didn't see a thing. See?" He waved at the paper in the typewriter. "Geranium star. Lots of chimneys. Local color, that's all. Unless you've got an ID for me?"

Ron sighed. "Don't push me on this, okay? The Russians find out there was press there, they'll make a formal protest and I'll have your ass out of here on the first truck."

Jake spread his hands. "I'll never go to Potsdam again. Okay? Now have a beer and tell us where the body is."

"The Russians have it. We're trying to get it released."

"Why the delay?"

"There's no delay. They're fucking *Russians.*" He paused. "It's probably the money. They're trying to figure out how much they can keep." He glanced at Jake. "You might as well be useful, since you were there. How much did he have?"

"No idea. A lot. Thousands. Double whatever they give you."

"I'm on tonight," Tommy said. "You going to have an official statement?"

"I don't have an official anything," Ron said. "As far as I know, somebody got drunk and fell in the lake. If you think that's a story, be my guest." Jake looked at him. No tags. No bullet. But Ron was rushing on. "We *will* have a release on the first session, though, in a couple of hours. If anybody cares."

"Warm greetings were exchanged by the Allies," Tommy said. "Generalissimo Stalin made a statement expressing a wish for a lasting peace. An agenda for the conference was approved."

Ron grinned. "And to think you weren't even there. No wonder you're the best."

"And a soldier happened to fall in the lake."

"That's what they tell me." He turned to Jake. "Stay in town. I mean it."

Jake watched him walk off. "When did the Russians close off Potsdam?" he said to Tommy.

"Over the weekend. Before the conference." He looked at Jake. "What?"

"He'd only been in the water a day."

"How do you know?" Tommy said, alert.

Jake waved his hand. "I don't, for sure. But he wasn't that bloated."

"So?"

"So how did he get into Potsdam? If it was closed off?"

"What the hell. You did," Tommy said, watching him. "Of course, you have an honest face."

The piano music was coming through the open windows, not Mendelssohn this time but Broadway, party songs. Inside, the house was filled with uniforms and smoke and the clink of glasses. Gelferstrasse was entertaining. Jake stood for a minute in the hall, watching. There was the usual hum of conversation, laced with Russian from a group standing near the spread of cold cuts, and the usual music, but it was a cocktail party without women, oddly dispirited, looking for someone to flirt with. Men stood in groups talking shop or sometimes not saying anything at all, lifting glasses from the trays passed by the old couple and tossing them back quickly, as if they knew already that nothing better was going to come along. The host seemed to be Colonel Muller, whose silver hair moved through the crowd as he introduced people, occasionally getting clamped on the shoulder by a friendly Russian, as awkward and unlikely in the role as Judge Hardy himself would have been. Jake headed for the stairs.

"Geismar, come in," Muller said, handing him a glass. "Sorry we had to requisition the dining room, but there's plenty of grub. You're welcome to whatever's left." In fact, the dining table, pushed against the wall, was still heaped with ham and salami and smoked fish, a banquet.

"What's the occasion?"

"We're having the Russians over," Muller said, making them sound like a couple. "They like parties. They invite us to Karlshorst, then we invite them here. Back and forth. It greases the wheels."

"With vodka."

Muller smiled. "They don't mind bourbon either."

"Let me take a rain check. I can't speak a word of Russian."

"A few of them speak German. Anyway, in a while it won't matter. It's always a little awkward at first," he said, looking toward the party, "but after they've had a few, they just say things in Russian and you nod and they laugh and we're all good fellows."

"Allies and brothers."

"Actually, yes. It's important to them, this stuff. They don't like being left out. So we don't." He took a drink. "This isn't what it looks like. It's work."

Jake held up his glass. "And somebody's got to do it."

Muller nodded. "That's right, somebody does. Nobody told me I'd end up feeding drinks to Russians, but that's what we do now, so I do it. And I could use a new face to liven things up." He smiled. "Besides, you owe me a favor. Lieutenant Erlich says I'm supposed to chew you out, but I'm going to let it pass."

"You're supposed to?"

"You mean, who am I? I guess we didn't meet. With the congressman giving speeches. I'm Colonel Muller. Fred," he said, extending his hand. "I work for General Clay."

"Doing what?"

"I look after some of the functional departments. Keep them in line when I have to. Lieutenant Erlich's one of them."

Jake smiled. "Somebody's got to do it."

Muller nodded again. "I'd take the Russians any day. They're touchy, but they don't write home. Your bunch is more trouble."

"So why are you going to let it pass?"

"You getting out to Potsdam? Ordinarily I wouldn't. But I don't see that it's done anybody any harm." He paused. "I served with General Patton. He said to look out for you, you were a friend to the army."

"Everybody's a friend to the army."

"You wouldn't know it from the papers back home. They come over here, don't know the first thing, just point fingers to get themselves noticed."

"Maybe I'm no different."

"Maybe not. But a man puts in time with the army, he's more likely to see the whole thing, not try to make a mountain out of a molehill," Muller said.

Jake looked over the rim of his glass. "I found a man's body, and so far nobody's even asked me about it. Is that the molehill you had in mind?"

Muller stared back. "All right, I'm asking you. Is there anything we should know?"

"I know he was shot. I know he was carrying a lot of cash. I may be a friend to the army, but you try to keep what I do know quiet and it's like waving red meat at a dog. I get curious."

Muller sighed. "Nobody's trying to hide anything." He looked away at the party, then back at Jake. "Nobody's going to start anything either. There are almost two hundred reporters assigned to Berlin. They're all looking for something to write about. So they go see the bunker, cash in some cigarettes over at Zoo Station. Next thing you know, everybody's in the black market. Well, maybe everybody is, a little. What's ordinary here isn't ordinary at home."

"Is it ordinary to get shot?"

"More than you'd think," he said wearily. "The war's not over here. Look at them," he said, indicating the Russians. "Toasts. Their men are still all over, drunk half the time. Last week a jeepload of them start waving guns down in Hermannplatz—our zone—and before you could say boo, one of our MPs starts shooting and we're back at the O.K. Corral. Three dead, one ours. So we protest to the Russians and they protest back and there are still three people dead. Ordinary."

He turned to face Jake, his eyes gentle. "Look, we're not angels here. You know what an occupation army does? It occupies. They pull guard duty. They stand in front of buildings. They've got nothing but time. So they bitch and chase girls and make a little money selling their PX rations, which they're not supposed to do but they figure they're entitled, they won the war, and maybe they're right. And sometimes they get into trouble. Sometimes they even get shot. It happens." He paused. "But it doesn't have to be an international incident. And it doesn't have to make the army look bad. It's what happens here."

"But they'll file a report. It's still not that ordinary, is it?"

"And you want to see it."

"I'm curious, that's all. I never found a body before."

Muller looked at him, appraising. "It might take a while. We don't know who he is yet."

"I know who he is."

Muller raised his eyes. "I thought there weren't any tags."

"I knew his face. We were on the plane together. Lieutenant Tully."

Muller said nothing, just stared, then slowly nodded his head. "Come to my office tomorrow. I'll see what I can do. Elssholzstrasse."

"Which is where?"

"Schöneberg. Behind Kleist Park. The drivers will know."

"The old Supreme Court?"

"That's right," Muller said, surprised. "It was the best we could find. Not too much damage. Maybe God has a soft spot for judges. Even Nazi judges."

Jake grinned. "By the way, did anyone ever tell you—"

"I know, Judge Hardy. I suppose it could be worse. I don't know, I haven't seen the movies." He glanced at Jake. "Tomorrow, then. That's two favors you owe me. Now come and meet some Russians. Sounds like things are revving up." He motioned toward the front room, where the piano had switched from Cole Porter to a thumping Russian song. "They're the real story in Berlin, you know. They've been running things for two months—it's their town. And look at it. Remind me to show you another report tomorrow. Infant mortality. Six out of ten babies are going to die here this month. Maybe more. Die. Of course, that's politics. Scandal sells papers."

"I'm not looking for any scandal," Jake said quietly.

"No? You might find some, though," Muller said, his voice weary again. "I don't suppose your lieutenant was up to much good. But if you ask me, that's not the real scandal. Six out of ten. Not just one soldier. Life's cheap in Berlin. Try that story. I have all the facts you need for that one." He stopped, catching himself, and finished off his drink. "Well. Let's go promote some Allied cooperation."

"They seem to be doing all right," Jake said, trying to be light. "It's turning into a Russian party."

"It always does," Muller said. "We just bring the food."

But language had divided the party into its own occupation zones. The Russians Jake met nodded formally, tried a few words in German, and retreated back into their steady drinking. The piano had returned to the American zone with "The Lady Is a Tramp," but the Russian player hovered behind, ready to reclaim the keyboard for his side. Even the laughter, getting louder, came from isolated pockets, separated by untranslatable jokes. Only Liz, gliding in with a quick wink to Jake, seemed to bring the party together, suddenly drawing both sets of eager uniforms around her like Scarlett at the barbecue. Jake looked around the room, hoping to find Bernie and his armload of questionnaires, but got caught instead by a burly Russian covered with medals who knew English and, surprisingly, also knew Jake.

"You traveled with General Patton," he said, his eyes twinkling. "I read your dispatches."

"You did? How?"

"It's not forbidden, you know, to read our allies." He nodded. "Sikorsky," he said, introducing himself, his voice accented but amused and sure of itself, an officer's gift of rank. "In this case, I confess, we were interested to know where you were. A very energetic soldier, General Patton. We thought he might even reach Russia." His face, fleshy but not yet sagging with jowls, creased with good humor. "I read your description of Camp Dora. Before the general pulled back to your own zone."

"I don't think he was thinking much about zones then. Just Germans."

"Of course, as you say," Sikorsky said gracefully. "You saw Nordhausen then. I saw it too. A remarkable place."

"Yes, remarkable," Jake said, the word absurdly inadequate. The underground rocket factory, two vast tunnels into the mountain crisscrossed with shafts, hollowed out by walking corpses in striped pajamas.

"Ingenious. To put it there, safe from bombs. How was it possible, we wondered."

"With slave labor," Jake said flatly.

"Yes," the Russian said, nodding solemnly. "But still remarkable. We called it Aladdin's cave." Whole production lines, some of the V-twos still waiting, assembled, machine shops and tunnels full of parts, dripping with moisture from the rock. Bodies scattered in dark corners, because no one had bothered to clear them away in the frantic last days. "Of course," the Russian went on, "there were no treasures in the cave when we got there. What could have happened, do you think?"

"I don't know. The Germans must have moved it all somewhere."

"Hmm. But where? You didn't see anything yourself?"

Just the endless line of American trucks hauling their spoils west—crates of documents, tons of equipment, pieces of rockets on flatbeds. Seen, but not reported—the general's request. When he became a friend to the army.

"No. I saw the gurneys where they hanged the prisoners. That was enough for me. And the camps."

"Yes, I remember. The hand you could not shake off."

Jake looked at him, surprised. "You did read the piece."

"Well, you know, we were interested in Nordhausen. Such a puzzle. So much, to vanish like that. What is the expression? A disappearing trick."

"Strange things happen in wartime."

"In peace too, I think. At our Zeiss works, for example—four people." He waved his fingers. "Like that, into thin air. Another disappearing trick."

"Telling stories out of school, Vassily?" Muller said, joining them.

"Mr. Geismar has not heard about our trouble at the Zeiss factory. I thought perhaps he would be interested."

"Now, Vassily, we'll save that for the council meeting. You know, we can't control what people do. Sometimes they vote with their feet."

"Sometimes they are given transportation," the Russian replied quickly. "Under *nacht und nebel.*" Night and fog, the old nighttime arrests.

"That was Himmler's technique," Muller said. "Not the American army's."

"Still, one hears these stories. And people vanish."

"We hear them too," Muller said carefully, "in the American zone. Berlin is full of rumors."

"But if they are true?"

"This one isn't," Muller said.

"Ah," the Russian said. "So it's a mystery. Like Nordhausen," he said to Jake, then lifted his empty glass in a mock toast and politely headed away for a refill.

"What was that?" Jake said.

"The Russians are accusing us of snatching some scientists from their zone."

"Which we wouldn't do."

"Which we wouldn't do," Muller said. "They would, though, so they always suspect the worst. They're still kidnapping people. Mostly political. Not as bad as in the beginning, but they still do it. We protest. So they protest."

"Like having each other over for drinks."

Muller smiled. "In a way."

"And what's Zeiss?"

"Optical works. Bomb sights, precision lenses. The Germans were way ahead of us there."

"But not for long."

Muller shrugged. "You never stop, do you? I can't help you with this one. A few engineers took off. That's all the story I know, if it is a story. Personally, I wouldn't blame anyone for trying to get out of the Russian zone."

"So our friend's just blowing smoke."

"Well, that's what they do best. Don't let him fool you. Just because he speaks English doesn't mean he's a friend."

"Who is he exactly?"

"Vassily? General Sikorsky. He's at the council. Does a little bit of everything, like all the comrades, but our counterintelligence boys know him, so I always thought he had a finger in that pie. Maybe even a kidnapping or two. I wouldn't put it past him."

"So I should watch my back."

"You?" Muller smiled, amused. "Don't worry. Even the Russians wouldn't want a reporter."

Jake moved past the front parlor, where a group had begun singing, and down the hall toward the French doors in the back, open to let the smoke drift out. It was still light, the late night of a northern summer, and he looked at the muddy garden where grass and canvas chairs must have been, now trampled over and uprooted, like everything else in Berlin. There had been mud at Nordhausen too, so much that the trucks had slid in it, spattering the work party as they roared away with Aladdin's treasures. No *nacht und nebel,* just gum-chewing T units, loading their convoys of steel prizes for the trip west. Where now? Somewhere over the Rhine, maybe even already in America, getting ready for the next war. If he asked now, he'd be told it had never happened. A disappearing trick. And he'd let that story go without a qualm, happy to oblige, because there was always another, until suddenly they were gone, all the big war stories, leaving nothing but rubble.

"Hey, Jackson," Liz said, standing hesitantly in the doorway, as if she were afraid to interrupt. "What's up?"

"Nothing. Just arguing with myself."

"Who won?" she said, coming over.

Jake smiled. "My better instincts."

"That must have been close." She lit a cigarette, offering him one. "Catch any flak about today?"

"Not much. Nobody seems to think it's anything special. They wonder why I care."

"Why do you?"

Jake shrugged. "It's an old superstition. If a story falls in your lap, it's bad luck to waste it."

"Old superstition." Liz sniffed.

"Sorry about the camera."

"No, I got it back. A nice Russian brought it to the press camp. Seemed to think I might go out with him, me being so grateful."

"They didn't use to ask, I hear." He looked over at her. "I wish I'd used it. In case I need to prove he was shot."

"They're denying it?"

"No, but they're not shouting about it either. I don't know why not. A soldier shot in the Russian zone—you'd think they'd be jumping up and down. They spend half the time here squawking at each other." He jerked a thumb toward the party. "So why not this time?"

Liz shook her head. "Nobody wants to raise a stink while the conference is on."

"No, I know the army. Something's—off. Nobody just gets shot. What was he doing here? You met him. He say anything to you on the plane?"

"No," she said. "He was too busy trying to keep his stomach in one place."

"I was thinking about that too. Why fly if you hate it so much? What was important enough to get him on a plane?"

"Oh, Jake, lots of people fly. Maybe he was ordered. He's in the army, you know."

"Was. Then why didn't somebody meet him, if he was ordered? Remember that, at the airport?"

"Frankly, no."

"Where was he? Everybody else had a ride." He took a breath. "There's something."

Liz sighed. "Okay, have it your way, Sherlock. You going to need some pictures? A little strong for *Collier's.*"

Jake smiled. "Maybe. I have something else in mind too." Liz raised her eyebrows. "Track down the old office staff, see what happened to them. Berlin stories. They'd use those pictures, if you're interested."

"You're on. Old friends," she said. "Not just one?"

"No," he said, ignoring it. "Everybody I can find. I want to know what happened here, not just in the bunker. This other thing—I don't know, maybe you're right, maybe there's nothing." He paused, thinking. "Except the money. There's always a story in money."

Liz dropped her cigarette and rubbed it out. "Well, you keep arguing with yourself. Let me know how it comes out. Looks like I'm off," she said, glancing through the door.

"Again?"

"Can I help it if I'm popular?" Before she could move away, a tall soldier, vaguely familiar, came to the door. "I'll be with you in a sec," she said to him, clearly not wanting him to come out. He lifted his beer bottle and turned back in to the house.

"The lucky guy?"

"Not yet. But he says he knows a good jazz club."

"I'll bet." Jake looked through the door. "Ah," he said, remembering. "The congressman's driver. Liz."

"Don't be a snob," she said, slightly flustered. "Anyway, he's not a driver. He's an officer."

"And a gentleman."

"Are any of you? At least this one doesn't talk with his mouth full."

Jake laughed. "That sounds like the real thing."

"No," she said, looking straight at him. "That's when somebody comes back for you. Four years later. But he'll do."

He started to follow her inside, but a roar of laughter, like a blast of warm air, caught him at the door and turned him around. He wanted to be in his Berlin, sipping beer in some fading garden light, not in this odd pocket of Allied goodwill, glasses clinking like fencing swords. But that Berlin had probably been gone for years, packed away with the garden lanterns into cellars.

He crossed the garden and opened the back gate. A footpath, not wide enough to be an alley, fed into the next street. All the houses were quiet—no dinner conversation coming through the windows, no radio—as if they were hunkered down, waiting for the party noise in

Gelferstrasse to become a brawl, another raid that might pass over. In the silence you could hear your feet.

He turned down one of the narrow roads that led to the institute grounds, where the streets were named for scientists, not generals and Hohenzollerns. Farradayweg. Emil had worked here, miles away from Pariserstrasse, in his own world. The district still had the leafy enclave feel of a university, but now windows were knocked out, the chemistry building half charred, a roof gone. At the far end of the street he could see lights in a modern brick building, but the institute itself was dark. Still, the main building was standing. Thielallee. A big folly of a building, spiked round turrets on each corner like Kaiser helmets. *Pickelhaubes.* He walked up the steps to look more closely. Maybe it was still operational, somewhere he could ask tomorrow.

"Nein, nein!" Jake started. In the quiet, a voice as surprising as a shot. He turned. An old man walking a scrawny dog, wearing a jacket and a tweed hunter's hat, as if he were expecting the summer evening to turn chilly. The dog made a noise, almost a growl, then leaned against the man's leg, too listless to make the effort. The man wagged his finger at Jake, correcting him, then pointed to the brick building across the intersection. "Kommandatura," he said loudly, pointing again. "Kommandatura," each syllable pronounced slowly, instructions to a lost foreigner.

"No, I was looking for the institute," Jake said in German.

"Closed," the man said automatically, but now it was his turn to start, surprised to hear German.

"Yes. Do you know when it opens in the morning?"

"It doesn't open. It's closed. *Kaput.*" He dipped his head, reflex manners. "Forgive me. I thought—an American. I thought you were looking for the Kommandatura. Come, Schatzie."

"The Berlin Kommandatura?" Jake said, coming down before he could move away. "That's it?" He looked toward the brick building, now taking in the flags, the windows with lights burning. Thin square columns to give it an entrance. "What was it before?" The dog began sniffing at his leg, so Jake leaned over and patted her, a gesture that seemed to surprise the old man more than his speaking German.

"An insurance company," the man answered. "Fire insurance. It was a joke, you know. The one building that didn't burn." He looked down at the dog, still sniffing Jake's hand. "Don't worry, she won't trouble you. Not so much energy these days. It's the food, you see. I have to share my ration with her, and it's not enough."

Jake stood up, noticing now the man's own skinny frame, a heartless illustration of the old saw that owners resembled their pets. But the scraps at Gelferstrasse were blocks away. Instead he took out a pack.

"Cigarette?"

The old man took it and bowed. "Thank you. You don't mind if I save it for later?" he said, carefully tucking it into his pocket.

"Here. Save that one. Smoke this," Jake said, suddenly wanting company.

The man looked at it, amazed at his windfall, then nodded and bent over to the lighter. "You are about to see something interesting—a cigarette in Berlin actually being smoked. It's another joke. One sells to another, and another, but who smokes them?" He inhaled, then leaned his hand against Jake's upper arm. "Forgive me. A little dizziness. Thank you. How is it that you speak German?" he said, making conversation, his tongue set loose by tobacco.

"I lived in Berlin before the war."

"Ah. It's not the best, you know, your German. You should study." A voice from a classroom.

Jake laughed. "Yes," he said, then nodded toward the man's pocket. "How much will you get for it?"

"Five marks, maybe. It's for her." He looked down at the dog. "I'm not complaining. Things are as they are. But it's difficult, to see her like this. How can you feed a dog, they say, when people are hungry? But what should I do? Let her die, an innocent? Who else is so innocent in Berlin? That's what I say to them—when you're innocent, I'll feed you too. That shuts them up. They're the worst, the golden pheasants."

Jake looked at him, lost now, wondering if he'd found not a man in the street but a crank. "Golden pheasants?"

"The big party members. Now, of course, they know nothing. You brought this on us, I say to them, and you want to eat? I'd rather feed a dog. A dog."

"So they're still around."

The old man smiled crookedly. "No, there are no Nazis in Berlin. Not one. Only Social Democrats. So many, all those years. How could the party have survived with so many against them? Well, it's a question." He took another drag and stared at the glowing tip. "All Social Democrats now. The bastards. They threw me out." He looked toward the institute building. "Years of work. I'll never make it up now, never. It's all *kaput.*"

"You're a Jew?"

He snorted. "If I were a Jew I'd be dead. They had to leave right away. The rest of us, they waited, hoping we would join, then it was an order—party member or out. So I was out. I really was a Social Democrat." He smiled. "Of course, you may not believe me. But you can check the records. 1938."

"You were at the institute?" Jake said, interested now.

"Since 1919," he said proudly. "They had places, you see, after the influenza, so I was lucky. It counted for something then, just to be here. Well, those days. I remember when we got the measurements from the eclipse. For Einstein's theory," he said, a teacher explaining, catching Jake's blank expression. "If light had mass, then gravity would bend the rays. Starlight. The eclipse made it possible to measure. Einstein said it would be 1.75 seconds of an arc, the angle. And do you know what it was? 1.63. So close. Can you imagine? In that one minute, everything changed. Everything. Newton was wrong. The whole *world* changed, right here in Berlin. Right here." He extended his arm toward the building, his voice following it in some private reverie. "So, then what? Champagne, of course, but the *talk.* All night talking. We thought we could do anything—that was German science. Until the gangsters. Then down the drain—"

"I had a friend at the institute," Jake said, breaking in before the old man could drift further. "I'm trying to locate him. That's why—perhaps you knew him. Emil Brandt?"

"The mathematician? Yes, of course. Emil. You were his friend?"

"Yes," Jake said. His friend. "I was hoping someone would know where he is. You don't—?"

"No, no, it's many years."

"But do you know what happened to him?"

"That I couldn't say. I left the institute, you see."

"And he stayed," Jake said slowly, piecing together dates. "But he wasn't a Nazi."

"My friend, anyone who was here after 1938—" He stopped, seeing Jake's face, and looked away. "But perhaps he was a special case." He dropped his cigarette. "Thank you again. I must say good evening now. The curfew."

"I knew him," Jake said. "He wasn't like that."

"Like what? Goering? Many people joined, not just the swine. People do what they have to do."

"You didn't."

He shrugged. "And what did it matter? Emil was young. A fine mind, I remember that. Numbers he could see in his head, not just on paper. Who can say what's right? To give up your work for politics? Maybe he loved science more. And in the end—" He paused, looking again at the building, then back at Jake. "You disturb yourself over this. I can see it. Let me tell you something, for the price of a cigarette. The eclipse? In 1919? The Freikorps were fighting in the streets then. I myself saw bodies, Spartakists, in the Landwehrkanal. Who remembers now? Old politics. Footnotes. But in that building we changed the world. So what's important? A party card? I don't judge your friend. We are not all criminals."

"Just the golden pheasants."

A mild smile, conceding the point. "Yes. Them I don't forgive. I'm not yet a saint."

"What does it mean, anyway? Golden pheasants?"

"Who knows? Bright feathers—the uniforms. The wives left in fur coats, before the Russians came. Maybe it was that they flew out of the bushes as soon as they heard the first shots. Ha," he said, the joke for himself. "Maybe that's why there are no Nazis in Berlin." He stopped and looked again at Jake. "It was a formality, you know. Just a formality." He tipped his hat. "Good night."

Jake stood for a minute in front of the gloomy institute, unsettled. Emil must have joined. There wouldn't have been any exceptions. But why did it surprise him? Millions had. A formality. Except Jake hadn't known. All that time, something unsaid. A pleasant man with gentle eyes, quiet at parties, diffident, who saw numbers in his head—someone Jake never thought about at all. Not a Nazi, one of the good Germans. Standing with his arm around Lena. Had she known? How could he not tell her? And how could she stay with him, knowing? But she had.

It was getting dark, so he started down Thielallee. A jeep had pulled up in front of the Kommandatura, dropping off two soldiers, who hurried up the stairs with briefcases. New politics, soon to be as old as the Freikorps. What was important? People do what they have to do. She had stayed. Jake had left. That simple. Except Emil wasn't simple anymore, which changed things. Had she known, those afternoons when they drew the shades to keep Berlin outside?

Jake felt suddenly disoriented, his mental map redrawn like the city's streets, no longer where they were supposed to be. When he turned right off Thielallee, he saw, confused, that he was literally lost. The side street didn't connect back to Gelferstrasse as he'd thought it would. And your German isn't the best either anymore, he thought to himself, smiling. But he had never known this part of town; the streets here had always gone this way. It was the other Berlin, the one he had known, where you now needed a compass to find your way, some needle pulled by gravity, strong enough to bend starlight.

CHAPTER FOUR

ALMOST ALL THE other buildings in Elssholzstrasse had been knocked out, so the Control Council headquarters stood even larger now. A massive hulk of Prussian stone, its grim streetfront must have seemed an appropriate way station in the old court days, when the judges inside, party members all, had sentenced their victims to worse prisons. The main entrance, however, around the driveway into Kleist Park, presented a lighter face, tall windowed doors flanked by carved floating angels who looked down across what had been a formal lawn bordered with hedges toward two symmetrical colonnades at the other end, an unexpected piece of Paris. The whole place was noisy with activity—cars crunching on the gravel, a work party repairing the roof, banging tiles—like a country house getting ready for a big weekend party. Four bright new Allied flags had been hung over the entrance; 82nd Airborne guards in white spats and shiny helmets were posted at the doorway. Even the dusty grounds were being tidied up, raked by a detachment of German POWs, the letters stenciled on their backs, while a handful of bored GIs kept watch, standing around idly and taking the sun. Jake followed a group of husky

Russian women in uniform through the chandeliered hall and up a grand marble staircase, an opera house entrance. He was met, surprisingly, by Muller himself.

"I thought you might like a look around," Muller said, heading them down the corridor. "We're still trying to get things in shape. Place took a fair amount of damage."

"Maybe not enough, given what it was."

"Well, we have to use what we can. Biggest place we could find. Over four hundred rooms, they say, although I don't know who's counting. Maybe they threw in a closet or two. Of course, only part of it's usable. This is where the council will sit." He opened the door to a large chamber, already converted to a meeting room with long tables arranged in a square. In each corner, near their respective flags, were desks with shorthand typewriters for recording secretaries. A stack of ashtrays and notepads sat on one table, waiting to be distributed.

"Nobody's been here yet," Muller said. "You're the first, if that means anything to you."

Jake looked around the empty room, feeling he was back at the Cecilienhof, counting chimneys. "No press section?"

"No press section. We don't want to encourage speeches—hard to resist with the press around. Give them an audience, they can't help themselves. We want working sessions."

"Nice and private."

"No." He nodded to the recording desks. "There'll be minutes. The council will meet once a quarter," he continued. "The Coordinating Committee once a month, the subcommittees—well, all the time. There's a lot to do."

Jake fingered the stack of notepads. "All organized."

"On paper," Muller said, leaning against the table, his back to the window, so that his silver hair developed a halo of light. "Actually, nobody knows how it's going to work. Until we do it. We're making it up as we go along. Nobody planned on this, running the country." He noticed Jake's raised eyebrows. "Not this way. They trained a few people, somewhere down in Virginia—to help the Germans with the transition," he said, drawing out the word. "Transition. I don't know what they expected. The last war, I suppose. Get a peace treaty, hand the country over to the good guys, and go home. But not this time. There wasn't anybody to hand it over *to.* Twelve years. Even the mailmen were Nazis. And the country—you've seen it, it's just shot to hell. Nobody expected them to fight to the end. Why would they? You don't expect a whole country to commit suicide."

"They had a little help from bomber command."

Muller nodded. "I don't say they didn't ask for it. But now it's flat and we've got it. No food, nothing running—Berlin HQ has got its hands full just fixing the water mains." He took a breath and looked directly at Jake. "We've got twenty million people to feed in our zone alone. The ones who aren't starving are stealing bicycles just to get around. We've got a winter coming with no coal. Epidemics, if we're not lucky, which we probably won't be. DPs—" He waved his hand as if, overwhelmed, he'd run out of words. "We didn't sign on for any of this," he said, his voice as tired as his eyes, "but we've got it anyway. So there's a lot to do." He glanced at the room. "Seen enough?"

Jake nodded. "Thanks for the look. And the speech," he added easily. "You wouldn't be trying to tell me something, by any chance."

Muller smiled patiently, Judge Hardy again. "Maybe just a little. I've been regular army all my life—we're used to protecting our flanks. People who write about MG, maybe they should have some idea what we're up against. A little perspective. We're not all—well, come on, I'll give you what you came for."

"How did you end up here, anyway?" Jake said, following him out into the long hall.

"Like everyone else—they don't need us in the field now, so we've got to serve our time out somewhere. I didn't volunteer, if that's what you mean. Tactical units don't have much use for MG, think we're just office boys. I wasn't any different. Nobody's going to get a promotion for fixing sewer lines. But nobody's getting promoted in the field now either—the war's over, they tell me—and I have a while to go before they pension me off. So. We're long on old farts here. The civilians, that's something else. Most of the time it's some lawyer who sat out the war in Omaha and now wants a commission so he can call himself captain—they won't sign on for the lower ranks. They get it too, the rank. What the rest of us had to work years for. It rubs a little, if you let it."

"But you don't."

"I did. But it's like anything else—the work takes over. You serve your country," he said flatly, without a hint of irony. "I didn't ask for it, but you know what? I think we're doing one helluva job here, given everything. Or does that sound like another speech to you?"

"No." Jake smiled. "It sounds like they ought to promote you."

"They won't," Muller said evenly, then stopped and faced him. "You know, this is probably my last post. I wouldn't want to see—any mess. If you're going to start flinging mud around, I'd appreciate a little early warning."

"I'm not—"

"I know, you're just curious. So are we. A man's been killed. And the truth is, we have no way of finding out what happened. We don't have Scotland Yard here, just some MPs arresting drunks. So we may never know. But if there's anything that might, well, be a problem for us, that we do need to know."

"What makes you think there is?"

"I don't. But that's what you're fishing for, isn't it?" He started walking again. "Look, all I'm asking is you meet me halfway on this. I don't have to release any information. If you hadn't been there at Potsdam—but you were, and you knew him. So now I've got a situation. I can't pretend it didn't happen. But I don't have to open this up to a lot of speculation either. I'm releasing it to you, not anybody else. If you do turn up something, okay, you've got yourself a story."

"But if I don't—"

"Then you don't guess out loud. No mystery body. No unsolved anything. You might get some mileage out of that in the papers. But all we'd get is a lot of questions we can't answer. That just *eats* time. We can't afford that. There's too much to do. All I'm asking is a little discretion."

"And tell you in advance what I'm going to say."

"I didn't say you couldn't say it. Just tell me if it's coming."

"So you can deny it?"

"No," Muller said, deadpan. "So I can duck." He stopped at a door paned with translucent glass. "Here we are. Jeanie should have the copies by now."

Jeanie was a pretty WAC whose red fingernails seemed too long for serious typing. She was putting carbon sheets into two beige folders and threw Muller a smile that Jake, amused, guessed was more than secretarial. Muller, however, was all business.

"Got those reports?"

She handed him one of the folders, then a message slip. "The general wants you at ten."

"Come on, then," he said to Jake, leading him into a plain office with an American flag in the corner. Muller belonged to the clean desk school—the only things on the empty surface were a pen set and a framed picture of a young soldier.

"Your boy?" Jake asked.

Muller nodded. "He was hit on Guadalcanal."

"I'm sorry."

"No, not killed. Wounded. At least he's out of it now." Then, avoiding any more intimacy, he opened the folder, took out two carbon flimsies, and pushed them across the desk to Jake. "Service record. Casualty report."

"You're calling it a casualty?"

"It's what we call the report," Muller said, slightly annoyed. "It's just a form. Anyway, now you know what we know."

Jake skimmed the first sheet, a spare listing of dates and assignments. Patrick Tully. Natick, Mass. A little older than the boy in the picture on the desk. The casualty report Jake could have written himself. "Not much, is it?" he said.

"No."

"What isn't here? Any trouble before that didn't make it into the record?"

"Not that I know of. Service record's clean, no flags. A distinguished member of the United States Armed Forces. That's what we're going to write to his mother, anyway."

"Yes," Jake said. A person, not a number, a kid with a family, not as lucky as young Muller. "What about the money?"

"She'll get that too, with his effects. APO money order. It was his, as far as we know. Let's hope she thinks he saved his back pay."

"How much was there? It doesn't say."

Muller looked at him, then nodded. "Fifty-six thousand marks. They convert at ten to one. So roughly five thousand dollars. That's what the Russians gave us, anyway. They say some of it blew away."

"So figure twice that. That's a lot of back pay."

"Maybe he was good at cards," Muller said.

"What brings in that kind of money? On the black market."

"Watches, mostly. If it ticks, the Russians'll buy it. A Mickey Mouse can go for five hundred bucks."

"That's still a lot of watches."

"That depends how long he was doing it. If he was doing it. Look, on the record? There is no black market. Sometimes supply depots come up a little short. Things disappear. One of the facts of wartime. The Germans are hungry. They'll buy food any way they can. It's about food. Naturally, we're doing what we can to stop it."

"And off the record?"

"Off the record, everybody does it. How do you stop a kid in a candy store? Want to do some quick arithmetic? A GI's allowed a carton of cigarettes a week at the PX. A nickel a pack, fifty cents a carton. On the street, it's worth one hundred dollars—that's five thousand dollars a year. Add in some chocolate, four bottles of liquor a month, another five thousand dollars. A package of food from home? Maybe some tuna fish, a can of soup? More. Lots more. It adds up. A guy can make a year's salary just from his rations. You try stopping that. Officially, there's no fraternization either. So how do we explain all the VD?"

Jake glanced down at the sheet. "He'd only been in Germany since May."

"What do you want me to say? Some of our boys are more enterprising than others. You don't have to be a big operator to make money in Germany. Last month our troops were paid about a million dollars. They sent three million home." He paused. "Off the record."

Jake stared, staggered by the figure. "I didn't think the Germans had that much money."

"The Germans. They're selling silverware for a stick of margarine. Whatever they've got left. The Russians have the money."

Jake thought of the ragtag guards at the Chancellery, the peasants wheeling carts through Potsdamerplatz, as primitive as a muddy village. "The Russians have that kind of money?" he said dubiously. "Since when?"

Muller looked at him. "Since we gave it to them." He hesitated. "How far off the record are we?"

"Farther every minute."

Muller sat back. "I'm going to hold you to that. You see, the original plan was to issue occupation marks. Something all the forces could use here and the locals would accept, not gum up the works with four different currencies. Fine. So the Treasury made up the engraving plates and, like idiots, gave a set to the Russians. Same money. Of course, the idea was they'd keep a strict accounting of theirs, since it would have to be convertible to hard currency—dollars, pounds, whatever. Instead they just started the presses and kept going. Nobody knows how much they made. Most of their troops hadn't been paid in three years. They got it all in occupation marks. The hitch is, they can't take them home—the Russians won't convert them—and now you've got a whole army with more money than they've ever seen before in their lives and one place to spend it. Here. So they buy watches and whatever else they can carry home. At any price. It's Monopoly money to them. And meanwhile, since the currency has to be honored, our boys take the marks they get and send them home as dollars and the Treasury has one hell of a drain on its hands. We yell and scream, of course, but I'd lay you even money—in dollars—that we're never going to see one ruble for those plates. The Russians say their marks just circulate in Germany, keeping the local wheels going—the Germans' tab. And we have a small problem explaining why so many are flooding back home, since there is no black market—so we pay. We're paying, in fact, for the Russian occupation here. But nobody wants to touch that story." He smiled. "And neither do you."

"I'm not even sure I understand it."

"Nobody understands money. Except what's in his pocket. Which is lucky for the Treasury. If we'd pulled a stunt like that, they'd court-martial us out of here in no time."

"So what are you going to do about it?"

"That's the ten o'clock meeting. General Clay wants to limit the amount a man can send home to his actual pay. It'll be a headache for the APO, just keeping track, and it won't solve everything, but at least it'll stop the worst of the bleeding. Of course they can still send goods home, but the money will stay here, where it belongs. Ultimately, the only thing that's going to work is a new currency, but don't hold your breath. How fast do you think the Russians would agree to that?"

"I mean, what are you doing on the ground? How do you police it?"

"Well, it's a problem. MP raids the worst spots from time to time, but that's just a little finger in the dike. Berlin's an open city—people go where they want. It's just administered in zones. So we can't patrol Zoo Station, that's the Brits. Alexanderplatz is in the Russian zone."

"Like Potsdam."

Muller looked up at him. "Like Potsdam. There's nothing we can do there."

"What about off the street? This much money—somebody must be running things."

"You mean gangs? Professionals? That I don't know. And I'd doubt it. You hear rumors about the DPs, but people like to blame the DPs for everything. Nobody polices them. The kind of thing you're talking about, you'd have to go back to Bavaria or Frankfurt, where there's still something to steal. Warehouses. Big hoardings. It happens, and I suppose Frankfurt must have somebody on it, if you're interested. But Berlin? It's been picked pretty clean. What you've got here is a lot of small money that adds up."

"That's a fair description of the numbers racket too."

A reluctant smile. "I guess." Muller paused, spreading his hands on the desk. "Look. A soldier sells a watch. Maybe he shouldn't, and maybe you don't think we're doing enough to stop him. But I'll tell you this—I've seen lots of men die in the last few years. Ripped up, holding their guts in. Good men. Kids. Nobody thought they were criminals then. Now they're picking up a few bucks. Maybe it's wrong, but you know what? I'm still a soldier. I think they're worth two million a month."

"So do I," Jake said slowly. "I just don't like to see them get shot. It doesn't seem right. For a watch."

Muller looked at him, disconcerted, then lowered his head. "No. Well. Is there anything else?"

"Lots, but you've got a meeting to get to," Jake said, standing up. "I don't want to wear out my welcome."

"Any time," Muller said pleasantly, also getting up, relieved. "That's what we're here for."

"No, you're not. I appreciate the time." Jake folded the flimsies into his pocket. "And these. Oh, one more thing. Can I see the body?"

"The body?" Muller said, literally taking a step back in surprise. "I thought you had seen it. Isn't that why we're here? It's—gone. It was shipped back to Frankfurt."

"That was fast. No autopsy?"

"No," Muller said, slightly puzzled. "Why would there be an autopsy? We know how he died. Should there have been one?"

Jake shrugged. "At least a coroner's report." He caught Muller's expression. "I know. You're not Scotland Yard. It's just a little skimpy, that's all," he said, patting the sheets in his pocket. "It might have helped to examine it. I wish you'd waited."

Muller looked at him, then sighed. "You know what I wish, Geismar? I wish you'd never gone to Potsdam."

Jeanie was arranging her set of carbons when he came out. She looked up and smiled without stopping, like a casino dealer, shuffling the third sheet to the bottom, then tossing the folder into an out box for filing. "All set?"

Jake smiled back. The army never changed, a world run in duplicate. He wondered if there was another girl to do the filing to save those wonderful nails. "For now," he said, still smiling, but she took it as a pass, arching her eyebrows and shooting him a look.

"We're here nine to five," she said, a dismissal.

"That's good to know," he said, playing along. "Colonel keep you pretty busy?"

"All the live-long day. Stairs are down the hall to your right."

"Thanks," he said, lifting his fingers to his forehead in a salute.

On the entrance steps he was blinded by the light and shaded his eyes to get his bearing. The sun, already hot, was streaming in from the east, filtering through the dust that hung over the ruins beyond the graceful colonnades. The work party, bent over their rakes, had got rid of their shirts but not, Jake noticed, their initials, P on one trouser leg, W on the other. The war had branded everybody, even Tully, now just some initials on a carbon flimsy.

He stood for a minute, his mind full of engraving plates and watch prices, all of which led him nowhere. Which was probably where Muller wanted him to go. He smiled to himself, thinking of Jeanie—two brush-offs in one morning, one more direct than the other. It was Muller who'd taken the circular way around, leaving him back on the steps not even sure he'd been through a revolving door. Except something nagged, a missing crossword piece that would leap to the eye if you looked at it long enough. He told the driver he wanted to walk.

"Walk?" the soldier said, amazed. "You mean back?"

"No, meet me at Zoo Station in about an hour. You know where that is?"

The soldier nodded. "Sure. It's a hike from here."

"I know. I like to walk. Helps me think." Explaining himself. He made a mental note to ask Ron for his own jeep.

But the soldier, like Jeanie, had been around. "I get it. You sure you don't want me to drop you? I mean, I don't care, it's your business."

Everybody does it, Jake thought as he headed across the battered park; a lot of small money that adds up. So whom had Tully done business with? A gun-happy Russian? A DP with nothing to lose? Anybody. Five thousand dollars, more. People got killed every day in Chicago for less, just for skimming a numbers collection. Life would be even cheaper than that here. But why come in the first place? Because the Russians were here, flush with cash. Not porcelain knickknacks and old silver to trade. Cash. Honey for bears. Everybody does it.

The park gates opened onto lower Potsdamerstrasse and a small stream of military trucks and civilians on rickety bicycles, all that was left of the traffic that used to roar by to the center. On foot Berlin was a different city, not the spectacle he'd seen from a touring jeep but something grittier, a wreck in closeup. He had loved walking in the city, exploring the miles of flat, irregular streets as if just the physical touch of shoe leather made it personal, brought him into its life. Sundays in the Grunewald. Afternoons wandering through districts where the other journalists never went, Prenzlauer or the tenement streets in Wedding, just to see what they were like, his eyes gliding from building to building, oblivious to curbs. Now he had to step carefully, skirting clumps of broken cement and picking his way through plaster and glass that crunched underfoot. The city had become a trail hike, full of obstacles and sharp things hidden under stones. Steel rods twisted into spiky shapes, still black from fire. The familiar rotting smell. At the corner of Pallasstrasse, the remains of the Sportpalast, where bicycles used to whiz by in the racing oval and Hitler promised the faithful a thousand years. Only the giant flak tower was standing, like the ones at the zoo, too sturdy even for bombs. A soldier was propped against the wall with one hand, talking to a girl and fondling her hair, the oldest black market in the world. Across the street, a few other girls in thin dresses leaned against a standing wall, gesturing to convoy trucks. At ten o'clock in the morning.

The side streets were clogged with debris, so he kept to the main roads, turning left on Bülowstrasse for the long walk up to the zoo. This was a part of town he'd known well, the elevated station hulking over Nollendorfplatz, with its ring of bars. A movie marquee had slid down to the pavement nearly intact, as if the building had been whipped out from under it, like the magic trick with a tablecloth. A few people were out, one of them pushing a baby carriage filled with household goods, and Jake realized that the dazed, plodding movement he'd seen from the jeep two days ago was the new pace of the city, as careful as his own. Nobody walked quickly over rubble. Why would anyone come to Berlin? Had Tully been before? There must be traveling orders, something to check. The army ran in duplicate.

More blocks of collapsed buildings, more groups of women in headscarves and old uniform pants, cleaning bricks. A woman in heels stepped out of one building, smartly dressed, as if she were heading up the street as usual for some shopping at KaDeWe. Instead she wobbled over some broken plaster to a waiting army car and straightened her nylons as she pulled her legs in, a different kind of excursion. And KaDeWe, in any case, was gone, ripped through by bombs and sagging into Wittenbergplatz, not even a window mannequin left. They used to meet here, sometimes by the *wurst* stands on the food floor, where you were likely to run into anybody, then leave separately for Jake's flat across the square. Taking different sides so that Jake could see her through the crowd as he waited at the stoplight, watching to see that no one followed. No one did. A game to make it more exciting, getting away with something. Then up the stairs where she'd be waiting, a ring to make sure Hal was out, and inside, sometimes grabbing each other even before the door clicked shut. The flat would be gone now too, like the afternoons, a memory.

Except it wasn't. Jake looked across the street, shading his eyes again. A piece of the building had been knocked out, but the rest was there, with his corner flat still facing west onto the square. He took a step, elated, then stopped. What would he say? 'I used to live here and I want to see it again'? He imagined another Frau Dzuris, looking puzzled and hoping for chocolate. A woman came to the window, opening it wider to the air, and for an instant he stopped breathing, straining to see. Why couldn't it be? But it wasn't Lena, wasn't anything like Lena. A truck went by, blocking the view, and when it passed, the broad back was turned to the window so that he couldn't see her face, but of course he'd know, just the movement of her arm at the window, even from across the square. He dropped his hand, feeling foolish. A friend of the landlord's, no doubt, eager to snap up the flat when Hal finally left. Someone who wouldn't know him, might not even believe he'd been there at all. Why should she? The past had been wiped out with the streets. But the flat was there, real, a kind of proof that everything else had happened too. If he looked long enough, maybe the rest of the square would come back with it, busy, the way it all used to be.

He turned away and caught a glimpse of himself in a broken shard of plate glass from the store window. Nothing was the way it used to be, not even him. Would she recognize him now? He stared at the reflection. Not a stranger, but not the man she had known either. A lived-in face, older, with two deep lines bracketing his mouth. Dark hair thinning back from the temples. A face he saw every day shaving, without noticing it had changed. He imagined her looking at him, smoothing away lines with her fingers to find him. But faces didn't come back either. They got cluttered with assignments and frantic telegrams, squint lines from seeing too much. They'd been kids. Only four years, and look at all the marks. His face was still there, like the flat, but scarred now too, not the one he'd had before. But the war had changed everybody. At least he was here, not dead or turned into a set of initials. POWs. DPs.

He stopped, a tiny, nagging jolt. Initials. He took out the carbon sheets and scanned them again. That was it. He put the top sheet under, glanced over the second, then automatically shuffled for the third and stopped, empty-handed. But Jeanie had had three carbons. He squinted, trying to remember. Yes, three, like a stacked deck. He stood for another minute thinking, then put the sheets away and started up the street again toward the zoo, where small amounts of money were being made.

The driver took him back to Bernie's office, a small room in the old Luftwaffe building crammed with files and stacks of questionnaires that spilled off the couch and rose in piles on the floor, a mare's nest of paper. How did he find anything? The desk was worse. More stacks and loose clippings, stale coffee cups, even an abandoned tie—everything, in fact, but Bernie, who was out again. Jake flipped open one of the files, a buff-colored *fragebogen* like one Lena might have filled out, a life on six typed pages. But this was Herr Gephardt, whose spotless record deserved, he claimed, a work permit.

"Don't touch anything," said a soldier at the door. "He'll know. Believe it or not."

"Any idea when he'll be back? I keep missing him."

"You the guy from yesterday? He said you might be by. Try the Document Center. He's usually there. Wasserkäfersteig," he said, breaking it into syllables.

"Where?"

The soldier smiled. "Mouthful, huh? If you hold on a sec, I'll take you—I was just going myself. I can find it, I just can't spell it."

They drove west past the press camp to the U-bahn station at Krumme Lanke, where a handful of soldiers and civilians huddled in a miniature version of the Reichstag market, then turned right down a quiet street. At the far end Jake could see the trees of the Grunewald. He thought of the old summer Sundays, with hikers in shorts heading out to the beaches where the Havel widened into the series of bays Berlin called lakes. Today, in the same hot sun, there were only a few people gathering fallen branches and loading them into carts. An axe chipped away at a broad stump.

"Pathetic, isn't it?" the soldier said. "They chop down the trees when nobody's looking. There won't be anything left by winter." A winter with no coal, according to Muller.

At the edge of the woods, they turned up a narrow street of suburban villas, one of which had been turned into a fortress with a high barbed-wire double fence, floodlights, and patrolling sentries.

"They're not taking any chances," Jake said.

"DPs camp out in the woods. Once it's dark—"

"What's in there, gold?"

"Better. For us, anyway. Party records."

He showed a pass at the door, then led Jake to a sign-in ledger in the entrance hall. Another guard was inspecting the briefcase of a soldier on his way out. Neither spoke. The council headquarters had had the busy shoe-clicking hum of a government office. This was quieter, the locked-in hush of a bank. One more ID check took them into a room lined with filing cabinets.

"Christ. Fort Knox," Jake said.

"Bernie'll be down in the vault," the soldier said, smiling. "Counting the bars. This way."

"Where'd you get it all?" Jake said, looking at the cabinets.

"All over. The party kept everything right to the end—membership applications, court records. Guess they never thought they'd lose. Then they couldn't destroy them fast enough." He spread his hand toward the cabinets as they walked. "We got the SS files too, even Himmler's personal one. The big haul, though, that's downstairs. Index cards. The central party registry in Munich kept duplicates of all the local cards—every single Nazi. Eight million and counting. Sent them to a paper mill in Bavaria finally, to pulp them, but before the owner could get around to it, the Seventh Army arrived. So, *voilà.* Now we've got them. Here we go." He went down a staircase to the basement. "Teitel, you here? I found your guy."

Bernie was bent over a broad table whose littered surface was a mirror image of the mess in his office. The room, an alcoved cellar that might once have held wine, was now walled from floor to ceiling with wooden drawers, like card catalogues in a library. When he looked up, his eyes were confused, as if he had no idea who Jake was.

"Sorry to barge in like this," Jake said. "I know you're busy. But I need your help."

"Oh, Geismar. Right. You're looking for a friend. I'm sorry, I forgot all about it." He picked up a pen, ready to work.

"Don't forget to sign him out," the driver said to Bernie, drifting back up the stairs.

"What was the name?"

"Brandt. But I need something else."

Bernie looked up, his pen still poised to write. Jake pulled out a chair.

"A soldier was killed in Potsdam yesterday—well, killed the day before. He washed up on the conference grounds yesterday. Hear about it?"

Bernie shook his head, waiting.

"No, I guess not," Jake said, "not down here. Anyway, I was there, so I got interested. He had some money on him, a lot, five thousand, maybe closer to ten. I thought that was interesting too, but apparently I'm the only one. MG just gave me the brush this morning—polite, but a brush. This one came with a lecture. Happens all the time. Black market's a nickel-and-dime game, no big players. Nobody gets excited when a Russian shoots one of our men, just when they do anything else. So go away, please. Now I'm even more interested. Then I hear the body's already been shipped back to Frankfurt. That's a little too efficient, especially for MG. Following me so far?"

"Who was the brush?"

"Muller," Jake said.

Bernie frowned. "Fred Muller? He's a good man. Old army."

"I know. So they say keep a lid on it and he keeps a lid on it. Look, I don't blame him. He's a time-server and he doesn't want any trouble. He probably thinks I'm a pain in the ass."

"Probably."

"But why keep a lid on it? He promises me an exclusive and gives me a casualty report. But not all of it. There's a sheet missing." Jake paused. "The kind of thing the DA's office used to pull."

Bernie smiled. "So why come to me?"

"Because you were a DA. I've never met one yet who stopped being a DA. Something's funny here. You can feel it in your gut."

Bernie looked over at him. "I don't feel anything yet."

"No? Try this. Muller wants me to think it's a GI making a few bucks on the side. Okay, not nice, but nothing special, either. But he wasn't just a GI. PSD, that's Public Safety Division, isn't it?"

"That's what it says on the charts," Bernie said slowly.

"Well, that's what it says on the casualty report too. PSD. He was one of you. Ever met a police department that couldn't be bothered when a cop got shot? That's one organization takes care of its own."

Bernie looked at him again, then reached over for his coffee cup. "We're not exactly a police department, you know," he said carefully. "It's not the same."

"But you run the MPs, you run the local police, you're responsible for law and order. Such as it is."

"I don't run anything. You're asking the wrong guy. I'm Special Branch. I just—"

"Chase rats, I know. But you're still in the department. You must know people. Anyway, you're the only one I know. So."

Bernie took another sip of coffee. "Berlin PSD?"

"No, he flew in from Frankfurt. Another interesting point, by the way."

"Then no wonder Fred sent him back. Put it in somebody else's In box. It's the MG way." He paused. "Look, I don't have time for this, whatever it is. You want somebody over in CID. Criminal Investigation."

Jake shook his head. "CID's army, not Military Government. Knife fights. This is being handled by Public Safety." He took the sheets out of his pocket. "Here, see for yourself."

Bernie put his hand up in a stop sign. "No, I mean it. I don't have the time."

"Somebody else's In box," Jake said.

Bernie put down the cup and sighed. "What are you looking for, anyway?"

"Why nobody wants to know. The way the story's supposed to go is the Russians loot, we just liberate a few souvenirs. I've told it that way myself. And Public Safety? The last place you'd expect to find a bad apple. Wrong barrel. But my guess is that he had something going, not just a couple of cartons of cigarettes, and I'll bet it's Muller's guess too. The difference is, he doesn't want to know and this time I do. So would a DA. Man's dead."

Bernie ran his hand through the tight waves of his hair and stood up, as if the chair had been confining him. He moved a folder onto a pile, then walked over to another, pretending to be busy. "I'm not a DA here," he said finally. "I'm MG too. Maybe Fred's right, you know. The guy closed his own case. Maybe we're all better off."

"Except for one thing. What if he wasn't acting solo? A man comes to Berlin to make a deal and ends up dead. So who was he coming to see?"

"A Russian, you said." He moved another pile.

"Must have been. But who set it up? He's operating all by himself? There have to be some other apples in that barrel. Chances are, he had friends. It's a friendly kind of business."

"Friends in Public Safety?" Bernie said, looking up.

"Somewhere. That's the way it used to work in Chicago."

"That's Chicago," Bernie said, waving his hand.

"And Berlin. It's always the same, more or less. Here's a big city with no police and a lot of money floating around. Put out that kind of cheese and the usual mice come out. And pretty soon somebody has to organize it, to make sure he gets a little more. It's always the same. The only question is whether Patrick Tully was one of the mice or one of the rats who took a little more."

"Who?"

"Patrick Tully. The victim." Jake handed over the sheet to Bernie. "Twenty-three. Afraid of flying. So why come to Berlin? Who was he coming to see?"

Bernie stared at the paper, then at Jake.

"That's the report," Jake said. "Half of it, anyway. Maybe the other half can tell me."

"I can tell you," Bernie said evenly, his body finally still. "He was coming to see me."

"What?" A word to fill time, too surprised to say anything else. For a second neither of them spoke. Bernie looked again at the sheet.

"Yesterday," he said quietly, thinking aloud. "That's why I canceled you. He never showed. I told Mike to keep an eye out. That's probably who he thought you were. Why he brought you here—we're off-limits to press."

"Tully was coming to see you?" Jake said, still taking it in. "Want to tell me why?"

"I have no idea." He glanced up. "That isn't a brush. I don't know."

"You didn't ask?"

Bernie shrugged. "People come through from Frankfurt all the time. Somebody from PSD requests a meeting, what am I supposed to say? No? Half the time they're just looking for an excuse to come to Berlin. Everybody wants to see it, but you're supposed to have a reason for being here. So they liaise and fart around in meetings nobody has time for and then go home."

"With five thousand dollars."

"He didn't get it from me, if that's what you're asking," he said irritably. "He didn't show, or do you want Mike to verify that?"

"Keep your shirt on. I'm just trying to figure this out. You didn't know him?"

"Not from Adam. PSD out of Frankfurt, that's all. Never worked with him on a case. I don't even know if he was Special Branch. I suppose I could find out." A crack in the door. Still a DA after all.

"But what did you think he wanted? Just like that, out of the blue."

Bernie sat down, ruffling his hair again. "A face meeting with Frankfurt? Out of the blue? It could have been anything. Grief, usually. The last time it was Legal complaining about my methods," he said, giving the word an edge. "They like to do that personally, bring you in line. Frankfurt thinks I'm a loose cannon. Not that I give a shit."

"Why a loose cannon?"

Bernie smiled slightly. "I've been known to break a regulation. Once or twice."

"So break another one," Jake said, looking at him.

"Because you have a gut feeling? I don't know you from Adam either."

"No. But somebody comes to see you, makes a stop along the way, and gets shot. Now two of us are interested."

Bernie met his eyes, then looked away. "You know, I didn't come to Germany to catch crooked soldiers."

Jake nodded, not saying anything, waiting for Bernie to pop up again. Instead, he stopped squirming and leaned forward, like a negotiator at the Cecilienhof, finally down to business.

"What do you want?"

"The other sheet. There's nothing here." Jake pointed at the report. "Not even ballistics. There must be someone you could ask. Quietly, just nosing around."

Bernie nodded.

"Then a call to Frankfurt. Naturally you'd be curious, someone doesn't show. So who was he, what did he want? Scuttlebutt. There should be talk all over the place now, somebody comes back in a box. Oh, did you know him? What the hell happened?"

"You trying to tell me how to do this?"

"Any rumors," Jake went on. "Maybe something valuable's gone missing. Some liberated souvenirs. It's a long shot, but you never know. And a picture would be nice."

"For publication?" Bernie said, wary.

"No, for me. There must be one in his file there, if you can get hold of it without upsetting the horses. I'm not sure how, but maybe something will come to you."

Bernie smiled. "Maybe something will."

"Traveling orders. Who authorized the trip? What for? You'd want to know. He was coming to see you."

"Yes," Bernie said, thoughtful again, then sprang up and began moving around the room, jiggling change in his pocket. "And what's all this supposed to get you?"

"Not much. It's not much to ask, either. Just what you'd want to know if you'd never talked to me. If an appointment turned up dead."

"So what else?"

"I need a partner. I can't work this alone."

Bernie held up his hand. "Forget it."

"Not you. A name. Who covers the black market for Public Safety? Who'd know the snitches, the people out on the street? If Tully had something big to sell, who would he have gone to see? He sure as hell didn't come to Berlin to stand on a corner. I need someone who knows the players."

"I can't help you with that."

"Can't?"

"There isn't anybody like that. Not that I've ever heard of. 'Covers' it. Like a beat? You're still back in Chicago."

"You could ask," Jake said, getting up now too, Bernie's restlessness contagious.

"No, I couldn't. I'm *in* Public Safety. Technically. You don't shit where you sleep. Not for long, anyway. Nobody else will either, once they know what you're after. Tully was PSD too. You think he had friends. Where do you think he had them? I have things to do here, not play cops and robbers with my own department. You do that one alone." He looked up with a hint of a smile. "We'll see how good you are."

"But you'll make the call. You'll do that."

"Yeah, I'll make the call," he said, busying himself again with the folder pile. "I hate it when people don't show up." He stopped and looked directly at Jake, his eyes friendly. "I'll call. Now how about clearing out of here and letting me get back to work."

Jake walked over to the card catalogues and fingered the brass pulls on the drawers. "Catching real criminals," he said. "In here."

"That's right, real criminals. Careful of the merchandise. That's the most valuable thing in Berlin."

"I heard about the paper mill. Some break."

"Maybe God figured he owed us one. Finally," he said, a gravelly voice.

"Mind if I have a look? See what they're like?" Jake said, pulling open a drawer before Bernie could answer. The Bs were near the back, a row of Brandts. Helga, Helmut, no Helene. He pulled his hand away, feeling relieved and ashamed at the same time. How could he have thought there would be? But how could you be sure who anyone was anymore? He remembered that first night, looking down on the old woman in the garden, wondering. What did you do? Were you one of them? The girls on Potsdamerstrasse, the bicycles going past KaDeWe, the woman in his old flat—everyone in Berlin had become a suspect. Who were you before? But Bernie knew. It was all here in black-and-white, typed on cards. His fingers flipped again. Perhaps he was a special case, the professor had said. Berthold. Dieter. There—Emil. Not a special case. But maybe a different Emil Brandt. He took out the card. No, his address. Her address. 1938. All the time Jake had known him. His eyes went down the card. A party decoration. For what? An SS appointment, in 1944. SS. Emil. A nice man who saw numbers in his head.

He looked up to find Bernie standing next to him.

"Your friend?"

"No. Her husband. Christ."

"You didn't know?"

Jake shook his head. "It says he was decorated. It doesn't say why."

"That would be in his party file. These are the registry cards. You want me to find out?" Chasing rats.

Jake shook his head again. "Just where he is."

"You mean if she's with him," Bernie said, studying his face.

"Yes. If she's with him." But he'd never imagined them together. Just Lena, opening the door, the surprised look in her eyes, throwing her arms around his neck. He put the card back and closed the drawer.

"What was her name?"

"Helene Brandt. She used to live in Pariserstrasse. I'll write it down for you." He went over to the desk for a piece of paper. "Can I give you a few others?" he said, writing. "I want to track down the old office staff. For a story. I know you're busy—"

Bernie spread his hands, a what-else-is-new gesture, then took the list. "I'll put Mike on it. It'll give him something to do. They'd have to be in Berlin, you know."

"Yes," Jake said. "Let me know what Frankfurt says."

"Get going before I change my mind," Bernie said, retreating behind the desk.

"But you'll make the call."

Bernie looked up. "You could get to be a real pain, you know that?"

Jake went back up the stairs and through the quiet archive room. Records of everything, just lying here waiting, millions of due bills. Maybe Emil had been decorated as part of a group, a ceremony with families, applauded for their services to the state. Doing what? Teaching mathematics? Now filed away in one of these cabinets, to make another case for the prosecution.

"Sign out, please." The indifferent guard, chewing gum.

Jake scribbled in the ledger, then stepped outside into the click of a photograph.

"Well, look who's here." Liz was bent on one knee, shooting up at the doorway and the tall blond soldier who stood posing in front of it. Last night's date. Jake stepped aside as she took another. The soldier pulled back his shoulders. Cool eyes, an illustrator's jaw, the kind of Aryan looks Emil's group would have liked.

"Okay," Liz said, finished. "Jake, meet Joe Shaeffer. Like the pen. Joe—"

"I know who you are," the soldier said, shaking hands. "Pleasure." He turned to Liz. "Five minutes," he said, then nodded stiffly at Jake and went inside.

"Something for your personal collection?" Jake said, pointing to the camera.

"It *was.*"

"How was the jazz?"

"Wouldn't you like to know. What's it like inside? Anything interesting?"

He thought of the files, every one a story, then realized she meant anything to photograph. "Like a library," he said.

"Great." A grimace. "Still, some trophy, huh? You know they got it all in a paper mill," she said, her voice as excited as the driver's. Jake looked at her. The war had become a kind of scavenger hunt. Rockets at Nordhausen. Engineers at Zeiss. Now even pieces of paper, decorations and promotions. The magazine spread would show tall Joe opening a file.

"Yeah, I heard," he said, moving away. "Watch yourself in there. Lots of dark corners."

"Aren't you funny."

He grinned and was about to start down the steps when he heard his name shouted inside. "Geismar!" A second shout, followed by Bernie in a mad dash, almost colliding with Liz, another piece of Gelferstrasse china. "Good. I caught you."

Jake smiled. "You know Liz? You share a bathroom."

Bernie barely managed a confused nod to her, then grabbed Jake's arm. "I need to talk to you." His face was flushed from the exertion of the run. "This list."

"That was fast," Jake said easily, then saw Bernie's eyes, holding him as firmly as the hand on his arm. "What?"

"Come here," Bernie said, moving them down the stairs, out of earshot. "Naumann," he said, holding the list up. "Renate Naumann. How do you know her?"

"Renate? She worked for me at Columbia. They all did."

"That's the first I've heard of it."

Jake looked at him, bewildered. "Off the books. I used her as a stringer. She had a great eye."

Bernie made a face, as if Jake had told a bad joke, then looked away. "Great eye. Yes," he said, his voice filled with disgust.

"You know her?" Jake said, still puzzled.

Bernie nodded.

"I thought she'd be dead. You know where she is?"

"She's in jail."

Bernie looked around, then took Jake's arm again and began walking out past the sentries. "I hate this fucking barbed wire. It gives me the willies." When they reached the jeep, Bernie leaned against it, his energy finally spent.

"What do you mean, jail?" Jake said.

"Some friends you've got." Bernie took out a cigarette. "She was a *greifer.* You know *greifer*?"

"Grabber. Catcher. Of what?"

"Jews."

"That's impossible. She was—"

"A Jew. I know. A Jew to catch Jews. They thought of everything. Even that."

"But she—" Jake started, but Bernie held up his hand.

"You want to hear this?" He took a pull on his cigarette. "The first big roundup here was in 'forty-two. February. After that, any Jew in Berlin was illegal, underground. They were called U-boats. There were still thousands, if you can imagine it. Some had a place—if a gentile was protecting them. The others, they had to move around. Place to place. During the day, you had to keep moving, so the neighbors wouldn't suspect. Wouldn't report you," he said, almost spitting the word. "Berlin's a big city. You could stay lost in the crowd, if you kept moving. Unless somebody knew you. A *greifer.*"

"I don't believe it."

"No? Ask the Jews she caught. A few survived. A few. Or we wouldn't have caught *her.* That's when I had to break a few regulations." He looked up. "It was worth it. To catch her? Worth it." He moved away from the jeep, pacing in a small circle. "How it worked? Some covered the railway stations. Renate liked the cafés. Usually Kranzler's or the Trumpf, over by the Memorial Church. The big one in Olivaerplatz, the Heil. A drink, you watch the people. Sometimes a Jew you actually knew, from the old days. Sometimes someone you just suspected, so some talk, a little fishing, a hint you were a U-boat yourself. Then snap. A visit to the ladies' room for the telephone. They usually took them on the street, so it wouldn't cause a disturbance in the café. Finish your drink, they're just rounding up some Jews. Everyone but Renate. The next day, another café. She had a great eye, you see," he said, glancing back at Jake.

"She said she could tell just by looking. Not even Streicher could do that—to him it was all cartoon noses. Renate was better than the Nazis, she didn't need the star patches. Not with that eye. And, you know, people are foolish. So careful, day after day—can you imagine what that's like?—and then the relief, a friendly face. If you can't trust another Jew— A few even asked her *out.* A date, under those conditions. 'Just let me powder my nose in the ladies'.'" He flicked the cigarette into the street.

"And then?" Jake said, helpless, wanting to know.

"The collection point. A Gestapo building, so disturbances didn't matter anymore. Lots of screaming there. They put them on the trucks. Then out to the trains for the trip east. The neighbors told us the noise was terrible. They'd keep their windows closed until the trucks left."

"Maybe she didn't know," Jake said quietly.

"She lived there. With the other catchers. They kept them on a short leash. Maybe a reminder—'You could be next.' But she wasn't. She saved herself." He paused. "I saw the room where she lived. It's on the courtyard. She could see them loading the trucks. So maybe she closed her window too." He looked harder at Jake. "She knew."

The day seemed to have stopped around them, the empty street as still as the archives inside. Birdless trees. Sentries standing motionless in the sun.

"That's—" Jake sputtered, then stopped, like a candle without air.

"The worst thing you ever heard?" Bernie prompted. "Stay in Germany. When you think you've heard the worst, there's something more. Always something worse."

Loaded into trucks while she watched. "How many?" Jake said.

"Does it matter?"

Jake shook his head. A girl with bright eyes and curly hair. But who was anybody anymore?

"Can I see her? Could you arrange that?"

"If you want. I should tell you, you won't be the first. Your buddies were all over this one. A Nazi? Old news. But a Jew? That they went for. *Ach.*" He waved his hand again, as if he were swatting the whole thing away like a gnat. "There's a trial coming up. If you have the stomach for it."

"Does she admit it?"

"There's no question about this one," Bernie said, looking at him. "We have witnesses."

"But if they forced her—"

"She did it. That's what matters, you know. She did it." He took a breath. "The people she caught are dead. Nobody made excuses for them."

"No."

"So," Bernie said, exhaling the word, case closed. "Not what you expected, is it?"

"No."

"No," Bernie said. "I'm sorry. It's a lousy business, all of it. Stick to the black market."

"I'd still like to see her."

Bernie nodded. "Maybe she'll tell you something. Why. I'll never understand it."

"We weren't here. We don't know what it was like."

"I had family here," Bernie snapped. "I know what it was like for them."

Jake looked back at the quiet villa, through the high barbed wire that gave Bernie the willies. "What'll happen to her?"

"Prison," Bernie said flatly. "She's a woman—they won't hang her. Maybe it's worse—she'll have to live with it."

"In a cell with the Nazis who made her do it."

"She decided that herself when she became one of them. I said it was a lousy business. How do you think I feel—her *greifer.* Another Jew. Was I right? You tell me."

Jake lowered his head. "I don't know."

"I don't either," Bernie said quietly, a tiny crack in his voice that left his face unguarded, for a second the boy again practicing Mendelssohn. "So you just do the job."

"It was you who got her?"

"Personally? No. Gunther Behn. Our bloodhound." He stopped, then grabbed Jake's arm. "Wait a minute. It didn't occur to me before. I kept thinking Public Safety. You're looking for someone who knows the streets? Gunther's ex-police. Every alley. You might try him. Assuming he's willing. You have any expense money to throw around?"

"Maybe. Berlin police?"

"A detective. Good, when he's sober."

"How do you know him?"

"I told you, he helped me with the Naumann case."

"I thought the police were Nazi."

"They were. They're not police anymore either. Not if they were lieutenant or higher."

"So he's out of a job. And you gave him a new one? I thought you weren't supposed to work with them."

"We're not. He's still out of a job. He just helped me out on this." He looked up. "I broke a regulation."

"You used a Nazi."

Bernie lifted his face, a slight thrust of the jaw. "We caught her."

"How much did you pay him?"

"Nothing. He had a special interest. Renate caught his wife."

"He was married to a Jew?"

"They divorced, so he could keep his job. Later—" He broke off, letting the pieces assemble themselves. Had he hidden her or just let her drift through the streets, waiting for the pounce? "You're in Berlin. There's always something worse."

"And you think he might help?"

"That's up to you. Take a bottle of brandy. He likes that. Maybe you can talk him into it."

"He knows the black market?"

"Well, that's the thing," Bernie said, with the first trace of a smile. "He's in it."

CHAPTER FIVE

GUNTHER BEHN LIVED as far east as you could go in Kreuzberg and still be in the American sector. In the old days it would have been a short walk to police headquarters in Alexanderplatz. Now the way was blocked by a hill of bricks and a gutted tram that had been upended as a tank barricade and never removed. The top of Behn's building had been blown away, leaving only Gunther's ground-floor flat and the floor above, half open to the sky. It took several knocks to bring him to the door, a pair of thick glasses peering suspiciously around the edge.

"Gunther Behn? My name is Geismar. Bernie Teitel sent me."

A surprised look, hearing German, then a grunt.

"Can I come in?"

Gunther opened the door. "You're an American. You can do whatever you want," he said, shuffling indifferently back to an armchair where a cigarette was burning. The room was crowded—a table, a daybed, an old console radio, shelves of books, and a giant map of Greater Berlin that covered an entire wall. In one corner, a stack of cans of PX supplies he hadn't bothered to hide.

"I brought you this," Jake said, holding out the brandy.

"A bribe?" he said. "What does he want now?" He took the bottle. "French." In the warm room, stale with smoke, he was wearing a cardigan. Close-cropped hair, almost as short as the gray stubble that covered his unshaven chin. Not yet old, probably early fifties. Behind the glasses, the glazed eyes of a drinker. A book lay open on the armchair. "What is it? Is there a date for the trial?"

"No. He thought you might be able to help me."

"With what?" he said, opening the bottle and sniffing.

"A job."

He looked at Jake, then put the cork in and handed back the bottle. "Tell him no. I'm finished with that business. Even for brandy."

"Not for Bernie. A job for me." Jake nodded at the bottle. "It's yours either way."

"What is it? Another *greifer*?"

"No, an American."

His cheek moved in a tic of surprise, which he covered by walking over to the table and pouring two fingers of brandy into a glass. "How is it you speak German?" he said.

"I used to live in Berlin."

"Ah." He tossed back a healthy swig. "How do you like it now?"

"I knew Renate," Jake said to his back, hoping for a point of contact.

Gunther took another gulp. "So did many people. That was the problem."

"Bernie told me. I'm sorry about your wife."

But Gunther seemed not to have heard, a willed deafness. In the awkward quiet Jake noticed for the first time that there were no pictures in the room, no reminders at all, the visual traces locked away somewhere in a closet, or thrown out after the divorce. "So what do you want?"

"Some help. Bernie said you were a detective."

"Retired. The Amis retired me. Did he tell you that?"

"Yes. He also said you were good. I'm trying to solve a murder."

"A murder?" He snorted. "A murder in Berlin. My friend, there were millions. Who cares about one?"

"I do."

Gunther turned, looking him up and down, a policeman's appraisal. Jake said nothing. Finally Gunther turned back to the bottle. "A drink?" he said. "Since you brought it."

"No, it's early."

"Coffee, then? Real coffee, not ersatz." Not grudging; an invitation to stay.

"You have it?"

"Another gift," he said, holding up the glass. "One minute." He headed toward the kitchen but detoured to peek out the window. "Did you disable the motor? The distributor cap?"

"I'll chance it."

"Don't take chances in Berlin," he said, scolding. "Not now." He shook his head. "Americans."

Jake watched him open the door to the kitchen. More packing cases, a pile of canned goods, cartons of cigarettes. Gifts. He was still sipping the brandy, but moved around the small space with steady efficiency, one of those drinkers who never seem affected until they pass out at night. Jake went over to the shelves. Rows of westerns. Karl May, the German Zane Grey. Gunfights in Yuma. Sheriffs and posses tracking through sagebrush. An unexpected vice at the edge of Kreuzberg.

"Where did you get the map?" Jake said. The whole city, dotted with pins.

"My office. It wasn't safe in the Alex, with the bombs. Now I like to look at it sometimes. It makes me think Berlin is still out there. All the streets." He came into the room with two cups. "It's important to know where you are in police work. The where, very important." He handed Jake a cup. "Where was your murder?"

"Potsdam," Jake said, glancing involuntarily at the map, as if the body would appear in the ribbons of blue lakes in the lower left corner.

"Potsdam? An American?" He followed Jake's eyes to the edge of the map. "With the conference?"

"No. He had ten thousand dollars," Jake said, baiting a hook.

Gunther looked at him, then motioned him to a table chair. "Sit." He sank into the armchair, moving the book aside. "So tell me."

It took ten minutes. There wasn't much to tell, and Gunther's expression discouraged speculation. He had taken off his glasses, his eyelids lowered to slits, and he listened without nodding, the only sign of life a steady movement of his hand from coffee cup to brandy glass.

"I'll know more when I hear back from Bernie," Jake finished.

Gunther pinched the bridge of his nose and rubbed it in thought, then put back his glasses.

"What will you know?" he said finally.

"Who he was, what he was like."

"You think that would be useful," Gunther said. "Who."

"Don't you?"

"Usually," he said, taking a drink. "If this were before. Now? Let me explain something to you. I saved the map." He cocked his head toward the wall. "But everything else was lost. Fingerprint files. Criminal picture files. *General* files. We don't know who anyone is in Berlin. No residency records. Lost. Something is stolen, you can't look in the hock shops, the usual places. They're gone. If it's sold to a soldier, he sends it home. No trace. No policeman in Berlin can solve a crime now. Not even a retired one."

"It's not a German crime."

"Then why come to me?"

"Because you know the black market."

"You think so?"

"You get a lot of gifts."

"Yes, I'm so rich," he said, lifting his hand to the room. "Tins of corned beef. A treasure."

"You know how it works, or you wouldn't be eating. You know how Berlin works."

"How Berlin works," Gunther said, grunting again.

"Even now. Germans run the market. Probably the same ones who ran things before. You'd know them. So which one did Tully know? He wasn't making a casual deal. He wasn't *in* Berlin, he came to Berlin."

Gunther slowly took out a cigarette and watched Jake as he lit it. "Good. That's the first point. You saw that. What else?"

A detective testing a recruit. Jake leaned forward.

"The point is the money. There's too much."

Gunther shook his head. "No, you missed the point. The point is that he still had it."

"I don't follow you."

"Herr Geismar. A man sells something. The buyer shoots him. Would he not take the money back? Why would he leave it?"

Jake sat back, disconcerted. The obvious question, overlooked by everybody except a bent cop, still on the job behind the brandy haze. "Meaning?"

"Meaning the buyer and the killer are not necessarily the same. In fact, not the same. How could it be? You're looking for the wrong man."

Jake got up and walked over to the map. "The one leads to the other. Has to. There's still the money."

"Yes, the money," Gunther said, following him with his eyes. "That interests you. It's the other point that interests me. Where."

"Potsdam," Jake said dully, looking at the map.

"Potsdam," Gunther repeated. "Which the Russians have closed off. No one has been there for days. Not even the people you think I know." He took another drink. "For them, a real inconvenience. No market day—a serious loss. But they can't get in. And your soldier can. How is that?"

"Maybe he was invited."

Gunther nodded. "The final point. But for you, also the end. A Russian? Children with guns. They don't need a reason to shoot. You will never find him."

"The black market doesn't work by sector. It's all over the city. This much money—even a Russian—someone will know something. People talk." Jake went back to his chair and leaned forward again. "They'd talk to you. They know you."

Gunther lifted his head.

"I can pay," Jake said.

"I'm not an informer."

"No. A cop."

"Retired," Gunther said sourly. "With a pension." He raised his glass to the packing cases.

"And how long do you think that will last? Once the MPs get started. An American killed—they have to do something about that. Clean things up. At least for a while. You could use a little insurance."

"From the Americans," Gunther said, deadpan. "To find someone they don't want found."

"They will. They'll have to, if somebody makes enough noise." He paused, holding Gunther's eyes. "You never know when a favor might come in handy."

"You are the noisemaker, I take it." Gunther looked away and took off his glasses again. "And what do I get? For my services. My *persilschein*?"

"Persil?" Jake said, confused, trying to translate. "Like the detergent?"

"Persil washes everything clean," Gunther said, rubbing the glasses on the cardigan. "Remember the advertisements? The *persilschein* washes everything too, even sins. An American signs a certificate and"—he snapped his fingers—"the record is clean. No Nazi past. Go back to work."

"I can't do that," Jake said, then hesitated. "Maybe I can talk to Bernie."

"Herr Geismar, I'm not serious. He won't *persil* me. I was in the party. He knows that. Now I'm in—business. My hands are—" He stopped, looking down at them. "Anyway, I don't want to go back to work. It's finished here. When you leave, the Russians will take over. Not even a *persilschein* would make me work for them."

"Then work for me."

"Why?" he said, more a dismissal than a question.

Jake glanced around the airless room, a short walk from the old office, all the teletypes and radio calls now just a map on the wall.

"Because you're not ready to retire. And I'll miss all the points." He nodded at the book. "You can't sit around all day reading Karl May. He isn't writing any new ones."

Gunther looked at him for a second, a bleary scowl, then put on his glasses and picked up the book. "Leave me alone," he said, retreating again behind the haze.

But Jake sat still, waiting him out. For a few minutes there was no sound but the quiet ticking of the wall clock, the silence of a standoff, like the one on the book jacket, six-shooters drawn. Finally Gunther peered over his glasses.

"There is maybe one more point."

Jake raised his eyebrows, still waiting.

"Did he speak German?"

"Tully? I don't know. I doubt it."

"A difficulty, then, for such a transaction," Gunther said carefully, working through a checklist. "If he was meeting a German. Who run the market. You say."

"All right. Then who else?"

"This talk—it would be private? I have to protect my pension," he said.

"Private as a confessional."

"You know Ronny's? On the Ku'damm?"

"I can find it."

"Try there tonight. Ask for Alford," he said, pronouncing the English correctly. "He likes Ronny's."

"An American?"

"A Tommy. Not German. So maybe he's heard something. Who knows? It's a start. Mention my name."

Jake nodded. "But you'll be there."

"That depends."

"On what?"

Gunther looked down at the page, dismissing him again. "Whether I finish the book."

He got back to Gelferstrasse to find a crowd halfway down the block from the billet, MPs in jeeps and a whole truckload of soldiers all milling around two women who stood looking at a house, hands to their cheeks, as if they were watching an accident. In the open truck, Ron stood next to some newsreel cameras, deserted by the rest of the press for the sidewalk show. The MPs were trying to get the women to move but without much success, barking in English while the women wailed in German. Plaster dust was floating out of the windows like smoke.

"He speaks German," Tommy Ottinger said to one of the MPs, waving Jake over.

"Tell them in kraut they can't go in," the MP said, frustrated. "One floor's gone already—the rest of it's going to cave."

"What happened?" Jake said to Tommy.

"They had a bomb in the back that weakened the house and now the whole thing's shaky. Kitchen ceiling just went and another wall's about to pop and they're still trying to get in."

The two women now shouted at Jake.

"They want to get their things," he translated. "Before it goes."

"No can do," the MP said. "Christ, these people don't know when they're lucky. They could have been in there. You got to hit them over the head to make them understand anything."

"My clothes," one of the women cried in German. "I have to have clothes. How do you live without clothes?"

"It's dangerous," Jake said to her. "Wait till it settles. Maybe it'll be all right."

The house answered with a groan, almost a human sound, the joists pressed down by weight. A piece of plaster fell inside, sending out another puff of dust.

"Helmut," the other woman said, holding herself, now really alarmed.

"What's that, her dog?" the MP said.

"I don't know," Jake said. "Is anybody coming to help?"

"Are you kidding? What are we supposed to do?"

"Prop the walls." He'd seen it done in London, support beams put against a damaged house like improvised flying buttresses. Just a few pieces of lumber.

"Buddy—" the MP said, then stopped, the idea too absurd to deserve a response.

"So what are they doing?" Jake said, indicating the soldiers.

"Them? They're on their way to the game. Why don't you take it easy and tell the krauts to come over here before they get hurt. Fuck their things."

Jake looked up at the truck where Ron was standing with his hands on his hips, obviously annoyed at the delay. "We're going to be late," he said to the men.

"What game?"

"Football," Ron said. "Come on, guys. Let's go."

A few of them moved, climbing reluctantly into the truck.

"The Brits'll wait," Tommy said.

"I can't leave him," the woman said.

"This could take all day," Ron said, but the house was groaning again, as compelling as a fire, working to some kind of end.

"Helmut," the woman said, hearing the rumble, and then, before anyone could stop her, bolted up the pavement to the door and raced inside.

"Hey!" the MP shouted, but no one moved, frozen like a crowd held at gunpoint. "Fuck," he said, watching her disappear. "Well, that's one less to worry about."

The words seemed to push Jake by the shoulders. He glared at the MP, then broke away without thinking and ran after her. The entryway was littered with plaster. *"Frau!"* he yelled. "Come. It's not safe." No one answered. He stopped, listening in the creaking house for an animal whimper, the terrified Helmut being rescued. Instead, a calm "One moment" came from the front room. She was standing in the middle, just looking around, holding a picture frame.

"You must come out," he said gently, going over to her. "It's not safe."

She nodded. "Yes, I know. It's all I have, you see," she said, looking down at the picture. A boy in a Wehrmacht uniform.

He took her elbow. "Please," he said, leading her away.

She began to walk with him, then stopped at an end table near the doorway and picked up a porcelain figurine, one of those pink-cheeked shepherdesses that gather dust in parlors. "For Elisabeth," she said, as if she were apologizing for taking her own things.

The house, having held its breath for a few minutes, now exhaled again with a loud thump in the back. She started, and Jake took her by the shoulder to keep her going, so that his arm was around her when they came out on the stoop.

"Hold it." The voice, oddly, of a policeman catching looters. But it was only Ron, next to the newsreel camera. For a brief moment, as they stood on the stoop, Jake realized that it was running and, worse, that what it had hoped to catch was his death. American journalist killed in Berlin—something finally worth filming.

"Anna!" the other woman shouted, hysterical. "Are you crazy? Are you crazy?"

But Anna was undisturbed now, the picture clutched to her chest. She left Jake's side, walked calmly down the steps, and handed the figurine to the other woman.

"Fucking Boy Scout," the MP said to him.

"Ain't he, though?" Tommy said. "Probably do the same for a cat."

"Where is fucking Helmut anyway?" the MP said, disgusted.

"It's her son," Jake said. He turned to the truck. "Get a good picture?" he said to Ron. "Sorry it didn't fall down for you."

"Maybe next time." Ron grinned. "Come on, hop up. Next stop, Allied games. The boys who fought together play together. *Collier's* will love it."

Jake looked up at him. The truth was, *Collier's* would. The Allies in peace, conference table to playing field. Not Nazi cops and homeless Berliners. He could file this week, before the impatient telegrams started coming.

"The Russians too?"

"They've been invited."

"Hey, buddy," said the MP, subdued now. "Ask them if they've got someplace to go."

Jake spoke with the women, standing now arm in arm, their backs to the soldiers.

"She has another sister in Hannover."

"She'll need a travel permit for that. Tell her we'll get her to the DP camp down in Teltowerdamm. It's not bad."

But the word, once translated, jolted them, the clang of a cell door closing. "Not a camp!" the woman with the figurine shrieked. "Not a camp. You can't make us." She clutched Jake's arm.

"What's *lager*?" the MP said.

"Camp. They're afraid. They think it's a concentration camp."

"Yeah, like the ones they used to run. Tell them it's an American camp," he said, certain this would be a comfort.

"They look to you like they ran anything?"

"What the hell. Krauts."

Before Jake could answer, the side wall finally gave way, collapsing inward and taking the weakened body of the house with it in a roar. There was a crack of wood splintering and masonry smashing down, all the sounds of an explosion, so that when the dust rose in a cloud from the center it seemed the house had been bombed after all. One of the women gasped, holding her hand over her mouth. Everyone stood still, mesmerized. In the truck the cameras were running again, grateful for a little spectacle after the dud rescue. Some of the neighbors had run over and joined the crowd, standing away from the two women, as if their bad luck were catching. No one spoke. A part of the back wall buckled. Another crash, more dust, then a series of thuds, like aftershocks, as bits of the house detached themselves and slid into the center heap, until finally the noise stopped and they were looking through the standing façade at another one of Ron's decayed teeth. The woman holding the figurine started to cry, but Anna simply stared at the wreck without expression, then turned.

"Okay, okay," the MP said, waving his white stick, "let's break it up. Show's over."

Jake looked at the house. Hundreds of thousands of them.

The truck driver started the engine, a signal to the others, and the soldiers began to climb on, shoving good-naturedly and joking.

"What about the women?" Jake said to the MP. "You can't just leave them."

"What are you, the Salvation Army?"

"Come on, Jake," Tommy said. "There's nothing you can do here."

And in fact, what could he do? Take them home and ask them to tell him their troubles for *Collier's*? The old couple from the billet had begun to lead them away. A night or two in the cramped basement, perhaps, living off the B rations from upstairs. Then a travel pass to Hannover and another basement. Or maybe not. Maybe just a tramp through the Tiergarten with the others, DPs because of a minute of falling plaster.

"You know, we didn't start the fucking war," the MP said, evidently reading his face.

"No. They did," Jake said, confusing him, and followed Tommy into the truck.

They drove up into the British sector, past the radio tower where Jake had made the Columbia broadcasts, and out to the Olympic Stadium. The area around it was the usual mess, trees blasted into stumps, but the stadium, even scarred by shelling, looked just the way Jake remembered it. It had probably been the best of the Nazis' monumental buildings, deceptively horizontal until you went through the gate and saw the long steps dropping down into the sunken amphitheater. He recognized the spot where he'd sat with the Dodds watching the games, his first job in Berlin. Miles of loudspeakers had been strung from the stadium out across the city to flash the news of each event to the center. Goebbels' idea, a modern marvel to impress the visitors. It was the first time he'd seen Hitler, taking the salute in his emperor's box. Fresh out of Chicago, years before Lena.

Today groups of soldiers were lying shirtless on the patchy grass, drinking beer and getting some sun before the game. The rows and rows of seats that had held thousands now had only a few hundred, but still a larger crowd than he'd expected, about the same as at a high school game back home. They were clustered at one end of the vast oval, where a football field had been chalked out in lime, British and Americans side by side, with a few French near the end, wearing hats with red pompoms. No Russians. On the sidelines a few soldiers sat in a circle playing cards, grumbling when they had to move for the newsreel camera crew. In the middle of the field, the players, in jerseys and shorts, were jumping up and down in warmup exercises. An occupying army with nothing to do but occupy.

"So the Russians didn't show," Jake said to Ron. "Who's playing the French?"

"They're here for the track events. That's all the Russians are scheduled for too, so they'll probably turn up. Want to interview some of the players?"

"I'll just watch. Where'd the Brits learn to play?"

Ron shrugged. "They say rugby's close. We're mixing the teams, just in case. Keeps things fair."

"You're a born diplomat."

"No. We've got the British reels to consider," he said, pointing to another crew with tripods. "They don't want to show their guys getting trounced, do they? Who'd watch that? Allied games, remember?"

But in fact after the kickoff it was an American show, GI quarterbacks calling the plays, the British blocking, and everyone getting scraped by the rough field in pile-up tackles. The crowd cheered every play, even the referees throwing red foul flags, and swapped money in side bets and whooped until finally the high spirits were infectious, like a Saturday somewhere in the Big Ten. A piece of home. Even the players, healthy and pink in the sun, seemed to be in another country, miles from the pasty, grim bodies in the streets outside.

Jake hadn't seen football in years, and now, unexpectedly, the sounds on the field took him back to sunny afternoons when nothing mattered except the next ten yards and who you might be seeing after the game. America, where all the houses were intact. But it was the homesickness of an exile—what you missed was your own youth, not a place. He'd been back only once since he'd first sat in this stadium, a week between assignments, and then all he'd known was the overseas America of the war, the field mess parties and USO shows that weren't really home but a movie of home. He'd be a stranger there now.

But wouldn't everybody? They'd all been gone too long, were all different, even the MP at the house, maybe a football player, who now thought a dead woman was one less German to worry about. He shifted in his seat, embarrassed by his own nostalgia. Leave the amber waves to Quent Reynolds, making his mother queen for a day at Toots Shor's. He knew better. The America he'd left, the late editions and cops on the take, was the same unholy mix as anywhere else. And yet there it was, the unexpected longing, triggered by a football game. Who he was, as inescapable and permanent as a birthmark.

A touchdown. The crowd jumped up around him, yelling and slapping backs. Someone passed him a beer. From the corner of his eye he saw Ron leave the cameras to greet Congressman Breimer. He introduced him to a small group of soldiers, presumably Utica boys, who shook hands and posed for army photographers. Souvenirs for the folks. Then he led Breimer over to the newsreel crew, positioning him in front of the play and testing a microphone. Jake left his seat and walked down to the sidelines. Breimer had already begun speaking.

"In this stadium, where that great American Jesse Owens exposed the Nazi lie of racial superiority, we're seeing today proof of another victory. This great Allied coalition that won the war is now winning the peace, still side by side, still determined to show the world we can work together. *And* play some pretty good football." A pause here as the soldiers around him laughed. "Our task here is not easy. But can anyone doubt, looking at these fine boys, that we're going to succeed? We're going to help this country up out of the ashes, extend our hands to the good Germans who've prayed for democracy during all these dark years, and make a world where war will never happen again. That's what they're fighting for now. Today these men are playing, but tomorrow they'll be back at work. Hard work. Building our future. If you could see them here in Berlin, as I can, you'd know they're going to win that one too."

Impromptu, without notes, the sort of thing he could rattle off without even thinking. Huffing and puffing. Another piece of home. Jake looked at him, wondering what he'd been like before—probably the kid waving his hand in class, volunteering to clap erasers and deliver the milk bottles, destined even then for better things.

"And now, I'm told, the Eighty-second Airborne has a little halftime entertainment for us."

Ron gave a stage manager's signal, and the cameras swerved to an opening beneath the tiers of seats. A row of white helmets came trooping out, playing a Sousa march. The soldiers cheered. The cameras tracked the band onto the scrubby playing field, brass horns shining as they lined up in formation. The noise was deafening.

"Where are the pompom girls?" Jake said to Ron.

"Very funny," Ron said. He pointed to the seats. "They love it."

And they did. Jake looked up at the crowd, stamping and whistling, winning the peace for Movietone News. Then he saw Brian Stanley a few tiers farther up, leaning back on his elbows in a patch of sun, eyes closed, the only still thing in the stands. The band started in on another march. Jake climbed back up the stairs.

"Enjoying the game?"

Brian opened his eyes for a second, then closed them again. "I was. Until The Honorable started in."

Jake sat down next to him, watching the band below. The music boomed through the stadium.

"My god," Brian said, "do you think they could turn it *down* a little?"

"Late night?"

Brian managed a small grunt, then slowly pulled himself up, wiping his forehead. "You know, I'm worried about Winston. He's been blathering on about the Polish borders. Why?"

"Why not?" Jake said, looking back from the field. The conference, almost forgotten, while he'd been taking coffee with Gunther.

"Because they were decided the minute Uncle Joe crossed them. All this carrying on. It's not like him."

"Maybe he's playing for time."

"No, he's distracted. The election, I expect. Pity, coming right during the conference. I think it's put him off his game. Not like your Honorable." He nodded toward Breimer, who was applauding the band coming off the field, still blaring. "Lovely piece of work, isn't he? Extending his hand," he said, doing a passable imitation.

"That's what he's usually doing. As long as you've got something to put in it."

Brian smiled. "That leaves the Germans out, then. 'Extend our hands.' On the plane I seem to remember they were getting what they deserve. Ah, peace at last." This to the field, where the band had finally been replaced by a referee's whistle beginning the third-quarter play, a background noise by comparison. Brian leaned on his elbows again. "And where've you been, by the by? I looked for you at the briefing. Chasing the furlines?"

"No, a story on the black market."

"You're not serious," Brian said, closing his eyes. "That's an old, old story."

"Well, so are the Polish borders."

Brian sighed and went back to the sun. Down on the field, Breimer was detaching himself from the press corps and walking over to a waiting soldier—Liz's date, alone now, his manner brisk and serious. Breimer put a hand on his shoulder, drawing him away from the crowd in a backroom huddle. Jake watched them for a few minutes, their heads nodding in conversation. More than just a driver.

"Thick as thieves, aren't they?" Brian said, following Jake's stare.

"Hmm."

"Why the interest?"

"He's seeing Liz."

"You can't blame him for that. I wouldn't mind a look-in myself."

The crowd suddenly started shouting—another touchdown—but the two heads didn't turn.

"So what's he doing with Breimer?"

Brian yawned, indifferent. "Building our future. Been at it for days, they have. He met him at the airport."

"He did?" Jake looked over at Brian, still as a lizard. "You don't miss much, do you?"

"Well, it's my job, isn't it? All you have to do is keep your eyes open," he said, closing his again.

Now the two men were moving apart, their business finished, Breimer signaling to a GI that he was ready to leave. Shaeffer hurried out of the stadium without even glancing at the game.

"Hey, Brian," Jake said, thinking. "You were on the plane. Remember the guy who was afraid of flying?"

"The boots?"

"Who met him? Did you notice?"

"No," Brian said. "Why?"

"Did you talk to him on the plane? Notice anything about him?"

Brian opened his eyes. "I take it there's a reason you're asking?"

"He turned up dead. At Potsdam."

"What, the one they fished out?"

Jake nodded.

"And?"

"And I'd like to know why. I think there's a story in it."

"Dear Jake. Back on the old beat. And here's poor Poland hanging in the balance—"

"So did you? Talk to him?"

"Not a word. I don't think anyone did. As I recall, The Hon did most of the talking. This your black market story?"

"He made a deal here. Picked up quite a bundle."

"That nice young man?" Brian said.

"Maybe not so nice. Five, ten thousand dollars."

"Really?" Brian said, interested now. "With what?"

"What do you mean?"

"Well, he didn't have any luggage. What was he trading?"

"He didn't have any luggage?" Jake said, trying to picture the scene at Tempelhof.

"No. I did notice that. I thought, that's odd. Then I thought, well, he's *from* Berlin."

"No. He wasn't. Notice anything else?"

"My boy, I didn't even notice that until you brought it up. A chap without luggage—what's there to that?"

Jake didn't answer. What would Gunther see, the obvious point overlooked? A deal with nothing to trade. But you didn't get ten thousand for nothing. Small enough, then, to carry in a pocket.

"Damn," Brian said to another roar from the field. "One of ours, too. Now I have to write it up." In the British stands, some soldiers held up a Union Jack.

"Suppose a Russian shot him?"

"Ah," Brian said slowly. "A little awkward just now, wouldn't it be?" He waved toward the game. "And just when we were all getting along so nicely. Is that where you're going with this? A little stink bomb for the conference?"

"I don't know."

"They wouldn't like that."

"Who?"

"Any of them."

Jake looked around the stadium. Any of them. The story nobody wanted him to do. Which meant it was the only one worth doing. He glanced toward the newsreel crew, half expecting to see Breimer winning the peace again. Instead he saw Bernie coming toward them, head down, in his usual terrier hurry. He searched the crowd, then smiled at Jake and waved him down. Jake took a breath. He'd tracked him here—news that couldn't wait. Elated, he left Brian and ran down the stairs.

"You found her?"

"What? Oh, the woman," Bernie said, looking flustered. "No. I'm sorry. She's not there." But he'd been smiling.

"You looked?"

"There's no record. I put in a query for the husband. He might be easier, if he's POW." He paused, letting the thought drift and watching Jake's face. "You might try the message boards. Sometimes it works."

Jake nodded, not really listening. Everyone filed a *fragebogen* if they wanted a ration card. Unless they were buried somewhere under a collapsed wall. No record.

"Well, thanks anyway," he said, his voice dropping. "I guess that's that." But what had he expected?

"People do turn up. I said it was—"

"I know. Anyway, nice of you to come."

"No," Bernie said, embarrassed again. "It wasn't that. I mean, there's something else."

Jake looked up.

"Something interesting," Bernie said, his five o'clock shadow creasing in another smile. "I found out why Muller didn't want you to see the other sheet. You were right. There was a ballistics report." He pulled a carbon from his pocket and paused, making Jake wait. "It was an American bullet."

CHAPTER SIX

IT WASN'T HARD to find Ronny's. The British had drawn the flashy stretch of the Kurfürstendamm in the partition, and the swarm of British army vehicles outside the club marked it like a neon sign. Drivers sat smoking on the fenders, keeping guard, catching snatches of music as officers pushed inside, holding girls by their waists, some of them already weaving from drink. In the street only a few cars passed the broken storefronts and gutted hotels. Bicycles had disappeared with the fading light. In an hour, the Ku'damm would be as dark as a country road, lit by a sliver of moon and the phosphorus strips left over from the blackout.

Jake parked behind a British jeep and walked along the cleared sidewalk to the entrance. The store next door was in ruins, the old plate glass replaced by plywood covered with pieces of paper and bits of cardboard with messages, set inside the window to shelter the ink from rain. It was just light enough to see. Some of them had been neatly written out in the formal Gothic script of the gymnasiums, but most were hastily scribbled, the scrawls carrying their own sad urgency. "Winter boots. Felt lined. Excellent condition. Will trade for children's shoes." "Any information Anna Millhaupt. Previously at 18 Marburgerstrasse." "Your future revealed. Madame Renaldi. Personalized charts. 25 marks or coupons." "War widow, two children. Attractive. Seeking German husband. Must have flat. Excellent cook." Jake turned away and opened the door to a blast of music.

He'd expected a basement cave, something out of the old Grosz drawings, but Ronny's was bright and noisy, decked out with white tablecloths and pictures on the wall. Waiters in starched shirts wriggled past the cramped tables like eels, carrying plates, holding them away from the jostling on the small dance floor. A five-piece band was playing an up-tempo "Sweet Lorraine," and a crowd of Allied uniforms and girls in summer dresses bumped around the packed floor in a quick foxtrot. The girls were dressed to go out—real dresses and bright lipstick and open-toed shoes, not the uniform trousers and kerchiefs of the rubble cleaners. But the familiar smell had penetrated even here, lying unmistakably under the smoke and perfume. It occurred to him, a detail for a piece, that on the raucous, crowded floor they were literally dancing on graves.

Gunther was sitting in a thick haze of smoke at the end of the raised bar that ran along the side wall. Jake walked past a burst of laughter and a rattle of glasses as a small group of Russians banged the table for service. The band, without a pause, switched to "This Year's Kisses."

Gunther was huddled with another civilian and barely acknowledged Jake when he reached the bar, giving a quick nod and then a jerk of his head toward a table in the corner.

"He's over there."

Jake followed his eyes to the table. A young soldier, thin hair slicked straight back like Noël Coward's, sat between two bottle blondes eating dinner, heads bent over their plates.

"But I have some news," Jake said.

"Let me finish my business," Gunther said. "I'll join you. A moment."

"The gun," Jake continued. "It was American."

Gunther looked at him directly, his eyes alert behind their brandy film. "So," he said, noncommittal.

"Who's this?" the other German said.

Gunther shrugged. "A new man from the Alex," he said, the old headquarters. "I'm breaking him in."

The other man found this funny. "From the Alex." He laughed. "That's good."

"I'll be with you in a minute," Gunther said, nodding again at the table with the blondes.

Jake squeezed between tables until he reached the English soldier. A kid, skinny and bright-eyed, not the grizzled thug he'd imagined.

"Alford?"

"Danny. You Gunther's friend? Have a drink," he said, pouring one. "Gunther said to fix you up. Anything you like."

"Is it okay to talk?" Jake said, looking at the girls as he sat down.

"Who, them? Right as rain. The only word they know is fuck. Isn't that right, Ilse?"

"Hello," one of the girls said, evidently her other word, and went back to her plate. A piece of gray meat and two potatoes the size of golf balls. Danny must have eaten elsewhere; there was nothing in front of him but a bottle of scotch.

"Don't know where she gets the appetite," Danny said. "Does the heart good, doesn't it, to see her go at it? Now, was there something special you like? Something a bit out of the way, or just straight up? You're an officer, right?" he said, glancing at Jake's shoulder patch. "They won't go unless it's an officer. But they're all clean. I insist on that. Checked once a week. We don't want to take any surprises home, do we? Was there something special?"

"No," Jake said, embarrassed, "it's not that. Not girls."

"Right," Danny said, picking up his glass but not missing a beat. "My mistake. Now, the boys are a bit more, you understand. They're only out once a night. Get used up otherwise. You know." He looked at Jake. "All Hitler Youth, every one of them. With uniforms, if you like." Cheerful as a street vendor in Whitechapel.

Jake, flustered, shook his head. "No, you don't understand. I'm looking for some information."

"You a copper?" Danny said, wary.

"No."

"Well, a friend of Gunther's. You'd have to be all right, wouldn't you?" He lit a cigarette, watching Jake while the end caught. "What sort of information?"

"A man made ten thousand dollars Monday. You hear about anything like that?"

"Ten thousand," he said, impressed. "In one go? That's very nice. Friend of yours?"

"An acquaintance."

"Why not ask him, then?"

"He's gone back to Frankfurt. I want to know where he made it."

"Want to do a little business yourself, is that it? What are you selling?"

Jake shook his head again. "I want to know what he was selling."

Behind them there was applause as the band stopped for a break, the vacuum of the sudden quiet soon filling with louder talk.

"Why come to me? Ten thousand, that's not girls, that isn't."

"Gunther said you're a guy hears things."

"Not this," Danny said firmly, squashing his cigarette in the ashtray.

"Want to ask around? I could pay."

Danny peered at him. "You could pick up a phone and get Frankfurt too."

"No. He's dead."

Danny stared at him. "You might have said. Shows a want of trust. Maybe you'd better piss off. I don't want any trouble."

"No trouble. Look, let's start over. Man I know came to Berlin Monday to do some business and got killed. I'm trying to find out who did it."

"Gunther know him too?"

"No. He's helping me. The man only spoke English. Gunther thought you might have heard something. A man gets killed, people talk."

"Not to me they haven't. Now piss off."

"I just want to know if you've heard anything."

"Now you know." Danny took out another cigarette. "Look, I make a nice little living here. A bit of this, a bit of that. No trouble. I don't have ten thousand dollars and I don't shoot people. And I keep my nose to myself. You get all kinds here. Live and let live and you live longer. Isn't that right, Ilse?"

The girl looked up and smiled blankly.

"If someone did have ten thousand dollars, what would he buy with it?" Jake said, switching tack.

"In one go? I don't know, I never had that much." But he was intrigued now. "The big stuff, that's more of a swap, like. Friend of mine got hold of a factory shipment—lovely cloth, parachute quality—and the next thing you know he's got trucks coming in from Denmark. Tinned ham. Now he's got something. You can sell that anywhere. But no money till it hits the street, if you see what I mean. Cash? Antiques, maybe. But, see, I wouldn't know one from another, so I steer clear of that."

"What else?"

"Medicine. They'd pay cash for that. But that's a dirty business, medicine. I won't touch that."

Jake looked at him, fascinated. Ham but not penicillin, a new kind of hair-splitting.

"He was carrying it with him, whatever it was," Jake said. "No truckloads, not even a box. Something small enough to carry."

"Jewelry, then. Now that's a specialty, of course," Danny said, as if he were referring to one of his girls. "You have to know what you're about."

"Would you ask around?"

"I might. As a favor to Gunther, mind. Ah, here we go again," he said, seeing the band come back on the stand. He poured Jake another drink, warming to the subject. "Small enough to carry? Not gold—too heavy. Paper maybe."

"What kind of paper?"

The band had started in on "Elmer's Tune," causing a new rush to the dance floor. Jake felt his chair pushed from behind. A Russian maneuvered through with his hand stuck firmly on a girl's behind. Another Russian now loomed over the table, smiling at Ilse and twirling his finger in the international sign language for dance.

"Piss off, mate. Can't you see the lady's eating?"

The Russian reared back, surprised.

"He didn't realize she was with you," a voice behind them said in accented English. "Apologies." Jake turned. "Ah, Mr. Geismar."

"General Sikorsky."

"Yes, an excellent memory. Excuse my friend. He thought—"

"He's a friend of yours?" Danny said to Jake. "Well, that's all right, then. Ilse, give him a whirl, there's a good girl."

"You dance?" she said to the Russian, getting up and taking him by the arm.

"Thank you," Sikorsky said. "Very kind."

"Don't give it a thought," Danny said, all geniality. "What about yourself?"

"Another time," he said, looking at the other blonde. "Good to see you again, Mr. Geismar. A different sort of party." He glanced toward the dance floor, where Ilse and the Russian were already locked together. "I enjoyed our conversation."

"Aladdin's cave," Jake said, trying to remember.

"Yes. Perhaps we can discuss it again one day, if you'd like to visit our sector. It is not so lively as this, though. Good night." He turned to Danny and made a little bow, preparing to move off. "My comrade thanks you for your help."

"Mind you bring her back," Danny said, teasing.

Sikorsky looked at him, then took out a wad of bills, peeled a few off, and dropped them next to Danny's glass. "That should cover it," he said, and walked away.

Danny stared at the bills, stung, as if someone had slapped his face. Jake looked away, his eyes following Sikorsky across the room to the bar, where he was saying hello to Gunther's friend.

"It bleeding well doesn't cover it," Danny was saying. "Red bastards."

"What kind of paper?" Jake said, turning back.

"What? Oh, all kinds. You ask me, what would you buy with ten thousand dollars, and it comes to me, I *have.* I buy paper. You know, deeds."

"You own property here?"

"A cinema. That was the first. Now it's flats. Of course, you want the right areas. But now a cinema, that's always worth something, isn't it?"

"What happens when you go home?" Jake said, curious.

"Home? No. I like it here. Lots of girls—they can't do enough for you. And I've got my property. What have I got in London? Five quid a week and thank you very much? There's nothing in London. You've got all the opportunity in the world right here."

Jake sat quietly for a minute, at a loss. Another *Collier's* piece they'd never want, the cheeky private with a corner table at Ronny's.

"I doubt he was selling deeds," he said finally.

"Well, that's just an example, isn't it? Here, have one more," he said, pouring, enjoying himself. "It's single malt, not your blended."

He sipped some. "Lots of valuable things on paper. IDs. Discharge papers. Get you an honorable, if you like. Fudged, but who's to know? Of course, the Germans are the ones for paper."

"Persilscheins," Jake said. "To wash away your sins."

"That's right. You might get two thousand for one of those, if it's good. Sell a few more and—" He stopped, putting down the glass. "Hang on a minute. I'll tell you what *has* been going around. Haven't seen one myself, of course, but I did hear—very good prices, too."

"What?"

"Camp letters. Character witnesses. Some Jewish bloke writes that so-and-so was in the camp with him, or so-and-so tried to keep him *out* of the camp. Best sort of *persilschein*—cleans the record up right away."

"If it's authentic."

"Well, the writer is. Of course, most won't do it, you can understand that. But if you really need the money—to get out of the country, say, something like that—well, what's one letter?"

Jake stared at his glass, appalled. Exonerate your own murderer. Always something worse. "Christ," he said, a sigh of disgust, almost inaudible under the noise of the band.

Danny shifted in his seat, uncomfortable again, as if Jake had thrown more money on the table.

"I don't see it that way. You can't hold a grudge in this life. I mean, look at me. Three years in that POW camp and it was hell, I can tell you. This'll never be the same." He touched his ear. "Deaf as a post. I picked that up there. But I picked up some German too, that's the bright side, I didn't know it would come in handy, and now that's all over and done with and what's the use of going on about it? You have to get on, that's what I think." For a wild moment, Jake heard Breimer's voice, an unlikely echo.

"It was a different kind of camp," Jake said.

"Let me tell you something, mate. When you spend three years POW, you tell me how different it was."

"Sorry. I didn't mean—"

"That's all right," Danny said expansively. "No offense taken. Tell you the truth, I'm not much for camp letters myself. Stinks, really, after what they've been through. I mean, it's not like they're volunteering, you know what I mean? Need the money is what it is. Poor bleeders—you can see them here, they've still got those pj's on, it tears you right up. So the letters—I won't touch stuff like that. It's taking advantage."

Jake looked at him, the man with boys in Hitler Youth uniforms. "Can you find out who's peddling them?"

"Why?"

An appointment with a Public Safety lawyer. Maybe a connection after all. He thought of Bernie's office, stacked high with paper.

"A hunch. It's not jewels—that doesn't feel right. Let's follow the paper trail." He glanced at Danny's dubious face. "I'd pay you, of course."

"Tell you what. Friend of Gunther's. I'd like to oblige, as far as it goes. Let me poke around a bit. No promises, mind. Anything turns up, I'll set you a price. You can't ask fairer than that, can you?"

"No."

"Hello, Rog," Danny said, looking up at a British private. "All set?"

"I've got the major outside."

"Right. That's you, darling," he said to the blonde, who put down her napkin and took out a lipstick. "Just as you are, love. No sense doing your mouth, given where it's going. Off you go."

"Wiedersehen," she said politely to Jake, getting up and following the private.

"Safe home," Danny called after her. "Choice goods, that one. Enjoys it. Sure you don't want a go?"

"Can I ask you something? Why—" Jake said, then stopped, not sure how to ask it. "I mean, I thought all it took was a couple of cigarettes. So why—"

"Well, some gents are shy, like. That's how it started. See, I'm not shy, so I was in a way to make a few introductions. Some appreciate that. The convenience. Officers, they don't want to pick something up off the street. You don't know what you're getting, do you? A little surprise for the wife. Hello, what's this? Nasty. It's the hygiene, really. I've got a doctor checks them. Decent chap. Takes care of any accidents too, if you know what I mean. Of course, the girls prefer it—saves wear and tear, all that walking about."

"Why only officers?"

Danny smiled. "Got the money, for a start. But, you know, it's really the girls. All the same, aren't they? Looking for love. And a ticket out. London, why not? Anywhere but here. Now, an enlisted man isn't going to do that, is he? You need an officer."

"And do they?"

"What? Take them home? Naw. Quick suck and a poke is what they like. Still, you never know. I always tell the girls, look on the bright side. There's always a chance. Just put your heart and soul into it and maybe something will come of it."

"And they believe you."

Danny shrugged. "They're not whores, see. Nice girls, some of them, temporaries. They're just trying to get by. You have to give them something to hope for."

"What do you tell the boys?"

"That's just a side," Danny said. He ran his hand over his slick hair, embarrassed again. "It takes all kinds."

"Are they really Hitler Youth?"

"'Course. Viktor, anyway. He's Ilse's brother."

"Quite a family."

"Well, you know, I think he *was* that way. The others, I don't know. Bit reluctant at first. But they're glad of the money, and who's to know, really? Viktor finds them—friends of his. As I say, it's just a side. Here, watch this one. He's good, he is. Regular Benny Goodman."

He pointed to the bandstand, where a clarinet player had stood up, licking his reed as he waited for the lead-in. When he started, he did play Goodman, "Memories of You," the sad opening notes mellow as liquid. Another sound of home, the music so unexpectedly beautiful that it seemed a kind of reproach in the smoky room. On the dance floor couples drew closer, swaying instead of bouncing, as if the clarinet were charming them. The player swayed too, eyes closed, blotting out the bright, ugly room to let the music take him somewhere else.

"Everything seems to bring . . ." The music of romance, not good times and quick gropes, a song for girls looking for love. Jake watched them move dreamily on the floor, heads leaning on uniformed shoulders, giving themselves something to hope for. At the tables people had grown quieter, pretending to watch the solo but really drawn by something else, the world they'd known before Ronny's, brought back, close enough to touch, by the sentimental notes. ". . . memories of you." Even here. There was Lena's dress, across the floor, the same deep blue, her going-out dress. He remembered the way she'd brush the back as she got up, a quick touch to smooth out the wrinkles, so that it clung to her afterward, moving with her. On the front there'd been a patch of glitter going up to the shoulder, little fingers of bright sequins, like a sprinkling of stars. But wool, too warm for a summer's night in a crowded room, and this one had a wet patch showing between the shoulder blades, stretched over a girl too big for it, with blond hair piled on top of her head like Betty Grable. Still, the same deep blue.

When the band came in behind the clarinet, ending the solo, there was a restless stirring at the tables, a kind of relief to be out of the spell, back to just music.

"What did I tell you?" Danny said, his eyes shiny, but Jake continued to watch the dress, the damp spot now covered by an American soldier's hand. *Fragebogen.* Message boards. Why not here, dancing at Ronny's? But the waist was too thick, bulging over the belt.

Gunther was making his way steadily across the room, skirting the dancers. There was a sudden roar at the door as a large party swept in, looking for tables. "Memories of You" floated away.

"Gunther, you old sod," Danny said, standing up, a show of respect. "Take a pew." He pulled out a chair. Gunther sat down and poured a drink.

"Meet the general?" Jake said, nodding in Sikorsky's direction.

"I know the general. Sometimes a useful source."

"But not this time," Jake said, reading his face.

"Not yet." He downed the glass and sat back. "So. You've had a good talk?"

"Danny's been telling me about his real estate. He's a landlord."

"Yes. A *kino* for parachute silk," Gunther said, shaking his head, amused.

"Steady," Danny said. "No tales out of school now."

Gunther, ignoring him, raised his glass. "You will dress half the women in Berlin. I salute you. Parachutes."

"You can't beat it for quality," Danny said.

But silk hadn't reached the dance floor yet, just the cheap cotton prints from the last wartime ration. Lena's dress was gone from the floor, hidden somewhere among the crowded tables. The band had started a jazzy version of "Chicago."

"You have the actual report?" Gunther said.

Jake pulled the flimsy from his breast pocket and watched Gunther look it over, sipping as he read.

"A Colt pistol," he said, nodding, a western fan. "M-1911."

"Is that special?"

"No, very common. Forty-five-caliber. Very common." He handed the paper back.

"So now what?" Jake said.

"Now we look for an American bullet. That changes everything."

"Why?"

"Not why, Herr Geismar. Where. Potsdam. All along, it's a problem. The Russians closed down the market. But there are two things in Potsdam. The market, but also the conference. With many Americans."

"He wasn't at the conference."

"But perhaps at the compound in Babelsberg. Invited there. What could be more likely? All the Americans are there, even Truman. Just down the road from the conference site. On the same lake, in fact." He looked pointedly at Jake. "He was *found* at the Cecilienhof, but was he shot there? The night before the conference? No one there, guards only?" He shook his head. "Bodies drift. An obvious point."

"Frigging Scotland Yard, isn't it?" Danny said, frankly admiring. "You're a caution, Gunther. No mistake."

"But what isn't obvious is the money," Jake said.

"Always with you the money," Gunther said.

"Because it was there. Let's say he did have a pass to the compound, that he saw an American. He still picked up ten thousand dollars. You only make that kind of money in the market. So, all right, an American in the market. Who's also at the conference? Most of those guys were just flown in. They're not allowed out. You don't see any of them here." He waved his hand toward the noisy room.

"That is to their credit," Gunther said dryly. "Nevertheless, he was in Potsdam. And so was an American bullet."

"Yes," Jake said.

"And who is at the conference? We can except Herr Truman."

"Washington people. State Department. Aides," Jake said, ticking them off.

"Not at the meeting. In Babelsberg."

"Everybody," Jake said, thinking of Brian's requisition list. The last blowout of the war. "Cooks. Bartenders. Guards. They've even got somebody to mow the lawn. Everybody except press."

"A wide net," Gunther said glumly. "So we eliminate. Not everybody can authorize. First you will find out who issued his papers. Then after—" He drifted off, back to his own list.

"That still doesn't tell me what he was selling."

"Or buying," Danny said casually.

"What did you say?" Gunther said, wide awake, putting his hand on Danny's arm.

"Well, any transaction, there's two sides, isn't there?"

Gunther said nothing for a second, then patted his arm. "Thank you, my friend. A simple point. Yes, two sides."

"I mean," Danny said, encouraged, "he'd have dollars, wouldn't he? An American. What—"

"It wasn't dollars," Jake said. "Marks. Occupation marks."

"Oh. You might have said. Russian or American?"

"I thought they were the same." Engraving plates, handed over.

"They're *worth* the same, of course, but now the look— Here." Danny picked up one of Sikorsky's dropped notes. "Now, this is Russian. See the little dash before the serial number? You won't see that on the American ones." Somebody in the Treasury Department, careful after all. Jake wondered if Muller knew.

"You sure?"

"Things like that, you notice," Danny said. "I thought it was fake, see, so I asked. Doesn't make any difference, really, just something to keep track, I reckon."

"Who has the money?" Gunther asked Jake.

"I've got one of the bills. Not on me." Back in the drawer of the frilly pink vanity, next to the still of Viktor Staal.

"Then look," Gunther said.

"But they circulate back and forth, don't they?"

Gunther nodded. "It might be suggestive, however." He turned to Danny, raising his glass. "Well, my friend. To your good eye. Most helpful."

"On the house, Gunther, on the house," Danny said, clinking glasses, pleased with himself.

"But if he was buying, what was he buying?" Jake said insistently.

"That's an interesting question," Gunther said as Danny poured another drink. "More difficult."

"Why?"

"Because whatever it was, he never got it. He still had the money," Gunther said, repeating an earlier point to a slow pupil.

Jake felt a door close. How could you trace what was never exchanged? "Now what?"

"Now we find out who he was. What would he buy? Has Teitel spoken to Frankfurt?"

"I don't know."

"Then we wait," Gunther said, sitting back, his eyes drooping. "A little patience."

"So we do nothing."

Gunther opened one eye. "No. *You* will play the policeman. Find out who authorized his pass. I'm retired. I'm going to have a brandy."

Jake put his drink down, ready to leave. The room was even more crowded, the bar almost invisible behind a wall of people, and the noise was rising now with the smoke, covering the band. "Sleepy Time Down South," the clarinet again, peppier, straining to be heard. A girl squealed somewhere, then laughed. He took a breath, claustrophobic. But no one else seemed to mind. They were all young, some as young as Danny, who was tapping the table in time to the music. He'd never taken Lena dancing in her blue dress. The clubs by then had become shadowy, dimmed by the Nazis, taking notes in the audience during the comedy sketches. No longer fun, just something to show the tourists, who wanted to see the Femina with the telephones on the tables. Nobody had been young then, not like this, and it only came once.

"Back in a sec," Danny said, standing up. "Goes right through you, don't it? Keep an eye on Gunther—he goes right out when he naps."

Jake watched the slick head move through the crowd. How many nights did Gunther sit here, finally oblivious even to the smell? The couples on the floor had taken on a kind of blur. This is probably what he saw, people bouncing through a haze, the music almost an echo. It occurred to Jake that he was probably a little drunk himself. Another dream song, "I'll Get By." There was the dress again, leaning against the soldier. The overweight blonde.

He narrowed his eyes. If you blocked out the rest, the dress would come into focus as it had been, without the bulges and damp spots, moving with her. He remembered the Press Club party when he'd sat watching across a different room, the dress finally turning, her eyes laughing at him in secret, a quick flash like the sequins.

The blonde turned, the dress hidden now by the uniform, only the shoulder visible, shimmering with sequins. Jake blinked. Not drunk, not a trick of the eye. The same dress.

He stood up and began to cross the room, a swimmer, people sweeping past him like water. When the blonde looked up, her face alarmed, he saw what he must look like, a drunk plowing through the crowd with the crazed, determined steps of a sleepwalker. Her eyes darted away, anxious with fear. No, not fear, recognition. Not as plump as she'd been in the office, but still a big girl. Fräulein Schmidt. A poor typist, Goebbels' spy.

"Hannelore," he said, going up to them.

"Go away." A rasp, nervous.

"Where did you get the dress?" he said in German.

The soldier had stopped dancing, annoyed. "Hey, buddy, get lost."

Jake grabbed her upper arm. "The dress. Where did you get it? Where is she?"

She wrenched her arm out of his grip. "What dress? Go away."

"It's hers. Where is she?"

The soldier placed himself between them, holding Jake's shoulder. "What's the matter with you, you deaf or something? Blow."

"I know her," Jake said, trying to get past him.

"Yeah? Well, she doesn't want to know you. Beat it," the soldier said, shoving him.

"Fuck off." Jake pushed him aside, and the soldier staggered a little. Jake took her arm again. "Where?"

"Leave me alone." A wail loud enough to draw attention, people around them stopping in midstep. She reached for her soldier. "Steve!"

The soldier grabbed Jake's shoulder, spinning him around. "Blow or I'll deck you, you fuck."

Jake swatted his hand away and moved toward her again. "I know it's hers."

"Mine!" she screamed, moving away.

His eyes were still on her so that he missed the punch, a hard jab to the stomach, making him double over, winded.

"Now beat it."

Chairs scraped behind them. Jake's mouth filled with the taste of sour whiskey. Without thinking, he lunged for the soldier, trying to push him away, but the soldier was waiting. He stepped aside, then smashed his fist into Jake's face, sending him backward. Jake heard the shouts around him as he reached out to grab the air, a stunned weightlessness, going down, until he felt his head crack against the floor. Another crash as the crowd moved back against a table, then everyone leaning over him, pushing away the soldier with his fist still raised. When Jake tried to lift his head, blood filling his mouth, he felt a surge of nausea and closed his eyes to hold it down. Don't black out. The band stopped. More yelling. Some men were dragging the soldier away. Another soldier bent down.

"You okay?" Then, to the crowd, "Give us some air, for Christ's sake." Jake tried to get up again, clenching his mouth against another taste of bile, dizzy. "Take it easy."

Faces bent over him. A girl with bright red lipstick. But not Hannelore.

"Wait. Don't let them go," Jake said, trying to rise. "I have to—"

The soldier held him down. "What are you, crazy?"

"He started it," someone said. "I saw it."

Then Gunther was there, alert, dabbing the corner of Jake's mouth with a handkerchief. He reached up, pulling a bottle from the next table and pouring whiskey over the cloth.

"Hey. Use your own fucking booze."

A sharp, cauterizing sting, as surprising as the first punch. Jake winced.

"Heroics," Gunther said, wiping Jake's mouth. "Can you move your head?"

Jake nodded, another sharp pain, then seized Gunther's arm and pulled himself up. "Don't let them get away," he said, looking around wildly and starting for the door.

A dozen hands grabbed him, pinning his arms. "Sit the fuck down. You want the MPs in here?" He was pushed into a chair. Someone motioned to the band to start playing.

"It was her dress," Jake said to Gunther, who looked at him dumbly.

"He with you?" the soldier said to Gunther. "We don't want any trouble here."

"You don't understand," Jake said, standing.

The soldier grabbed him again. "No, you don't. It's over, *verstehe*? You make one move and I'll fucking deck you too."

"I'll take him home," Gunther said calmly, moving the soldier's hand away. "No more trouble."

He clutched Jake's arm and forced him to walk slowly toward the door. People stared as they squeezed past the tables.

"I have to find her," Jake said.

Outside, the same parked cars and drivers, the street black. Jake looked in both directions, everything swallowed up in the dark.

"Now, my friend, what happened?"

Jake felt the back of his head, a trickle of blood. "There isn't time. Go back. I'll be all right." He went over to one of the drivers. "You see a blonde in a blue dress?"

The driver looked at him suspiciously.

"Come on, it's important. Big girl with a soldier."

"What's it to you?"

"Tell him," Gunther barked, suddenly a cop.

The driver jerked his thumb east, toward the Memorial Church.

Gunther held him. "They're gone," he said simply. "It's not safe."

But Jake had already thrown off his hand and started to run. He could hear Gunther call out behind him, then even that died away, covered by the ragged sound of his own breathing.

Clouds had covered what little moon there was, so that the dark seemed tangible, like a fog you could brush away. They'd been gone only a few minutes, not long enough to vanish, but there was no one in the street. What if the driver was lying? He ran faster, then rammed his foot into a stray brick lying on the pavement. The pain shot up through him, joining the dull ache in his head, and he stopped, holding his stomach to catch his breath. They couldn't be far. They'd stick to the Ku'damm, hoping for the lights of a cellar bar. The side streets would be impossible, clogged with unseen rubble. Assuming they went this way at all.

Up ahead, a tiny light flickered in a doorway. Jake started again, limping slightly, his sore foot slowing him like a brake.

"Hello, Tommy." A soft voice called out where the light had been, then another flicker, a flashlight shining up under the whore's chin, bathing her tired face in a ghost's light.

"Did you see a couple go by?" he said in German. "A blond girl."

"Come with me. Why not? Fifty marks."

"Did you?" he said, insistent.

"Go to hell." She snapped off the flashlight, saving batteries, and disappeared in the dark.

He could make out the jagged edges of the bombed church against the sky as a truck swept around the intersection. The old heart of the west end, flashing with theater lights, now just dark shadows. He remembered London in the blackout, buses appearing out of nowhere, headlights dimmed to slits like crocodile eyes. He had always hated it, the blindness, stumbling over curbs, but the ruins here made it worse, disturbing, twisted shapes in a nightmare. A jeep swung out of the broad Tauentzienstrasse, lighting up the sidewalk for a second. A pack of soldiers coming out of a bar, and there, beyond them, holding a flashlight, a tall soldier with a fleshy blonde.

Jake picked up his pace, ignoring the pain in his foot. They were heading toward Wittenbergplatz, the way he used to go home, down past the KaDeWe windows. Don't lose her now. They had walked, so it couldn't be far. Maybe another club. Hannelore Schmidt, Goebbels' spy, who didn't want to be recognized, arm in arm with the new order. He wondered what she'd put on her *fragebogen.* Not the calls to Nanny Wendt. Where had she got the dress? Ransacking the old flat in Pariserstrasse. Maybe a trade for food coupons. She'd know something. Not a pointless search through Bernie's files, a real connection.

Jake saw them crossing the street now, guided by the weaving flashlight, which picked up a group of DPs huddled in the square. She'd be safe with Steve, a handy man to have around in a fight. Jake touched the corner of his mouth, tender, still streaked with blood. They were across Wittenbergplatz.

It was then he stopped, in front of the broken plate glass window, watching the tiny beam of light move toward the familiar heavy door.

Almost a joke, there all along. His old flat, passed around the Columbia staff until finally Hal Reidy had left too. Had Hal given it to her, a farewell bonus? Or had she simply moved in, another spoil to pick up, like the French cognacs and Danish hams that flooded into the city that last year. The meek inherited after all, even Hannelore Schmidt. Now what? Race up the stairs for another punching session with Steve? Now he knew where she was. He could come back tomorrow, bring some coffee, a peace offering, and talk to her calmly. A light went on in his window. His window. He imagined Hannelore draped over his couch with her GI, Lena's dress flung aside, sequins crumpled on the floor. Where did she get it?

He crossed the square, warily circling the DPs, and went into his street. A walk he'd taken a million times. He pushed open the tall wooden door. Pitch dark, the hall light either gone out or stolen. In one corner he could hear the dripping of water in a bucket. But this was home, stairs he could climb with his eyes closed. He felt his way up the banister. A turn at the landing, then up to his floor, along the railing to the door. He knocked, not loud, a force of habit. The most terrifying sound in Germany, a knock on the door. Harder now. "Hannelore." What if she refused to open? He tried the doorknob. Locked. His flat. He knocked again, then banged his open palm against the door, a steady pounding. "Hannelore!" Finally the sound of the lock clicking, the door opening a crack, then wider. A woman with frightened eyes standing with the light behind her. Not Hannelore, a gaunt woman with stringy hair, sickbed pale, another ruin. But over the dark circles her eyes widened.

"I'm sorry," he said, embarrassed, turning away.

"Jacob," she whispered.

He glanced back, startled. Her voice. And now the face, familiar, was taking shape too, behind the pale skin. Not the way he'd imagined it. The same weightless feeling, falling into Ronny's tables.

"Lena. My god." His voice also a whisper, as if sound would chase her away, a ghost not yet real.

"Jacob." She reached up her hand, touching the blood at the corner of his mouth, and he realized that he was the ghost, wild-eyed and bloody, someone from another world. "You came back."

He took her hand from the streak of blood and moved it to his mouth, kissing it, grazing the fingers, not yet able to take in any more. Just the fingers, real. Alive.

She moved them along his lips, a Braille touch, trying to make sense of the ridges.

"You came back."

He nodded, too happy to say anything, weightless but not falling, rising now, a balloon, watching her eyes fill, still too startled to smile.

"You're hurt," she said, touching him, but he took her fingers away, holding them as he shook his head.

"No, no. It doesn't matter. Lena, my god." And then he reached out for her, drawing her to his chest, arms around her. He kissed the side of her face, moving his head with hers, kissing her everywhere, as if he were still afraid she'd evaporate unless he touched her. "Lena." Just saying it. Then he held her tightly, his face in her hair, feeling her press against him, holding him down, until suddenly she let go, slumping, a dead weight, and he realized she'd fainted.

CHAPTER SEVEN

JAKE CARRIED HER inside. There was a pillow on the couch where Hal used to flop—evidently her bed. Struggling under her weight, he moved past the bathroom to the bedroom door. No hands free to open it, so he kicked. The door was flung open by Steve, down to dog tags and boxer shorts, his socks still on. Behind him, Hannelore, in a slip, let out a squeak.

Steve started toward him. "Boy, you don't quit, do you?"

"She passed out. Help me get her on the bed."

Steve looked at him, dumbfounded.

"It's all right. I'm an old friend. Ask her." He cocked his head toward Hannelore. "Come on, give me a hand."

Steve stepped aside. "Who is he?" he said to Hannelore.

"From before the war. No," she said to Jake as he carried Lena in. "That's my bed. She's on the couch. A few days, she said, and now look."

"Go fuck in the hall for all I care. She's sick—she needs the bed." He put her down gently, stepping on the blue dress lying on the floor. "Do you have any brandy?"

"Brandy. Where would I get brandy?"

Steve walked over to his dropped uniform, took out a pint bottle, and handed it to Jake. A few drops on her lips, then a faint choke, eyes half open. He wiped sweat from her forehead. Feverish.

"You going to tell me what's going on here?" Steve said.

"What's wrong with her?" Jake asked Hannelore.

"I don't know. I took her in, she was all right. I thought, well, two rations. It's a help, you know? Now this. She just lies there all day. It's always the same when you're kindhearted. People take advantage." Her voice hard and aggrieved.

"Has she seen a doctor?"

"Who has money for doctors?"

"You look like you're doing all right."

"You can't talk to me like that. What do you know about it? Coming here like this. It's not your flat. It's mine now."

"This your place?" Steve asked.

"It was. She used to work for me," Jake said, looking at Hannelore. "And Dr. Goebbels. She tell you that?"

"That's not true. You can't prove anything." She looked at Steve, then walked over to the nightstand and lit a cigarette, defiant. "I knew it was trouble when I saw you. You never liked me. What did I do? I take in a friend. Kindhearted. Now you're going to make trouble."

"Jacob," Lena said faintly, then clutched his hand, holding it with her eyes closed.

"Get her something to drink. She's burning up. Some water. You can spare that, can't you?"

Hannelore glared at him, then started for the kitchen. "Maybe it's good you're here. You can feed her now. I'm finished with this business."

"Nice girl," Jake said as she left. "Friend of yours?"

Steve shrugged. "A few times. She's all right."

Jake glanced over at him. "I'll bet."

"Here," Hannelore said, returning with a glass of water.

Jake raised Lena's head and made her drink, then dipped his handkerchief in the water and put it on her forehead. Her eyes were open now.

"You came back," she said. "I never thought—"

"It's all right now. We'll get you a doctor."

"No, don't leave," she said, still holding his hand.

He looked up at Steve. "Listen, I need your help. We have to get a doctor."

"She's German, isn't she? Army docs don't treat civilians."

"There's a man back at Ronny's. He knows me. Ask for Alford."

"Alford? I know Alford," Hannelore said.

"Good. Then you go with him. Tell him it's urgent—tonight. And have his doctor bring medicine. Penicillin, I guess, whatever he has. Say it's a personal favor to me." He stood up, pulling out his wallet. "Here. Tell him it's a down payment. If it's more, I'll pay him tomorrow. Whatever he wants."

Hannelore's eyes widened at the sight of the money.

"Don't even think about it," Jake said. "Every mark. I'll check."

"Go to hell," she said, offended. "Go get him yourself, then."

"Listen, Hannelore, for two cents I'd turn you in. They'll make you a rubble lady. It's hell on the nails." He looked at her red fingertips. "Now get dressed and do it."

"Hey, you can't talk to her—"

"And I'll have you up for fraternizing with a Nazi. And assaulting an officer. I can do it, too."

Steve stared at him. "Tough guy," he said finally.

"Please," Jake said. "She's sick, for Christ's sake, you can see that."

Steve glanced over at the bed, then nodded and began to put on his pants.

"I'm not a Nazi," Hannelore said. "I was never a Nazi. Never."

"Shut up and get dressed," Steve said, throwing her the dress.

"You were always trouble for me," she said to Jake, still disgruntled, pulling the dress over her head. "Always. And what made you so perfect? Sneaking around with her. I knew all the time. Everybody knew."

"Here," Jake said, handing Steve the money, "you take it. He's a young guy. Slick hair." He took a key from his pocket. "My jeep's there, if you want to drive back."

Steve shook his head. "She can walk."

"What do you mean, she can walk? Where are you going?" Hannelore said, still arguing with him as they went out the door.

"You mustn't be angry with her," Lena said in the sudden quiet. "She's had a hard time."

Jake sat on the bed, looking at her, still trying to take her in. "You've been here. All the time," he said, as if that were the remarkable thing. "I passed the other day—"

"I knew she had the flat. There was nowhere else. The bombs—"

He nodded. "Pariserstrasse, I know. I looked for you everywhere. I saw Frau Dzuris. Remember?"

She smiled. "Poppyseed cakes."

"She's not fat anymore." He wiped her brow, letting his hand rest on the side of her face. "Have you been eating?"

"Yes. She's good to me. She shares her ration. And of course she gets a little extra from the soldiers."

"How long has that been going on?"

She shrugged. "We eat."

"How long have you been sick?"

"A little while. I don't know. The fever this week."

"Do you want to sleep?"

"I can't sleep. Not now. I want to hear—" But in fact she closed her eyes. "How did you find me?"

"I knew the dress."

She smiled, her eyes still closed. "My good blue."

"Lena," he said, smoothing her hair. "My god."

"Oh, I must look terrible. Do you even recognize me?"

He kissed her forehead. "What do you think?"

"That's a nice lie."

"You'll look even better after the doctor fixes you up. You'll see. I'll bring some food tomorrow."

She held her hand to his head, looking at him. "I thought I'd never see you again. Never." She noticed his uniform. "Are you a soldier? Were you in the war?"

He turned slightly and pointed to his shoulder patch. "Correspondent."

"Tell me—" She paused, blinking, as if caught by a sudden pain. "Where to begin? Tell me everything that happened to you. Did you go back to America?"

"No. Once, a visit. Then London, all over."

"And now here."

"I told you I'd come back. Didn't you believe me?" He took her by the shoulders. "Everything's going to be the same."

She turned her head. "It's not so easy, to be the same."

"Yes, it is. You'll see. We're the same."

Her eyes, already shiny with fever, grew moister, but she smiled. "Yes, you're the same."

He brushed the bare hairline above his temple. "Almost, anyway." He looked down at her. "You'll see. Just like before."

She closed her eyes, and he busied himself wetting the handkerchief, disconcerted by his own words. Not like before.

"So you found Hannelore," he said, trying to be conversational, then, "Where's Emil?"

"I don't know," she said, her voice curiously detached. "Dead, maybe. It was terrible here, at the end."

"He was in Berlin?"

"No, up north. For the army."

"Oh," he said, not trusting himself to say more. He stood up. "I'll get some more water. Try getting a little sleep before the doctor gets here."

"Like a nurse," she said, closing her eyes.

"That's right. I'm going to take care of you. Go to sleep. Don't worry, I'll be here."

"It seems impossible. I just opened the door." Her voice drifting.

He turned to leave, then stopped. "Lena? What makes you think he's dead?"

"I would have heard." She moved her hand up, covering her eyes. "Everyone's dead. Why not him?"

"You're not."

"No, not yet," she said wearily.

He glanced at her. "That's the fever talking. I'll be right back."

He walked through the main room to the kitchen. Everything the same. In the bedroom, littered with Hannelore's clothes and bottles of lotion, he could imagine being somewhere else, but here it was his flat, the couch against the wall, the little table by the window, not even rearranged, as if he'd simply gone away for the weekend. The kitchen shelves were bare—three potatoes and a few cans of C rations, a jar of ersatz coffee. No bread. How did they live? At least Hannelore had her dinner at Ronny's. Surprisingly, the gas ring worked. A kettle to make coffee. No tea. The room itself felt hungry.

"It's cold," she said when he put a new wet cloth on her forehead.

"It's good for the fever. Just keep it there."

He sat for a minute looking at her. An old cotton wrapper dotted with patches of sweat, wrists thin enough to snap. Like one of the grim DPs he'd seen plodding across the Tiergarten. Where had Emil been?

"I went to the Elisabeth," he said. "Frau Dzuris said you worked there."

"With the children. There was no one to help, so—" She winced. "So I went there."

"Did they get out? Before the raid?"

"Not bombs. Shells. The Russians. Then the fire." She turned her head, eyes filling. "No one got out."

He turned the cloth over, feeling helpless.

"Don't think about it now."

"No one got out."

But she had, somehow. Another Berlin story.

"Tell me later," he said softly. "Get some sleep."

He smoothed her hair again, as if it would empty her head, and in a few minutes it seemed to work. The little gasps evened out and became almost soundless, so that only the faint movement of her chest showed she was breathing at all. Where was Hannelore?

He watched her sleep for a while, then got up and looked around the jumbled room. Clothes had been flung over the chair, a pair of shoes resting on top. Without thinking, he began putting things away, filling time. A messy room is the sign of a messy mind—his mother's old saying, ingrained after all. He realized, absurdly, that he was tidying up for the doctor. As if it mattered.

He opened the closet door. He had left a few things with Hal, but they were gone, traded perhaps on one of the message boards. In their place, a fur coat was hanging next to some dresses. A little ragged, but still fur, the kind of thing he'd heard they collected to send to the troops on the eastern front. But Hannelore had kept hers. A present, no doubt, from a friend in the ministry. Or maybe just salvaged after one of the bombing raids, when the owner hadn't got out.

He went into the living room. There wasn't much to straighten here—the lumpy couch, a suitcase neatly set underneath, some stray cups that hadn't been washed. Near the window table, something new—an empty birdcage, Hannelore's one addition to the room. Otherwise, just as before. He washed the cups in cold water, then wiped off the sink counter, settling in. When there was nothing left to do, he stood by the window smoking, thinking about the hospital. What else had she seen? All the time he'd imagined her in the old flat, getting dressed to go out, frowning at herself in the mirror, safe under some bell jar of memory. The last four years were only supposed to have happened to him.

A few cigarettes later, he heard Hannelore on the stairs.

"Leave the door open," she said, switching off her flashlight. "He'll never find it otherwise."

"Where's the doctor?"

"He's coming. They had to get him. How is she?"

"Sleeping."

She grunted and went into the kitchen, pulling down a bottle hidden over the top shelf.

"Where's Steve?" Jake said.

"You ruined that for me," she said, pouring a drink. "He'll never come back now."

"Don't worry, there're plenty more where he came from."

"You think it's so easy. What am I supposed to do now?"

"I'll make it up to you. I'll pay for the room, too. She can't sleep out here."

"No, only me, is that it? How can I bring people to a couch?"

"I said I'd pay. You can take a vacation, give yourself a rest. You could use it."

"Go to hell," she said, then noticed the washed cups on the counter. "Ha. Maid service too. My ship has come in." But she sounded mollified now, already counting the money. "You have a cigarette?"

He gave her one and lit it.

"I'll move her out as soon as she's better. Here, take this." He handed her some money. "I can't move her now."

"All right, all right, nobody's throwing anybody out. I like Lena. She was always nice to me. Not like some," she said, looking at him. "She used to come sometimes during the war, bring coffee, have a little visit. Not for me. I knew why she came. She wanted to be here, just sit in the flat. Make sure it was still here. It reminded her, I suppose. Such foolishness. Everything just so. 'Hannelore, you moved the chair. Didn't you like it over here?' I knew what she was up to. And my god, what did it matter, with the bombs every night, where a chair was? 'If it makes you so happy, move it back,' I'd say, and you know, she would? Foolishness." She finished off the drink.

"Yes," Jake said. Another bell jar. "Did Hal give you the apartment?"

"Of course. He was a friend of mine, you know."

"No, I didn't know," he said, genuinely surprised.

"Oh you, you never noticed anything. Just her. That's all you could see. Hal was very nice. I always liked the Americans. Even you, a little. You weren't a bad sort. Sometimes," she added, then paused. "Don't make trouble for me. I was never a Nazi, I don't care what you think. Never. The BDM only—all the girls in school had to join. But not a Nazi. Do you know what they'll do? They'll give me a Number V ration card—that's a death card. You can't live on that."

"I don't want to make trouble for you. I'm grateful to you."

"Huh," she said, putting out her cigarette. "But I'm still on the couch. Well, let me get my things."

When she came back she was in a silk nightgown, her heavy breasts bulging. Hal's friend.

"Does it embarrass you?" she said, almost coquettish. "Well, I can't help that if I'm out here." She spread a sheet on the couch.

"Is she still sleeping?"

Hannelore nodded. "She doesn't look so good," she said.

"How long has she been sick?"

"A week, maybe two. When she came, I thought she was just tired. You know, everyone looks tired now. I didn't know. What could I do? There wasn't much to eat."

"I'll bring some food tomorrow. For both of you."

"And some cigarettes maybe?" She had begun wiping her face with a damp cloth, taking off years with the rouge. How old would she be now, twenty-five?

"Sure."

"Herr Geismar," she said to herself, shaking her head. "Back in Berlin. Who would have thought? Even the old room, eh?"

"I'll wait up," Jake said. "Sleep if you like."

"Oh, with a man in the room. Not likely. Maybe just a little rest."

But in a little while she was out, her mouth open, the sheet barely covering her breasts, the unconcerned sleep of a child. More waiting, staring out into the eerie darkness of Wittenbergplatz. He made mental lists—food, medicine if he could get it from the dispensary, faking an illness. If not, Gunther, who could get anything. But what medicine? He glanced at his watch. One-thirty. What kind of doctor came at two in the morning?

He came at three, a little tapping up the stairs, then a skeletal frame in the doorway, clearing his throat as if he were ringing a bell. He was almost grotesquely thin, with sunken concentration camp eyes. Where had Danny found him? A rucksack for a medicine bag.

"You're the doctor?"

"Rosen." He nodded formally. "Where is she?"

Jake pointed to the bedroom, watching Rosen take in the sleeping Hannelore on the couch.

"First, somewhere to wash my hands."

Jake assumed it was a euphemism, but in the bathroom Rosen really did wash his hands, then dry them methodically, like a surgeon.

"Should I boil some water?" Jake said, at a loss.

"Why? Is she having a baby?"

In the bedroom, Jake woke her gently, then stepped aside as Rosen felt her throat with his clean hands, presumably testing for swelling. A palm on her forehead instead of a thermometer.

"How long?"

"I don't know. She said a week or so."

"Too long. Why didn't you call before?"

But that was too complicated to explain, so Jake just stood there, hovering. "Can I do something?"

"You can make some coffee. I'm not often up at this hour."

Jake went to the kitchen, sent off like an expectant father, superfluous. Filling the kettle, a small pop as the gas lit. In the living room, Hannelore moaned and turned over.

He went back to the bedroom and stopped at the door. Rosen had opened her robe so that she lay naked on the bed, his hands spreading her legs to examine her, an unexpected intimacy. The body Jake had seen so many times, stroking it to life, now being prodded like a slab.

She's not one of Danny's girls, he wanted to shout, but Rosen had already caught his look of dismay.

"I'll call you," he said curtly. "Go make the coffee."

Jake backed out of the doorway. Why examine her there? The only thing Danny's doctor would know. But who else could he have called? He saw the hands on her white thigh.

In the kitchen, he stirred the fake coffee in a cup. No sugar, nothing. He heard them talking down the hall, questions, Lena's faint replies. He picked up the cup to take it in. But Rosen didn't want him there. Instead he put it on the table and sat watching it grow cold. Hannelore's hair had come undone, a messy girl even in her sleep.

When Rosen finally came out, he washed his hands again under the kitchen tap. Jake started for the bedroom.

"No. I've given her something to sleep." He poured some of the kettle water into another cup and dropped in a syringe needle. "She should be in a hospital. Why did you wait?"

"What's wrong with her?"

"These girls," Rosen said, shaking his head. "Who did the abortion?"

"What abortion?" Jake said, stunned.

"You didn't know?" He went over to the table and sipped some coffee. "They shouldn't wait so long."

"Is she all right?"

"Yes, it's done. But there was an infection. Lack of hygiene, perhaps."

Jake sat down, feeling sick. Another bed, hands probing, not washed.

"What kind of infection?"

"Don't worry. Not venereal. She can work again."

"You don't understand. She's not—"

Rosen held up his hand. "That's your affair. I don't ask. But she'll need more penicillin. I only had the one dose. Can you make an injection? No, I thought not. I'll come back. Meanwhile, use these." He put some tablets on the table. "Not as strong, but you need to bring the fever down. Make her take them, never mind the taste."

"Thank you," Jake said, taking them.

"They are expensive."

"That doesn't matter."

"A valuable girl," Rosen said wryly.

"She's not what you think."

"It doesn't matter what I think. Just give her the tablets." He glanced toward the couch. "You have two here?"

Jake turned away, feeling like Danny stung by Sikorsky's money. But who cared what Rosen thought?

"Did she tell you she had an abortion?" Jake said.

"She didn't have to. That's what I do."

"Are you a real doctor?"

"You're a fine one to ask for credentials," Rosen said, then sighed and took another gulp of coffee. "I was a medical student in Leipzig, but of course I was thrown out. I became a doctor in the camp. No one asked for a degree there. Don't worry, I know what I'm doing."

"And now you work for Danny."

"You have to live somehow. You learn that in the camp too." He put down the coffee cup, ready to go. "So, the tablets, don't forget," he said, getting up. "I'll come tomorrow. You have something on account?"

Jake handed him some money. "Is this enough?"

He nodded. "The penicillin will be more."

"Anything. Just get it. But she'll be all right?"

"If you keep her off the streets. At least no Russians. They're all diseased."

"She's not a whore."

"Well, I'm not a doctor, either. Such niceties." He turned to go.

"What time tomorrow?"

"After dark. But not so late as this, please. Not even for Danny."

"I can't thank you enough."

"You don't have to thank me at all. Just pay me."

"You're wrong about her," Jake said, wondering why it mattered. "She's a respectable woman. I love her."

Rosen's face softened, surprised at the words, something from a forgotten language. "Yes?" he said. He turned away again, his eyes weary. "Then don't ask about the abortion. Just give her the tablets."

Jake waited until the steps had died away in the stairwell before he closed the door. Don't ask. But how could he not? Worth putting your life at risk. A matter of hygiene. He put the cup in the sink, then turned out the light and started down the hall, exhausted.

She was sleeping, her face smooth in the soft glow of the lamp. The way he had imagined it, the two of them in bed, his bed even, holding each other as if the war hadn't happened. But not yet. He sank onto the chair and took off his shoes. He'd wait here until it was light, then wake Hannelore to keep watch. But the chair was springy, poking at him like thoughts. He went over and lay down on his side of the bed, still in uniform. On top of the sheet, so he wouldn't disturb her. When he reached over to switch off the light, she stirred with a kind of dreamy restlessness. Then, as he lay staring up at the dark, she took his hand and held it.

"Jacob," she whispered.

"Ssh. It's all right, I'm here."

She tossed a little, her head moving in a slow rhythm, so that he realized she was still asleep, that he'd become part of the dream.

"Don't tell Emil," she said, her voice not quite in the room. "About the child. Promise me."

"I promise," he said, and then her body relaxed, her hand still locked in his, peacefully, while he lay staring at the ceiling, wide awake.

Lena slept through most of the next day, as if his being there had finally allowed her to be really sick, not to have to make the effort to get up. He took the time out to get things: the jeep, miraculously still there; money from his army account; supplies at the PX, goods bulging on the shelves and piled high on the floor; a change of clothes at Gelferstrasse. Life errands. He threw his battered portable into the bag with his clothes, then told the old couple he'd be away for a day or two and was there any food he could take? More cans. The old man handed him something wrapped in paper, about the size of a bar of soap.

"Nobody in Germany has had butter for a long time," he said, and Jake nodded, a conspirator.

At the press camp, where he went to collect messages, there were sandwiches and doughnuts. He filled another bag.

"Well, somebody got lucky, I see," Ron said, handing him a press release. "Today's schedule, if you care. And details on the U.S. dinner—

a good time was had by all. It was, too. I hear Churchill got pissed. Take the ham sandwiches, it's what they like. Can't get enough ham, the *fräuleins.* Need any rubbers?"

"Somebody ought to spank you."

Ron grinned. "You'll thank me later, believe me. You don't want to go home with pus between your legs. By the way, they loved you in the newsreel. Maybe they'll use it."

Jake looked at him, puzzled, then shrugged it off, not wanting to talk.

"Don't be a stranger," Ron said as he hurried out.

But he already was. Potsdam, even tiddly Churchill, felt a million miles away. When he passed the flags in front of the headquarters building, he felt he was leaving a foreign country, saluting itself, a provider of tins. He glanced at the full sacks on the seat beside him. They'd eat out of cans, but they'd eat. In the bright sunshine, the villas and trees in Grunewald were as lovely as ever. Why hadn't he noticed before? He didn't see the rubble as he sped up the Kurfürstendamm, just the happy morning light. For a moment it seemed still lined with shops. The important thing was to get fluids into her to prevent dehydration. Soup, every mother's remedy.

As Ron had predicted, Hannelore fell on the sandwiches.

"Ham, my god. And white bread. No wonder you won the war, to eat like this. We were starving."

"Save one, okay?" he said, watching her gobble it down. "How's Lena?"

"Sleeping. How she can sleep, that one. What's that?"

"Soup," he said, putting the pot on the ring.

"Soup," she said, a child at Christmas. "Is there another tin, maybe? My friend Annemarie, she would be so grateful."

The thought of getting her out of the house made him generous. He handed her two cans, then a pack of cigarettes.

"These are for you."

"Luckies," she said in English. "You're not a bad sort."

When he took the soup in, Lena was awake, looking out the window. Still pale. He felt her forehead. Not as bad as before, but still feverish. He began to spoon soup for her, but she took it from him, sitting up.

"No, I can feed myself."

"I like doing it."

"You'll make me an invalid. I feel so lazy."

"Never mind. I've got nothing better to do."

"You should work," she said, and he laughed—a sign of life, the way she used to scold him back to the typewriter.

"Would you like anything?"

"A bath, but there's no hot water. It's terrible, how we all smell."

"I hadn't noticed," he said, kissing her forehead. "Let me see what I can do."

It took forever. The boiling water seemed to turn cold the minute it touched the porcelain, so he had to carry more pots from the gas ring like a slow conveyor belt, until finally he had a shallow bath, not really hot but a little better than tepid. He thought of Gelferstrasse and its steaming tub.

"Soap," she said. "Where did you get it?"

"U.S. Army. Come on, hop in."

But she hesitated, the old self-consciousness. "You don't mind?" she said, indicating the door.

"You didn't use to be so shy."

In the same tub, bubbles covering her breasts, laughing at him when he patted her dry, getting himself wet.

"Please. I'm so thin."

He nodded and closed the door behind him, then went into the bedroom. Musty, despite the open window; rumpled sheets Hannelore probably hadn't changed in weeks. But how could she have washed them? The smallest household task had become an ordeal. He found another set in the closet and changed the bed while he listened to the splashing next door. Hospital corners, everything stretched tightly.

He was in the kitchen, washing up, when she came out, toweling her hair. She looked brighter, as if the dark circles under her eyes had been merely dirt.

"I'll do that," she said.

"No, you get into bed. I'm going to spoil you for a few days."

"Your typewriter," she said, moving to the table and touching the keys.

"Not the same one, though. That's still in Africa somewhere. I had a hell of a time getting this one."

She touched the keys again. He saw that her shoulders were shaking, and he went over to her, turning her around.

"So silly," she said, crying, "a typewriter." Then she fell against his shoulder, holding him, so that his face was in her hair, a fresh smell now, and he burrowed into it.

"Lena," he said, feeling her shudder against him, still crying, the way it should have been at the train station, some involuntary release.

Her head nodded against him and they stood that way for a minute, just holding each other, until he felt the heat through her hair and pulled away, brushing tears from the corners of her eyes with his fingers.

"Maybe some rest, huh?"

She nodded again. "It's the fever, this," she said, wiping her eyes, collecting herself. "So silly."

"That's what it is," he said.

"Just hold me," she said, "like you used to."

And for a moment he didn't want to do anything else, so happy the room around him seemed to melt away. But her hair was damp with sweat again and he could feel her sag.

"Come on, we'll put you to bed," he said, his arm around her as he walked her down the hall. "Clean sheets," he said, pleased with himself, but she didn't seem to notice. She slipped into bed and closed her eyes.

"I'll let you sleep."

"No, talk to me. It's like medicine. Tell me about Africa. Not the war. What it was like."

"Egypt?"

"Yes, Egypt."

He sat on the bed, brushing back her hair. "On the river it's beautiful. You know, sailboats."

She frowned, as if trying to see it. "Boats? In the desert?"

"And temples. Huge. I'll take you someday," he said, and when she didn't respond, he went on, describing Cairo and the old *souk,* the pyramids of spices, until he saw that she had finally drifted off, another sailboat.

He finished washing up, then out of habit sat down at the typewriter. Lena was right; he should work, they'd expect something in a day or two, and here was the old table, where he used to type out the broadcasts, looking into the busy square. The street was almost deserted now, just the usual thin stream of army trucks and refugees, but the spell had caught him, all the familiar props. When he started typing, the clicking sound filled the room like an old phonograph record, found at the bottom of the pile.

"Potsdam Up Close," something he could make up from hearsay and pictures, but with a chance to put himself on the spot, face-to-face with the Big Three, almost as if he'd been at the baize table too, talking to them, the only journalist there, something *Collier's* would like. Maybe even a cover line. Dressed up with eyewitness details—the Red star of geraniums, the chimneys, the patrolling Russians. Then the contrast to central Berlin, his trip that first day, Churchill at the Chancellery, putting himself in Brian Stanley's place, who wouldn't mind and who probably wouldn't see it anyway. Our man in Berlin. Not what had really happened—a squalid murder, getting his life back—but what mattered to *Collier's,* enough to keep the contract going. The football game as a finish, building the peace even while the Big Three negotiated. When he finished, it was a thousand words too long, but *Collier's* could worry about that. He was back in business. Let them cut Quent Reynolds.

Rosen came before dinner, not furtive this time, even apologetic.

"Mr. Alford explained the situation. Forgive me if I—"

"Never mind. You're here, that's what matters. She's been sleeping."

"Yes, good. You didn't say anything—what I told you? Sometimes it's a little sensitive, even after everything. Their sweethearts come back, they think everyone waits. It's difficult."

"I don't care."

"No? It's not always the case."

Another Berlin story that didn't make the piece, arguments and tears. He thought of the soldiers crossing the Landwehrkanal that day, almost home.

This time Rosen had brought a thermometer.

"A little better," he said at the bed, reading it. "The penicillin must be working. A miracle drug. From mold. Imagine."

"How much longer?"

"Until she's better," he said vaguely. "You can't kill the infection with one shot. Not even a miracle drug. Now you, *gnädige frau,* drink, sleep, that's all—no shopping." A friendly bedside phrase, as if there were shops. "Think good thoughts. Sometimes that's the best."

"He's taking care of me," Lena said. "He changed the sheets." Noticing after all.

"So," Rosen said, amazed, still a German man.

Outside, Jake gave him money. "Do you need any food?" he said, pointing to the cans on the counter. "PX."

"Perhaps some tinned meat, if you can spare."

Jake handed him a can.

"I remember," Rosen said, looking down at it. "When we got out, the Americans gave us these. We couldn't eat—too rich. It wouldn't stay down. We threw up everything, right in front of them. They were offended, I think. Well, how could they know? Excuse me for last night. Sometimes it's not only the body that vomits. The spirit goes too."

"You don't have to explain. I saw Buchenwald."

Rosen nodded and turned to the door. "Keep up with the tablets, don't forget."

Lena insisted on getting up for dinner, so the three of them sat around the table, Hannelore bubbling over with high spirits, as if the ham sandwich had been another kind of injection.

"Wait till you see what I got at Zoo Station, Lena. For ten cigarettes. She wanted the pack, and I said, who gets a pack for a dress? Even ten was too many, you know, but I couldn't resist. In good condition, too. I'll show you."

She got up and held the dress to her body.

"See how well cut? She must have known somebody, I think. You know. And see how it fits. Not too small here."

She took off her dress without a hint of embarrassment, and slid the new one over her slip.

"See? Maybe a tuck here, but otherwise perfect, don't you think?"

"Perfect," Lena said, eating soup. A little more color than before.

"I couldn't believe the luck. I can wear it tonight."

"You're going out?" Jake said. An unexpected bonus to the shopping trip, the flat to themselves.

"Of course I'm going out. Why not? You know, they opened a new cinema in Alexanderplatz."

"The Russians," Lena said grimly.

"Well, but some are nice. They have money, too. Who else is there?"

"No one, I guess," Lena said indifferently.

"That's right. Of course the Americans are nicer, but none of them speak German, except for the Jews. Are you not going to finish that?"

Jake handed her his piece of bread.

"White bread," she said, a child with a sweet. "Well, I'd better get ready. You know, they're on Moscow time, everything so early. Isn't that crazy, when they have all those watches? Leave the dishes, I'll do them later."

"That's all right," Jake said, knowing she wouldn't.

In a minute he heard a trickle of water in the bathroom, then a spray of perfume. Lena sat back, finished, looking out the window.

"I'll get coffee," Jake said. "I have a treat for you."

She smiled at him, then looked again out the window. "There's no one in Wittenbergplatz. It used to be so busy."

"Here, try this," he said, bringing her the coffee and giving her a doughnut. "It's better if you dunk."

"It's not polite," she said, laughing, but dipped it daintily and took a bite.

"See? You'd never know they were stale."

"How do I look?" Hannelore said, coming in, hair pinned again like Betty Grable's. "Doesn't it fit well? A tuck here." She pinched the side, then gathered up her purse. "Feel better, Lena," she said, unconcerned.

"Don't bring anyone back," Jake said. "I mean it."

Hannelore made a face at him, oddly like a rebellious teenager, and said, "Ha!," too full of herself to be annoyed. "Look at you, an old couple. Don't wait up," she said, pulling the door behind her.

"An old couple," Lena said, stirring her coffee. "I'm not yet thirty."

"There's nothing to thirty. I'm thirty-three."

"I was sixteen when Hitler came. Think of it, my whole life, Nazis, nothing else." She looked out again at the ruins. "They took everything, didn't they?" she said moodily. "All those years."

"You're not ready for a cane yet," Jake said, and when she managed a smile he took her hand across the table. "We'll start over."

She nodded. "It's not so easy sometimes. Things happen."

He looked away. Why bring it up at all? But it seemed an opening.

"Lena," he said, still not looking at her, "Rosen said you had an abortion. Was it Emil's?"

"Emil?" Almost a laugh. "No. I was raped," she said simply.

"Oh," he said, just a sound.

"Does that bother you?"

"No." A quick lie, without missing a beat. "How—"

"How? The usual way. A Russian. When they attacked the hospital, they raped everybody. Even the pregnant mothers."

"Christ."

"Not so unusual. It was ordinary then, at the end. Look how squeamish you are. Men do the raping, but they never want to talk about it. Only the women. That's all we talked about then—how many times? Are you diseased? I was afraid for weeks that I had been infected. But no, instead a little Russian. Then, when I got rid of it, a different infection."

"Rosen says it isn't venereal."

"No, but no more children either, I think."

"Where did you get it done?" he asked, picturing a dark alley, the cliché warning of his youth.

"A clinic. There were so many, the Russians set up a clinic. 'Troop excesses.' First they rape you, then they—"

"Wasn't there a doctor?"

"In Berlin? There was nothing. My parents were in Hamburg—god knows if they're alive. There was nowhere else to go. A friend told me about it. Free, she said. So, another gift from the Russians."

"Where was Emil?"

"I don't know. Dead. Anyway, not here. His father's still alive, but they don't speak. I couldn't go to him. He blames Emil for all this, if you can imagine."

"Because he joined the party?"

She nodded. "For his work. That's all it was. But his father—" She looked up. "You knew?"

"You never told me."

"No. What would you have said?"

"Do you think it would have made a difference to me?"

"Maybe to me, I don't know. And this room, when we came here, it was away from all that. Emil, everything. Somewhere away. Do you know what I mean?"

"Yes."

"Anyway, he wasn't one of *them.* Not political. The institute, that's all he cared about. His numbers."

"What did he do during the war?"

"He never said. It wasn't allowed, to talk about such things. But of course it was weapons. That's what they all did, the scientists—make weapons. Even Emil, his head always in a book. What else could they do?" She looked up. "I don't apologize for him. It was the war."

"I know."

"He said, stay in Berlin, it's better. He didn't want me to be part of all that. But then the bombing got so bad, they allowed the wives to go there with them. So the men wouldn't worry. But how could I leave then?" she said, staring into the cup, her eyes beginning to fill. "What did it matter? I couldn't leave Berlin. Not after Peter—" Her voice caught, drifting into some private thought.

"Who's Peter?"

She looked up. "I forgot. You don't know. Peter was our son."

"Your son?" he said, stung in spite of himself. A family, with someone else. "Where is he?"

She stared back at the cup. "He was killed," she said, her voice flat. "In a raid. Almost three." Her eyes filled again.

He put his hand on hers. "You don't have to tell me."

But she hadn't heard him, the words spilling out now, a purge.

"I left him in the kindergarten. Why did I do that? In the shelter all night I had him with me. He would sleep in my lap, not cry like the others. And I thought, well, that's over, another night. But then the Americans came. That's when they started like that—the British at night, the Americans in the day. No let-up. Eleven o'clock, I remember. I was shopping when the warning came, and of course I ran back, but the wardens caught me—everyone into the shelter. And I thought, the nursery's safe, they had a deep cellar." She stopped for a moment, looking away to the window. "Then after the raid, I went there and it was gone. Gone. All buried. The mothers—we had to dig them out. All day digging, but maybe there was a chance. Then the screaming when they brought them out, one after another. We had to identify them, you see. Screaming. I went a little crazy. 'Be quiet, be quiet, you'll frighten them.' Imagine saying such a thing. And the crazy thing was—Peter, not a scratch, no blood, how could he be dead? But of course he was. Blue. Later they told me it was asphyxiation, you just stop breathing, no pain. But how do they know? I just sat there in the street with him all day. I wouldn't move, not even for the wardens. Why? Do you know what it's like, to lose a child? Both of you die. Nothing's the same after that."

"Lena," he said, stopping her.

"All you can think is, why did I leave him there? Why did I do that?"

He got up and stood behind her, smoothing his hands on her shoulders, calming her.

"It'll pass," he said quietly.

She took out a handkerchief and blew her nose.

"Yes, I know. At first I didn't believe it. But he's dead, I know, that's all there is to it. Sometimes I don't even think about it anymore. Isn't that terrible?"

"No."

"I don't think about anything. That's what it's like now. You know what I used to think, during the war? That you would come and rescue me—from the bombs, everything here. How? I don't know. Out of the sky, maybe, something crazy. You'd just appear at the door, like yesterday, and take me away. A fairy tale. Like the girl in the castle. Now you're here and it's too late."

"Don't talk like that," he said, turning her chair and bending down, looking up at her. "It's not too late."

"No? You still want to rescue me?" She ran her fingers across his hair.

"I love you."

She stopped. "To hear that again. After all these terrible things."

"That's over. I'm here."

"Yes, you're here," she said, her hands at the sides of his face. "I thought nothing good would ever happen to me again. How can I believe it? You still love me?"

"I never stopped. You don't stop."

"But such terrible things. And now I'm an old woman."

He reached out and touched her hair. "We're an old couple."

That night they slept close together, his arm around her, like a shield even bad dreams couldn't get through.

CHAPTER EIGHT

EACH DAY WAS better, so that by the following weekend she was able to go out. Hannelore had found a friend "temporarily" and they'd been alone for days, a reclusive happiness that had finally become confining. Jake had done a second piece—"Adventures in the Black Market," Russians and Mickey Mouse watches, the food situation, Danny and his girls discreetly left out—and Lena had slept and read, getting stronger. But the weather had grown sultry; the humid Berlin summer that used to drive everyone to the parks now just swirled the rubble dust, coating the windows with grit. Even Lena was restless.

Neither of them had seen the Russian sector, Lena because she refused to go there alone, so Jake drove east through the Mitte, past Gendarmenmarkt, then Opernplatz, where they'd made bonfires of books. Everything gone. When they saw the caved-in Berliner Dom in the distance, they were too dispirited to go on and decided to stroll up the Linden instead, the old Sunday outing. No one was out walking now. In the ruins, a makeshift café that had been set up just before Friedrichstrasse was crammed with Russians sweating in the heat.

"They'll never leave," Lena said. "It's finished here now."

"The trees will grow back," Jake said, looking at the black stumps.

"My god, look at the Adlon."

But Jake was looking at the figure coming through the door, the building evidently only partially ruined. Sikorsky noticed him at the same time and came over.

"Mr. Geismar, you decided to visit us after all," he said, shaking hands. "For the afternoon tea, perhaps."

"They still have it?"

"Oh yes, it's a tradition, I'm told. Not so formal now, but more democratic, yes?"

In fact everyone Jake could see at the door brimmed with medals and decorations. A generals' playground.

"In the back there are still some rooms. From mine you can see Goebbels' garden. Or so they tell me it was. Excuse me," he said, turning to Lena, "I am General Sikorsky." A polite bow.

"I'm sorry," Jake said. "Fräulein Brandt." Why not *frau*?

"Brandt?" he said, looking at her carefully. "It's a common name in Germany, yes?"

"Yes."

"You're a Berliner? You have family here?"

"No. All killed. When the Russians came," she said, an unexpected provocation.

But Sikorsky merely nodded. "Mine too. My wife, two children. In Kiev."

"I'm sorry for that," Lena said, embarrassed now.

He acknowledged this with another nod. "The fortunes of war. How is it a beautiful woman is still unmarried?"

"I was. He's dead."

"Then I am sorry for that," Sikorsky said. "Well, enjoy your walk. A sad sight," he said, looking at the street. "So much to do. Goodbye."

"So much to do," Lena said after he walked away. "And who made it like this? Russians. Did you see the way he looked at me?"

"I don't blame him. He has an eye for a pretty girl." Jake stopped and put his hand to the side of her head, touching her hair. "You are, you know. Look at you. You've got your color back. Like before."

She looked up at him, then shook her head, embarrassed again. "No, not that. Something else. Suspicious. The Russians are suspicious of everything."

"I heard he was in intelligence. They look at everybody that way. Come on."

They walked past the Brandenburg Gate, still plastered with giant posters of the Big Three.

"No trees," she said. "Oh, Jake, let's go back."

"Tell you what, we'll go out to the Grunewald, take a walk in the woods. You up for that?"

"It's not like this?"

"No. Cooler too, I'll bet," he said, wiping sweat from his face.

"Something for the lady?" A German in an overcoat and fedora, detached from the group milling around the Reichstag.

"No," Lena said, "go away."

"Prewar material," the man said, opening his coat and pulling out a folded garment. "Very nice. My wife's. Scarcely worn. See?" He was unfolding the dress.

"No, please. I'm not interested."

"Think how she'll look," he said to Jake. "For summer, light. Here, feel."

"How much?"

"No, Jake, I don't want it. Look how old, from before the war."

But that's what had caught his eye, the kind of dress she used to wear.

"You have cigarettes?" the man said eagerly.

Jake held it up against her. Cinched waist, blouse top; the way she had always looked.

"It's nice," he said. "You could use something."

"No, really," she said, flustered, as if she were being dressed in public, where everyone could see. She looked around, expecting MPs with whistles. "Put it away."

"It'll look pretty on you."

He took out a fresh pack of cigarettes. What had Hannelore said was the going rate? But just then MPs did appear, British soldiers with white sticks, beginning to scatter the crowd like chickens. The German snatched the pack, flinging the dress at Jake. "A thousand thanks," he said, hurrying. "A bargain—you won't regret it." He began to run toward the arch, his overcoat flapping.

"Oh, such foolishness. Anyway, it's too much. A whole pack."

"That's all right. I feel rich." He looked at her. "I haven't bought you anything in a long time."

She began folding the dress. "Look, it's wrinkled."

"It'll steam out. You'll look nice." He put his hand up to her hair. "With your hair down."

She looked up at him. "I don't wear it that way anymore."

"Maybe once. A few pins," he said, taking one out.

She brushed his hand away. "Oh you, you're impossible. Nobody wears it that way anymore."

Back in the jeep, they drove through Charlottenburg, down more long avenues of ruins, dust hanging in the heavy air, until finally they could see trees at the edge of the Grunewald and beyond them the water, where the river widened to make the lakes. It was cooler, but not much, the sun blocked by clouds now, turning the water to slate, the air still thick with listless heat. At the old yacht club, Union Jacks hung from flagpoles, not even stirred by a breeze. They could see two boats on the water, becalmed, their sails as motionless as two white dabs in a painting. But at least the city was behind them, nothing now but the broad water and, across it, suburban houses in Gatow poking through the trees. They took the road rimming the water, ignoring the charred patches in the forest and smelling pines, the clean air of before.

"The boats should come in, it's going to storm. My god, it's hot." She patted her face with a handkerchief.

"Let's put our feet in."

But the little stretch of beach, deserted, was littered with bottles and pieces of artillery shells that had washed up on shore, a bathtub ring of debris, so they crossed the road to the woods. The air was sticky but peaceful, no hikers shouting out to each other, no clomping horses on the riding trails. Alone in a way they'd never been before, hiding from the Sunday crowds. Once they'd made love here behind some bushes, the sound of trotting horses just a few yards away, the threat of being discovered as exciting as flesh. Getting away with something.

"Remember the time—" he started.

"Yes. I know what you're thinking. I was so nervous."

"You liked it."

"You liked it."

"Yes, I did," he said, looking at her, surprised to find himself aroused. Just remembering it.

"I'm sure they saw."

"There's no one here now," he said, moving her against a tree, on impulse, kissing her.

"Oh, Jake," she said, a light scold, "not here," but she let him kiss her again, opening her mouth, then suddenly felt him against her and gasped, breaking away. "No, I can't."

"It's all right. There's no one—"

"Not that," she said, shaking her head, distressed. "Anybody touching there—"

"I'm not anybody."

"I can't help it." She lowered her head. "It's the same. Please."

He touched her face. "I'm sorry."

"You don't know what it was like," she said, still looking down.

"It won't be like that," he said softly, but she broke away, leaving the tree.

"Like a knife," she said, choking a little. "Tearing—"

"Stop."

"How can I stop? You don't know. You think everything goes away. It doesn't go away. I can still see his face. One touch there and I see his face. Is that what you want?"

"No," he said quietly. "I want you to see me."

Now she did stop, and she rushed over to him, putting her hand on his chest. "I do. It's just— I can't."

He nodded.

"Oh, don't look like that."

How did he look? A flush of shame and disappointment? The first bright day out of the sickroom, as murky now as the overcast sky.

"It's not important," he said.

"You don't mean that."

He put his finger under her chin, lifting it. "I want to make love to you—there's a difference. I'll wait."

She leaned her face into his chest. "I'm sorry. I still—"

"We'll take it a little bit at a time." A light kiss. "See?" He stopped and held her by the shoulders. "It won't be like that."

"For you," she said, stinging him, so that he drew away a little. Something new, a voice he hadn't heard before. But who knew her better, every part of her?

"A little bit at a time," he said, kissing her again, easing her out of it.

"And then what?" she said moodily.

"A little more," he said, but before he could kiss her the sky finally broke, a loud crackle and streak of light, and he smiled, laughing at the cue. "Then that. That's what happens. See?"

She looked at him. "How can you joke?"

He stroked her face. "It's supposed to be fun." The first drops fell. "Come on, we don't want you to get wet."

She looked down again, biting her lower lip. "What if it never happens." She stopped and clutched at his shirt, ignoring the rain. "I'll do it if you want to," she said flatly. "Right here, like the other time. If you want."

"With your eyes closed."

"I'll do it."

He shook his head. "I don't want to be somebody else's face."

She looked away. "Now you're angry. I thought you wanted—"

"The way it used to be. Not like this." He put his finger to her hair. "Anyway, I'm getting wet. There's nothing like a cold shower to take your mind off things," he said, trying to be light but watching her, still uneasy.

"I'm sorry," she said, head down.

"No, don't," he said, wiping the rain off her cheek. "We have lots of time. All the time we want. Come on, you're soaked."

She kept her head down, preoccupied, as he led her back to the road. The rain had picked up, drenching the jeep, and it cut into them when they started to drive. He left the open road for the woods, as if, crazily, the trees would shelter them, forgetting that the trails were dirt at this end of the park, full of ruts and puddles. He went faster when they hit the straight road heading east, worried now that the wet would chill her, make her sick again. She had crouched down behind the windshield, curled up against the rain, an excuse to withdraw into herself.

The woods were dreary and somber, and he cursed himself for taking the shortcut, no drier and filled with shadows, like the rest of the day. What had he expected, sunlit meadows and a picnic rug wet with sex? Too soon. But what if it was always going to be too soon? When she had stood by the tree, shuddering, he'd felt he was back in the collapsing house, its joints creaking, too wounded to be propped up again. A gasp, just at a touch. It won't be like that. How did he know? Only one of them had gone through it. And he had pushed, maybe ruined things, like some kid eager to get laid. Except he hadn't planned anything, it had just happened, trying to get it back, one of those afternoons when everything had been good, when they both wanted it. Too soon.

He stopped to take cover at the Avus underpass, army trucks roaring on the concrete trestle over their heads, but she was shivering, no warmer than out in the rain. Walls dripping, clammy. Better to make a run for it, change clothes, not huddle in the wet. But where? Wittenbergplatz was miles. At least get out of the woods. They passed Krumme Lanke, almost through now, and he saw the street leading to the Document Center. Maybe Bernie was there, snug in his cellar of index cards, but what good would he be? Jake looked over at her, alarmed. Still hunched and shivering, all the healing of the past week about to be undone. A hot bath. He remembered carrying pots to the tepid tub. Speeding now, past the press camp. Maybe Liz had something dry to wear. No civilians in the billets. But who would stop him, the old couple?

He was lucky. There was no one at Gelferstrasse, the house so empty you could hear the clock. She hesitated at the door.

"Is this where you live? It's allowed?"

"Say you're my niece," he said, pulling her in.

Their wet shoes squeaked up the stairs, leaving prints.

"In there," he said, pointing to his door. "I'll start a bath for you."

Water so hot it steamed. He opened the tap as far as it would go, then saw a jar of bath salts Liz had left on the shelf and poured some in. A little foam, the smell of lavender—maybe a present from tall Joe.

She was standing inside the door, looking around, her dress dripping.

"Your room, it's so funny. Pink. Like a girl's."

"It was. Here." He handed her a towel. "Better get those off. The bath's all yours."

He went over to his closet, stripping down and throwing the wet clothes in a pile. He pulled out a clean shirt and went over to the drawer for underwear. When he turned, he found her watching him and, suddenly shy, held up the shirt to cover himself.

"You're still dressed," he said.

"Yes," she said, and he realized she was waiting for him to leave, modest again, afraid to reveal anything.

"Okay, okay," he said, grabbing his pants. "I'll be downstairs. Take as long as you want—the heat'll do you good."

"I'd forgotten," she said, "what you looked like."

He glanced up at her, disconcerted, then picked up dry shoes and headed for the door. "That'll give you something to think about in the tub. Come on, off," he said, pointing to her dress. "Don't worry, I won't look. There's a woman lives next door. She won't mind if you borrow something."

"No, I have my new dress," she said, unfolding it. "Only a little damp here."

"See, a bargain," he said, closing the door.

Downstairs, he put on his shoes, then sat staring out the window at the rain. A little bit at a time. And yet there they'd been, almost naked in a room, looking at each other. He could hear the water running, but more slowly now, keeping it hot while she soaked. Like strangers, as if they'd never been to bed. Lying there afterward, watching her at the mirror. But that had been before.

He got a drink from one of the labeled bottles in the dining room—Muller, who could certainly spare it—and brought it back to the window. The rain was falling straight, not even hitting the open sill, the kind of steady rain that could go on for hours, good for crops and staying indoors. There was a phonograph near the piano, and he went over and flipped through the stack of records. V Discs, the Nat Cole Trio, clearly somebody's favorite. He took a record out of its sleeve and put it on. "Straighten Up and Fly Right." Light and silly, American. He sat down with a cigarette and put his feet on the windowsill, brooding despite the music. The last thing he'd anticipated. So sure how it would be.

When the song repeated itself, he frowned and got up to take it off. No water now, no sounds upstairs. She'd be drying herself, toweling her hair, pinning it back up. He heard a soft movement, like mice, and knew she must be crossing the hall. In his room. He took a handful of records and put them on in a stack so he wouldn't hear anything else, no rustling, nothing to make his thoughts dart back and forth. Just a piano, bass, and guitar, and the steady rain. He put his feet back up on the sill. The old afternoons had never been long enough—a rush to get dressed, back into the city. Now the minutes stretched out with nowhere to go, as formless and lazy as the cigarette smoke curling up in the empty house.

He didn't hear her when she came in, just felt some change in the air behind the music, a smell of lavender. He turned his head and saw that she was standing still, waiting for him to see her. Making an entrance, tentative. He stood up, staring, his mind turning over. The bath had given her color, pink as his room, her old face. But there was more. The dress was a little big and she had belted it tightly, making it blouse over on top, a 1940 dress. She had combed out her hair to go with it, letting it fall down around her face in the old style. All arranged, like an invitation, everything he'd asked for. She smiled shyly, taking his silence for approval, and took a few steps toward him, then turned to the phonograph, a girl on a date looking for something to say.

"What does it mean, 'you're the cream in my coffee'?" she said, looking at the record.

"That they go together," he said absently, still staring at her.

"It's a joke?" she said, making small talk.

He nodded, hearing the lines now because she seemed to be listening. "Like that. 'My Worcestershire, dear.'"

"Worcestershire?" Stumbling over it in English.

"A sauce."

She glanced over at him. "Do I look all right?"

"Yes."

"I borrowed the shoes."

And then nothing, just looking at him while the record changed, waiting. A slower song now, "I'll String Along with You," the kind they dreamed to at Ronny's. She came over to him, swaying a little in the unfamiliar shoes, and put her hand on his shoulder.

"Do you still know how? I think I forget."

He smiled and put his hand on her waist, beginning to move with her.

They danced in a small circle, not close, letting the song lead. Through the thin material he could feel that she had nothing on underneath and it startled him, as if she were naked, past the fumbling hooks and snaps of getting undressed, all ready. He moved away slightly, still unsure of her, but she held him, her eyes on his, keeping him with her. No sound but the rain.

"You didn't have to do this," he said, touching her hair.

"I wanted to. You like it this way."

A smile, pleased with herself, still looking up at him, until finally he didn't know what it meant, what had happened upstairs, except that questions would ruin it and they were moving together. Just dance, a little bit at a time. The record changed. She moved closer, warm against him, so that he could feel the swell of her down below, the faint scratch of her hair through the material, teasing him. He started to move back.

"It's all right," she said. "I want to feel you."

But she had blinked, like the gasp at the tree, and when she put her head on his shoulder it was to close her eyes, willing herself against him.

"Lena, you don't—"

"Just hold me."

They danced through the song, not hearing it, their feet moving by themselves, an excuse for being close, and the music worked, he felt her let go, an easy leaning into him. A little bit more. But she surprised him again, pressing tighter to feel him there and putting her arms around his back, her mouth to his ear.

"Let's go upstairs," she whispered.

"You're sure?"

She didn't answer, just led him slowly across the room so that their going seemed another part of the dance, rhythmic and dreamy, one leg after another up the stairs. Now it was he who was tentative, not sure what to do, following her, watching her stop halfway up to take off the shoes, a slow, erotic gesture, undressing for him, bending gracefully to pick them up, then the bare feet, pale white, as if they were the most intimate thing about her. He followed the rest of the way, watching her skirt brush against her legs, and then they were in his room, the music went away, distant, and he could hear himself breathing. He stood waiting, still at a loss, while she let the shoes fall and turned to him and opened the top button of his shirt, then the next, movements as deliberate as steps. She opened the shirt, smoothing her hands across his chest, making his skin tense at the surprise of it, then went back to the buttons, down, almost to the last, when she stopped and leaned her head against his bare skin, resting there.

"Help me," she said.

He put his hand to her neck, moving the hair aside and stroking it gently until she tipped her head back to look up at him again, nodding for him to go on. He undid her belt, hearing it drop to the floor, then slowly began pulling the dress up, gathering it until she raised her arms, trancelike, and it was over her head and off, then somewhere on the floor, and she was naked. Both hands now along her neck as he kissed the top of her head, rubbing his face in her hair. He moved his hands down her back, resting at the bottom, then walked her to the bed, sitting her down on the pink spread.

He started to undo his belt buckle, but she reached up and did it for him, the shirt falling away, then pulled the zipper and put her hands on his hips, pushing pants and underwear down at the same time until he sprang free and she was looking at him. She touched his penis, moving her hand over it slowly, making it familiar, and he stood rigidly, his eyes closed, trying not to feel her. Finally he took her hand away and dropped to the bed, moving next to her so that they were facing each other, his hand on her hip as they kissed.

Slowly, a little bit at a time. He began stroking her softly, every piece of skin familiar, the curve of her back, the hollow just before her hip, the underside of her breast, brushing it with the back of his hand until it rose with her breathing, trying to imagine her feeling it, to do it for her. Everything familiar. Except the pleasure, the feeling itself, always new, different every time, like the sky, too immediate to hold in memory. You remembered skin, the shape of a curve, but the rest disappeared and you spent your whole life coming back to it, again and again, only to find it was never the same, each time a surprise. So private no one else could ever feel it. He tried to hold himself back, emptying his mind, but she pressed up against him and there it was again, insistent. But not now; a little at a time, the grateful luxury of simply touching her. All this time and he hadn't remembered anything, just the outline, just enough to want it again.

"Lena," he said, a whisper, "are you sure?" but she covered his mouth, an open kiss, willing them quiet, and he wondered where she was, not lost in the feeling with him but somewhere inside her head, maybe in the past, where they no longer needed to go.

He moved his hand down to her thigh, trying to reach her. The soft inside, the most vulnerable place in the world, gently, light enough to coax her back. When he ran his finger along her bush, trying to open the lips, he could feel she was still dry, still closed away, for all the kissing and rubbing against him. Not ready. A little more. He put his finger in his mouth, wetting it, then placed it over her clitoris, just resting it, until he heard her intake of breath, a connection, and began moving it lightly in a circle, the merest graze, moistening it, circling wider and moving smoothly now, getting slick with her own wet. Her pelvis moved against him, as if she were trying to close her legs, but instead they went slack, opening to his finger. "Oh," she said, an involuntary sigh, as he slipped it farther down, still rubbing lightly back and forth until it was wet enough, then farther, parting the lips, slipping finally inside her, feeling the heat as she closed around him. He paused to let her catch her breath, but she put her hand over his, forcing him to keep moving it, and his finger continued in a steady back and forth, lingering near the top to circle the nub, then down, the lips spreading wider until she was open and wet everywhere, riding his finger. She turned to open her mouth to him again, as wet as below, reaching behind his head to lock him to her as her hips kept moving. When she broke away, gasping for air, shaking a little, it was to take hold of his penis. "With you," she said, drawing it to her, the head jumping when it touched the slick open skin.

Slowly. He covered her, resting above her on his arms, and she guided him in. He could feel the walls give way and forced himself to stop, letting it slide in slowly, a little at a time, so that it felt she were doing it, pulling him in deeper. When their bodies met, all the way in, she put her arms around him, holding his head down next to hers, and they lay still for a moment, listening to each other breathe. Then a slight movement, so small it seemed impossible it could cause the feeling that went through him, and he was determined now to make it last, not give in to it, because he wanted her with him. Slowly, like a dancer practicing steps, not going faster even when he heard her in his ear, her breath almost a pant. A long stroke in and out, as slow as a tease, then the short, steady movements inside again, one after another, so far in they seemed joined and suddenly he felt her rippling around him, not waiting anymore, and there was a gasp in his ear so that he knew she was coming, grabbing his back. He held still for a moment to make sure, her head turned away as her insides clutched him, an unmistakable spasm.

She turned her head back to kiss him, her breathing still ragged, opening her eyes. I see you. And when they kissed he started moving again, still slowly, because now there was no urgency, they were there, and he felt they would never have to stop if he didn't go faster and they'd never have to let the feeling go. More. His face was in her hands now as she kissed him, his body still suspended over her, and he realized that she was moving faster, hurrying him, even wetter. "It's all right," she said, "it's all right," almost a sob, but smiling, freeing him to pleasure himself. Except that it was already everything he wanted, the intimacy, both of them there, and he kept moving the same way, not even aware anymore that his prick was filled with blood to bursting. Just keep moving. No end. He felt her hands on his buttocks, clasping him, pushing him in deeper because she was still moving too, something he hadn't expected, rocking, and now he had to hold out because he heard little cries, could feel her wrapped around him, the feeling no longer individual, spreading over them both, so that when she came again, a series of shudders, it spurted out of him too and he saw that what he thought he wanted before wasn't everything after all, this was everything, even as it went away.

He wasn't aware of falling down next to her, his arm still around her, not even of his penis slipping out, only of her shoulders shaking beside him.

"Don't cry," he said, touching her hair.

"I'm not crying. I don't know what it is. Nerves."

"Nerves."

"It's so long—"

He ran his hand over her shoulder, feeling the shaking begin to subside. "I love you. You know that?"

She nodded, wiping her eyes. "I don't know why. I do such terrible things. How can you love a person who does terrible things?"

Babbling. He continued stroking her shoulder.

"It must be your jokes," he said softly.

"My jokes. You say I never make jokes."

"Then I don't know why."

She smiled a little, then sniffed. "Is there a handkerchief?"

"In my pants."

He watched her get up, languid, walk over to the pile of clothes, and take out his handkerchief and gently blow her nose, her body still flushed with patches of red, love marks. She stood for a minute, letting him look at her, then held up the pants.

"Do you want a cigarette? You always used to like a cigarette."

"I left them downstairs. Never mind. Come here."

She curled up next to him, her head on his chest.

"You didn't notice the curtains were open."

"No, I didn't notice," she said and even now made no move to cover up or try to draw the spread around her.

"Why did you—"

"When I saw you before," she said easily. "So white. Like a boy."

"A boy."

"My lover," she said, putting her hand on his chest. "I thought, I know him. I know him. He's my lover."

"Yes."

"Maybe I can feel that again." She turned her head to look at him. "How I was with you."

The words went through him, a flush of well-being so complete that all he ever wanted to do was lie there, holding her and listening to the rain.

"It used to frighten me," she said. "How it made me feel. I thought it was wrong to feel that way. I wanted to have a normal life. Be a good woman. I was raised for that."

"No," he said, stroking her, "for this."

"And now it's all gone anyway, that life. It doesn't matter anymore." She put her head back, lying quietly, looking across his chest at the room. "What's going to happen?" she said.

"We'll go to America."

"Germans are so popular there?"

"The war's over."

"I don't think for us. Even here, the Americans look at you— What do they think we did?"

"Never mind them. Somewhere else, then, where nobody knows who we are. Africa," he said, playing.

"Africa. What would you do there?"

"This. All day long. If it's hot, we'll close the shutters."

"We can do this anywhere."

"That's the idea," he said, pulling her up and kissing her.

She hung over him, her hair falling around his face. "Somewhere new," she said.

"That's right." He ran his hand over her buttocks. "No more terrible things."

Her face clouded and she turned away, facing the wall. "There's no place like that."

"Yes, there is." He kissed her shoulder. "You'll forget."

"I can't," she said, then turned back to face him. "I killed him. Do you know what that means? I can't forget the blood. It was everywhere, in my hair—"

"Ssh," he said, then put his hand up to stroke her head. "It's not there anymore. It's gone."

"But to kill somebody—"

"You had to."

"No. It was finished. I couldn't stop him from that. Then I killed him anyway. With his gun, while he was still on me. Killed him. And I didn't have to. You think I'm the same person." She lowered her head. "I wanted to be. Pretending to look like before. But it's not before."

"No, it's now. Lena, listen to me. He raped you. He might have killed you. We all had to do terrible things in the war."

"Did you?"

"Yes."

"What things?"

He took her face between his hands and looked straight at her. "I forget."

"How can you forget?"

"Because I found you again. I forget the rest."

She looked away. "You mean you want me to."

"You will. We're going to be happy. Isn't that what you want?"

She smiled a little.

"We'll start here." He turned her face and began kissing it, the cheek, then the lips, drawing a map of their place. "We've already started. You forget everything when you make love. That's why they invented it."

Finally they drifted off, not quite asleep but hazy, like the vapor that hung outside after the rain. They were still lying there, holding each other, when he heard a door close, footsteps next door, the world coming back.

"We should get dressed," she said.

"No, wait a little," he said, his arm around her.

"I have to wash," she said, but she didn't move either, content to lie there, still drifting, until they heard the quick knock on the door. "Oh," she said, flipping the end of the spread up to cover them, only halfway there when Liz opened the door and stopped in surprise, eyes wide with embarrassment.

"Oh, sorry," she said, a gulp, ducking away and closing the door behind her.

"My god," Lena said, swinging out of bed, grabbing clothes and holding them up in a bunch. "You don't lock the door?"

He looked at her from the bed, grinning.

"How can you laugh?"

"Look at you, covering yourself. Come here."

"Like a farce," she said, ignoring him. "What will she think?"

"What do you care?"

"It's not nice," she said, then, hearing herself, began to smile too. "I'm a respectable woman."

"You were."

She put her hand to her mouth to cover her smile, a girlish gesture, then tossed his pants over to the bed and started wriggling into her dress.

"What will you say to her?"

"Tell her to knock longer next time," he said, up now and putting on his pants.

"It happens so often, is that it?"

"No," he said, coming over and kissing her. "Just this once."

"Get dressed," she said, but smiling. She turned to the mirror. "Oh, look at me. My hair's a mess. Is there a comb?"

"In the drawer." He nodded at the frilly vanity. He buttoned his shirt and started tying his shoes, watching her at the mirror, the same absorbed concentration. She opened a drawer, searching. "On the right," he said.

"You shouldn't leave your money around," she said. "It's not safe."

"What money?"

She held up Tully's hundred-mark note. "And no lock either. Anyone could—"

He went over to the dressing table. "Oh, that. It's not money. It's evidence," he said easily, the word as far from his thoughts as Tully or anything else.

"What do you mean, evidence?"

But he wasn't listening now, looking at the bill. What had Danny said? A dash before the number. He turned the bill over. A dash, Russian money. He stood for a second, trying to think what it could mean, then gave it up, indifferent, his mind still hazy, not wanting anything to interrupt the day. He put the note back in the drawer and leaned down to kiss her head. The lavender was still there, mixed now with the smell of them.

"I'll be down in two minutes," she said, eager to leave, as if the billet were a hotel room they'd rented for the afternoon.

"All right. We'll go home," he said, pleased at the sound of it. He picked up Liz's shoes on the way out.

In the hall he waited until she answered his knock.

"Hey, Jackson," she said, still looking embarrassed. "Sorry about that. Next time put a tie on the door."

"Your shoes," he said, handing them to her. "I borrowed them."

"I'll bet you looked swell."

"Hers were wet."

She looked up at him. "It's against the house rules, you know."

"It's not what you think."

"No? You could have fooled me."

"What did you want, anyway?" he said, feeling too good to want to explain.

"Mostly to see if you were alive. You still live here, don't you?"

"I've been busy."

"Uh-huh. And here I was, worried. Men. People have been asking for you, by the way."

"Later," he said, unconcerned. "Thanks again for the shoes."

She tipped one to her head in a salute. "Anytime. Hey, Jackson," she said, stopping him as he turned to go. "Don't let it throw you. It's only—"

"It's not what you think," he said again.

She smiled. "Then stop grinning."

"Am I?"

"Ear to ear."

Was he? He went down the stairs, wondering if his face were really a flushed sign, giving them away. Slap-happy. All the intimacy reduced to a popular song lyric. But who cared?

He turned off the phonograph and finally had a cigarette, pacing now instead of lying in bed, the usual ritual turned around like everything else. How long since she'd come down the stairs dressed like that, wanting to? Outside, the wet leaves were gleaming in the new light, shiny as coins. Russian money. Tully'd had Russian money. His mind, still vague, was toying with it when he heard stamping at the door. Bernie, wiping his feet on the mat and shaking out an umbrella, a careful boy who practiced piano.

"Where the hell have you been?" he said, hurrying in. "I've been looking for you. For days." A faint accusation.

"Working," Jake said, the only legitimate excuse. Was he grinning?

"I've got other things to do, you know. Playing errand boy. And you take a powder," Bernie said, his voice as raspy as an alarm clock.

"You heard from Frankfurt?" Jake said, waking to it.

"Plenty. We need to talk. You didn't tell me there was a connection." He put the files he'd been carrying on the piano, as if he were about to roll up his sleeves and start to work.

"Can it wait?" Jake said, still elsewhere.

Bernie stared at him, surprised.

"Okay," Jake said, giving in, "what did they say?"

But Bernie was still staring, this time beyond him, to Lena coming down the stairs, her hair pinned back up, proper again, but the dress swaying with her, another entrance. She stopped at the door.

"Lena," Jake said. "I want you to meet someone." He turned to Bernie. "I found her. Bernie, this is Lena Brandt."

Bernie kept staring, then nodded awkwardly, as embarrassed as Liz.

"We got caught in the rain," Jake said, smiling.

Lena mumbled a polite hello. "We should go," she said to Jake.

"In a minute. Bernie's been helping me with a story." He turned. "So what did they say?"

"It can wait," Bernie said, still looking at Lena, flustered, as if he hadn't seen a woman in weeks.

"No, it's all right. What connection?" Curious now.

"We'll talk later," Bernie said, looking away.

"I won't be here later." Then, taking in his embarrassment, "It's all right. Lena's—with me. Come on, give. Any luck?"

Bernie nodded reluctantly. "Some," he said, but he was looking at Lena. "We've located your husband."

For a minute she stood still, then slumped to the piano bench, holding on to the edge.

"He's not dead?" she said finally.

"No."

"I thought he was dead." Her voice a monotone. "Where is he?"

"Kransberg. At least he was."

"It's a prison?" she said, her voice still flat.

"A castle. Near Frankfurt. Not a prison, exactly. More like a guest-house. For people we want to talk to. Dustbin."

"I don't understand," she said, confused.

"That's what they call it. There's another near Paris—Ashcan. Dustbin's where they've stashed the scientists. You know he was part of the rocket team?"

She shook her head. "He never talked to me about his work."

"Really."

She looked at him. "Never. I don't know anything."

"Then you'll be interested," Bernie said, his voice hard. "I was. He did the numbers. Trajectories. Fuel capacity. Everything but the casualties in London."

"You blame him for that? There were casualties in Berlin too."

Jake had stood following them as if he were at a tennis match and now looked at her, surprised at the strength of her return. A kindergarten covered with concrete slabs.

"Not from flying bombs," Bernie said. "We didn't have the benefit of his expertise."

"And now you will," she said, unexpectedly bitter. "In prison." She got up and went over to the window. "Can I see him?"

Bernie nodded. "If we find him."

The phrase shook Jake awake. "What do you mean?"

Bernie turned to him. "He's missing. About two weeks now. Just up and left. It's got them all foaming. Apparently he's a particular favorite of von Braun's," he said, glancing toward Lena. "Can't do without him. I made a routine query, and half of Frankfurt jumped down my throat. They seem to think he was coming to see you," he said to Lena. "Von Braun, anyway. Says he tried it before. There they were, safe and sound down in Garmisch, waiting for the end, and he makes a beeline for Berlin to get his wife out before the Russians got here. Is that right?"

"He didn't get me out," Lena said quietly.

"But he was here?"

"Yes. He came for me—and his father. But it was too late. The Russians—" She glanced over to Jake. "He didn't get through. I thought they killed him. Those last days—it was crazy, to take that risk."

"Maybe it was worth it to him," Bernie said. "Anyway, that's what they think now. In fact, they're looking for you."

"For me?"

"In case they're right. They want him back."

"Do they want to arrest me too?"

"No, I think the idea is that you're the bait. He'll come looking for you. Why else would he want out? Everyone else is trying to get in. Kransberg's for special guests. We like to keep the big Nazis comfortable."

"He's not a Nazi," Lena said dully.

"Well, that's a matter of opinion. Don't worry, I can't touch him. The technical boys put Kransberg off-limits. Scientists are too valuable to be Nazis. Whatever they did. He should have stayed where he was, nice and cozy. A little Ping-Pong in the evenings, I hear. Makes you wonder, doesn't it?"

"Bernie—" Jake began.

"Yeah, I know, leave it alone. You can't fight city hall. Every time we start getting somewhere on one of them, the tech units yank the file. Special case. Now I hear they want to take them to the States, the whole fucking team. They're arguing over salaries. Salaries. No wonder they wanted to surrender to us." He nodded to Lena. "Let's hope he finds you soon—you don't want to miss the boat." He paused. "Or maybe you do," he said, glancing at Jake.

"You're out of line," Jake said.

"Sorry. Don't mind me," Bernie said to Lena. "It comes with the job. We're a little shorthanded." He looked at Jake again. "Now the tech units, that's something else. Nothing but manpower there." He turned back to Lena. "If he turns up, give one of them a call. They'll be glad to hear from you."

"And if he doesn't?" Jake said. "You said two weeks."

"Then start looking. I think you'll want to find him."

Jake looked at him, puzzled. "What exactly is he accused of?"

"Strictly speaking, nothing. Just leaving Kransberg. A little rude, for an honored guest. But it makes the rest of them jumpy. They like to stick together—improves their bargaining position, I guess. And of course the tech boys have had to beef up security, which takes away from the country club feel of the thing. So they'd like him back."

"He just walked out?"

"No. That's the part that will interest you. He had a pass, all official."

"Why would that interest me?"

Bernie walked over to the piano and flipped open a file folder. "Take a look at the signature," he said, handing Jake a carbon sheet.

"Lieutenant Patrick Tully," Jake said, reading aloud, his voice falling. He raised his eyes to find Bernie watching him.

"I was wondering if you knew," Bernie said. "I guess not. Not with that face. Interested now?"

"What is it?" Lena said.

"A soldier who was killed last week," Jake said, still looking at the paper.

"And you blame Emil for that?" she said to Bernie, anxious.

He shrugged. "All I know is, two men went missing from Kransberg and one of them's dead."

Jake shook his head. "You're off-base. I know him."

"That must keep things friendly," Bernie said.

Jake looked up at him, then passed over it. "Why would Tully sign him out?"

"Well, that's the question, isn't it? What occurred to me was, it's a valuable piece of paper. The only problem with that is the guests don't have any money—at least, they're not supposed to. Who needs cash when you've got room service courtesy of the U.S. government?"

Jake shook his head again. "It wasn't Emil's money," he said, thinking of the dash before the serial number, but Bernie had leaped elsewhere.

"Then somebody else's. But there must have been some deal. Tully wasn't the humanitarian type." He picked up another folder. "Here, bedtime reading. He's been in one racket or another since he hit the beach. Of course, you wouldn't know it from this—just a series of transfers. The usual MG solution—make him somebody else's problem."

"Then why send him to a place like Kransberg?"

Bernie nodded. "I asked. The idea was to get him away from civilians. He was MG in a town in Hesse, and things got so bad even the Germans complained. Hauptmann Toll, they called him—crazy. He'd prance around in those boots carrying a *whip.* They thought the SS was back. So MG had to get him out of there. Next, a detention camp in Bensheim. No market there, maybe a few cigarettes, but what the hell? What I hear, though, is that he was selling discharge papers. Don't bother to look—record just says 'relieved.' That was sweet. The way they nailed him is he ran out of customers, so he started having them arrested once they were out—figured they'd pay again. One of them screams bloody murder and the next thing you know he's off to Kransberg. They probably thought, what harm could he do there? No one *wants* to check out."

"Except Emil," Jake said.

"Evidently."

"But what did they say? When Emil didn't come back. People just come and go?"

"The guards figured it must be okay if he had papers. And Tully drove him. See, the idea is, it's not a prison—once in a while the scientists go into town with an escort. So nobody thought anything of it. Then, when he didn't come back, Tully says he's as surprised as anybody."

"Wasn't he supposed to stay with him?"

"What can you do? Tully had a weekend pass—he didn't want to play nursemaid. He says he trusted him. It was personal—a family matter. He didn't want to be in the way," Bernie said, glancing again at Lena.

"And nobody says anything?"

"Oh, plenty. But you can't court-martial a man for being stupid. Not when he thinks he's doing one of the guests a favor. Best you can do is transfer him out. I'd lay you even money it was just a matter of time before those papers were in the works again. But then he went to Potsdam. Which is where you came in."

Jake had flipped open the folder and was staring at the photograph stapled to the top sheet. Young, not bloated from a night of drifting in the Jungfernsee. He tried to picture Tully striding through a Hessian village with a riding crop, but the face was bland and open, the kind of kid you found on a soda fountain stool in Natick, Mass. But the war had changed everybody.

"I still don't get it," he said finally. "If it was that loose, why pay to get out? From the sound of it, he could have jumped out a window and run. Couldn't he?"

"Theoretically. Look, nobody's trying to *escape* from Kransberg— it doesn't occur to them. They're scientists, not POWs. They're trying to get a ticket to the promised land, not run away. Maybe he wanted the pass—you know what they're like about documents. So officially he wouldn't be AWOL."

"It's a hell of a lot to pay for a pass. Anyway, where did the money come from?"

"I don't know. Ask him. Isn't that what you wanted to know in the first place?"

Jake looked up from the picture. "No, I wanted to know why Tully was killed. From the sound of it, there could have been a hundred reasons."

"Maybe," Bernie said slowly. "And maybe just one."

"Just because a man signed a piece of paper?"

Bernie spread his hands again. "Maybe a coincidence. Maybe a connection. A man gets out of Kransberg and heads for Berlin. A week later the man who gets him out comes to Berlin and ends up killed. I don't believe in coincidence. It has to connect somewhere. You add two and two—"

"I know this man. He didn't kill anybody."

"No? Well, I'd sure like to hear it from him. Ask him about the SS medal while you're at it, since you know him so well." He went over to the piano. "Anyway, he's your lead. You won't even have to go looking. He's coming to you."

"He hasn't turned up yet."

"Does he know where you are?" Bernie said to Lena.

She had slumped onto the bench again, staring at the floor. "His father, maybe. His father knows."

"Then sit tight. He'll show up. Or maybe you'd rather he didn't," he said to Jake. "A little inconvenient, all things considered."

"What's gotten into you?" Jake said, surprised at his tone.

"I don't like putting Nazis in hotels, that's all."

"He didn't do it," Jake said.

"Maybe. Maybe you don't want to do the math anymore. Add it up. Two and two." He gathered the other folders off the piano. "I'm late. Frau Brandt," he said, a courtesy nod that became a parting shot. He turned to Jake. "It connects."

He was halfway across the room before Jake stopped him.

"Bernie? Try this one. Two and two. Tully comes to Berlin. But the only one we know he was coming to see was you."

Bernie stood quietly for a moment. "Meaning?"

"Numbers lie."

When Bernie left, the room seemed as still and airless as a vacuum tube, the only movement the ticking of the hall clock.

"Don't mind him," Jake said finally. "He just talks tough. He likes to be mad."

Lena said nothing, then got up and went over to the window, folding her arms over her chest and staring out. "So now we're all Nazis."

"That's just Bernie. Everybody's a Nazi to him."

"And it's better in America? Your German girlfriend. Was she a Nazi too? That's how he looks at me. And he's your friend. Frau Brandt," she said, imitating Bernie.

"That's just him."

"No, I am Frau Brandt. I forgot, for a little while." She turned to him. "Now it's really like before. There are three of us."

"No. Two."

She smiled weakly. "Yes, it was nice. We should go now. The rain's finished."

"You don't love him," he said, a question.

"Love," she said, dismissing it. She turned to the piano. "I've scarcely seen him. He was away. And after Peter, everything changed. It was easier not to see each other." She looked back. "But I won't send him to prison either. You can't ask me to do that."

"I'm not."

"Yes. I'm the bait—isn't that what he said? I saw your face—like a policeman. All those questions."

"He's not going to prison. He didn't kill anybody."

"How do you know? I did."

"That was different."

"Maybe it was different for him too."

He looked at her. "Lena, what is it? You know he didn't."

"And you think that matters to them? A German? They blame us for everything." She stopped and looked away. "I won't send him to prison."

He went over to her, turning her face with his finger. "Do you really think I'd ask you to do that?"

She looked at him, then moved away. "Oh, I don't know anything anymore. Why can't we leave things as they are?"

"This is the way they are," he said quietly. "Now stop worrying. Everything's going to be all right. But we have to find him. Before the others do. You see that."

She nodded.

"Would he really go to his father? You said they didn't speak."

"But there's no one else. He came for him, you know, even after everything. So."

"Where were you? Pariserstrasse?"

She shook her head. "It was bombed already. The hospital. He said to wait for him there, but then he didn't get through."

"So he wouldn't know where else to look. He'd try his father."

"Yes, I think so."

"Anyone else? Frau Dzuris hadn't seen him."

"Frau Dzuris?"

"I tried her first, remember? You're not so easy to find." He paused. "Wait a minute. She said there'd been a soldier. Maybe that's why Tully came—to find you."

"Me?"

"Well, Emil. To get him back. That would explain why he wanted to see Bernie, too—to check the *fragebogens*. That's Bernie's department. Maybe he thought he'd find yours there. Except you didn't fill one out. Why didn't you, by the way?"

She shrugged. "A party member's wife? They would have made me work on the rubble. I couldn't, I was too weak. And for what, a class V card? I had that much from Hannelore."

"But Tully wouldn't have known. I didn't. So he'd want to check."

"If he was looking for me."

"It makes sense. Finding Emil would get him out of a lot of hot water."

"But if he'd already paid?"

Jake shook his head. "Bernie's wrong. He didn't get money from Emil. Russian marks aren't floating around Frankfurt. He got it in Berlin."

"Then why did he let him out?"

"That's what I want to ask Emil."

"Now you're a policeman again."

"A reporter. Bernie's right about one thing. Emil's the only lead I've got. There must be a connection—just not the one he thinks."

"He wants to make trouble for Emil. You can see that. It's so important, this soldier? Who was he?"

"Nobody. Just a story. At least he was. Now he's something else. If you really want to keep Emil out of trouble, we'd better find out who did kill him."

Lena took this in, brooding, then went over to the phonograph and fingered one of the records as if she were waiting for the music to start again.

"A little while ago, we were going to Africa."

He came up behind her, touching her shoulder. "Nothing's changed."

"No. Except now you're a policeman. And I'm bait."

CHAPTER NINE

THE NEXT DAY was hot again. Berlin was literally steaming, the rain that had washed the dust from the air now rising in wisps over the wet ruins, making the smell worse. Emil's father lived in Charlottenburg, a few streets away from the *schloss,* in what was left of an art nouveau block of flats, divided into rooms for bombed-out families. The street hadn't been cleared, so they'd had to leave the jeep on Schloss Strasse and thread their way through the rubble on a footpath dotted with house-number sticks planted in the debris like trail markers. They were sweating when they arrived, but Professor Brandt was dressed in a suit and a high starched collar from the Weimar era, stiff even in the wilting heat. His height took Jake by surprise. Emil had been Jake's size, but Professor Brandt towered over him, so tall that when he kissed Lena on the cheek, he bent at the waist, an old officer's bow.

"Lena, it's good of you to come," he said, more polite than warm, as if he were receiving a former student.

He looked at Jake, taking in the uniform, and his eye twitched. "He's dead," he said flatly.

"No, no, a friend of Emil's," Lena said, and introduced them.

Professor Brandt offered a dry hand. "From happier days, I think."

"Yes, before the war," Jake said.

"You are welcome, then. I thought perhaps—an official visit." A flicker of relief even his composed face couldn't hide. "I'm sorry, I have nothing to offer guests. It's difficult now," he said, indicating the cramped room whose light came in shafts through a boarded-up broken window. "Perhaps you would care to walk in the park? It's more pleasant, in this weather."

"We can't stay long."

"Well, a little walk, then," he said, clearly embarrassed by the room and eager to go out. He turned to Lena. "But first, I must tell you. I'm so sorry. Dr. Kunstler was here. You know I asked him to inquire in Hamburg. Your parents. I'm sorry," he said, his words as formal as a eulogy.

"Oh," she said, the sound catching in her throat like a whimper. "Both?"

"Yes, both."

"Oh," she said again. She sank to a chair, covering her eyes with a hand.

Jake expected Professor Brandt to reach out to her, but instead he moved away, leaving her isolated, alone with her news. Jake looked at her awkwardly, stuck helpless in his role, a friend of the family unable to do more than be silent.

"Some water?" Professor Brandt said.

She shook her head. "Both. It's certain?"

"The records—there was so much confusion, you can imagine. But they were identified."

"So now there's no one," she said to herself in a small voice.

Jake thought of Breimer looking out of the plane window at the wrecked landscape. What they deserved. Seeing buildings.

"Are you all right?" Jake said.

She nodded, then stood up, smoothing out her skirt, visibly putting herself in order. "I knew it must be. It's just—to hear it." She turned to Professor Brandt. "Perhaps a walk would be better. Some air."

He picked up a hat, clearly relieved, and led them down the hall, away from the front entrance. Lena drifted behind, ignoring Jake's arm. "We'll go out the back. They're watching the building," he said.

"Who?" Jake said, surprised.

"Young Willi. They pay him, I think. He's always in the street. Or one of his friends. With cigarettes. Where do they get them? He was always a sneak, that one."

"Who pays him?"

Professor Brandt shrugged. "Thieves, perhaps. Of course, they may not be watching *me.* Someone else in the building. Waiting for their chance. But I prefer they don't know where I am."

"Are you sure?" Jake said, looking at the white hair. An old man's imagination, protecting a boarded-up room.

"Herr Geismar, every German is an expert at that. We've been watched for twelve years. I would know in my sleep. Here we are." He opened the back door to the blinding light. "No one, you see."

"I take it Emil hasn't been here?" Jake said, still thinking.

"Is that why you've come? I'm sorry, I don't know where he is. Dead, perhaps."

"No, he's alive. He's been in Frankfurt."

Professor Brandt stopped. "Alive. With the Americans?"

"Yes."

"Thank God for that. I thought the Russians—" He started walking again. "So he got out. He said the Spandau bridge was still open. I thought he must be crazy. The Russians were—"

"He left Frankfurt two weeks ago," Jake said, interrupting him. "For Berlin. I was hoping he'd come to you."

"No, he wouldn't come to me."

"To find Lena, I mean," Jake said, awkward.

"No, only the Russian."

"A Russian was looking for him?"

"For Lena," he said, hesitant. "As if I would help him. Swine."

"Me?" Lena said, listening after all.

Professor Brandt nodded, avoiding her eyes.

"What for?" Jake said.

"I didn't ask questions," Professor Brandt said, his voice almost prim.

"But he didn't want Emil," Jake said, thinking aloud.

"Why would he? I thought—"

"He give you a name?"

"They don't give names. Not them."

"You didn't ask? A Russian making inquiries in the British sector?"

Professor Brandt stopped, upset, as if he'd been caught in an impropriety. "I didn't want to know. You understand—I thought it was personal." He looked at Lena. "I'm sorry, don't be offended. I thought he was perhaps a friend of yours. So many German women—one hears it all the time."

"You thought that?" she said, angry.

"It's not for me to judge these things," he said, his voice correct and distant.

She looked at him, her eyes suddenly hard. "No. But you do. You judge everything. Now me. You thought that? A Russian whore?" She looked away. "Oh, why am I surprised? You always think the worst. Look how you judge Emil—your own blood."

"My own blood. A Nazi."

Lena waved her hand. "Nothing changes. Nothing," she said and strode ahead, visibly walking off her anger.

They crossed the street quietly, Jake feeling like an intruder in a family quarrel.

"She's not herself," Professor Brandt said finally. "It's the bad news, I think." He turned to Jake. "Is there some trouble? This Russian—it's to do with Emil?"

"I don't know. But let me know if he comes back."

Professor Brandt looked at Jake closely. "May I ask what exactly you do in the army?"

"I'm not in the army. I'm a reporter. They make us wear the uniform."

"For your work. That's what Emil said too. You're looking for him—as a friend? Nothing else?"

"As a friend."

"He's not under arrest?"

"No."

"I thought perhaps—these trials. They're not going to put him on trial?"

"No, why should they? As far as I know, he hasn't done anything."

Professor Brandt looked at him curiously, then sighed. "No, just this," he said, gesturing toward the gutted *schloss.* "That's what they've done, him and his friends."

They were approaching the palace from the west, the ground still covered with pieces of glass from the smashed orangerie. Berlin's Versailles. The building had taken a direct hit, the east wing demolished, the rest of the standing pale yellow walls scorched with black. Lena was walking ahead into the formal gardens, now unrecognizable, a bare field of mud littered with shrapnel.

"It was always going to end this way," Professor Brandt said. "Anyone could see that. Why couldn't he see that? They destroyed Germany. The books, then everything. It wasn't theirs to destroy. It was mine, too. Where's my Germany now? Look at it. Gone. Murderers."

"Emil wasn't that."

"He worked for them," he said, voice rising as if they were in court, the case he'd been arguing for years. "Be careful when you put on a uniform. It's what you become. Always the work. You know what he said to me? 'I can't wait for history to change things. I have to do my work now. After the war, we can do wonderful things.' *Space.* We. Who? Mankind? After the war. He says this while the bombs are falling. While they're putting people on trains. No connection. What are you going to do in space, I said, look down on the dead?" He cleared his throat, calming himself. "You agree with Lena. You think I'm harsh."

"I don't know," Jake said, uncomfortable.

Professor Brandt stopped, looking at the *schloss.* "He broke my heart," he said, so simply that Jake winced, as if a bandage had been lifted off the old man's skin, exposing it. "She thinks I judge him. I don't even know him," he said, his words seeming to droop with him. But when Jake looked up, he stood as stiffly as before, his neck still held up by the high collar. He started into the park. "Well, now the Americans will do it."

"We didn't come here to judge anybody."

"No? Then who else? Do you think we can judge ourselves? Our own children?"

"Maybe nobody can."

"Then they will get away with it."

"The war's over, Professor Brandt. Nobody got away with anything," Jake said, looking at the charred remains of the building.

"Not the war. No, not war. You know what happened here. I knew. Everybody knew. Grunewald Station. You know they liked to send them from there, not in the center, where people would see. Did they think we wouldn't see there? Thousands of them in the cars. The children. Did we think they were going on holiday? I saw it myself. My god, I thought, how we will pay for this, how we will pay. How could it happen? Here, in my country, a crime like this? How could they do it? Not the Hitlers, the Goebbelses—those types you can see any day. In a zoo. An asylum. But Emil? A boy who played with trains. Blocks. Always building. I've asked myself a million times, over and over, how could this boy be a part of that?"

"And what answer did you get?" Jake said quietly.

"None. No answer." He stopped to remove his hat, then took out a handkerchief and patted his forehead. "No answer," he said again. "You know, his mother died when he was born. So there were just the two of us. Just two. I was too strict maybe. Sometimes I think it was that. But he was no trouble—quiet. A wonderful mind. You could see it working when he played—one block after another, just so. Sometimes I would sit there just watching his mind."

Jake glanced over at him, trying to imagine him without the collar, stretched out on a child's floor in a jumble of building blocks.

"And later, of course, at the institute, a wonder. Everyone predicted great things, everyone. Instead, this." He spread his hand, taking in the past along with the torn-up garden. "How? How could such a mind not see? How can you see only the blocks, nothing else? A missing piece. Like all the rest of them, some missing piece. Maybe they never had it. But Emil? A good German boy—so what happened? To be with them."

"He came back for you at the end."

"Yes, do you know how? With SS. Do you expect me to get in that car, I said, with them?"

"The SS came for you?"

"For me? No. Files. Even then, with the Russians here, they came to get files out—imagine it. To save themselves. Did they think we didn't know what they did? How can you hide something like that? Foolishness. Then here. 'It's the only way,' Emil said, 'they have a car, they'll take you.'" He switched voices. "'Tell the old shit to hurry or we'll shoot him too,' they said. Drunk, I think, but they did that, shot people, even in those last days, when everything was lost. Good, I said, shoot the old shit. That will be one bullet less. 'Don't talk like that,' Emil says. 'Are you crazy?' You're the crazy one, I said. The Russians will hang you if you're with these swine. 'No, Spandau's open, we can get to the west.' I'd rather be with the Russians than with scum, I said. Arguing, even then." The SS voice again. "'Leave him. We don't have time for this.' And of course it was true—you could hear the artillery fire everywhere. So they left. That's the last I saw him, getting into a car with SS. My son." His voice grew faint and stopped, as if he were rewinding a spool of film in his head, the scene played out again.

"Trying to save you," Jake said.

But Professor Brandt ignored him, retreating back to conversation. "How is it you know him?"

"Lena worked with me at Columbia."

"The radio, yes, I remember. A long time ago." He glanced toward Lena, waiting for them near the edge of the garden where the sluggish water of the Spree made its bend. "She doesn't look well."

"She's been sick. She's better now."

Professor Brandt nodded. "So that's why she hasn't come. She used to, after the raids, to see if I was all right. The faithful Lena. I don't think she told him."

She turned as they approached. "Look at the ducks," she said. "Still here. Who feeds them, do you think?" A kind of apology for her outburst, simply by not mentioning it. "So, have you finished?"

"Finished?" Professor Brandt said, then peered at Jake. "What is it you want?"

Jake took the photograph of Tully out of his breast pocket. "Has this man been here? Have you seen him?"

"An American," Professor Brandt said, looking at it. "No. Why? He's looking for Emil too?"

"He may have been. He knew Emil in Frankfurt."

"He's police?" Professor Brandt said, so quickly that Jake looked up in surprise. What was it like to be watched for twelve years?

"He was. He's dead."

Professor Brandt stared at him. "And that's why you want to see Emil. As a friend."

"That's right, as a friend."

He looked at Lena. "It's true? He's not trying to arrest him?"

"Do you think I would help with that?" she said.

"No," Jake said, answering for her, "but I'm worried. Two weeks is a long time to be missing in Germany these days. This is the last man who saw him, and he's dead."

"What are you saying? You think Emil—"

"No, I don't think. I don't want to see him end up the same way, either." He paused, taking in Professor Brandt's startled expression. "He may know something, that's all. We need to find him. He hasn't been to Lena's. The only other place he'd go is to you."

"No, not to me."

"He did before."

"Yes, and what did I say to him? That day with the SS," he said, running the film again. "'Don't come back.'" He looked away. "He won't come here. Not now."

"Well, if he does, you know where Lena is," Jake said, putting the picture back.

"I sent him away," Professor Brandt said, still in his own thoughts. "What else could I do? SS. I was right to do that."

"Yes, you were right. You're always right," Lena said wearily, turning away. "Now look."

"Lena—"

"Oh, no more. I'm tired of arguing. Always politics."

"Not politics," he said, shaking his head. "Not politics. You think it was politics, what they did?"

She held his eyes for a moment, then turned to Jake. "Let's go."

"You'll come again?" Professor Brandt said, his voice suddenly tentative and old.

She went over and put her hand near his shoulder, then brushed the front of his suit as if she were about to adjust his tie, a gesture of unexpected gentleness. He stood straight, letting her smooth out the material, a substitute for an embrace. "I'll press it for you next time," she said. "Do you need anything? Food? Jake can get food."

"Some coffee, perhaps," he said, hesitant, reluctant to ask.

Lena gave his suit a final pat and moved away, not waiting for them to follow.

"I'll walk a little now," Professor Brandt said, then glanced toward Lena's back. "She's like a daughter to me."

Jake simply nodded, not knowing what to say. Professor Brandt drew himself up, shoulders back, and put on his hat.

"Herr Geismar? If you find Emil—" He stopped, choosing his words carefully. "Be a friend to him, with the Americans. There is some trouble, I think. So help him. You're surprised I ask that? This old German, so strict. But a child—it's always there, in your heart. Even when they become—what they become. Even then."

Jake looked at him, standing tall and alone in the muddy field. "Emil didn't put people on trains. There's a difference."

Professor Brandt lifted his head toward the scorched building, then turned back to Jake, lowering the brim of his hat. "You be the judge of that."

When they got back to the jeep, Jake took a minute to look into Professor Brandt's street, but no one was there, not even young Willi, keeping watch for cigarettes.

Nothing had changed at Frau Dzuris'—the same dripping hallway, the same boiling potatoes, the same hollow-eyed children watching furtively from the bedroom.

"Lena, my god, it's you. So you found her. Children, look who's here, it's Lena. Come."

But it was Jake who drew their attention, pulling out chocolate bars, which they snatched up, tearing off the shiny Hershey wrappers before Frau Dzuris could stop them.

"Such manners. Children, what do you say?"

A mumbled thanks between bites.

"Come, sit. Oh, Eva will be sorry to miss you. She's at church again. Every day, church. What are you praying for, I say, manna? Tell God to send potatoes."

"She's well, then? And your son?"

"Still in the east," she said, dropping her voice. "I don't know where. Maybe she prays for him. But there's no God there. Not in Russia."

Jake had expected to stay two minutes, a simple question, but now sat back at the table, giving way to the inevitable visit. It was a Berlin conversation, comparing survivor lists. Greta from downstairs. The block leader who chose the wrong shelter. Frau Dzuris' son, safe from the army, then trapped at the Siemens plant and hauled off by the Russians.

"And Emil?" Frau Dzuris said with a sidelong glance at Jake.

"I don't know. My parents are dead," Lena said, changing the subject.

"A raid?"

"Yes, I just heard."

"So many, so many," Frau Dzuris said, shaking her head, then brightened. "But to see you together again—it's lucky."

"Yes, for me," Lena said with a weak smile, looking at Jake. "He saved my life. He got me medicine."

"You see? The Americans—I always said they were good. But it's a special case with Lena, eh?" she said to Jake, almost waggish.

"Yes, special."

"You know, he may not come back," she said to Lena. "You can't blame the women. The men made the war and then it's the women who wait. But for how long? Eva's waiting. Well, he's my son, but I don't know. How many come back from Russia? And we have to eat. How will she feed the children without a man?"

Lena looked over at them still eating the chocolate, her face softening. "They've grown. I wouldn't recognize them." She seemed for a moment someone else, back in a part of her life Jake had never known, that had happened without him.

"Yes, and what's to become of them? Living like this, potatoes only. It's worse than during the war. And now we'll have the Russians."

Jake took this as an opening. "Frau Dzuris, the soldier who was looking for Lena and Emil—he was a Russian?"

"No, an Ami."

"This man?" He handed her the picture.

"No, no, I told you before, tall. Blond, like a German. A German name even."

"He gave you his name?"

"No, here," she said, putting her finger above her breast, where a nameplate would have been.

"What name?"

"I don't remember. But German. I thought, it's true what they say. No wonder the Amis won—all German officers. Look at Eisenhower," she said, floating it as a light joke.

Jake took the picture back, disappointed, the lead suddenly gone.

"So he wasn't looking for Emil," Lena said to the picture, sounding relieved.

"Something's wrong?" Frau Dzuris said.

"No," Jake said. "I just thought it might be this man. The American who was here—did he say why he came to you?"

"Like you—the notice in Pariserstrasse. I thought he must be a friend of yours," she said to Lena, "from before, when you worked for the Americans. Oh, not like you," she said, smiling at Jake. She turned to Lena. "You know, I always knew. A woman can tell. And now, to find each other again. Can I say something to you? Don't wait, not like Eva. So many don't come back. You have to live. And this one." To Jake's embarrassment, she patted his hand. "To remember the chocolate."

It took them another five minutes to get out of the flat, Frau Dzuris talking, Lena lingering with the children, promising to come again.

"Frau Dzuris," Jake said to her at the door, "if anyone should come—"

"Don't worry," she said, conspiratorial, misunderstanding. "I won't give you away." She nodded toward Lena, starting down the stairs. "You take her to America. There's nothing here now."

In the street, he stopped and looked back at the building, still puzzled.

"Now what's the matter?" Lena said. "You see, it wasn't him. It's good, yes? No connection."

"But it should have been. It makes sense. Now I'm back where I started. Anyway, who did come?"

"Your friend said the Americans would look for Emil. Someone from Kransberg, maybe."

"But not Tully," he said stubbornly, still preoccupied.

"You think everyone's looking for Emil," she said, getting into the jeep to leave.

He started around to his side, then stopped, looking at the ground. "Except the Russian. He was looking for you."

She glanced over at him. "What do you mean?"

"Nothing. Trying to add two and two." He got in the jeep. "But I need Emil to do that. Where the hell is he, anyway?"

"You were never so anxious to see him before."

Jake turned the key. "Nobody was murdered before."

Emil didn't come. The next few days fell into a kind of listless waiting, looking out the window, listening for footsteps on the quiet landing. When they made love now, it seemed hurried, as if they expected someone to come through the door at any minute, their time run out. Hannelore was back, her Russian having moved on, and her presence, chattering, oblivious to the waiting, made the tension worse, so that Jake felt he was pacing even when he was sitting still, watching her lay out cards on the table hour after hour until her future came out right.

"You see, there he is again. The spades mean strength, that's what Frau Hinkel says. Lena, you have to see her—you won't believe it, how she sees things. I thought, you know, well, it's just fun. But she knows. She knew about my mother—how could she know that? I never said a word. And not some gypsy either—a German woman. Right behind KaDeWe, imagine, all this time. It's a gift to be like that. Here's the jack again—you see, two men, just as she said."

"Only two?" Lena said, smiling.

"Two marriages. I said one is enough, but no, she says it always comes up two."

"What's the good of knowing that? All during the first, you'll be wondering about the second."

Hannelore sighed. "I suppose. Still, you should go."

"You go," Lena said. "I don't want to know."

It was true. While Jake waited and worked the crossword puzzle in his head—Tully down, Emil across, trying to fit them together—Lena seemed oddly content, as if she had decided to let things take care of themselves. The news of her parents had depressed her and then seemed to be put aside, a kind of fatalism Jake assumed had come with the war, when it was enough to wake up alive. In the mornings she went to a DP nursery to help with the children; afternoons, when Hannelore was out, they made love; evenings she turned the canned rations into meals, busy with ordinary life, not looking beyond the day. It was Jake who waited, at loose ends.

They went out. There was music in a roofless church, a humid evening with tired German civilians nodding their heads to a scratchy Beethoven trio and Jake taking notes for a piece because *Collier's* would like the idea of music rising from the ruins, the city coming back. He took her to Ronny's, to check in with Danny, but when they got there, drunken shouts pouring out to the street, she balked, and he went in alone, but neither Danny nor Gunther was there, so they walked a little farther down the Ku'damm to a cinema the British had opened. The theater, hot and crowded, was showing *Blithe Spirit,* and to his surprise the audience, all soldiers, enjoyed it, roaring at Madame Arcati, whistling at Kay Hammond's floating nightgown. Dressing for dinner, coffee and brandy in the sitting room afterward—it all seemed to be happening on another planet.

It was only when the lush color changed to the grainy black-and-white of the newsreel that they were back in Berlin—literally so, Attlee arriving to take Churchill's place, another photo session at the Cecilienhof, the new Three arranged on the terrace just as the old Three had been that first time, before the money started blowing across the lawn. Then the Allied football game, with Breimer at the microphone winning the peace and fists raised in the end zone as the British made their unlikely score. Jake smiled to himself. In the jumble of spliced film, at least, they had won the game. The clip switched to a collapsing house. "Another kind of touchdown, as an American newsman makes a daring rescue—"

"My god, it's you," Lena said, gripping his arm.

He watched himself on the porch, arm around the German woman as if they had just emerged from the wreck, and for an instant even he forgot what had really happened, the film's chronology more convincing than memory.

"You never told me," she said.

"It didn't happen that way," he whispered.

"No? But you can see."

And what could he say? That he only appeared to be where he was? The film had made it real. He shifted in his seat, disturbed. What if nothing was what it seemed? A ball game, a newsreel hero. How we looked at things determined what they were. A dead body in Potsdam. A wad of money. One thing led to another, piece by piece, but what if you got the arrangement wrong? What if the house collapsed afterward?

When the lights came on, she took his silence for modesty.

"And you never said. So now you're famous," she said, smiling.

He moved them into the swarm of British khaki in the aisle.

"How did you get her out?" Lena said.

"We walked. Lena, it never happened."

But from her expression he could see that it had, and he gave it up. They moved into the lobby with a crowd of British officers and their Hannelores.

"Well, the man of the hour himself." Brian Stanley, tugging at his sleeve. "A hero, no less. I *am* surprised."

Jake grinned. "Me too," he said, and introduced Lena.

"Fräulein," Brian said, taking her hand. "And what do we think of him now? Very *Boy's Own,* I must say. Come for a drink?"

"Another time," Jake said.

"Oh, it's like that. Enjoy the film? Apart from yourself, that is."

They passed through the door to the warm evening air.

"Sure. Make you homesick?" Jake said.

"Dear boy, that's the England that never was. We're the land of the common man now, haven't you heard? Mr. Attlee insists. Of course, I'm common myself, so I don't mind."

"It still looks pretty cushy on film," Jake said.

"Well, it would. Made before the war, you know. Couldn't release it while the play was on and of course it ran forever, so they're just now getting around to it. You see how young Rex looks."

"The things you know," Jake said. Another trick of chronology.

Brian lit a cigarette. "How are you getting on with your case? The chap in the boots."

"I'm not. I've been distracted."

Brian glanced at Lena. "Not by the conference, I gather. I never see you around at all. The thing is, you got me thinking a bit. About the luggage and all that. What occurred to me was, how did he get on the plane in the first place?"

"What do you mean?"

"Well, it was a scramble. You remember. Had to pull strings just to get on the damn thing."

"So what strings did he pull?" Jake said, finishing for him.

"Something like that. There we were, packed in like sardines. The Honorable and everyone. And then one more. All very last-minute.

No bags, as if he hadn't expected to go. More like he'd been *summoned,* if you see what I mean."

But Jake had leaped ahead to something else—how had Emil managed it? No one just walked onto a plane, certainly not a German.

"I don't suppose they found any travel orders?" Brian was saying.

"Not that I know of."

"Of course, it may have been the old greased palm—I've done it myself. But if someone okayed it? I mean, if you're so curious about him, it might be useful to know."

"Yes," Jake said. Who had okayed Emil?

"You never know with the army—they keep a record of everything except what's useful. But there must have been some kind of manifest. Anyway, it's just a thought."

"Keep thinking for a minute," Jake said. "How would a German get here?"

"How does anybody? Military transport—he'd have to hitch a ride. There isn't any civilian transport. I supposed he could bicycle in, if he didn't mind the Russians running him off the road. They do it for fun, I hear."

"Yes," Lena said. Brian looked at her, surprised that she'd been following the conversation.

"Anyone particular in mind?" he said to Jake.

"Just a friend of mine," Jake said quickly, before Lena could interrupt. "He's been due for over a week."

"Well, there's nothing to that. Do you have any idea what it's like out there?" He swept his hand in a broad gesture to the dark space beyond the city. "Chaos. Absolute bloody chaos. Seen the autobahns? Refugees going this way and that. Poles going home. And good luck to *them.* Sleep anywhere you can. He's probably in a hayloft somewhere, rubbing his feet."

"A hayloft."

"Well, a bit of color. I shouldn't worry, he'll turn up."

"But if he flew—" Jake said, still thinking.

"A German? Need to pull some big strings for that. Anyway, he'd be here, wouldn't he?"

Jake sighed. "Yes, he'd be here." He looked at the thinning crowd as if Emil might suddenly appear, strolling down the Ku'damm.

"Well, I've got a drink waiting. Fräulein." He nodded at Lena. "Mind you stay out of falling houses," he said, winking at Jake. "Once lucky. Lovely how we won the game, wasn't it?"

"Lovely," Jake said, smiling.

"There's a thing, by the way. What's he up to, the Honorable?"

"Why would he be up to anything?"

"He's still here. Now your average poobah, they're in and out. Not that I blame them. But there's the Honorable, lingering, lingering. Makes you wonder, doesn't it?"

Jake looked at him. "Does it?"

"Me? No. Made Tommy Ottinger wonder, though. Says he's really just a point man for American Dye."

"And?"

"And Tommy's going home. I hate to see a story go to waste. You might want to look into it—if you've got the time, that is." Another quick glance at Lena.

"Tommy's giving away stories now?"

"Well, you know Tommy. A few drinks and he'll tell you anything. Strictly an American affair, of course, so no good to me. Anyway, there's a tip. I have to say, I rather like the idea of catching the Honorable with his hand in the till."

"His hand in what till?"

"Well, Tommy thought he might be up to some private reparations. Just a little something for American Dye. Which, to their way of thinking, is pretty good for the country too, so it's patriotic looting, really. They talk their heads off at Potsdam about reparations and meanwhile they're stripping the place clean."

"I thought it was the Russians doing the stripping."

"And not your clean-cut American boys. Football players one and all, if you believe the films. No, this is the game. The Russians don't know what to take—just pack up the power plants and anything shiny and hope for the best. But the Allies—oh, we're doing it too, God bless us—now, that's something different. Experts, we've got. Tech units all over the country, just hauling off the good bits. Blueprints. Formulas. Research papers. Picking their brains, you might say. You were at Nordhausen. They got all the documents there—fourteen *tons* of paper, if you can believe it. And of course you can't, because nobody can get the story—you get near it and *poof,* off it goes. Classified. Ghosts. There's a thought—maybe we should give Madame Arcati a go, *she* might get somewhere."

He stopped, his expression serious. "That's what I'd look into, Jake. This is a real story, and no one's got it—just a whiff once in a while. The Russians get fussed and bark at us—you kidnapped the engineers at Zeiss!—then of course they turn around and do the same thing. And on it goes. Until there's nothing left to steal, I guess. Reparations. That's the story I'd go after."

"Why don't you?"

"I don't have the legs for it. Not anymore. Needs someone young who doesn't mind a bit of trouble."

"Why Breimer?" Jake said. "What makes you think he's doing anything but making dumb speeches?"

"Well, the man at the stadium, for one thing. Remember him? Thick as thieves. He's with one of the tech units."

"How do you know?"

"I asked," Brian said, raising an eyebrow.

Jake looked at him steadily, then grinned. "You don't miss a thing, do you?"

"Not much," he said, returning the smile. "Well, I'm off. You've got a tired young lady wanting to go home and here I am, blathering on. Fräulein." He nodded to Lena again, then turned to Jake. "Think about it, will you? Be nice to see you back at work again."

Jake put his arm around Lena and headed them toward Olivaerplatz, away from the streetwalkers and cruising jeeps. There was moonlight, so that you could see the broken tops of buildings against the sky, spiky, like jagged pieces of gothic script.

"Is it true what he says? About the scientists? They want to pick Emil's brain too?"

"That depends on what he knows," he said, evasive, then nodded. "Yes."

"Now them. Everybody wants to find Emil."

"He must have flown," Jake said, still thinking. "Nobody walks from Frankfurt. So either he hasn't got here yet or he's hiding somewhere."

"Why would he hide?"

"A man's dead. If they did meet—"

"Still the policeman."

"Or he got a ride. He did before."

"When he came for me, you mean."

"With the SS. Some ride."

"He wasn't SS."

"He came with them. His father told me."

"Oh, he'll say anything. So bitter. To think, the only family I have now, a man like that. To send away a child."

"He's not a child anymore."

"But SS. Emil?"

"Why would he lie, Lena?" he said gently, turning to her. "It must be right."

She took this in, then turned away, literally not facing it. "Right. He's always right."

"You like him, though. I could see."

"Well, I feel sorry. There's nothing for him now, not even his work. He resigned when they fired the Jews. That's when the fighting started, with Emil. So he was right, but now look."

"What did he teach?"

"Mathematics. Like Emil. They said at the institute he was their Bach—passing the gift, you know? Just alike. The two Professor Brandts. Then one."

"Maybe Emil should have resigned too."

She walked for a minute, not answering. "It's easy to say now. But then—who knew it would end? Sometimes it seemed the Nazis would be here forever. It was the world we lived in, can you understand that?"

"I was here too."

"But not a German. There was always something else for you. But Emil? I don't know—I can't answer for him. So maybe his father's right. But your friend, he wants to make him a criminal. He was never that. Not SS."

"They gave him a medal. It's in his file. I saw it. Services to the state. You didn't know?"

She shook her head.

"He never told you? But didn't you talk? You were married. How could you not talk?"

She stopped, looking across Olivaerplatz, empty and moonlit. "So you want to talk about Emil? Yes, why not? He's here. Like in the film, the ghost who comes back. Always in the room. No, he never told me. Maybe he thought it was better. Services to the state. My god. For numbers." She looked up. "I didn't know. What can I say to you? How can you live with someone and not know him? You think it's hard. It's easy. At first you talk and then—" She trailed off, back in her head again. "I don't know why. The work, I think. We didn't talk about that—how could we? I didn't understand it. But he lived for that. And then, after the war started, everything was secret. Secret. He wasn't allowed. So you talk about daily things, little things, and then after a while not even that, you don't have the habit anymore. There's nothing left to talk about."

"There was a child."

She looked at him, uncomfortable. "Yes, there was a child. We talked about him. Maybe that's why I didn't notice. He was away so much. I had Peter. That's how things were with us. Then, after Peter—even the talking stopped. What was there to say then?" She turned away. "I don't blame him. How can I? He was a good father, a good husband. And me, was I a good wife? I tried that once. And all the time we were—" She faced him again. "It wasn't him. Me. I stopped."

"Why did you marry him?"

She shrugged, making a wry smile. "I wanted to be married. To have my own house. In those days, you know, it wasn't so easy. If you were a nice girl, you lived at home. When I came to Berlin, I had to live with Frau Willentz—she knew my parents—and it was worse, she was always waiting at the door when I came in. You know, at that age—" She paused. "It seems so silly now. I wanted my own dishes. Dishes. And, you know, I was fond of Emil. He was nice, came from a good family. His father was a professor—even my parents couldn't object to that. Everybody wanted it. So I got my dishes. They had flowers—poppies. Then, one raid and they were gone. Just like—"

She looked at the crumbled buildings, then picked up the thread again. "Now I wonder why I wanted them. All that life. I don't know—who knows why we do what we do? Why did I go with you?"

"Because I asked."

"Yes, you asked," she said, still looking at the buildings. "I knew, even that first time. At the Press Club, that party. I remember thinking, nobody ever looked at me this way. As if you knew a secret about me."

"What secret?"

"That I would say yes. That I was like that. Not a good wife."

"Don't," Jake said.

"So I couldn't be faithful to him," she said, as if she hadn't heard. "But I don't want to hurt him. Isn't it enough to leave him? Now we have to be policemen too? Waiting here, like spiders, to trap him."

"Nobody's trying to trap him. According to Bernie, they want to offer him a job."

"Picking his brain. And then what? Oh, let's go now. Leave Berlin."

"Lena, I can't get you out of Germany. You know that. You'd have to be—"

"Your wife," she finished, a resigned nod. "And I'm not."

"Not yet," he said, touching her. "It'll be different this time." He smiled at her. "We'll get new dishes. Stores in New York are full of them."

"No, you only want that once. Now it's something else."

"What?"

She turned her head, not answering, then leaned against him. "Let's just love each other. It's enough now," she said. "Just that." She started walking again, pulling his hand lightly with hers. "Look where we are."

They had turned without noticing into the end of Pariserstrasse, the heaps of rubble like pockets of shadow along the moonlit street. The washbasin was still perched on the mound of bricks where Lena's building had been, its porcelain dull in the faint light, but Frau Dzuris' notice had fallen over, the ink now streaked by rain.

"We should put up a new one," he said. "In case."

"Why? He knows I'm not here. He knew it was bombed."

Jake looked at her. "But the American who went to Frau Dzuris didn't know that. He came here first."

"So?"

"So he hasn't talked to Emil. Where did you go after?"

"A friend from the hospital. Her flat. Sometimes we just stayed at work. The cellars were safe there."

"What happened to her?"

"She died. In the fire."

"There must be someone. Think. Where would he go?"

She shook her head. "His father. He would go there. Like always."

Jake sighed. "Then he's not in Berlin." He went over and righted the notice stick, wedging it in the bricks. "Well, we should do it for her, so her friends can find her."

"Friends," Lena said, almost snorting. "All the other Nazis."

"Frau Dzuris?"

"Of course. During the war she always had the pin, you know, the swastika. Right here." She touched her chest. "She loved the speeches. Better than the theater, she used to say. She'd turn the radio up loud so everyone in the building would hear too. If they complained, she'd say, 'Don't you want to hear the Führer? I'll report you.' Always the busybody." She looked away from the rubble. "Well, that's finished too. At least no more speeches. You didn't know?"

"No," he said, disconcerted. A lover of poppyseed cakes.

A truck roared into the street, catching Lena in its headlights.

"Look out." He grabbed her hand and pulled her toward the bricks.

"Frau! Frau!" Guttural shouts, followed by laughs. In the open back of the truck, a group of Russian soldiers, holding bottles. *"Komme!"* one of them shouted as the truck slowed.

Jake could feel her freeze beside him, her entire body rigid. He stepped into the street so that his uniform was visible in the light.

"Get lost," he said, jerking his fingers at the truck.

"Amerikanski," one of them shouted back, but the uniform had its effect. The men who had started to get off the back stopped, one of them now raising a bottle to toast Lena, someone else's property. A joke in Russian went around the truck. The men saluted Jake and laughed.

"Beat it," he said, hoping his tone of voice would be the translation.

"Amerikanski," the soldier said again, taking a drink, then suddenly pointed behind Jake and shouted something in Russian. Jake turned. In the moonlight, a rat had stopped on the porcelain basin, nose up. Before he could move, the Russian took out a gun and fired,

the noise exploding around them, making Jake's stomach contract. He ducked. The rat scampered away, but now other guns were firing too, a spontaneous target practice, hitting the porcelain with a series of pings until it cracked, a whole piece of it lifting up and flying away like the rat. Behind him, he could feel Lena clutching his shirt. A few steps and they would be in the line of fire, as unpredictable as a drunken aim. And then, abruptly, it stopped and the men started laughing again. One of them banged the roof of the cab to get the truck moving and, looking at Jake, threw a vodka bottle to him as it drove off. Jake caught it with both hands, a football, and stood looking at it, then tossed it onto the bricks.

Lena was shaking all over now, as if the smash of the bottle had released everything her fear had kept still. "Pigs," she said, holding on to him.

"They're just drunk," he said, but he was rattled. You could die here in a second, on a trigger-happy whim. What if he hadn't been there? He imagined Lena running down the street, her own street, being chased into shadows. As his eyes followed the truck, he saw a basement light go on—someone waiting in the dark until the shooting passed. Only the rats could run fast enough.

"Let's go back to the Ku'damm," she said.

"It's all right. They won't come back," he said, holding her. "We're almost at the church."

But in fact the street frightened him too, sinister now in the pale light, unnaturally still. When they passed a standing wall, the moon disappeared behind it for a minute and they were back in the early days of the blackout, when you picked your way home by the eerie glow of phosphorus strips. But at least there'd been noise, traffic and whistles and wardens barking orders. Now the silence was complete, not even disturbed by Frau Dzuris' radio.

"They never change," Lena said, her voice low. "When they first came, it was so terrible we thought, it's the end. But it wasn't. It's still the same."

"At least they're not shooting people anymore," he said easily, trying to move away from it. "They're soldiers, that's all. It's just their way of having fun."

"They had their fun then too," she said, her voice bitter. "You know, in the hospital they took the new mothers, the pregnant women, they didn't care. Anybody. They liked the screaming. They laughed. I think it excited them. I'll never forget that. Everywhere in the building. Screams."

"That's over now," he said, but she seemed not to hear.

"Then we had to live under them. Two months—forever. To know what they did and then see them in the street, wondering when it would start again. Every time I looked at one, I heard the screams. I thought, I can't live like this. Not with them—"

"Ssh," Jake said, reaching up to her hair the way a parent soothes a sick child, trying to make it all go away. "That's over."

But he could see in her face that it wasn't. She turned away. "Let's go home."

He looked at her back. He wanted to say something more, but her shoulders were hunched away from him, waiting now for more soldiers in the shadowy street.

"They won't come back," he said, as if it made any difference.

CHAPTER TEN

TOMMY OTTINGER'S FAREWELL party coincided with the end of the conference and so became, without his intending it, a Goodbye Potsdam bash. At least half the press corps were leaving Berlin too, as much in the dark about the actual negotiations as when they arrived, and after two weeks of bland releases and cramped billets, they were ready to celebrate. By the time Jake got to the press camp, it already had the deafening noise and littered bottles of a blowout. The typing tables had been pushed to one side for a jazz combo, and a sprinkling of WACs and Red Cross nurses took turns like prom queens on the makeshift dance floor. Everyone else just drank, sitting on desks or propped up against the wall, shouting over each other to be heard. In the far corner, the poker game that had begun weeks ago was still going on, oblivious to the rest of the room, cut off by its own curtain of stale smoke. Ron, looking pleased with himself, was circulating with a clipboard, signing up people for tours of the Cecilienhof and the Babelsberg compound, finally open to the press now that everyone was gone.

"See the conference site?" he said to Jake. "Of course, you've already been."

"Not inside. What's in Babelsberg?"

"See where Truman slept. Very nice."

"I'll pass. What are you so happy about?"

"We got through it, didn't we? Harry's gone back to Bess. Uncle Joe's—well, who the fuck knows? And everybody behaved himself. Almost everybody, anyway," he said, glancing at Jake, then grinning. "Seen the newsreel?"

"Yeah. I want to talk to you about that."

"Just part of the service. I thought you looked pretty good."

"Fuck."

"The thanks you get. Anybody else'd be pleased. By the way, you ought to check your messages. I've been carrying this for days." He pulled out a cable and handed it to Jake.

Jake unfolded it. "Newsreel everywhere. Where are you? Wire firsthand account rescue ASAP. *Collier's* exclusive. Congrats. Some stunt."

"Christ," Jake said. "I ought to make you answer it."

"Me? I'm just the errand boy." He grinned again. "Use your imagination. Something will come to you."

"I wonder what you'll do after the war."

"Hey, the movie star." Tommy came over, putting his hand on Jake's shoulder. "Where's your drink?" The top of his bald head was already glistening with sweat.

"Here," Jake said, taking the glass out of Tommy's hand. "You look like you're drinking for two."

"Why not? *Auf wiedersehen* to this hellhole. So who gets my room, Ron? Lou Aaronson's been asking."

"What am I, the desk clerk? We've got a list this long. Of course, some people don't even use theirs." Another glance at Jake.

"I hear Breimer's still around," Jake said.

"Take an act of Congress to get that asshole out," Tommy said, slurring his words a little.

"Now, now," Ron said. "A little respect."

"What's he up to?" Jake said.

"Nothing good," Tommy said. "He hasn't been up to anything good since fucking Harding was president."

"Here we go again," Ron said, rolling his eyes. "Bad old American Dye. Give it a rest, why don't you?"

"Go shit in your hat. What do you know about it?"

Ron shrugged pleasantly. "Not much. Except they won the war for us."

"Yeah? Well, so did I. But I'm not rich and they are. How do you figure that?"

Ron thumped him on the back. "Rich in spirit, Tommy, rich in spirit. Here," he said, pouring a drink and handing it to him, "on the house. I'll see you later. There's a nurse over there wants to see where Truman slept."

"Don't forget about the room," Tommy said to his back as he melted into the crowd. He took a drink. "To think he's just a kid, with years to go."

"So what do you know, Tommy? Brian said you might have a story for me."

"He did, huh? You care?"

"I'm listening. What about Breimer?"

Tommy shook his head. "That's a Washington story." He looked up. "Mine, by the way. I'll crack the sonofabitch if I have to go through every patent myself. It's a beaut, too. How the rich get richer."

"How do they?"

"You really want to hear this? Holding companies. Licenses. Fucking paper *maze.* Half the time their own lawyers can't trace it. American Dye and Chemical. You know they were like that with Farben," he said, holding up two fingers folded over each other. "Before the war. *During* the war. Share the patents and one hand washes the other. Except there's a war on and you don't trade with an enemy company. Looks bad. So the money gets paid somewhere else—Switzerland, a new company. Nothing to do with you, except, funny, there are the same guys on the board. You get paid no matter who wins."

"Not very nice," Jake said. "Can you prove it?"

"No, but I know it."

"How?"

"Because I'm a great newspaperman," Tommy said, touching his nose, then looking down into his drink. "If I can get through the paper. You'd think it would be simple to find out who actually owns something, wouldn't you? Not this time. It's all fuzzy, just the way they like it. But I know it. Remember Blaustein, the cartel guy? Farben was his baby. He said he'd give me a hand. It's all there somewhere in

Washington. You just have to get your hands on the right piece of paper. Of course, you have to want to find it," he said, lifting his glass to his colleagues in the noisy room, dancing with WACs.

"So what's Breimer doing in Berlin, then?"

"Plea bargaining. Help his old friends. Except he's not getting very far." He smiled. "You have to hand it to Blaustein. Make enough noise and somebody finally listens. Hell, even we listen once in a while. Result is that nobody wants to go near Farben—the stink's too strong. MG's got a special tribunal set up just for them. They'll nail them, too—war crimes up the kazoo. Not even Breimer's going to get the biggies off. He's trying to kick the teeth out of the de-Nazification program with all those speeches he makes, but even that won't do it this time. Everybody knows Farben. Christ, they built a plant at Auschwitz. Who's going to stick out his neck for people like that?"

"That's it? Speeches?" Jake said, beginning to feel that Ron might after all be right, that Tommy was riding a hobbyhorse, barely touching the ground. What else would Breimer be doing?

"Well, he does what he can. The speeches are part of it. Nobody's really sure what de-Nazification means—where do you draw the line?—so he keeps whittling away at that and pretty soon you're a lot less sure than you were. People want to go home, not try Nazis. Which of course is what American Dye is hoping, so their friends can go back to work. But not everybody's in jail. What I get is that he's offering employment contracts."

Jake raised his head. "Employment contracts?"

"They already have the patents. The idea is to get the personnel. Nobody wants to stay in Germany. The whole place'll probably go Commie anyway, and then where are we? Problem now is getting them *in.* The State Department has this funny idea about not giving visas to Nazis, but since everybody *was* a Nazi and since the army wants them anyway, the only way in is to find a sponsor. Somebody who can say they're crucial to their operations."

"Like American Dye."

Tommy nodded. "And they'll have the War Department contracts to prove it. The army gets the eggheads and American Dye gets a nice fat contract to put them to work and everybody's happy."

"We're talking about Farben people? Chemists?"

"Sure. They'd be a natural fit for American Dye. I talked to one. He wanted to know what Utica was like."

"Anybody else? Not Farben?"

"Could be. Look, put it this way. American Dye will do anything the army wants—their *business* is the army. Army wants a wind tunnel expert, they'll find a use for him, especially if the army gives them a wind tunnel contract. You know how it works. It's the old story."

"Yeah, with a new wrinkle. Jobs for Nazis."

"Well, that depends what kind of stink comes off the record. Nobody's finding work for Goering. But most of them, you know, just kept their heads down. Nominal Nazis. What the hell, it was a Nazi country. And the thing is, they're good—that's the kicker. Best in the world. You talk to the tech boys, their eyes get all dreamy just thinking about them. Like they're talking about pussy. German science." He shook his head, taking another drink. "It's a helluva country when you think about it. No resources. They did it all in laboratories. Rubber. Fuel. The only thing they had was coal, and look what they did."

"Almost," Jake said. "Look at it now."

Tommy grinned. "Well, I never said they weren't crazy. What kind of people would listen to Hitler?"

"Frau Dzuris," Jake said to himself.

"Who?"

"Nobody—just thinking. Hey, Tommy," he said, brooding. "You ever hear of any money actually changing hands?"

"What, to Germans? Are you kidding? You don't have to bribe them—they want to go. What's here? Seen any chemical plants with Help Wanted signs out lately?"

"And meanwhile Breimer's recruiting."

"Maybe a little on the side. He's the type likes to stay busy." He looked up from his drink. "What's your interest?"

"He'd have a lot of money to throw around," Jake said, not answering. "If he wanted something."

"Uh-huh," Tommy said, peering at Jake. "What are you getting at?"

"Nothing. Honestly. Just nosing around."

"Now why is that? I know you. You don't give a flying fuck about Farben, do you?"

"No. Don't worry, the story's all yours."

"Then why are you pumping me?"

"I don't know. Force of habit. My mother always said you learn something every time you listen."

Tommy laughed. "You didn't have a mother," he said. "Not possible."

"Sure. Even Breimer's got one," Jake said lightly. "I'll bet she's proud as anything."

"Yeah, and he'd sell her too if you put the money in escrow." He put the glass down on the table. "Probably runs the goddamn garden club while her boy's collecting envelopes from American Dye. It's a great country."

"None better," Jake said easily.

"And I can't wait to get back to it. Figure that one out. Listen, do me a favor. If you come up with anything on Breimer, let me know, will you? Since you're just nosing around."

"You get the first call."

"And don't reverse the fucking charges. You owe me."

Jake smiled. "I'm going to miss you, Tommy."

"Me and your bad tooth. Now what the hell is he up to?" he said, cocking his head toward a drum roll coming from the band.

Ron was standing in front of the combo, holding a glass.

"Listen up. Can't have a party without a toast."

"Toast! Toast!" Shouts from around the room, followed by a chorus of keys tinkling against glasses.

"Come on up here, Tommy."

Groans and whistles, the good-natured rumble of a frat party. Soon people would be balancing bottles on their heads. Ron started in on something about the finest group of reporters he'd ever worked with, then grinned as the crowd shouted him down, held up his hand, and finally gave in just by raising his glass with a "Good luck." Some airplanes made of folded yellow typing paper floated in from the crowd, hitting Ron's head, so that he had to duck, laughing.

"Speech! Speech!"

"Go fuck yourselves," Tommy said, which hit the right note, making the crowd whistle again.

"Come on, Tommy, what do you say?" A voice next to Jake—Benson, from *Stars and Stripes,* slightly hoarse from shouting.

Tommy smiled and lifted his glass. "On this historic occasion—"

"Aw!" More hoots and another paper plane gliding by.

"Let's drink to free and unrestricted navigation on *all* international inland waterways."

To Jake's surprise, this brought down the house, prompting a whoop of laughter followed by chants of "Inland waterways! Inland waterways!" Tommy drained his glass as the band started playing again.

"What's the joke?" Jake said to Benson.

"Truman's big idea at the conference. They say the look on Uncle Joe's face was worth a million bucks."

"You're kidding."

"Who could? He actually insisted they put it on the agenda."

"I thought the sessions were secret."

"That one was too good to keep quiet. They had five leaks in about five minutes. Where've you been?"

"Busy."

"Couldn't get him off it. The way to lasting peace." He laughed. "Open up the Danube."

"I take it this didn't make the final agreement?"

"You nuts? They just pretended it wasn't there. Like a fart in church." He looked over at Jake. "Busy with what?"

After that, the party grew louder, a steady din of music and voices that kept rising until it finally became one piercing sound, like steam whistling out of a valve. Nobody seemed to mind. The nurses were getting the rush on the dance floor, but the noise had the male boom of all the occupation parties, nearly stag, civilian girls confined by the nonfraternization rules to the shadow world of Ku'damm clubs and groping in the ruins. Liz waved from the dance floor, signaling for Jake to cut in, but he gave a mock salute and went to the bar instead. Fifteen more minutes, to be polite, and he'd go home to Lena.

The whole room was jumping now, as if everyone were dancing in place, except for the poker game in the corner, whose only movement was the methodical slapping of cards on the table. Jake looked down at the end of the bar and smiled. Another pocket of quiet. Muller was putting in a reluctant appearance, more than ever Judge Hardy, silver-haired and sober, like a chaperone at a high school dance.

Jake felt an elbow, then a slosh of beer on his sleeve, and moved away from the bar to make a last circuit around the room. A burst of laughter from a huddle nearby—Tommy at it again. Near the door, a corkboard hung on the wall, cluttered with pinned-up sheets of copy and headlines clipped out of context. His Potsdam piece was there, the margins, like all the others, filled with scribbled comments in code. NOOYB, not one of your best. A story on Churchill leaving the conference. WGWTE, when giants walked the earth. The back-slapping acronyms of the press camp, as secret and joky as the pass-words in a schoolboys' club. How he'd spent the war.

"Admiring your handiwork?"

He turned to find Muller standing behind him, his uniform army crisp in the sweaty room.

"What's it mean, anyway?" Muller said, pointing to the scribbles.

"Reviews. In shorthand. OOTAG," Jake said, pronouncing it as a word. "One of the all-time greats. NOOYB—not one of your best. Like that."

"You men have more initials than the army."

"That'll be the day."

"The only one I hear these days is FYIGMO—fuck you, I got my orders. Home, that is," he said, as if Jake had missed it. "I suppose you'll be heading home too, now that Potsdam's over."

"No, not yet. I'm still working on something."

Muller looked at him. "That's right. The black market. I saw *Collier's*. There's more?"

Jake shrugged.

"You know, every time there's a story like that, it's an extra day's work for somebody, explaining it."

"Maybe somebody should clean it up instead."

"We're trying, believe it or not."

"How?"

Muller smiled. "How do we do anything? New regulations. But even regulations take time."

"Especially if some of the people making them are sending money home too."

Muller threw him a sharp look, then backed off. "Come for a smoke," he said, a gentle order.

Jake followed him out. A line of jeeps stretched along the dusty broad sweep of Argentinischeallee, but otherwise the street was deserted.

"You've been busy," Muller said, handing him a cigarette. "I saw you in the movies."

"Yeah, how about that?"

"I also hear somebody's been making inquiries in Frankfurt about our friend Tully. I assume that's you?"

"You forgot to mention what a colorful character he was. Hauptmann Toll."

"Meister Toll, since you like to be accurate. Not that it matters. Comes to the same thing." Another weak smile. "Not one of *our* best."

"The whip's a nice touch. He ever use it?"

"Let's hope not." He drew on his cigarette. "Find what you were looking for?"

"I'm getting there. No thanks to MG. Want to tell me why you're holding out on me? For the sake of accuracy."

"Nobody's holding out on you."

"How about a ballistics report? On a second sheet that wasn't there. I suppose that got mislaid."

Muller said nothing.

"So let me ask you again. Why were you holding out?"

Muller sighed and flicked his cigarette toward the street. "That's easy. I don't want you to do this story. Clear enough? Some low-life gets in trouble in the black market and the papers start yelling corruption in the MG. We don't need that." He glanced at Jake. "We like to clean up our own mess."

"Including murder? With an American bullet."

"Including that," Muller said evenly. "We've got a criminal investigation department, you know. They know what they're doing."

"Keeping it quiet, you mean."

"No. Getting to the bottom of it—without a scandal. Go home, Geismar," he said wearily.

"No."

Muller looked up, surprised at the abrupt answer.

"I could make you go home. You're on a pass here, just like everyone else."

"You don't want to do that. I'm a hero—it's in the movies. You don't want to run me out of town now. How would that look?"

Muller stared for a minute, then smiled reluctantly. "I admit there are better options. At the moment."

"Then why not stop being army brass for five seconds and give me a little cooperation? You've got an American dead. The CID isn't going to do a damn thing and you know it. You could use the help."

"From you? You're not a policeman. You're just a pain in the ass." He grimaced. "Now, how about letting me serve out my time in peace? Go make trouble somewhere else."

"While you're waiting, would it interest you to know the money on him was Russian?"

Muller's head snapped up, then held still. The one thing that always got the MG's attention. "Yes, it would," he said finally, looking steadily at Jake. "How do you know?"

"The serial numbers. Ask the boys in the CID, since they're so professional. Still want me off the case?"

Muller looked down at the ground, moving his foot in a small circle, as if he were making a decision.

"Look, nobody's trying to hold out on you. I'll get you the ballistics report."

"That's all right. I've seen it."

Muller raised his head. "I won't ask how."

"But while you're being so friendly, you could do me another favor. Kind of make it up to me. You didn't find any travel orders on him."

"That's right."

"What about an airport okay? Who got him on the plane? I need somebody to check the dispatchers. July sixteenth."

"But that could take—"

"I figure your secretary might have some time on her hands. If she could call around for me, I'd appreciate it. They'd listen to you. Me, it might take weeks."

"You haven't had any problem so far," Muller said, looking at him carefully.

"But this time I'd have some help from the top. For a change. You know how it is. And while she's at it, one more thing? Check a flight listing for an Emil Brandt. Previous week and since." He took in

Muller's blank expression. "He's a scientist Tully sprang from Kransberg. Dustbin. Heard of it?"

"Where are you going with this?" Muller said quietly.

"Just have her do it."

"Dustbin's a secret facility."

Jake shrugged. "People talk. Hang around the press camp more. You'd be surprised what you pick up."

"You can't write about it. It's classified."

"I know. Don't worry, I'm not interested in Dustbin. Just Meister Toll."

"I'm not sure I understand the connection."

"If I'm right, just wait a little and you can read all about it in the papers."

"That's one thing I have no intention of doing."

Jake smiled. "Why don't you wait and see how it comes out? You might change your mind." He glanced up at him, serious now. "No black eyes."

"Do I have your word on that?"

"Would you take it? Why not just say you have my best intentions and leave it at that? But I'd appreciate the calls."

Muller nodded slowly. "All right. But I want you to do something for me—work with the CID on this."

"Carbons in triplicate? No thanks."

"I won't have you running around like a loose cannon. You work with them, understand?"

"Now I'm on the team? A minute ago you were sending me home."

Muller's shoulders sagged. "That's before the Russians were involved," he said glumly. "Now we need to know. Even if that means using you." He paused, thinking. "You're sure about the money? The serial numbers? That's the first I've heard of it. I thought it was all the same."

"There's a little dash. A friend in the black market tipped me off. It's the sort of thing they notice. Turns out the Treasury Department isn't as dumb as you thought."

"That makes me feel a whole lot better." Muller straightened up. "I wish you did. All right, let's go back in before I change my mind," he said, leading Jake to the door. They stopped on the threshold, hit by the blast of noise. A conga line was snaking through the room, legs flying out on the one-two-three-kick, nobody quite on the same beat. "The ladies and gentlemen of the press," Muller said, shaking his head. "My god, I wish I was back in the army. Drink?"

"You have mine. I'm on my way home."

"Where is that these days? I haven't seen you at dinner lately. Keeping company somewhere?"

"Colonel. There are rules about that."

"Mm. Strictly enforced," he said wryly. "Like everything else." He turned to go, then stopped. "Geismar? Don't make me regret this. I can still kick your ass home."

"I'll keep that in mind," Jake said. "Just make the calls, please."

He said goodbye to Tommy, now in a sloppy, bear-hugging mood. The conga line had broken up and with it the rest of the dancing, but the party showed no signs of slowing down. The drinking had reached the stage when jokes could turn into arguments without anyone noticing. Liz was taking some group shots, a line of reporters with their arms draped over each other's shoulders and their faces fixed in bleary grins. A cheer went up when someone arrived with more ice. It was time to go. He was almost at the door when Liz caught up with him.

"Hey, Jackson. How's your love life?" She was carrying her shoes in one hand and a camera case in the other, her eyes shiny with drink.

"Okay. How's yours?"

"Away, since you ask."

"No more tall Joe?"

"Keep your shirt on. He's back tomorrow." She made a face. "They always come back. How about a lift? I don't think I can make it in these," she said, holding up the shoes.

"Little unsteady on your feet?" Jake said, smiling.

"These? They gave out about an hour ago."

"Come on."

"Here," she said, handing him the shoes. "Let me get my bag."

He stood there, shoes dangling from his fingers, and watched her weave over to the table and struggle with a strap that kept missing her shoulder as she tried to fling it in place. Finally he went over and took the bag from her, sliding it onto his own shoulder.

"Well, aren't you nice? Stupid thing."

"Come on, you could use some air. What have you got in here?"

She giggled. "Oh, I forgot. You. I've got you in there. Wait a minute," she said, stopping him and fumbling with the zipper. "Fresh out of the darkroom. Well, fresh. I've been carrying these around for days." She pulled out some glossies and shuffled to find the right one. "Here we are. Our man in Berlin. Not bad, considering."

He looked at himself stepping into the right half of the picture, leaving the Document Center behind. Thinning over the temples, a surprised expression. "I've looked better," he said. The same feeling he'd had seeing his reflection in KaDeWe's window—someone else, no longer the young man in his passport photo.

"That's what you think."

Off to the left Joe stood posing, as tall and blond as a poster Aryan. One of the tech boys, according to Brian. Breimer's friend. Jake dropped the picture on the pile, then stopped and pulled it back, looking again.

"Hey, Liz," he said, staring at it, "what's Joe's last name again?"

"Shaeffer. Why?"

A German name.

He shook his head. "Nothing, maybe. Can I keep this?"

"Sure," she said, pleased. "I've got a million more where that came from."

Blond, like a German, Frau Dzuris had said. The right fit. But was it? In the picture, another camera trick, he and Jake were standing on the steps as if they'd been together all along. Nothing was what it seemed.

He glanced at his watch. Frau Dzuris would be getting ready for bed, disturbed by a knock on the door. But not asleep yet. He grabbed Liz's arm and began tugging her across the floor.

"Where's the fire?"

"Let's go. I have to see somebody."

"Oh," she said, an exaggerated drawl. She reached over and took her shoes. "Not this time. Let her wear her own."

Jake ignored her, hurrying them to the jeep.

"You know, it's none of my business—" she began as she got in.

"Then don't say it."

"Touchy," she said, but let it go, leaning back in her seat as they started down the road. "You know what you are? You're a romantic."

"Not the last time I looked."

"You are, though," she said, nodding her head, having a conversation with herself.

"What's Joe doing in Berlin?" Jake said.

But the drink had taken her elsewhere. She laughed. "You're right. *He's* not. Anyway, what do you care?" She turned to him. "It's not serious, you know. With him. He's just—around."

"Doing what?"

She waved her hand. "He's just around."

She put her head back against the seat, cushioning it, as if it were too much trouble to hold it upright on the bumpy road. For a second Jake wondered if she was going to pass out, but she said idly, "I'm glad you like the picture. It's a fast shutter. Zeiss. No blurs."

The blur instead seemed to be in her speech. They had circled the old Luftwaffe building and were heading into Gelferstrasse, almost there. In front of the billet, he idled the motor and reached for the shoulder bag.

"Can you manage?" he said, fitting the strap in place.

"Still in a hurry, huh? I thought you lived here."

"Not tonight."

"Okay, Jackson," she said softly. "I'll take a hike." And then, surprising him, she leaned over and kissed him on the mouth, a full kiss.

"What was that for?" Jake said when she broke away.

"I wanted to see what it was like."

"You've had too much to drink."

"Yeah, well," she said, embarrassed, gathering her bag and getting out. "My timing isn't the best, either." She turned to the jeep. "Funny how that works. It might have been nice, though, don't you think?"

"It might have been."

"A gentleman," she said, hitching up the bag. "I'll bet you're the type who'll pretend to forget about it in the morning, too."

But in fact it stayed with him all the way to Wilmersdorf, the unexpected mystery of people, who they really were. He'd been right about Frau Dzuris, ready for bed and clutching her wrapper, frightened by the knock. And he'd been right about the picture. "Yes, you see, like a German," Frau Dzuris said. "That's the one. You know him? He's a friend?" But in the dim light of the doorway, his eyes never went to the photo, caught instead by the empty space on the cloth over her left breast, where a pin once would have been.

The next day it was Liz who didn't remember. She was on her way to Potsdam with one of Ron's tour groups, thinned out by hangovers, and seemed surprised that he mentioned Joe at all.

"What do you want to see him for?"

"He has some information for me."

"Uh-huh. What kind of information?"

"Missing persons."

"You going to tell me what you're talking about?"

"You going to tell me where he is?"

She shrugged, giving up. "He's meeting me, as a matter of fact. In Potsdam."

"Why Potsdam?"

"He's getting me a camera."

Jake pointed to the one she was carrying, with the prized fast shutter. "He get you that too?"

"What's it to you?" She smiled, palms up. "He's a generous guy."

Jake grinned. "Yeah, with requisitioned cameras. He say where he got it?"

"Ask him yourself. You coming or not?" She pointed to Ron's car, an old Mercedes. Two reporters were dozing in the back, legs spread out, waiting for the trip to start.

"Too crowded. I'll follow."

"Better stick with me. Look what happened the last time we went."

So in the end she rode with him. They followed Ron's car until they reached the Avus, then lost it when it jerked into autobahn speed, weaving in and out of the stream of cars heading out of Berlin. The traffic surprised him. In the bright sunshine it seemed everyone was going to Potsdam—trucks and jeeps and cars like Ron's, snatched from garages for new owners. Behind them an old black Horch filled with Russians barely kept up, but the others were racing on the open highway, prewar driving, with the trees of the Grunewald rushing past.

When they got into town, the bomb damage he'd missed before leaped to the eye. The Stadtschloss, a roofless ruin, had taken the worst of it, and only sections of the long colonnade were left facing the market square. The Nikolaikirche opposite had lost its dome, the four corner towers looking more than ever like odd minarets. Only the

Palladian Rathaus seemed likely to survive, with Atlas still perched on top of its round tower, holding up a gilded ball of the world, a kind of bad joke—the British bombers had spared the kitsch.

The Alten Markt, however, was lively. A rickety tram was running in front of the obelisk, and the huge open square was crammed—hundreds, perhaps a thousand people milling between stacks of goods, bargaining openly, as noisy as the medieval market that had given the space its name. It reminded him, improbably, of the *souk* in Cairo, a dense theater of exchange, hawkers grabbing buyers by the sleeve, the air full of languages, but drained of color, no open melons and pyramids of spices, just scuffed pairs of shoes and chipped Hummel knickknacks and secondhand clothes, closets stripped for sale. But at least there was none of the furtiveness of the Tiergarten market, one eye keeping watch for raiding MPs. The Russians were buying, not guarding, eager to be back in business after the hiatus of the conference. No one whispered. Two soldiers walked by with wall clocks balanced on their heads. None of this would have been here when Tully came. Jake imagined instead a meeting in some quiet corner. Maybe even in the Neuer Garten, just steps from the water. Selling what?

They left the jeep near the empty space in the colonnade where the Fortuna Portal had been and wandered into the crowd, Liz snapping pictures. Ron's car was nowhere in sight, probably still headed for Truman's villa, but Jake noticed, amused, that the Horch had had to squeeze in behind the jeep, the only place in Berlin with a parking problem.

"Where are you meeting him?" Jake said.

"He said by the colonnade. We're early. Look at this—do you think it's real Meissen?"

She picked up the soup tureen, gilt-edged handles and pink apple blossoms, the kind of thing you could have found by the dozen in Karstadt's before the war. But the German woman selling it, gaunt and sagging, had come to life.

"Meissen, ja. Natürlich."

"What are you going to do with that?" Jake said. "Make soup?"

"It's pretty."

"Lucky Strike," the woman said in accented English. "Camel."

Liz handed it back and motioned to the woman to pose. As the camera clicked, the woman smiled nervously, holding out her dish, still hoping for a sale, and Jake turned uneasily, feeling ashamed, as if they were stealing something, the way primitive people feared a camera took souls.

"You shouldn't do that," he said as they moved off, the woman shouting after them in disappointment.

"Local color," Liz said, unconcerned. "Why do they all wear pants?"

"They're old uniforms. The men aren't allowed, so the women wear them."

"They aren't," she said, pointing to two girls in summer dresses talking to French soldiers, whose red berets flashed like bird feathers in all the khaki and gray.

"They're selling something else."

"Really?" Liz said, curious. "Right out in the open?"

But they posed too, arms around the soldiers' waists, less self-conscious than the woman with porcelain.

They had made a half-circle to the obelisk, past the cigarette dealers and watch salesmen and piles of PX cans. On the steps of the Nikolai a man had spread out carpets, a surreal touch of Samarkand. Nearby a one-armed veteran was offering a box of now useless hand tools. A woman with two children at her side held out a pair of baby shoes.

They found Shaeffer near the north end of the colonnade, looking at cameras.

"You remember Jake," Liz said breezily. "He's been looking for you."

"Oh yes?"

"Find anything?" she said, taking the camera from him and putting it to her eye.

"Just an old Leica. Not worth it." He turned to Jake. "You looking for a camera?"

"Not unless it's got a Zeiss lens," Jake said, nodding at Liz's case. "You pick that one up at the plant?"

"The plant's in the Soviet zone, last I heard," Shaeffer said, looking at him carefully.

"I heard one of our tech units paid it a visit."

"Is that a fact?"

"I thought they might have picked up some souvenirs."

"Now why would they do that? You can get anything you want right here." Shaeffer spread his hand toward the square.

"So you haven't been there?"

"What is this, twenty questions?"

"Don't race your motor," Liz said to him, handing back the Leica. "Jake's always asking questions. It's what he does."

"Yeah? Well, go ask them somewhere else. You ready?" he said to Liz.

"Hey, the babe with the camera." Two American soldiers, running over to them. "Remember us? Hitler's office?"

"Like it was yesterday," Liz said. "How you boys doing?"

"We got our orders," one of the soldiers said. "End of the week."

"Just my luck," Liz said, grinning. "Want a shot for the road?" She held up the camera.

"Hey, great. Get the obelisk in, can you?"

Jake followed the camera's eye to the GIs, the market swirling behind them. He wondered for a second how they'd explain it at home, Russians holding wristwatches to their ears to check the ticking, tired German ladies with tureens. At the church, two Russians were holding up a carpet, a general with medals hovering off to one side. As a tram pulled in, dividing the crowd, the Russian turned his face toward the colonnade. Sikorsky, holding a carton of cigarettes. Jake smiled to himself. Even the brass came to market day for a little something on the side. Or was it payday for informants?

The GI was scribbling on a piece of paper. "You can send it there."

"Hey, St. Louis," Liz said.

"You too?"

"Webster Groves."

"No shit. Long way from home, huh?" he said, looking toward the bombed-out *schloss.*

"Say hi to the folks," Liz said as they moved off, then turned to Shaeffer. "How do you like that?"

"Let's go," he said, bored.

"One more question?" Jake said.

But Shaeffer had begun to walk away.

"Why are you looking for Emil Brandt?"

Shaeffer stopped and turned. For a second he stood still, staring, his face a question.

"What makes you think I'm looking for anybody?"

"Because I saw Frau Dzuris too."

"Who?"

"The neighbor. From Pariserstrasse."

Another hard stare. "What do you want?"

"I'm an old friend of the family. When I tried to look him up, I found your foot sticking in the door. Now why is that?"

"An old friend of the family," Shaeffer said.

"Before the war. I worked with his wife. So let me ask you again—why are you looking for him?"

Shaeffer kept his eyes on Jake, trying to read his face. "Because he's missing," he said finally.

"From Kransberg, I know."

Shaeffer blinked, surprised. "Then what's your question?"

"My question is, so what? Who is he to you?"

"If you know Kransberg, you know that too. He's a guest of the U.S. government."

"On an extended stay."

"That's right. We're not finished talking to him."

"And when you do, he's free to go?"

"I don't know about that. That's not my department."

"Which is what, exactly?"

"None of your fucking business. What do you want, anyway?"

"I want to find him, too. Just like you." He glanced up. "Any luck?"

Shaeffer looked sharply at him again, then eased off, taking a breath. "No. And it's been a while. We could use a break. Maybe you're the break. A friend of the family. We don't know anything personal about him, just what's in his head."

"What is?"

Shaeffer looked down. "A lot. He's a fucking walking bomb, if he talks to the wrong people."

"Meaning Russians."

Shaeffer nodded. "You say you knew his wife? Know where she is now?"

"No," Jake said, avoiding Liz's eye. "Why?"

"We figure he's with her. He kept talking about her. Lena."

"Lena?" Liz said.

"It's a common name," Jake said to her, a signal that worked, because she looked away, quiet. He turned again to Shaeffer. "What if he doesn't want to be found?"

"That's not an option," Shaeffer said stiffly. He looked down at his watch. "We can't talk here. Come to headquarters at two."

"Is that an order?"

"It will be if you don't show up. You going to help or not?"

"If I knew where he was, I wouldn't have asked you."

"His background—you can brief us on that. There must be someone he'd see. Maybe you're the break," he repeated, then shook his head. "Christ, you never know, do you?"

"It's been a long time. I don't know who his friends are—I can tell you that now. I didn't even know he'd been a Nazi."

"So? Everyone was a Nazi." Shaeffer looked over at Jake, suspicious again. "You one of those?"

"Those what?"

"Guys still fighting the war, looking for Nazis. Don't waste my time with that. I don't care if he was Hitler's best friend. We just want to know what's up here," he said, putting a finger to his temple.

An echo from another conversation, at a dinner table.

"One more question," Jake said. "First time I saw you, you were picking Breimer up. Gelferstrasse, July sixteenth. Ring a bell? Where'd you go?"

Shaeffer stared again, his mouth drawn thin. "I don't remember."

"That's the night Tully was killed. I see you know the name."

"I know the name," Shaeffer said slowly. "PSD at Kransberg. So what?"

"So he's dead."

"I heard. Good riddance, if you ask me."

"And you don't want to know who did it?"

"Why? To give him a medal? He just saved somebody else from having to do it. The guy was no good."

"And he drove Emil Brandt out of Kransberg. And that doesn't interest you."

"Tully?" Liz said. "The man we found?"

Jake glanced at her, surprised at the interruption, then at Shaeffer, a jarring moment, because it occurred to him for the first time that it might have been Shaeffer's interest all along, a flirtation to see what she knew. Who was anybody?

"That's right," he said, then turned to Shaeffer. "But that doesn't interest you. And you don't remember where you took Breimer."

"I don't know what you think you're getting at, but go get it somewhere else. Before I paste you one."

"All right, that's enough," Liz said. "Save it for the ring. I came here to get a camera, not to watch you two square off. Kids." She glared at Jake. "You take some chances. Now how about giving me a nice smile—I want to finish off this roll—and then you run along like a good boy. That means you too," she said to Shaeffer.

Surprisingly, he obeyed, turning to face the camera with Jake. "Two o'clock. Don't forget," he said out of the side of his mouth.

"Quiet," Liz said, crouching a little to frame the picture. "Come on, smile."

As she bent, the sound of a shot cracked through the square, followed by a scream. Jake looked over her shoulder. A Russian soldier was running past the obelisk, dodging people who flew out of his way like startled geese. Another shot, off to the right, from a handful of Russians near the parked Horch, guns out. But in the split second of his glance, Jake saw that the guns weren't pointing at the obelisk but had tracked farther along, aiming now at Liz's back.

"Down!" he yelled, but instead she jerked up, surprised, so that when the bullet came it thudded into her neck. A frozen second, then another crack, a sharp whistle. Shaeffer staggered backward, hit, and crumpled to the ground. Before Jake could move, he felt Liz's body falling forward, toppling him against the colonnade, its weight forcing him back until he was falling too, his head hitting the column as he went down. Screams everywhere now in the square, the sound of feet running on stone, another shot glancing off the colonnade. He tried to breathe under the weight, then realized that what stopped his mouth was blood pumping out of her throat, coating him. More shots, the market erupting with guns, so many guns that they seemed fired at random, not aimed, people hugging the paving stones to get out of the crossfire.

In a panic Jake tried to roll Liz away, pushing her hips as another rush of blood spurted into his face. He wriggled out from under and reached over to grab Shaeffer's pistol from its holster, then snaked behind the column, breathing in gulps. The Russians by the Horch were still firing, shooting in all directions now as soldiers around the square crouched and fired back. Jake aimed the gun, trying to steady his weaving hand, but when he fired the shot missed, smashing the headlight of the car. A bullet from somewhere else caught one of the Russians instead, flinging his body back against the car.

And then, before Jake could fire again, it was suddenly over, the other Russians scurrying away behind the Horch, quick as rats, and gone, the square empty except for a body lying near the obelisk, everything still. He heard a gurgle next to him, then a shout in German near the Nikolai. He crawled over to Liz, feeling his shirt sticky with blood. Her eyes were open, still wide with terror but moving, and the blood had stopped gushing, just a steady flow into the pool next to her head. He pressed his hand on her neck to stop it, but a trickle oozed through his fingers, wetting them.

"Don't die," he said. "We'll get help."

But who? Shaeffer rolled slightly and groaned. No one moved in the square.

"Don't die," he said again, his voice catching. Her eyes were looking straight at him, and he wondered for a second if she could see, if he could will her to hold on simply by looking back at her. A girl from Webster Groves.

He turned his head to the square. "Somebody help!" he shouted, but who knew English? *"Hilfe!"* As if an ambulance might come screeching down the street, where there were no ambulances.

He looked at her eyes again. "It's going to be all right. Just hold on." He pressed harder on her neck, his hand now completely red. How much blood had she lost? Footsteps behind him. He looked up. One of the tourist GIs, stunned by the blood.

"Jesus Christ," he said.

"Help me," Jake said.

"They got Fred," he said, groggy, as if it were an answer.

"Ask one of the Germans. We have to get her to a hospital. Krankenhaus."

The GI looked at him, bewildered.

"Krankenhaus," Jake said again. "Just *ask.*"

The boy moved away unsteadily, a sleepwalker, and sank to his knees by the obelisk where the other GI lay. A few people had crept back into the square, looking left and right, wary of more fire.

"Don't worry," he said to Liz. "Just hold on. We'll make it."

But at that moment he knew, a shudder through his body, that they wouldn't, that she was going to die. No ambulance was going to come, no doctor in a white coat to make everything better. There was only this. And he saw that she knew, wondered how you filled those last minutes—a roar in the head or was it utterly still, taking in the sky? In the time it took to snap a picture. Her eyes moved, frightened, and his moved with them, keeping her here, and then she opened her mouth as if she were about to speak, and he heard the gasp, not dramatic, quiet, a little intake of ragged air that stopped and didn't come back, trapped somewhere. None of the noisy theater of birth, just an interrupted breath of air and you left your life.

Her eyes had stopped moving, the pupils fixed. He took his hand away from her neck and wiped it on his pants, smearing blood. The thick smell of it. He picked up the camera lying next to her, still dazed, every movement an effort. Everything gone in a second, one flash at a time, too fast even for a Zeiss lens.

Shaeffer groaned again and Jake wobbled over, still on his knees. More blood, a patch spreading across the left shoulder.

"Take it easy," Jake said. "We'll get you to a hospital."

Shaeffer reached up with his good arm to grab Jake's and squeeze it. "Not Russian," he said in a hoarse whisper. "Get me out of here."

"It's too far."

But Shaeffer clenched his arm again. "Not Russian," he said, almost violent. "I can't."

Jake looked toward the square, filling up now, people shuffling aimlessly, the moment after an accident. Russians everywhere; a Russian town.

"Can you move?" Jake said, reaching behind Shaeffer's head. Shaeffer winced but lifted himself slowly, stopping halfway, like someone sitting up in bed. He was blinking, dizzy with shock. Jake reached under his shoulder and began pulling him up, straining under the weight. "The jeep's over there. Can you stand?"

Shaeffer nodded, then fell forward, stalled. Jake glanced again toward the square. Anybody.

"Hey, St. Louis!" he shouted, waving the GI over, keeping Shaeffer propped up as he waited. "Here, give me a hand. Get him in the jeep."

Together they managed to drag Shaeffer to his feet and lugged him forward, each step a mile, panting. Fresh blood seeped out of the wound. "Not Russian," Shaeffer mumbled again, sounding delirious, then yelled in pain when his body hit the passenger seat, a final heave, and passed out, head drooping down on his chest.

"Is he going to make it?" the GI said.

"Yes. Help me with the girl."

But when they got there and saw Liz lying in her pool of blood, the GI balked, staring at her. Impatient, Jake reached under and lifted her by himself, his knees shaking, and staggered back to the jeep, as if he were carrying somebody over the threshold, with her head dangling down. He laid the body in gently and went back for the gun. The GI was still standing there, pale, holding Liz's camera in his hand.

"You got blood on you," he said stupidly.

"Stay with your buddy. I'll send somebody," Jake said, taking the camera.

The GI looked at the soldier lying on the ground. "Jesus Christ Almighty," he said, his voice breaking. "I don't even know what happened."

A new group of Russians had arrived, surrounding the Horch like MPs, examining the dead Russian. The running soldier who had started it all was gone, swallowed up in Potsdam. No other bodies, just Liz and the boy going home at the end of the week. When Jake got to the jeep, anxious now to leave, one of the Russians started toward him, gesturing at Shaeffer slumped in the front seat. There would be questions, a Soviet doctor—what he'd wanted to avoid. Jake got in and started the jeep. The soldier called out to him, presumably telling him to stop. No time now. The closest army hospital would be HQ in Lichterfelde, miles away.

The Russian stood in front of the jeep, holding up his hand. Jake raised the gun, aiming it. The Russian cowered and stepped aside. A kid no older than the GI, scared, who saw a madman covered in blood with a gun in his hand. The others looked up, then ducked away too.

The power of a gun, as heady as adrenaline. Nobody stopped you when you held a gun. They were still backing away toward the Horch as the jeep spun out of the square and headed toward the bridge.

Shaeffer's body swayed with the initial jolt, then fell limply against Jake's side, leaning on him as they drove out of Potsdam. When they sped past the sector crossing, Jake could see the guards' alarmed expressions and realized his face was still bloody. He wiped it with his sleeve, sweat streaked with dark red. Now that they were on the road, racing, he found himself gulping in air, his chest heaving, as if he'd been holding his breath underwater. A dream, except for the body in the back and the heavy soldier lying against him, head bobbing. I don't even know what happened. But he did. When he played the dream again in his mind, it stopped after the soldier ran to the obelisk, when he saw the guns pointing beyond the soldier, at Liz. A diversionary run, the guns always intended for someone else. But who would want to kill Liz? A mistake. He looked over to Shaeffer. Someone else. A man who'd rather risk his life than be taken away by Russians.

CHAPTER ELEVEN

LIZ'S BODY WAS shipped home by military transport and Shaeffer's lay in a hospital bed, mending, without visitors. MG filed an official complaint with the Russians, who promptly sent one back, and the incident floated between In trays, waiting for the Kommandatura to meet and quarrel. Jake retreated to the flat and tried to write a piece about Liz, then gave it up. In *Stars and Stripes* she had already become a kind of soldier on the front lines; why say anything else? It was the newsreel all over again, more real than real. If you watched it on the screen, what would you actually see? An accident in crossfire, not a girl stepping into someone else's bullet. Only Jake had looked over her shoulder at the pointing gun.

When he went to Gelferstrasse, he was unnerved to hear footsteps next door, but it was only Ron, folding her clothes onto a pile near an open satchel.

"Give me a hand, will you?" he said, holding up some underwear. "It feels funny, going through this stuff."

"Never seen panties before?"

"It feels funny, that's all," Ron said, strangely subdued, and Jake knew what he meant. As each piece of silk dropped into the satchel, he felt finally that Liz was really gone, now just a bundle of neatly folded effects.

"Why don't you get the woman downstairs to do it?"

"A German? There wouldn't be much left. You know what they're like."

Jake held up a pair of shoes, the ones Lena had danced in, and stood for a second looking at them.

"Take them if you want," Ron said. Why not? A whole suitcase of things Lena could use, impossible to buy. He'd become a Berliner, scavenging the dead. He dropped the shoes in the satchel.

"They might mean something to somebody. Is there family?"

Ron shrugged. "What about these?" he said, pointing to a small collection of cosmetics. "Christ, women."

A half tube of lipstick, some powder, a jar of cream—all ordinary, not worth sending back.

"Let downstairs have them."

"The old lady?"

"She can trade them."

"I'll bet she's got her eye on the cameras. They're already making noises about the storage room in the basement—you know, where she set up a darkroom. They say they need the space."

"I'll clear it out," Jake said, picking up a camera from the bed. The one she'd used in Potsdam, still flecked with blood. He twisted the knob to the end, then popped out the last roll. "You'd better clean this before you pack it," he said, holding the camera out to Ron, who looked at it squeamishly. "Where's it all going, anyway?"

"Home."

"Not CID?"

"Why CID?" Ron said, surprised.

"Well, she was killed, wasn't she?"

"She might have been hit by a bus, too. We don't send them the bus. What are you talking about?"

Well, what? Jake looked at the lipstick, a folded blouse, none of it evidence, only what had flashed in his eyes, as unreliable as a newsreel. He walked over to the desk, stacked with photographs.

"Hell of a way to go, though," Ron was saying, finishing the packing. "All through the war without a scratch, and then *bam.*"

Jake started flipping through the pictures. Churchill at the Chancellery. Ron at the airport in a blur of uniforms. Another of Joe.

"What about Shaeffer?"

"He lost some blood, but they stitched him up all right."

"They said no visitors."

"It was a lot of blood," Ron said, looking at him. "Since when were you two so friendly?"

"Just asking. What happens to these?" Jake said, holding up the pictures.

"Damned if I know. The news service, I guess, technically. Think there's anything the family would want?"

"I doubt it. She's not in any of them." The other side of the camera, so that you left without a trace.

"Well, have a look. Just get them out of here—we're going to need the room." He snapped the satchel shut. "That's that. Not a lot, is it?"

"She liked to travel light."

"Yeah, except for her goddamn equipment," he said, nodding at the packed case by the door. "Some girl, though."

"Yes."

Ron looked over at him. "You two ever—"

"Ever what?"

"You know. I always thought she had a soft spot for you."

"No." It might have been nice.

"Just old Shaeffer, huh? You saved the wrong one, if you ask me."

"She was already dead."

Ron shook his head. "Fucking Dodge City. Nobody's safe out there."

Jake thought of Gunther, reading westerns, going through his points. "So we fire the police," he said.

"We're the police," Ron said, looking at him curiously. "Anyway, what difference would it make?" He turned to go. "You never know, do you? When your number's up, that's it."

"That wasn't it. Somebody shot her."

"Well, sure," Ron said, then turned back. "What are you saying?"

"I'm saying somebody shot her. Not an accident."

Ron peered at him. "Are you all right? There were only about a hundred witnesses, you know."

"They're wrong."

"Everyone but you. Then who did it?"

"What?"

"Who did it? Somebody shoots, not an accident, it's the first thing I'd want to know."

Jake stared. "You're right. Who was he?"

"Some Russian," Ron said, at a loss.

"Nobody's just some Russian. *Who* was he?" he said to himself, then gathered up the photographs to leave. "Thanks."

"Where are you going?"

"To see a policeman. A real one."

But it was Bernie who answered the door in Kreuzberg.

"You picked a fine time. Come on, as long as you're here. We have to get him on his feet."

Jake looked around the room—the same messy hodgepodge as before, everything smelling of fresh coffee. Gunther was bent over a mug, breathing in the steam, head nodding, the map of Berlin behind him.

"What's up?"

"The trial. He's in the witness box in an hour, so what does he do? Goes on a bender. I get here, he's on the fucking *floor.*"

"What trial?"

"Your pal Renate. The *greifer.* Today's the day. Here, help me get him up."

"Herr Geismar," Gunther said, looking up from the mug, eyes bleary.

"Drink the coffee," Bernie snapped. "All these weeks and now he pulls this." Gunther was rising unsteadily. "Think you can manage a shave, or should we do it for you?"

"I can shave myself," Gunther said stiffly.

"What about clothes?" Bernie said. "You can't go looking like that." A dirty undershirt marked with stains.

Gunther nodded toward the closet, then turned to Jake. "So how goes your case? I thought you had given up."

"No. I've got lots to tell you."

"Good," Bernie said. "Talk to him. Maybe that'll wake him up." He opened the closet and pulled out a dark suit. "This fit?"

"Of course."

"It better. You're going to make a good impression if I have to hold you up."

"It's so important to you?" Gunther said, his voice distant.

"She sent your wife to the ovens. Isn't it important to you?"

Gunther looked down and took another sip of coffee. "So what is it you want, Herr Geismar?"

"I need you to talk to your Russian friends. Find out about somebody. There was a shooting in Potsdam."

"Always Potsdam," Gunther said, a grunt.

"A Russian shot a friend of mine. I want to know who he is. Was." Gunther raised his eyes. "Somebody shot back."

"His name isn't on the report?" Gunther said, a cop's question.

"Not just his name. Who he was."

"Ah, the who," Gunther said, drinking more coffee. "So, another case."

"The same case."

"The same?" Bernie said, following the conversation from the closet. "They said it was an accident. A robbery. It was in the papers."

"It wasn't a robbery," Jake said. "I was there. It was a setup." He looked at Gunther. "The shooting was the point. They just happened to get the wrong person."

"That was your friend."

Jake nodded. "The man they wanted took one in the shoulder."

"Not a sharpshooter, then," Gunther said, using the western term.

"It's easy to miss in a crowd. You know what the market's like. All hell broke loose. Shooting all over the place. Ask your friend Sikorsky."

Gunther looked up from his coffee. "He was in the market? In Potsdam?"

Jake smiled. "Peddling cigarettes. Maybe he was buying a rug, I don't know. He got out fast enough when the shooting started, just like everybody else."

"Then he didn't see the first shots."

"I saw them."

"Go on," Gunther said.

"Talk while you shave," Bernie said, nudging him toward the bathroom. "I'll get more coffee."

Gunther shuffled to the sink, obedient, and stood for a minute in front of the mirror looking at himself, then started to lather his face with a brush. Jake sat on the edge of the tub.

"Don't be long," Bernie said from the other room. "We have to go over your testimony one last time."

"We've been over my testimony," Gunther said to the mirror grimly, his grizzled face slowly disappearing under a film of soap.

"You don't want to forget anything."

"Don't worry," Gunther said, to himself now, leaning on the sink. "I won't forget."

He picked up a straight-edge razor, his hand shaking.

"Are you going to be all right?" Jake said quietly. "Do you want me to do that?"

"You think I might hurt myself? No." He held up the razor, looking at it. "Do you know how many times I've thought how easy it would be? One cut, that's all, and it's over." He shook his head. "I could never do it. I don't know why. I tried. I put the razor here," he said, touching his throat, "but I couldn't cut. You think it would cut me now? An accident?" He turned sideways to look at Jake. "I don't believe in accidents." He faced the mirror again. "So tell me about our case."

Jake shifted on the tub rim, disconcerted. Not the drink talking, the voice behind the drink, suddenly naked, not even aware of being exposed, like someone in a window taking off his clothes. What goes through your head when you feel a razor on your throat? But now it was there again, taking a calm, neat stroke upward through the soap, guided by a survivor's steady hand.

Jake started to talk, his words following the rhythmic scraping, trying to match the logical path of the shave, down one cheek, curving around the corners of the mouth, but soon the story went off on its own, darting from one place to another, the way it had actually happened. There was a lot Gunther didn't know. The serial-number dash. Kransberg. Frau Dzuris. Even young Willi, loitering in Professor Brandt's street. At times Jake thought Gunther had stopped listening, stretching his skin to draw the razor closer without nicking, but then he would grunt and Jake knew he was registering the points, his mind clearing with each swipe of his soapy face.

Bernie came in with more coffee and stayed, leaning against the door and watching Gunther's expression in the mirror, for once not interrupting. A Russian kneeling in front of a Horch, gun out. Meister Toll. Gunther rinsed the blade and splashed his face clean.

"Is this presentable enough for you?" he said to Bernie.

"Just like new. Here's a shirt," he said, handing it over.

"So what do you think?" Jake said.

"Everything's mixed up," Gunther said absently, wiping his face.

"I've confused you."

"It's more, I think, that you have confused yourself."

Jake looked at him.

"Herr Geismar, you cannot do police work by intuition. Follow the points, like a bookkeeper. You have two problems, so you make two columns. Keep them separate, don't leap from column to column."

"But they connect."

"Only at Kransberg. Who knows? Maybe the one coincidence. The obvious point, you know, is that Tully *wasn't* looking for Herr Brandt. The others, yes. Not him." He shook his head, slipping into the shirt. "No, put your numbers down in order, each in its own column. It is only when the same number comes up that you have a match, the connection."

"Maybe they connect at Potsdam. That keeps coming up."

"Yes, and why?" Gunther said, buttoning the shirt. "I've never understood about Potsdam. What was he doing there? And that day, a closed city."

"You asked me to check on that," Bernie said. "Passes into the American compound. Zero. No Tully."

"But he was found there," Jake said. "Russian sector, Russian money."

"Yes, the money. It's a useful point." Gunther picked up the coffee cup again, drinking. "If he got Russian money, it must have been here. But not from an Ivan buying watches, I think. Who has so much? Have you heard anything from Alford?"

"No."

"Try again. The tie also?" he said to Bernie.

"You want to look your best for the judge," Bernie said.

Jake sighed, stymied. "Danny won't get us anywhere. We have to find Emil."

Gunther turned to the mirror, slipping the tie underneath his collar. "Keep your columns separate. There isn't yet the connection."

"And I suppose the shooting in Potsdam wasn't connected either."

"No. There a number matches."

"Shaeffer, you mean."

"Herr Geismar, you have a gift for ignoring the obvious. A gift." He leaned toward the mirror, knotting his tie. "There are three people standing in the market. Close. When you describe it, you see a gun pointing at the photographer. But I see her bending down. I see it pointing at you."

For a second Jake just stared at Gunther, the sharp eyes no longer cloudy, now cleared by caffeine. "Me?" he said, little more than a surprised intake of air.

"A man who finds a body, who investigates a murder. Do you mean this hasn't occurred to you? Who else? A soldier, for raiding the Zeiss works? Perhaps. The lady? And it might be, you know—you're quick to look away from her. The person shot is usually the one intended. But let's say this time you're right, a piece of luck. Luck for you."

Stepping into his bullet, dead because he was lucky.

"I don't believe it."

"When did you first see the Horch? On the Avus, you said. Soon after you left Gelferstrasse."

"That doesn't mean anything. Try this point. Nobody started shooting until we met Shaeffer."

"Away from the crowd. And if you had both been shot? An incident. No longer just you."

"But why—"

"Because you are dangerous to someone, of course. A detective is."

"I don't believe it," Jake said, his voice less sure than before.

Gunther picked up a hairbrush and ran it back over his temples. "Have it your way. But I suggest you move. If they know Gelferstrasse, they may know the other. I take it this is where the lady friend lives, the good Lena? It's one thing to put yourself in danger—"

Jake cut him off. "Do you really believe this?"

Gunther shrugged. "A precaution."

"Why should Lena be in any danger?"

"Why was a Russian looking for her? You didn't find it interesting, that point? The Russian at Professor Brandt's asks for her, not for the son."

"To find the son," Jake said, watching Gunther's face.

"Then why not ask for him?"

"All right, why not? Another obvious point?"

Gunther shook his head. "More a possibility. But it suggests itself." He looked up at Jake. "They already know where he is."

Jake said nothing, waiting for more, but Gunther turned away, taking the coffee cup with him into the other room. "Is it time?" he said to Bernie.

"You sober? Hold out your hands."

Gunther stretched one arm out—a mild trembling. "So I'm on trial now," he said.

"We want a credible witness, not a drunk."

"I'm a policeman. I've been in a courtroom before."

"Not this kind."

Jake had followed them, brooding. "That doesn't make sense," he said to Gunther.

"Not yet. As I say, a possibility." He put down the cup. "But I would move her. I would hide her."

Jake glanced at him, disturbed. "I still want to talk to Shaeffer," he said. "He's the one they shot. And he couldn't wait to get out of there. Even wounded, it's all he cared about." He paused. "Anyway, where could we go? It's not easy to move in Berlin."

"No. Unless you have to. I moved Marthe fourteen times," Gunther said, looking down at the floor. "Fourteen. I remember every time. You don't forget. Güntzelstrasse. Blücherstrasse. Every time. Will they ask me about that?" he said to Bernie.

"No," Bernie said, "just the last time."

"With the *greifer,*" he said, nodding. "A coffee. We thought it was safe. She had papers. Safe."

Jake looked at him, surprised. A U-boat trail, Gunther helping. "I thought you divorced her," he said.

"She divorced me. It was better." He looked up. "You think I abandoned her? Marthe? She was my wife. I did what I could. Flats. Papers. For a policeman, not so difficult. But not enough. The *greifer* saw her. By chance, just like that. So it was all for nothing. Every move." He stopped and turned to Bernie. "Forgive me, I'm not myself."

"You going to be sick?"

Gunther smiled weakly. "Not sick. A little—" His voice trailed off, suddenly frail. "Perhaps one drink. For the nerves."

"Nothing doing," Bernie said.

But Jake glanced at him, his body shrunken in the old suit, eyes uneasy, and walked over to the table and poured out a finger of brandy. Gunther drank it back in one gulp, like medicine, then stood for a second letting it work its way through him.

"Don't worry," he said to Bernie. "I won't forget anything."

"Let's hope not." He reached into his pockets and pulled out a mint. "Here, chew this. The Russians'll smell it on you a mile off."

"The Russians?" Jake said.

"It's a Russian trial. To show us they can do it too, not just string people up. Especially when we help catch them. Come on, we'll be late."

"Can I get in? I'd like to see this. See Renate."

"The press slots were gone days ago. Everybody wants to see this one."

Jake looked at him, feeling like Gunther asking for a drink.

"All right," Bernie said. "We'll put you on the prosecution team. You can keep an eye on our friend here. Which is getting to be a job." He glanced at Gunther. "No more."

Gunther handed the glass back to Jake. "Thank you." And then, as a kind of return favor, "I'll talk to Willi for you."

"Willi?"

"It's a type I know well. He'll talk to me."

"I mean, why him?" Jake said, intrigued to see Gunther still working, behind everything.

"To keep the figures neat. The little details. What's the English? Dot the *i*'s and cross the *t*'s."

"Still a cop."

Gunther shrugged. "It pays to be neat. Not overlook anything."

"What else did I overlook?"

"Not overlook—ignore, perhaps. Sometimes when it's not pleasant, we don't want to see."

"Such as?"

"The car."

"The Horch again? What's so important about the Horch?"

"No, Herr Brandt's car. That week—to drive into Berlin, how was it possible? The city was burning, at war. And yet he comes to get his wife. How was that allowed?"

"It was an SS car."

"Yes, his. You think the SS was offering lifts? While the city was falling? Either he was one of them or he was their prisoner. But they stop to collect the father, so not a prisoner. One of them. A mission for the SS—what kind? Even the SS didn't send cars for relatives those last days."

"His father said they were picking up files."

"And they risk coming to Berlin. What files, I wonder."

"That's easy to find out," Bernie said. "They surrendered in the west. There'll be a record somewhere. One thing we've got plenty of is files."

"More folders," Gunther said, looking at the stack Bernie had brought with him for the trial. "For all the bad Germans. Let's see what they say about Herr Brandt."

"What makes you think he's in them?" Jake said.

"What do you save when a city's on fire? You save yourself."

"He was trying to save his wife."

"But he didn't," Gunther said, then looked away, somewhere else. "Of course, sometimes it's not possible." He picked up his jacket and put it on, ready to go. "That last week—you weren't here. Fires. Russians in the streets. We thought it was the end of the world." He looked back at Jake. "But it wasn't. Now there's this. The reckoning."

The courtroom had an improvised look to it, as if the Russians had set up a stage without knowing where the props went. Their de-Nazification program had run to group executions, not trials, but the *greifer* was a special case, so they'd taken over a room near the old police headquarters in the Alex, built a raised platform of raw wooden boards for the judges' bench, and assigned the press haphazard rows of folding chairs that squeaked and scraped the floor as reporters leaned forward to hear. The prosecution attorneys and their Allied advisers were crammed together at one table, a lopsided stacking of cards against the defense lawyer and his one assistant, who sat by themselves at another. Along the wall, female Soviet soldiers made transcripts with steno machines, handing them to two civilian girls for translation.

The trial was in German, but the judges, three senior officers shuffling papers and trying not to look bored, evidently understood only a little, so the lawyers, also in uniform, occasionally switched to Russian, afraid to let their points drift away to the steno keys unheard. There was a heavy chair for witnesses, a Soviet flag, and not much else. It was the format of an inquisition, starker even than the rough-and-ready frontier courtrooms of Karl May, not a robe in sight. People were frisked at the door.

Renate stood behind a cagelike railing of new plywood next to the bench, facing the room, as if her expression during the testimony would be recorded as a kind of evidence. Behind her stood two soldiers with machine guns, gazing stolidly at her back. Bernie said she had changed, but she was recognizably the same—thinner, with the hollowed-out look you saw everywhere in Berlin, but still Renate. Only her dark hair was different, cropped close and turned a premature, indeterminate pale. She was dressed in a loose gray prison shift, belted, her collarbones sticking out, and the face he remembered as pretty and animated seemed rearranged—beaten, perhaps, or somehow disfigured by her life. But there were the eyes, sharp and knowing, glancing defiantly around the crowd as if she were even now looking for news items. The same way, Jake thought, she must have hunted for Jews.

She spotted him instantly, raising her eyebrows in surprise, then dropping them in bewilderment, a friend sitting at the table of her accusers. Did she think he was there to testify against her? What would he have said? A girl with a quick smile who liked to take chances, bold enough to cadge a cigarette from a Nazi on a train platform. A sharp eye, trained for snatching prey in the street. How could she have done it? But that was always the question—how could any of them have done it? He wanted suddenly to signal some absurd reassurance. I remember who you were. Not a monster, not then. How can I judge? But who could? Three Russian soldiers on a makeshift platform, whose fleshy faces seemed to ask no questions at all.

They were only minutes into the trial before Jake realized they hadn't come to establish guilt, just the sentence. And was there any doubt? The Germans had kept records of her activity, more columns of numbers. As the prosecution read out its indictments, Jake watched her lower her head, as if she too were overwhelmed by the sweep of it, all the snatches, one by one, until finally there were enough to fill boxcars. So many. Had she known them all, or just guessed, smelling fear when it walked into one of her cafés? Each number a face-to-face moment, real to her, not anonymous like a pilot opening the bomb bay.

The method was as Bernie had described—the sighting, the hurried call, the nod of her head to make the arrest, her colleagues bundling people into cars as she walked away. Why hadn't she kept walking? Instead she'd gone back to the collection center, her room there its own kind of short leash, but still not a prison. Why not just keep walking away? Gunther had moved his wife fourteen times. But he had had papers and friends prepared to help. No U-boat could survive alone. Where, after all, would she have gone?

The Russian prosecutor then switched, oddly, to a detailed account of Renate's own capture, the manhunt that finally ran her to ground in a basement in Wedding. For a moment Jake thought the Soviets were simply congratulating themselves for the press, now busily taking notes. Then he noticed Bernie in a lawyer's huddle, heard Gunther mentioned by name as the hunter, and saw that it was something more—the old DA's ploy, establishing your witness, the good guy in the neat jacket and tie. He needn't have bothered. The story, with its breathless chase, seemed lost on the first judge, who shifted in his seat and lit a cigarette. The Russian next to him leaned over and whispered. The judge, annoyed, put it out and gazed at the window, where a standing fan was lazily moving the stuffy air. Apparently an unexpected western custom. Jake wondered how long it would take to call a recess.

He'd assumed from the buildup that Gunther would be the star witness. Who else was there? The records supplied the mechanics of the crime, but its victims were dead, no longer able to accuse. Gunther had actually seen her do it. And a DA always started with the police, to weight his case at the beginning. The first person called, however, was a Frau Gersh, a more theatrical choice, a frail woman who had to be helped to the witness chair on crutches. The prosecutor began, solicitously, with her feet.

"From frostbite. On the death march," she said, halting but matter-of-fact. "They made us leave the camp so the Russians wouldn't find out. We had to walk in the snow. If you fell, they shot you."

"But you were fortunate."

"No, I fell. They shot me. Here," she said, pointing to her hip. "They thought I was dead, so they left me. But I couldn't move. In the snow. So the feet."

She spoke simply, her voice low, so that chairs creaked as people strained forward to hear. Then she looked over at Renate.

"The camp where she sent me," she said, louder, spitting it out.

"I didn't know," Renate said, shaking her head. "I didn't know."

The judge glared at her, startled to hear her speak but unsure what to do about it. No one seemed to know what the rules were supposed to be, least of all the defense attorney, who could only silence her with a wave of his hand and nod at the judge, an uneasy apology.

"She did!" the woman said, forceful now. "She knew."

"Frau Gersh," the prosecutor said deliberately, as if the outburst hadn't happened, "do you recognize the prisoner?"

"Of course. The *greifer.*"

"She was known to you personally?"

"No. But I know that face. She came for me, with the men."

"That was the first time you saw her?"

"No. She talked to me at the shoe repair. I should have known, but I didn't. Then, that same afternoon—"

"The shoe repair?" one of the judges said, confusing the past with the crutches now on display.

"One of her contacts," the prosecutor said. "People in hiding wore out their shoes—from all the walking, to keep moving. So Fräulein Naumann made friends with the shoe men. 'Who's been in today? Any strangers?' She found many this way. This particular shop—" He made a show of checking his notes. "In Schöneberg. Hauptstrasse. That's correct?"

"Yes, Hauptstrasse," Frau Gersh said.

Jake looked at Renate. Clever, if that's what you were after, collecting items from cobblers. All her news-gathering tricks, offered to murderers.

"So she talked to you there?"

"Yes, you know, the weather, the raids. Just to talk. I didn't like it—I had to be careful—so I left."

"And went home?"

"No, I had to be careful. I walked to Viktoria Park, then here and there. But when I got back, she was there. With the men. The others—good German people, helping me—were already gone. She sent them away too."

"I must point out," the defense lawyer said, "that at this time, 1944, it was against the law for German citizens to hide Jews. This was an illegal act."

The judge looked at him, amazed. "We are not interested in German law," he said finally. "Are you suggesting that Fräulein Naumann acted correctly?"

"I'm suggesting that she acted legally." He looked down. "At the time."

"Go on," the judge said to the prosecutor. "Finish it."

"You were taken away then. On what charge?"

"Charge? I was a Jew."

"How did Fräulein Naumann know this? You hadn't told her?"

Frau Gersh shrugged. "She said she could always tell. I have papers, I said. No, she told them, she's a Jew. And of course they listened to her. She worked for them."

The prosecutor turned to Renate. "Did you say this?"

"She was a Jew."

"You could tell. How?"

"The look she had."

"What kind of look was that?"

Renate lowered her eyes. "A Jewish look."

"May I ask the prisoner—such a skill—were you ever mistaken?"

Renate looked at him directly. "No, never. I always knew."

Jake sat back, feeling sick. Proud of it. His old friend.

"Continue, Frau Gersh. You were taken where?"

"The Jewish Old Age Home. Grosse Hamburger Strasse." A precise detail, coached.

"And what happened there?"

"We were held until they had enough to fill a truck. Then to the train. Then east," she said, her voice dropping.

"To the camp," the prosecutor finished.

"Yes, to the camp. To the gas. I was healthy, so I worked. The others—" She broke off, then looked again at Renate. "The others you sent were killed."

"I didn't send them. I didn't know," Renate said.

This time the judge held up his hand to silence her.

"You *saw.* You saw," the woman shouted.

"Frau Gersh," the prosecutor said, his calm voice a substitute for a gavel, "can you positively identify the prisoner as the woman who came to your house to arrest you?"

"Yes, positive."

Bernie leaned over in another huddle.

"And did you see her again?"

Jake glanced at the prosecutor, wondering where he was heading.

"Yes, from the truck. She was watching us from her window. When they took us away. Watching."

An echo of the story from Bernie. A shoe shop in Schöneberg, the American sector. So Bernie had found her too, another gift to the Russians.

"The same woman. You're positive."

Now the woman was shaking, slipping out of control. "The same. The same." She started to rise from the chair, staring at Renate. "A Jew. Killing your own. You watched them take us away." The beginning of a sob, no longer in court. "Your own people. Animal! Eating your own, like an animal."

"No!" Renate shouted back.

The judge slapped the desk with his palm and said something in Russian, presumably calling a recess, but the prosecutor hurried up to the bench and began whispering. The judge nodded, slightly taken aback, then said formally to the room, "We will stop for fifteen minutes, but first the photographers will be allowed in. The prisoner will remain standing."

Jake followed the prosecutor's signal to the back of the room, where Ron appeared from the press section, opening the door to let the photographers in. A small group filed down the center of the room. Flashing lights went off in Renate's face, causing her to blink and turn, shaking her head as if they were flies. The judges sat erect, posing. A soldier helped Frau Gersh onto her crutches. For a second

Jake expected to see Liz, snapping history. Then the flashbulbs died out and the judge stood.

"Fifteen minutes," he said, already lighting a cigarette.

In the corridor outside, the crowd of reporters had to press against the wall to let Frau Gersh pass on her crutches. Evidently there would be no cross-examination. Brian Stanley was standing off to one side, drinking from a pocket flask.

"Not up to Moscow standards, is it?" He offered Jake a drink. "Not the same without the confessions. That's what they like—all that bloody hand-wringing. Of course, they've got a lot to confess, the Russians have."

"It's a farce," Jake said, watching Frau Gersh leave.

"'Course it is. Can't expect the Old Bailey here." He looked down at his bottle. "Still, not the nicest girl in Berlin, is she?"

"She used to be. Nice."

Brian looked at him, confused, unaware of the connection.

"Yes, well," he said, at a loss, then slowly shook his head. "Never mistaken. Brought out the best in everybody, didn't it? By the way, I found you a boat."

"A boat?"

"You asked about a boat, didn't you? Anyway, they've got a few still. Over at the yacht club. Just mention my name." He looked up. "You did ask."

The afternoon he'd promised Lena, sailing on the lake, away from everything.

"Yes, sorry, I forgot. Thanks."

"Mind you don't sink it. They'll make me pay."

"Is that a drink?" Benson said, appearing with Ron.

"It was," Brian said, handing him the flask.

"What are you doing here?" Benson said to Jake, then turned to Ron. "And you promised. *Stars and Stripes* exclusive."

"Don't look at me. How did you get in?" he said to Jake. "They said no more passes."

"I'm helping the prosecution. She used to be a friend of mine."

An embarrassed silence.

"Christ," Ron said finally. "You always turn up one way or the other, don't you?"

"Can you get me an interview?"

"I can request one. So far, nothing. She hasn't been in a talking mood. I mean, what do you say after that? What can you?"

"I don't know. Maybe she'll say it to me."

"You'd have to share," Ron said, working. "Everybody wants this story."

"Fine. Just get me in." He looked at Benson. "That was a good piece on Liz. She would have liked it."

"Thanks," Benson said, a little uncomfortable with the compliment. "Hell of a thing. I hear the boyfriend's all right, though. He got out this morning."

Jake's head snapped up. "What? Yesterday he couldn't have visitors and today's he out of there? How did that happen?"

"What I hear is he's got friends in Congress," Benson said, trying to make a joke. "Who the hell wants to stay in the infirmary? They kill more than they cure. Anyway, he's sitting pretty. Got a nurse in his billet and everything. What's it to you?"

Jake turned to Ron, still agitated. "Did you know about this?"

"What are you talking about?"

"I told you," he said, grabbing Ron's arm. "She took a bullet for him—somebody wants him dead. Are there guards? Who's with him in the billet?"

"What do you mean, took a bullet?" Benson said, but Ron was moving Jake's hand away, staring.

"The U.S. Army," Ron said to Jake, "that's who. Pull fucking guard duty yourself, if it makes you so nervous."

"What's wrong?" Benson said.

"Nothing," Ron said. "Geismar's been seeing things, that's all. Maybe you ought to check into the infirmary yourself, have them give you a once-over. You're not making a lot of sense these days."

"There's someone there all the time?"

"Uh-huh," Ron said, still looking at him. "No Russians allowed. Ever."

"So I can see him?"

"That's up to you. He isn't going anyplace. Why don't you take him some flowers and see what it does for you? Christ, Geismar." He glanced toward the crowd shuffling back into the courtroom. "There's the bell. You coming, or do you want to run right over and play nurse?" he said, then looked at Jake seriously. "I don't know what this is all about, but you don't have to worry about him. He's as safe as you are." He nodded at the Russians by the door. "Maybe safer."

"I didn't know you and Shaeffer were friends," Benson said, still curious.

"Geismar's got friends stashed all over Berlin, haven't you?" Ron said, beginning to move. "How do you know this one, by the way?" he said, jerking his thumb toward the court.

"She was a reporter," Jake said. "Just like the rest of us. I trained her."

Ron stopped and turned. "That must give you something to think about," he said, then followed Benson through the door.

Bernie was standing at the end of the table with Gunther but came over as Jake took his seat. The judges were just returning, walking in single file.

"So," he said to Jake. "How do you think it's going so far?"

"Jesus, Bernie. Crutches."

Bernie's face grew tight. "The crutches are real. So was the gas."

"Why not just take her out and shoot her?"

"Because we want it on the record—how they did it. People should know."

Jake nodded. "So she's what? A stand-in?"

"No, she's the real thing. No different from Otto Klopfer. No different." He took in Jake's blank expression. "The guy who wanted the exhaust pipe fixed. Or maybe you forgot already. People do." He looked back to the press section, a restless scraping of chairs. "Maybe they'll listen this time."

"They made her do it. You know that."

"That's what Otto says too. All of them. You believe it?"

Jake looked up. "Sometimes."

"Which gets you where? Everybody's got a sad story, and the end's always the same. One thing I learned as a DA—you start feeling sorry for people, you never get a conviction. Don't waste your sympathy. She's guilty as hell."

The prosecutor began by calling Gunther to the stand, but before he could take the chair the defense attorney jumped up, stirred finally to some activity.

"May I address the court? What is the purpose of these witnesses? This emotionalism. The nature of the prisoner's work is not in question here. She herself has described it for the court." He held up a transcript. "Work, I would add, that she performed under the threat of her own death. She has also, let us remember, helped us identify her employers, given her full cooperation so that the Soviet people can bring the real fascists to justice. And what is her reward? This? We have here a matter for the Soviet people to decide, not the western press. I ask that we dispense with these theatrics and proceed with the serious business of this court."

This was so clearly unexpected that for an instant the judges just sat expressionless. Then they turned to each other. What they asked, however, was that he repeat his statement in Russian, and Jake wondered again how much of the trial they really understood. Renate stood impassively as the pleas rolled out again in Russian. Her full cooperation. Beaten out of her? Or had she sat down willingly and filled sheets with names? A new assignment, catching the catchers. When the lawyer finished, the judge dismissed him with a scowl. "Sit down," he said, then looked at Gunther. "Proceed."

The lawyer lowered his head, a schoolboy reprimanded for speaking out of turn, and Jake saw that he had missed the point. The business of the court was the theater. What happens when it's over, the summer after the war. Not clearing the rubble, not the shuffling DPs—peripheral stories. What happened was this season of denunciations, personal reprisals, all the impossible moral reparations. Tribunals, shaved heads, pointed fingers—auto da fés to purge the soul. Everyone, like Gunther, would have his reckoning.

They started his testimony carefully, a slow recitation of the years of police service, his voice a calm monotone, a return to order after Frau Gersh's crying. Bernie knew his audience. You could soften them with crutches, but in the end they would respond to this, the sober reassurance of authority. The judges were listening politely, as if, ironically, they had finally recognized one of their own.

"And would it be fair to say that these years of training had made you a good observer?"

"I have a policeman's eye, yes."

"Describe for us, then, what you saw that day at the—" He broke off to check his notes. "Café Heil, Olivaerplatz." Down the street from Lena's flat, where the world had gone on around them. "The café was familiar to you?"

"No. That's why I paid particular attention. To see if it was safe."

"For your wife, you mean."

"Yes, for Marthe."

"She was in hiding."

"At that time she had to walk during the day, so the landlady would think she was at work. Public places, where people wouldn't take notice. Zoo Station, for instance. Tiergarten."

"And you met her during these walks?"

"Twice a week. Tuesdays and Fridays," Gunther said, precise. "To make sure she was all right, give her a meal. I had coupons." Every week, for years, waiting for a tap on the shoulder.

"And this was where?"

"Usually Aschinger's. By Friedrichstrasse Station. It was always crowded there." The big cafeteria where Jake had often gone himself, grabbing a bite on his way to the broadcast. Jake saw them pretending to meet, jostled by the lunch crowd at the stand-up tables, eating blue-plate specials. "But it was important to change places. Her face would become familiar. So, that day, Olivaerplatz."

"This was in 1944?"

"March seventh, one-thirty."

"What is the importance of this?" the defense attorney said, standing.

"Sit down," the judge said, waving his hand.

The big roundups had started in '42. Two years of fading into crowds.

"Your memory is excellent, Herr Behn," the prosecutor said. "Please tell us the rest."

Gunther glanced toward Bernie, who nodded.

"I arrived first, as always, to make sure."

"The prisoner was there?"

"In the back. With coffee, a newspaper—ordinary. Then Marthe came. She asked me if the chair was free. A pretense, you see, so we would not seem to be together. I noticed the prisoner looking at us, and I thought perhaps we should go, but she went back to her paper, nothing wrong, so we ordered the coffee. Another look. I thought, you know, she was looking at *me,* perhaps she was someone I had arrested—this happened sometimes—but no, just a busybody. Then she went to the toilet. There is a phone there—I checked later—so that was when she called her friends."

"And did she come back?"

"Yes, she finished her coffee. Then she paid the bill and walked right past us to the door. That's when they came for Marthe. Two of them, in those leather coats. Who else had leather coats in 'forty four? So I knew."

"Excuse me, Herr Behn. You know for a fact the prisoner called them? How is that?"

Gunther looked down. "Because Marthe talked to her. A foolish slip, after being so careful. But what difference did it make in the end?"

"She talked to her?"

"She knew her. From school. Schoolgirls. 'Renate, is it really you?' she said. Just like that, so surprised to see her. Marthe must have thought she was in hiding too. Another U-boat. 'So many years,' Marthe said, 'and just the same.' Foolish."

"And did Fräulein Naumann recognize her?"

"Oh yes, she knew. 'You're mistaken,' she said, and of course that was right. Marthe shouldn't have said anything. It was dangerous to be recognized. They tortured the U-boats sometimes, to find the others, to get names. But she knew." He stopped, his eyes moving away, then began to talk more quickly, wanting it over. "She tried to leave then, of course, but they came, the coats, so she couldn't get out. And that's when I saw. They looked at *her,* one of them. First around the room, searching, then at her. To tell them. She could have said, she's gone, she just left. She could have saved her. Her old school friend. But no. 'That's the one,' she says. 'She's a Jew.' So they grabbed Marthe. 'Renate,' she said, that's all, the name, but the *greifer* wouldn't look at her."

"And you?" the lawyer said in the quiet room. "What did you do?"

"Of course people were looking then. 'What is this?' I said. 'There's some mistake.' And they said to her, the *greifer,* 'Him too?' And she had no idea who I was, you see. So they were ready to take me too, but then Marthe saved me. 'He's nobody,' she said. 'We were just sharing the table.' Nobody. And she moved away with them so they wouldn't even think about it. Quietly, you know. No commotion. Not even another look to give me away."

Jake sat up, his mind darting. Of course. If you didn't know your victim, someone had to point him out. Mistakes could be made. A crowded café. A crowded market square. But nobody had been there to save Liz.

"Herr Behn, I'm sorry to ask again. So there's no confusion—you state positively that you saw and heard the accused identify your wife for deportation. A woman known to her. There is no doubt?"

"No doubt. I saw it." He looked at Renate. "She sent her to her death."

"No," Renate said quietly. "They said a labor camp."

"To her death," Gunther said, then looked back to the prosecutor. "And she went with them in the car, the same car. All the *greifer*s together."

"I didn't want to," Renate said, a stray detail.

"Thank you, Herr Behn," the lawyer said, dismissing him.

"And then—do you know what?" Gunther said.

Bernie raised his head, surprised, something outside the script.

"What?" the lawyer said uncertainly.

"You want to know what it was like? Those days? The waitress came over. 'Are you paying for both?' she said. 'You ordered two coffees.'" He stopped. "So I paid." The end of the column, his final point.

"Thank you, Herr Behn," the lawyer said again.

The defense attorney rose. "A question. Herr Behn, were you a member of the National Socialist Party?"

"Yes."

"Let it be entered that the witness is an admitted fascist."

"All policemen were required to join the party," the prosecutor said. "This is irrelevant."

"I suggest that this testimony is biased," the defense attorney said. "A Nazi official. Who enforced the criminal laws of the fascist regime. Who testifies for personal reasons."

"This is absurd," the prosecutor said. "The testimony is the truth. Ask her." He pointed to Renate. Now both lawyers were standing, what formal procedures there had been slipping away in a crossfire that darted from lawyer to witness to accused. "Were you at the Café Heil? Did you report Marthe Behn? Did you identify her? Answer."

"Yes," Renate said.

"Not a stranger. A woman you knew," the prosecutor said, his voice rising.

"I had to." She looked down. "You don't understand. I needed one more that week. The quota. There were not so many left then. I needed one more."

Jake felt his stomach move. A number to fill the truck.

"To save yourself."

"Not for myself," she said, shaking her head. "Not for myself."

"Fräulein Naumann," the defense said, formal again. "Please tell the court who was also being held in custody in Grosse Hamburger Strasse."

"My mother."

"Under what conditions?"

"She was kept there so that I would come back in the evening, when my work was finished," she said, resigned now, aware that it wouldn't matter. But she had lifted her head and was looking at Jake, the way a public speaker pinpoints a face in an audience, talking only to him, a private explanation, the interview they probably would never have. "They knew I wouldn't leave her. We were taken together. First to work at Siemenstadt. Slaves. Then, when the deportations started, they told me they would keep her name off the list if I worked for them. So many every week. I couldn't send her east."

"So you sent other Jews," the prosecutor said.

"But then there were not so many left," she said, still to Jake.

"To—what did you call them?—labor camps."

"Yes, labor camps. But she was an old woman. I knew the conditions were hard. To survive that—"

"But that's not all you did, is it?" the prosecutor said, pressing now. "Your superior"—he glanced at a paper—"Hans Becker. We have testimony that you were intimate with him. Were you intimate with him?"

"Yes," she said, her eyes on Jake. "That too."

"And did he keep your mother off the list? For your good efforts?"

"At first. Then he sent her to Theresienstadt. He said it was easier there." She paused. "He ran out of names."

"Tell the court what happened to her there," the defense said.

"She died."

"But you continued your work after that," the prosecutor said. "You still came back every night, didn't you?"

"By then, where could I go? The Jews knew about me—I couldn't hide with them. There was no one."

"Except Hans Becker. You continued your relations with him."

"Yes."

"Even after he deported your mother."

"Yes."

"And you still say you were protecting her?"

"Does it matter to you what I say?" she said wearily.

"When it's the truth, yes."

"The truth? The truth is that he forced me. Over and over. He liked that. I kept my mother alive. I kept myself alive. I did what I had to do. I thought, there's nothing worse than this, but it will end, the Russians will come. Not much longer. Then you came and hunted me down like a dog. Becker's girlfriend, they called me. Girlfriend, when he did that to me. What is my crime? That I'm still alive?"

"Fräulein, that's not the crime here."

"No, the punishment," she said to Jake. "Still alive."

"Yes," Gunther said unexpectedly from the witness chair, but not looking anywhere, so that no one was sure what he meant.

The Russian prosecutor cleared his throat. "I'm sure we're all enlightened to hear that the Nazis are to blame for everything, fräulein. A pity, perhaps, that you did their work so well."

"I did what I had to do," she said, still staring, until finally Jake had to look away. What did she expect him to say? "I forgive you"?

"Are you finished with the witness?" the judge said, restless.

"One more question," the defense said. "Herr Behn, you're a large man. Strong. You did not struggle with the men in the café?"

"With Gestapo? No."

"No, you saved yourself." A pointed look at Renate. "Or, to be exact, your wife saved you. I believe that's what you said."

"Yes, she saved me. It was too late for her, once they knew."

"And after this you remained on the police force?"

"Yes."

"Enforcing the laws of the government that had arrested your wife."

"The racial laws were not our responsibility."

"I see. Some of the laws, then. Not all. But you made arrests?"

"Of criminals, yes."

"And they were sent where?"

"To prison."

"So late in the war? Most were sent to 'labor camps,' weren't they?"

Gunther said nothing.

"Tell us, how did you decide which laws to enforce for the National Socialists?"

"Decide? It wasn't for me to decide. I was a policeman. I had no choice."

"I see. So only Fräulein Naumann had this choice."

"I object," the prosecutor said. "This is nonsense. The situations were not at all similar. What is the defense trying to suggest?"

"That this testimony is compromised from start to finish. This is a personal grievance, not Soviet justice. You hold this woman accountable for the crimes of the Nazis? She had no choice. Listen to your own witness. No one had a choice."

The only possible defense left. Everyone was guilty; no one was guilty.

"She had a choice," Gunther said, his voice thick.

The defense nodded, pleased with himself, finally where he wanted to be.

"Did you?"

"Don't answer," the prosecutor said quickly.

But Gunther raised his head, unflinching—a moment he'd expected, even if Bernie hadn't, the other reckoning. Not to be put off, even by a bottle to blot himself out. He gazed straight ahead, eyes stone.

"Yes, I had a choice. And I worked for them too," he said, his voice as firm and steady as the hand on the razor. "Her murderers. Even after that."

The room, suddenly embarrassed, was silent. Not the answer any of them had wanted, a little death, pulled out of him like Liz's gasp. One cut.

He turned to Renate. "We all did," he said, his voice lower now. "But you—you could have looked away. Your friend. Just the once."

At this she did look away, facing the stenographers, so that her words were almost lost.

"I needed one more," she said, as if it answered everything. "One more."

Another awkward silence in the room, broken finally by the judge.

"The witness is not on trial here," he said. "Are you disputing what he saw?"

The defense shook his head, as eager as everyone else now to move on.

"Good. Then you're finished," the judge said to Gunther. "Step down." He glanced at his wristwatch. "We will meet tomorrow."

"But we have other witnesses," the prosecutor said, anxious not to let his momentum stall.

"Then call them tomorrow. It's enough for today. And next time stick to the facts."

Which were what, Jake wondered. Another column of numbers.

When no one moved, the judge waved his hand at the room. "Adjourned, adjourned," he said irritably, then rose, motioning for the other two to follow.

Jake heard the sound of chairs being moved, a low buzz, lawyers gathering papers. Gunther stayed in his chair, still looking straight ahead. The guards, surprised by the abrupt dismissal, nudged Renate away from her railing and began to lead her at gunpoint out of the room. Jake watched her pass in front of the bench, her eyes meeting his as she approached the prosecution table. She stopped.

"So it's really you," she said to him, her old voice. "You came back."

The guards, not sure whether she was allowed to speak, looked around for instructions, but the judges had gone, the room emptying with them.

Jake nodded, not knowing what to say. It's good to see you again? Collarbones sticking out.

"It wasn't for myself," she said to Jake, her eyes on him, waiting.

Jake looked down, unable to respond. Bernie was watching from the side, waiting too. But what could anyone say? A guard took her arm. In a minute she'd be gone. One word, something.

He fell back on the empty courtesy of a prison visit. "Can I get you anything?"

She looked at him for another moment, disappointed, then shook her head. More Russian, insistent now. The guards pushed her away from the table.

Jake stayed until the room was almost cleared, just a hum coming in from the hall. Gunther was still in his chair. When Bernie went over to get him, he looked up once, then brushed him aside, getting up stiffly, and walked toward Jake, one deliberate foot in front of the other.

"I'll give you a lift," Bernie said, but Gunther ignored him.

He stopped for a second at the table. "I'll talk to Willi," he said to Jake, then kept walking out of the room.

Bernie, disconcerted, went over and began putting files back in his briefcase.

"What about you?" he said.

Jake looked up. "I have the jeep." He stood up to leave, then turned. "Still think all the stories end the same way?" he said.

Bernie shoved the last file in the case. "Marthe Behn's did."

CHAPTER TWELVE

OUTSIDE, JAKE AVOIDED the Alex, where everyone had parked, and took one of the side streets instead, too numb to face Ron and the others swapping notes. Gunther had already disappeared somewhere in the rubble. A walk, anything to get away. But the courtroom followed him, a dead hand on his shoulder. What happens when it's over. He looked around. No one in the street, not even the usual children climbing over bricks. The raids had done their worst here—not a wall standing, the air still thick with sour dust. Flies buzzed over a deep bomb crater, now a gray pond of sewage from a broken main. But poison had been seeping into Berlin for years. When had Hans Becker told Renate about her mother? While they were in bed? Always something worse, even when it was ordinary. A waitress collecting her check, knowing. What it was like, day after day. For the first time Jake wondered if Breimer might be right, if this wasteland was what they deserved, some biblical retribution to wipe out the poison once and for all. But here it still was, a giant hole filling with sludge.

"Uri."

The Russian startled him, coming out of nowhere.

"Uri," the soldier said again, pointing to Jake's arm.

"No watch."

The Russian scowled. *"Ja, uri,"* he said, pointing to the old Bulova on Jake's wrist. He pulled a wad of bills from his pocket and held them out.

"No. Now piss off."

A hard stare, menacing, so that suddenly Jake felt his blood jump, a spurt of fear. A deserted street. It could be this easy, capricious, like shooting at rats. Another incident. But the Russian was turning away, disgruntled, stuffing the notes back in his pocket.

As Jake watched him go, breathing again, the street felt even emptier. No market crowds here. If Gunther was right, if he'd been the target, they could pick him off easily now. Not even a witness. If they wanted him. He stood still for a moment, back in Potsdam. A shell game of a crime, knowing the killer but not the victim. Three of them. What if it *had* been him? He moved his hand to his hip, an involuntary reflex, wishing he had a gun. Not that it had done Liz any good. He stopped. But she hadn't been wearing it that day, her cowgirl holster. Where was it? On the way back to Webster Groves? He tried to remember Ron in her room, folding clothes. No gun. Did it matter? But something unexplained.

He looked at the pond, unsettled. Follow the points. You play a shell game by elimination. Three of them in the market. Usually the one intended. But why would anyone want to kill Liz? Which left two. One of them now ready for visitors in Gelferstrasse. He turned and started back up the street, hand still on his hip. When he reached the jeep, another Russian, reading a newspaper, glanced up at him uneasily and moved away, as if he were in fact carrying a gun.

He found Breimer reading what seemed to be the same paper at Shaeffer's billet, a villa across the street from the collapsed house. An army nurse was flicking through *Life,* half listening as Breimer read snatches out loud, apparently unable to stop talking even outside a sickroom door.

"Two thousand times more than the Townbuster. That was the biggest we had. Two thousand *times.*" He looked up as Jake walked in. "Ah, good. He's been asking for you. Well, it's a great day, isn't it?

It won't be long now." When Jake said nothing, confused, he handed him the paper. "I see you haven't heard," he said. "And you call yourself a newspaperman. We'll all be going home after this. Twenty thousands tons of TNT. Size of a fist. Hard to imagine."

Jake took the paper. *Stars and Stripes.* U.S. REVEALS ATOM BOMB USED FIRST TIME ON JAPS. The other war, almost forgotten. A city he'd never heard of. Two square miles wiped out in one blast, the mess behind the Alex a warmup by comparison.

"It's over now for sure," Breimer said, but what Jake saw was the Russian's face by the jeep, uneasy.

"How does it work?" he said, scanning the page. A chart of the other bombs, getting bigger toward the bottom.

"You'll have to ask the eggheads that. All I know is, it did. They say you still can't see through the smoke. Two days. No wonder old Harry was playing hardball with the Reds. You have to hand it to him—he sure kept this one close to the vest."

Jaunty in a double-breasted suit on the Cecilienhof terrace, smiling for Liz's camera. With an ace up his sleeve.

"Yes sir, a great day," Breimer said, still excited. "When I think of all those boys—coming home. They'll all be coming home now. In one piece too, thank the Lord."

Jake looked at the fleshy face moving into another Kiwanis speech. But wasn't it true? Who would wish a single Marine dead on a Honshu beach? On Okinawa, they'd had to drag the Japs out of caves with flamethrowers, one by one. Still, something new, worse than before. Breimer was starting in again.

"How's the patient?" Jake said, interrupting.

"On the mend, on the mend," Breimer said. "Thanks to Corporal Kelly here. Too pretty to be a nurse, if you ask me. But you should see her make them hop to. No monkey business with this one."

"Not with a hypodermic in your hand, anyway," she said dryly, but her plain face was smiling, flattered.

"Can I see him?"

"Joe would want to see *him,*" Breimer said to the nurse, clearly in charge. He put his hand on Jake's shoulder. "That's a hell of a thing you did, getting him out of there. We're all grateful, I can tell you that."

"We who?"

"We everybody," Breimer said, dropping the hand. "Americans. That's an important boy we've got in there, one of the best. You don't want the Russkies getting their hands on him."

"He's not a favorite of theirs?"

Breimer took this as a joke and smiled. "Not exactly. Not Joe." He lowered his voice. "Shame about the girl."

"Yes." Jake moved to the door. "She's on duty when?" he said, nodding toward the nurse.

"Twice a day. Make sure everything's all right. I come when I can, of course. Least I can do. Joe's been a real help to me."

"Can you get someone round the clock? Use some pull? There ought to be someone here."

Breimer smiled. "Now don't get all excited. He's not that sick. Main trouble's keeping him in bed. Wants to do things too soon."

"The Russians took a shot at him once. They can do it again." Jake spread his hand toward the front door, wide open to the street.

Breimer looked at him, troubled. "They said it was an accident."

"They weren't there. I was. I'd get somebody, just in case."

"Maybe you're a little jumpy. We're not in the Russian zone here."

"Congressman, the whole city's a Russian zone. You want to take the chance?"

Breimer met his eyes, all business now. "Let me see what I can do." Not even a quibble.

"Armed," Jake said, then opened the door.

Shaeffer was propped up in bed, bare-chested, with a wad of gauze and adhesive tape covering one side. They'd given him a haircut in the hospital and now, with his ears sticking out, he seemed ten years younger, no longer a poster Aryan, smaller out of uniform, like a high school athlete without the shoulder pads. He was reading the newspaper too, but dropped it on the sheet when Jake came in.

"Well, finally. I was hoping you'd come. I wanted to thank—"

"Save it," Jake said easily, casing the room. Ground floor, an open window facing the bed. The room had been a library; a few books were still leaning on their sides on the shelves, evidently not worth ransacking. "You should have stayed in the hospital."

"Oh, I'm all right," Shaeffer said, cheerful, taking it for medical concern. "You hang around there long enough, some sawbones wants to take a leg off. You know the army."

"I mean it's safer. Any rooms upstairs?" He walked over to the window and looked out.

"Safer?"

"I asked Breimer to get a guard out front."

"What for?"

"You tell me."

"Tell you what?"

"Why the Russians took a potshot at you."

"At me?"

"The congressman seemed to think they don't like you very much."

"Breimer? He sees Russians in his dreams."

"Yeah, well, I saw them in Potsdam. Shooting—at you. Now suppose you tell me why they'd want to do that." He pulled up a chair next to the bed.

"I haven't the faintest idea."

Jake said nothing, staring at him from the chair. Finally Shaeffer, restless, looked away.

"Got a smoke?" he said. "The nurse took mine. Says I'll live longer."

"Not the way you're going," Jake said, lighting the cigarette and handing it to him, still staring.

"Look, I owe you something, I guess, but I don't owe you a story. I can't. The work's classified."

"I don't have any notebooks out. This one's for me, not the papers. You almost got me killed out there too. I figure I'm entitled to know why. Now, how about it?"

Shaeffer took another drag, following the smoke up with his eyes as if he were leaving the room with it. "You know FIAT?"

"No."

"Field Information Agency Technical. Fancy way of saying we take care of the scientists. Debriefing. Detention centers. Whatever."

"Like Kransberg," Jake said.

Shaeffer nodded. "Like Kransberg."

"And what's the whatever?"

"Finding them in the first place. It's possible we set up a team to cover Berlin. It's possible the Russians don't like that."

"Why? They've been here since May. What's left?"

Shaeffer smiled, expansive. "Plenty. The Russians were so busy shipping out the hardware, it took them a little while to realize they needed the guys who ran it. By that time a lot of them had disappeared—gone west, maybe into hiding. The Russians have a hard time recruiting. People aren't falling over themselves to travel east."

"Not when they can get a fat contract from American Dye," Jake said, nodding to the door.

Shaeffer looked at him, then stubbed out the cigarette. "Don't push me. He's out of it, or we stop here. Understood?"

"I hear you."

"Anyway, that's not it. The Russians have been offering good salaries too. If you want to go to work in the fucking Urals."

"Instead of beautiful Utica."

Shaeffer looked again. "I mean it."

Jake held up his hand. "Okay, they don't go to Utica."

"No, they don't. Dayton, since you want to know. There's a facility near Wright Field." He stopped, aware that he'd given something for free, then shrugged. "The first group goes to Dayton. If we can get them over. Satisfied?"

"I don't care one way or the other. What's the holdup?"

"De-Nazification. Those guys—we'd be lucky to get Ike cleared. They want the good Germans. So find me one. You don't think the Russians give a rat's ass."

Jake got up and walked toward the shelf. "But they do about you—assuming your team exists."

"Assuming."

"Been doing anything you shouldn't?"

"From their point of view? Winning. The Russians have been here two months and they're still going through their wanted list. We've been here three weeks and we're picking it clean. Once you start, one leads you to another. They've been waiting for us to come. Just holding on. Luftwaffe—the whole aeromedical staff. They even kept the research papers. KWI—still a lot of warm bodies over there if you can dig them out. It's not hard—their friends help. They're around, all right." Out for a stroll, walking the dog.

"Engineers at Zeiss?" Jake said.

"That's in the eastern zone. We don't go into the eastern zone."

"That's not what the Russians say."

"They like to make a stink. What I hear is, the engineers wanted to come."

"They just needed a helping hand."

Shaeffer's eyes followed him to the bookshelf, then looked away.

"It's possible their bombsight optics were years ahead of ours. Years ahead—worth a risk to get. It's possible someone wanted to send the Russians a message. They have this habit of kidnapping people. Maybe we wanted to show them we could do it too. Make them think twice next time."

"And did it?"

"More or less. Nobody's gone missing lately, anyway."

"Except Emil Brandt."

"Yes, except Emil."

"So now he's on your list."

"He's on everybody's list. He did all the calculations—he knows the whole program. I told you, we don't want to lose this one. Not now, for sure."

Jake raised his eyebrows. "Why not now?"

"The rocket team?" Schaeffer picked up the newspaper. "Can you imagine if the V-twos had carried one of these babies?"

"No, I can't," Jake said. London, gone.

"They're everybody's top pick," Shaeffer said. "But we got them. And we're going to keep them. All of them."

"What if they don't want to go?"

"They do. Even Brandt. He just wants to take his wife. Always the wife. We almost lost him once, after Nordhausen. We get the rockets, the blueprints, the team's stashed away in Oberjoch. And he gives the slip and takes off for Berlin on some fucking wild goose chase. He was lucky to get out alive."

"With his files," Jake said casually, a shot.

Shaeffer waved his hand. "Admin. Not worth a damn thing. All the tech files were at Nordhausen. That was just an excuse to get his wife."

"Admin? I thought they were SS files."

"It was an SS program. They took it over. By that time they were taking over everything. For what it was worth."

"They gave him a medal."

"They gave everybody a medal. The scientists weren't too thrilled about the SS taking over. Not the coziest guys you could think of. But what the hell, who gets to pick his boss? So they hand out some medals and it's smiles again. They had a ton of them." A floor in the Chancellery, heaped with Iron Crosses.

"Finally we get them to Kransberg," Shaeffer was saying. "Keep them together, see? And he does it again. The others, we tell them the dependents'll come later and they don't like it much. But this one, no. He has to go shack up with her somewhere, have a little reunion. As if we don't have enough to do. Go chasing her now. And we're short-handed as it is. And now this." He gestured to his wound.

"He's not with his wife," Jake said. "She doesn't know where he is."

Shaeffer looked at him, not saying anything for a moment. Then he took another cigarette from the pack on the bed, still buying time.

"Thanks for saving me the legwork," he said calmly. "Want to tell me where she is?"

"No."

"In our zone?"

Jake nodded. "She doesn't know anything."

"Well, that's a relief, anyway."

"What is?"

"Where she is. What do you think's been keeping me up nights—what if the Russians get her first? That'd be an offer we couldn't compete with. We'd lose him for sure."

Bait. Jake looked out the window, feeling another jump of blood, as if the soldier behind the Alex had appeared again.

"She'd be better off with us, you know," Shaeffer said, still calm.

"She's all right where she is."

But was she? The Russian had asked for her.

"Want to tell me how you found her?" Shaeffer said, watching him. "We tried everything. No *fragebogen,* no neighbors, nothing."

"You might have tried his father. Why didn't you, by the way?"

"His father?" Shaeffer said, surprised. "His father's dead."

"Where'd you get that idea?"

"Brandt told me so himself. I'm the one who debriefed him."

"You never mentioned that."

"You didn't ask," Shaeffer said, moving a checker into place.

"Well, he's alive. I saw him. Why would Emil say that?"

Shaeffer shrugged. "Why didn't you tell me where his wife was? People like to keep a little something back. Question of trust, maybe. He know anything?"

"No, he hasn't seen him either. Nobody has. Nobody since Tully. But you're not interested in him."

Shaeffer looked down, smoothing out the sheet. "Look, let's smoke a little pipe here. Since you've got your nose under the tent. I could use the help."

"Doing what?"

"What you've been doing. We still have to find him. I'm out of commission. You're not."

"No thanks to you. Let's start with Tully and see how we do."

"They were friends at Kransberg. Well, friends. Brandt spoke English and Tully liked to listen. Late-night stuff. Brandt was the moody type. Depressed. How everything had gone wrong. You know, booze talk."

"Tully told you this?"

"Well, it's possible the rooms were bugged. So we could hear what the guests had to say."

"Nice."

"The Nazis put the taps in. We just took them over when we moved in."

"Some difference."

"I don't think you understand how it is there. The scientists are bargaining. They want to make sure there's work, some deal to get them out. So they don't give everything all at once. A little at a time, to keep us interested. They check with von Braun before they tell us anything. I don't blame them—they're just looking out for number one. But we've got to know. Not just what's on paper—what's up here." He tapped his temple.

"All right, so they're pals."

"And Brandt waltzes out of there and Tully drives him and no one tells *us.* So that by the time we do hear about it, he's Mr. Innocent and Brandt's gone and still nobody's making the right connection."

"Which is?"

"They think it's a fuckup. Brandt cons Tully into giving him a pass. Just a nice guy."

"And you don't think so?"

"I don't believe in the Easter Bunny either. I checked. The guy's an operator. You know he was selling releases to Germans?"

"I heard."

"A real piece of work. Twice sometimes—that's how it came out. But they couldn't prove it. His word against theirs. A bunch of Germans squealing. Who's got time to investigate that? But Brandt—that's something else. I get interested. And here's the thing—it was *Tully's* idea, skipping out. So I figure he's up to his old tricks."

"Tully's idea?"

"Nobody thinks to check the taps," Shaeffer said. "We only make transcripts when the guests are talking science. The rest of the time, our guys are reading a comic or taking a leak or something. So I get the monitor for that night and ask him what they were talking about. Nothing, he says, personal stuff. Like what? Nothing, Tully just told him they'd found his wife. Nothing," he said sarcastically.

"But they hadn't."

"No. But I didn't know that then. What I knew was that Tully'd got himself a paying customer. The one thing Brandt wanted. So I figure they negotiate a little private business. Brandt never made any noises about leaving before. He doesn't clear it with von Braun—he just goes. Tully even drives him out. So when I hear that, I blow some whistles to yank Tully in, but by that time he's gone too."

"To Berlin. Why?"

"Payday, probably. They didn't have money at Kransberg. I figured Brandt got the cash from his wife."

"But he never found her."

"Then Tully had one pissed-off German on his hands."

"No," Jake said, shaking his head, thinking. "They didn't meet up again in Berlin. Why would Tully want to do that if he'd lied about the wife?"

"Well, I didn't know he *had.* See? I told you we could use you." He leaned back, turning it over. "But he came."

"Anything in the taps about friends in Berlin? Tully know anybody here?"

Shaeffer glanced up at him. "He knew Emil Brandt."

"You trying to say Emil killed him?"

"I'm trying to say I don't care. I just want him back. Tully's not important."

"He was important enough to shoot."

"Him? Maybe he just got in the way," Shaeffer said irritably, adjusting his bandage.

"Maybe," Jake said. Like a girl taking pictures. "Be useful to know."

"Not anymore," Shaeffer said, wincing now, distracted by the bandage. "All I know is, he was going to lead me to Brandt and he didn't." He looked up. "Glad to hear about the wife, though. That's something. At least the bastard didn't get paid."

"No, he got paid." Jake looked again out the window, another jolt. With Russian money.

"Yeah, I guess," Shaeffer said, meaning the bullet. "What is it?" he said, following Jake's stare.

"Nothing. Just thinking." Move her. He picked up his cap. "I'd better go. You want the nurse for that?" He nodded at the bandage.

"Just thinking, huh?" Shaeffer said, studying him. Then his face hardened, back in the poster. "Don't think too much. I want him back. I don't care what he did."

"If he did."

"You just find him," he said evenly, then smiled. "Christ, the wife. We could make a good team, the two of us."

Jake shook his head. "People get shot around you." He looked out the window again. "What if the Russians already have him?"

"Then I'd want to know that too. Where."

"So you can organize another raiding party? The Russians wouldn't like that."

"So what?"

"You might not be so lucky next time. Liz won't be there to take one for you."

Shaeffer glared at him. "That's a hell of a thing to say."

"All right, skip it."

He looked down. "I liked Liz. She was a good egg." A kid in a soda fountain booth.

"All right," Jake said again, an apology.

"You've got some fucking nerve. Anyway, what makes you so sure it was me? You can't tell anything with the Russians. How did they even know I'd be there? Tell me that."

"Why were you? Shopping in the Russian zone—not the smartest idea in your line of work."

"That was Liz. She wanted a camera. I figured, why not? How would they know? How *did* they know?"

"Maybe a *greifer* spotted you."

"What's that? A kraut word?"

"Sort of a lookout scout." Jake started for the door, then turned. A *greifer.* "The name Sikorsky mean anything to you?"

"Vassily?"

"That's right. He was in the market that day. Would he know you by sight?"

Shaeffer looked away, silent.

Jake nodded. "Make sure Breimer gets the guard."

"Don't worry, I can take care of myself." He pulled a gun out from under the sheet and patted it.

Jake stood still for a second. Just a casual extension of his hand, like a fielder's mitt. "You always keep one in bed? Or just lately?" He reached for the doorknob. "Better stay away from the window."

Shaeffer aimed the gun there, target practice. "A Colt 1911 will stop anything at this range."

Jake looked over at him. "A Colt 1911 stopped Tully too."

Shaeffer turned, frowning, still holding the gun. "Says who?"

"The ballistics report."

"So? It's a standard-issue piece of equipment. There are only about a million of them around."

"Not in German hands. Or do you think Tully gave him one with the pass?"

"What's that supposed to mean?"

"That Emil didn't do it. Not with one of those."

Shaeffer glanced up, then smirked. "That's right, I remember. You think I did. 'Where were you and Breimer on the night of—' whatever the fuck it was."

"July sixteenth," Jake said. "And where were you?"

Shaeffer lowered the gun. "Go fuck yourself." He put it back under the covers. "You don't listen. I'm the only one who wanted him alive. He was going to lead me to Brandt, remember?" He stared at Jake for another second, then let it pass, shaking his head. "You've got a funny way of making friends."

"Are we? I'm still trying to figure that one."

Another sharp look. "Just find him." Shaeffer sank back against the pillows with a grunt, forcing a smile. "You're all alike, you guys. Smart talk. Always something smart." He looked up, his eyes steel again, Aryan gray. "Just don't forget whose uniform you've got on. We're on the same team over here. The same team."

"Is that the same one Liz was on?"

"Yeah, well," he said, looking down. "Things happen, don't they? Wartime."

"We're not at war with the Russians."

Shaeffer looked over at the newspaper with its black headline, then raised his head. "Says who?"

Afternoon light was streaming into the flat, but Hannelore was already putting on lipstick to go out.

"A little early, isn't it?" Jake said, watching her lean into the mirror.

"It's a tea party. It's supposed to be early. A *jause,* no?"

"A Russian tea party?" he said, amused. A table of stolid commissars, with the Mad Hatter pouring out.

"No. My new friend, a Tommy. A real tea party, he said. You know, like before, with cups and everything."

Spiked, followed by another party on the couch.

She blotted her lips. "You just missed Lena. She's at Frau Hinkel's. You should go too. You can't imagine what she knows."

"She went to a fortune-teller?"

"It's not like that. Not a gypsy. She knows things, she really does."

Jake looked out the window toward Wittenbergplatz, searching the street. Windows fronting the square, exposed, the wonderful light suddenly a liability. "Hannelore? Have you noticed anyone hanging around outside? A Russian?"

"Don't be silly," she said, gathering her purse. "He went back. He's not looking for me."

"No, I meant—" he said, then stopped. Why would Hannelore notice anything?

"Come on, I'll show you," she said. "It's behind KaDeWe."

He locked the door behind them and followed her down the stairs. "Your friends," he said. "Anyone know about another flat?"

She turned, stung. "You want me to leave? This is my flat, you know. Mine. Just because I'm kindhearted—"

"No, not for you. For Lena. Her own place. It's an inconvenience for you like this."

"Oh, I don't mind really. I'm used to it. It's cozy, you know? And you're so good about the food. How would we eat? And where would she go? Nobody has a flat unless—"

"Unless what?"

"Unless she has a friend. You know, important."

"Not like me," he said, smiling.

"No. A general, maybe. Someone big. That's who has flats. And the whores." A world of difference in her mind.

A work party was clearing one edge of Wittenbergplatz, women in army trousers loading carts. In the hot sun, everything smelled of smoke.

"He's from London," Hannelore said as they crossed the street, her high heels wobbling on the torn pavement. "Would I like it there, do you think?"

"I did."

"Well, but it's all the same now." She spread her hand to take in the ruined square. "All like this."

"Not like this."

"Yes, they said so on the radio. During the war. Everything was bombed."

"No. Just a few parts."

"Why would they lie about that?" she said, sure of herself, Goebbels' audience. "There," she said when they reached KaDeWe. "In the next street. There's a sign with a hand. How do I look?"

"Like an English lady."

"Yes?" She fluffed her hair, looking in the shard of plate glass, still there, then waved him off. "Oh you," she said, laughing, and teetered away toward the west.

The sign was a crudely drawn palm with three lines sketched in—Past running along the top, Present through the middle, and a spur with Future snaking across the heel. How many wanted the upper part read now? Frau Hinkel was on the second floor, marked with a zodiac, and he opened the door to a crowd of women sitting quietly in chairs like patients in a doctor's waiting room. Berlin had become a medieval city again, black markets to transmute watches into gold, witches to glimpse the future in a pack of cards. A few years ago they had measured the curve of light.

But what did it matter? There was Lena, a surprised smile spreading across her face as he entered. A woman happy to see you, he thought, like nothing else, even better than good fortune. "Jacob," she said. The others looked up at him, frankly interested, then lowered their eyes, the familiar reaction to a uniform. The woman next to Lena moved, making a place. "How did you know I was here?"

"Hannelore."

"I know it's silly, but she kept after me," she said, still smiling, leaning close in a whisper, away from the others. "What's wrong? You look so—"

He shook his head. "Nothing. Just the day. I went to a trial."

"What trial?"

But it was the smile he wanted, not another terrible story. Not Renate, not Gunther, not any of them. Blue skies. He glanced at his watch. "Let's get out of here. Someone found me a boat. It's still light—we could go for a sail."

"A boat," she said, delighted, then frowned. "Oh, but I can't. We're expecting some children at the nursery. I have to help Pastor Fleischman. Don't be disappointed. Tomorrow, all right? Look how dusty you are," she said, brushing his arm, proprietary. "What?"

"Just looking."

She flushed, then busied herself again with his sleeve. "You should have a bath."

"Hannelore's just gone out," he said, an invitation. "We'd have the flat to ourselves."

"Ssh." She glanced over at the others.

"You could take one with me."

She stopped moving her hand and made a face, mischievous, darting her eyes to signal that they were being overheard.

He leaned closer, whispering. "I'll tell you your fortune."

A small laugh, tickled by his breath in her ear. "Yes?" she said, then grinned. "All right. I'll come some other time. It's such a wait here."

But as they got up, a small boy, presumably a little Hinkel, darted behind the curtain into the other room, and before they could reach the door Frau Hinkel herself appeared, holding back the curtain and looking at Jake. "Come," she said. "You."

Jake looked at the line of customers, embarrassed, but no one said a word, resigned to ceding place to soldiers. Lena pulled him toward the curtain, eager.

The room, like Frau Hinkel, was plain and ordinary—no beads, no turbans and crystal balls, just a table with some chairs and a worn deck of cards.

"The cards can tell us what is and what might be, but not what *will* be. Do you understand?" she said as they sat, a seer's insurance policy, but simply delivered, her voice soft and comforting. She held the deck out to Lena to shuffle.

"You go first," Lena said, nervous, not touching the cards.

"I don't—" Jake started, but Frau Hinkel had put them in his hands. An old deck, slick with use, the face cards looking like Hohenzollerns.

When she started laying them out in rows, he felt an unexpected prick of apprehension, as if, despite all reason, they might actually reveal something. He knew it was just theater, a fairway con, but he found himself wanting to hear good news whether it was real or not, a fortune cookie's message of happy journeys and long life, cloudless. But didn't everybody? He thought of the tired faces outside, all hoping for a lucky sign.

"You have lucky cards," Frau Hinkel said, as if she had heard him. "You have been lucky in life."

Absurdly, he felt relieved. But was anyone unlucky here for twenty-five marks?

"Yes, it's good. Because you have been close to death." A safe guess after years of war, he thought, beginning to enjoy the act. "But protected. Here, you see? By a woman, it seems."

He glanced up at her, but she was laying out more cards, covering the first set, absorbed in them.

"A woman?" Lena said.

"Yes, I think so. But perhaps simply by this luck, I can't tell. A symbol. Now it's the opposite," she said, staring at the fresh row. "Now you are the protector. A risk, some danger, but the luck is still there. A house."

"The newsreel," Lena said quietly.

"There, again. The protector, like a knight. A sword. Perhaps a rescue. You are a warrior?" she said easily, the archaic word natural to her.

"No."

"Then a judge. The sword of a judge. Yes, that must be it. There is paper all around you. Lots of paper."

"There, you see?" Lena said. "He's a writer."

Frau Hinkel pretended not to hear, busy with the cards. "But it's difficult for you, the judge. You see here, the eyes face in two directions, not just one, so it's difficult. But you will." She laid out another set. "You have interesting cards. Contradictions. The paper keeps coming up. The luck. But also deception. That explains the eyes, looking both ways, because there is deception around you." Speaking as if she were working it out for the first time, what must have been a routine. "And always a woman. Strong, at the center. The rest—it's hard to say, but the woman is always there, you keep coming back to her. At the center. May I see your hand?"

She reached over and traced a line down his palm. "Yes, I thought so. My god, such a line. In a man. So deep. You see how straight. One, your whole life. You have a strong heart. The rest, contradictions, but not the heart." She looked up at him. "You must be careful when you judge. The heart is so strong." She turned to Lena, still holding his hand. "The woman who finds this one will be lucky. One love, no others." Her voice sentimental, a professional after all. Lena smiled.

She laid out one more set. "Let's see. Yes, the same. Death again, close. Still the luck, but take care. We have only what might be. And deception again."

"Does it say who?"

"No, but you will see. The eyes face one way now. You will see it."

Jake shifted in his seat, uncomfortable. "Is there travel?" he said, leading them back to the fortune cookie.

"Oh yes, many trips." Offhand, as if it were too obvious to bother about. "A trip on water soon." Another safe guess for an American.

"Home?"

"No, short. Many trips. You will never be home," she said softly, an abstraction. "Always somewhere else. But it's not a sadness for you. The place is not important. You will always live here." She tapped the heart line in his open palm. "So it's a lucky life, yes?" she said, turning over the cards and handing them to Lena to shuffle.

"Then mine will be lucky too," Lena said, cheerful.

Count on it, Jake wanted to say, just pay the twenty-five marks.

But when Frau Hinkel laid out Lena's set, she looked at it for a moment, puzzled, then gathered up the cards again.

"What does it say?"

"I can't tell. Sometimes when there are two of you it confuses the cards. Try again." She handed the deck to Lena. "They need to have your touch only."

Jake watched her shuffling, earnest, the way Hannelore must have listened to the radio.

"Yes, now I see," Frau Hinkel said, laying down the rows. "A mother's cards. Very loving—so many hearts. It's important to you, children. Yes, two of them."

"Two?"

"Yes, two," Frau Hinkel said, sure, not even looking up for confirmation.

Jake glanced at Lena, wanting to wink, but she had grown pale, disconcerted.

"Two of everything," Frau Hinkel said. "Two men. Kings." She looked up, intimate. "There was another?"

Lena nodded. Frau Hinkel took her hand just as she had Jake's, getting a second opinion.

"Yes, there. Two. Two lines running there."

"They cross each other," Lena said.

"Yes," Frau Hinkel said, then moved on, not explaining. "But only one in the end. One perhaps has died?" Another safe guess for anyone in the waiting room.

"No."

"Ah. Then you have decided." She turned the hand to its side. "There are the children. You see, two."

She went back to another row of cards.

"Much sorrow," she said, shaking her head. "But happiness too. There is an illness. Have you been ill?"

"Yes."

"But no longer. You see this card. It fights the illness."

"The one with the sword?" Jake said.

Frau Hinkel smiled pleasantly. "No, this one. It usually means medicine." She looked up. "I'm glad for you. So many these days—no medicine, even in the cards."

Another row.

"You were in Berlin during the war?"

"Yes."

Frau Hinkel nodded her head. "Destruction. I see this all the time now. Well, they don't lie, the cards." She placed down a black card, then quickly drew out another to cover it.

"What does that mean?" Lena said, alert.

Frau Hinkel looked at her. "In Berlin? It usually means a Russian. Excuse me," she said, suddenly shy, a shorthand message. "But that is the past. See how they come now? More hearts. You have a kind nature. You must not look at the past. You see how it tries to come back—see this one—but never strong, not as strong as the hearts. You can bury it," she said oddly. "You have the cards." Laying them on, another row of red.

"And now? What will happen?"

"What might happen," Frau Hinkel reminded her, fixed on the cards. "Still two. Decide on the man. If you have done that, then you will be at peace. You have had sorrow in your life. Now I see—" She stopped, scooping her cards together, and when she began again her voice had become airier, now truly the voice of a fortune cookie. Good health. Prosperity. Love given and received.

When Lena gave her the money, smiling, Frau Hinkel patted her hand in a kind of benediction. But as she opened the curtain for them, it was Jake's arm she took, holding him back.

"A moment," she said, waiting until Lena was in the other room. "I don't like to say. What will be. It's not my place."

"What is it?"

"Her cards are not good. You cannot hide everything with hearts.

Some trouble. I tell you this because I see your cards mixed with hers. If you are the protector, protect her."

For a second, flabbergasted, Jake didn't know whether to laugh or be furious. Was this how she got them all to come back, time after time, some worrying trick? Thoughts that go bump in the night. A *hausfrau* with a waiting room full of anxious widows.

"Maybe she'll meet a handsome stranger instead. I'll bet you see a lot of those in the cards."

She smiled weakly. "Yes, it's true. I know what you think." She glanced toward the other room. "Well, what's the harm?" She turned to him again. "But who's to say? Sometimes it's right. Sometimes the cards surprise even me."

"Fine. I'll keep an eye out—looking both ways."

"As you wish," she said, dismissing him by turning her back.

"What did she want?" Lena said at the door.

"Nothing. Some American cigarettes."

They started down the stairs, Lena quiet.

"Well, there goes fifty marks," Jake said.

"But she knew things," Lena said. "How did she know?"

"What things?"

"What did she mean—close to death, a woman?"

"Who knows? More mumbo-jumbo."

"No, I saw you look at her. It meant something to you. Tell me." She stopped at the doorway, away from the glare of the street.

"Remember the girl in Gelferstrasse? At the billet? She was killed the other day. An accident. I was standing next to her, so I thought she meant that. That's all."

"An accident?"

"Yes."

"Why didn't you tell me before?"

"I didn't want to worry you. It was just an accident."

"Frau Hinkel didn't think so."

"Well, what does she know?"

"She knew about the children," Lena said, looking down.

"Two."

"Yes, two. My Russian child. How could she know that?" She looked away, upset. "A mother's cards. And I killed it. No hearts for that one."

"Come on, Lena." He put his hand to her chin and lifted it. "It's all foolishness. You know that."

"Yes, I know. It was just the child. I don't like to think about that. To kill a child."

"You didn't. It's not the same thing."

"It feels the same. Sometimes I dream about it, you know? That it's grown. A boy."

"Stop," Jake said, smoothing her hair.

She nodded into his hand. "I know. Only the future." She raised her head, as if she were physically pushing the mood away, and took his hand in hers, tracing the palm with her finger. "And that's me?"

"Yes."

"Such a line. In a man," she said, doing Frau Hinkel's voice.

Jake smiled. "They have to get something right or people won't come. Now, how about the bath?"

She turned his hand over to see his wristwatch. "Oh, but look. Now it's late. I'm sorry." She leaned up and kissed him, a peck. "I won't be long. And what will you do?" she said as they started for the square.

"I'm going to find us a new place to stay."

"Why? Hannelore's not so bad."

"I just think it's a good idea."

"Why?" She stopped. "There's something else you're not telling me."

"I don't want you to be bait anymore."

"What about Emil?"

"Hannelore's still there, if he comes."

She looked up at him. "You mean you don't think he's coming. Tell me."

"I think it's possible the Russians have him."

"No, I won't believe that," she said, so quickly that Jake looked over at her, disturbed. Two lines.

"I said it's possible. The man who got him out of Kransberg had Russian money. I think he was selling information—where Emil was. I don't want them getting to you."

"Russians," she said to herself. "They want me?"

"They want Emil. You're his wife."

"They think I would go with them? Never."

"They don't know that." They started again across the square, where the women were still sorting bricks. "It's just a precaution."

She looked up at their building, standing whole in the stretch of damage. "It's not safe anymore? I always felt safe there. All during the war, I knew it would be all right."

"It's still safe. I just want something safer."

"The protector," Lena said wryly. "So she was right."

"Come on, get in," he said, swinging up into the jeep.

She glanced again at the building, then climbed in, waiting for him to start the motor. "Safe. At the hospital they wanted me to be a nun. Wear the robes, you know? 'Put this on, you'll be safe,' they said. But I wasn't."

Pastor Fleischman had lost whatever flesh he'd had—rail thin, with an Adam's apple jutting out over his white collar. He was waiting in front of Anhalter Station with a handcart, so that in his clerical suit he looked, oddly, like a porter.

"Lena. I was getting worried. See what I found." He pointed to the cart. "Oh, but a car—" He looked eagerly at the jeep.

Lena turned to Jake, embarrassed. "You wouldn't mind? I don't like to ask—I know it's not permitted. But they're so tired after the train. It's such a long way to walk. You'll help?"

"No problem," he said to the pastor, then extended his hand and introduced himself. "How many are you expecting?"

"I'm not sure. Perhaps twenty. It's very kind."

"We'll have to take them in shifts, then," Jake said, but the pastor merely nodded, unconcerned with details, as if the Lord would multiply the jeep, like the loaves and the fishes.

They waited on the crowded platform, open to the sky through a rib cage of twisted girders. Fleischman had brought another woman to help, and while she and Lena talked, Jake leaned back against a pillar, smoking and watching the crowd. People sitting around in clumps, dispirited, holding on to rucksacks and bags, the usual station clamor slowed to a kind of listless stupor. A pack of teenage boys, feral, looking for something to snatch. A Russian soldier wandering up and down, probably after a girl. Tired women. Everything ordinary, what passed for peace. He remembered his going-away party, the platform alive with champagne and crispy uniforms, Renate winking, getting away with something.

"How is it you speak German?" Fleischman asked, something polite to pass the time.

"I used to live in Berlin."

"Ah. Do you know Texas?"

"Texas?"

"Well, forgive me. An American. Of course, it's a large country. There's a church, you see. Fredericksburg, Texas. A Lutheran church, so I think maybe German people once. They've offered to take some of the children. Of course, it's a chance for them. A future. But to send them so far, after everything—I don't know. How do I select?"

"How many do they want?"

"Five. They can take five." He sighed. "Now we send our children. Well, God will take care of them."

Just as he did here, Jake thought, looking at the scorched wall.

"They're orphans?"

Fleischman nodded. "From the Sudeten. The parents were killed during the expulsion. Then Silesia. Now here. Tomorrow, who knows? Cowboys."

"I'm sure they're good people, if they offered."

"Yes, yes, I know. It's the selection. How do I select?"

He moved away, not expecting an answer, before Jake could say anything. Names in a hat. Outside, the light was fading. People were still milling aimlessly. The train was now an hour late.

"I'm sorry," Lena said. "I didn't know. Do you want to leave?"

"No, I'm fine. Here, sit. Get some rest." He sank to the bottom of the pillar, pulling her down with him, her head against his shoulder.

"It's boring for you."

"No, gives me time to think."

But what he thought about, his mind drifting in the half wakefulness of waiting, was the cards, eyes facing in two directions. Deception. Nonsense. He wished he had a crossword puzzle, where one clue led to another, rational. A man gets on a plane, one across. With no baggage but a piece of information, the one thing you didn't have to carry. Worth money. Russian. So information to a Russian. In Potsdam.

Where he's dead by nightfall. How did he spend the rest of the day? Not looking for Emil. But neither was the Russian at Professor Brandt's. A possibility, Gunther had said, they already know where he is. But then who wanted Tully dead? Not the paymaster, presumably, or why pay in the first place? Maybe he just got in the way. Whose?

His head dropped onto his chest, nudging his eyes open. For a second he wondered if he was really awake. The station had grown black, dotted with harsh little pools of light from a row of bare bulbs strung between the pillars, a dream landscape where things crept in the dark. Lena was still leaning against him, breathing softly, safe. He closed his eyes. You couldn't solve a crossword without the key. No matter which way he worked it, the central piece was always Emil, who knew where the columns met. Without him, it was just tea leaves, the chance arrangement of cards. Sometimes they surprise even me. But people heard what they wanted to hear.

The shriek of the train whistle woke everybody. People scrambled to their feet, the dim rails suddenly growing brighter as the engine headlight inched its way toward the platform, as if the weight were too much for the engine to pull. People covered the roofs of the cars and hung along the sides, perched on running boards or just holding on to whatever piece of metal was available, like the trains he'd seen in Egypt, bursting with *fellaheen.* A few boxcars with feet dangling from the open sliding doors. Everyone worn and stiff, so that when they dropped onto the platform they moved slowly, awkward with cramps. A hiss, finally, of exhausted steam, and a clang of brakes. Now the platform crowd moved forward with their bundles, shoving to get on even before the train had emptied. In the confusion, Pastor Fleischman was running back and forth, trying to locate his charges. He waved Lena over. Frau Schaller, the other helper, was already lifting children off the train.

Their heads had been shaved for delousing, skeletal. Short pants, legs like sticks, slips of paper hanging on strings around their necks as makeshift IDs, faces dazed. As people pushed around them, they stood fixed, blinking. A few had dark blotches on their skin.

"Look at that. Have they been beaten?" Jake said.

"No, it's the edema. From no food. Any sore will bruise."

Pastor Fleischman began loading the smaller ones into the handcart while the others looked on blankly, huddled together. No luggage.

A little girl with mucus crusted under her nose. Another story *Collier's* would never run—who had really lost the war.

Jake leaned over to help with the loading, reaching for one of the younger boys, but the child reared back, screaming, *"Nein! Nein!"* Some of the platform crowd turned in alarm. Lena stepped between them, bent down, and spoke softly to the boy. She looked back over her shoulder at Jake.

"It's the uniform. He's afraid of soldiers. Say something in German."

"I only want to help," Jake said to him. "But you can go with the lady if you like."

The boy stared at him, then hid behind Lena.

"It's like this sometimes," she said, apologetic. "Any uniform."

Jake turned to another child. "Are you afraid of me?"

"No. Kurt's afraid. He's young. See how he wet himself?" Then he pointed to Jake's pocket. "Do you have chocolate?"

"Not today. I'm sorry. I'll bring you some tomorrow."

The boy looked down—too long away to imagine.

Frau Schaller had opened a bag and was handing out chunks of bread, which the children held to their chests as they ate. They began moving down the platform, Pastor Fleischman pulling the cart, the others straggling behind, Lena and Frau Schaller herding from the rear. The older children were looking around, eyes wide. Not the Berlin they'd heard about all their lives, Ku'damm lights and leafy boulevards. Instead, swarms of refugees and fire-blackened walls and, through the arches, dark mounds of brick. But the grown-ups were reacting in the same way, literally staggering through the doors. Now that they were here, where did they go? Jake thought of the weary DPs in the Tiergarten that first day, just moving.

They managed to squeeze the youngest group into the jeep, Lena holding the boy who'd wet himself. The nursery was in a church in Schöneberg, and before they were halfway there the children had begun to nod off, back in the rocking motion of the train. No sense of where they were, the streets a maze of moonlit ruins. What about the people who hadn't been met? Jake remembered walking out of Tempelhof that day, as confused as the refugees tonight, getting lost in the streets on the way to Hallesches Tor. And he knew Berlin. But of course they had been met, Breimer bundled into his official car, Liz and Jake piling in with Ron, everyone taken care of. Except Tully. How was it possible? A hasty trip, as if he'd been summoned, Brian thought. Left to find his way through the debris, someone who didn't know Berlin? He must have been met. Berlin sprawled. Potsdam was miles away. No taxis here, Ron had said. Certainly not to Potsdam. Someone in the crowd at Tempelhof. He thought of Liz's picture of Ron, a fuzzy background of uniforms. Why couldn't she have taken one of Tully, made everything easier? He must have been there somewhere, one of the blurs in the doorway. While Jake had been staring across the street at rubble, missing it. Take another look. Maybe it was there, the connection. No one just arrived in Berlin, except refugees from Silesia.

The church basement had been fitted out with a few cots and rows of mattresses scavenged from bomb sites. In one corner an old woodstove was heating soup. The room was bare—no crayoned drawings or cutouts, no piles of toys. As he watched Lena settle the children, he saw for the first time how exhausting the work must be, keeping them busy with imaginary games. Kurt still clung to her, burying his head whenever Jake caught his eye, but the others raced for the stove. "I'd better get the rest before the soup goes," Jake said, relieved to have an excuse to get out.

The return trip took longer. Fleischman insisted on bringing the cart and hanging it over the back with his body wedged against it for support, so that each bump in the road threatened to dislodge it with a crash. They seemed to move by inches, as slow as the train. At the church, it finally did fall, then needed a heave to turn it upright.

"Thank you. It's for the wood, you see. Otherwise, the stove—"

Jake imagined him working his way through the rubble in his white collar, picking up splintered pieces of furniture.

They had to carry the sleeping children in, dead weight, even the thinnest of them heavy. When he got to the basement doorway, a boy's head against his chest, Lena looked up and smiled, the same unguarded welcome as at Frau Hinkel's, but softer now, as if they'd already been to bed and were holding each other.

The soup was watery cabbage thickened by a few chunks of potato, but the children finished all of it and sprawled on the mattresses, waiting for sleep. A line for the one toilet, some squabbling, refered by an exhausted Fleischman. Lena washing faces with a damp cloth. An endless night. The girl with the mucus was crying, comforted by Frau Schaller stroking her hair.

"What will happen to them?" Jake asked Fleischman.

"The DP camp in Teltowerdamm. It's not bad—there's food, at least. But still, you know, a camp. We try to find places. Sometimes people are willing, for the extra rations. But of course it's difficult. So many."

The few children still awake were given books, the old bedtime ritual, Lena and Frau Schaller reading to them in murmurs. Jake picked one up. A children's picture book of Bible stories, left over from Sunday school. His German could manage that. He sat down with the chocolate eater and opened the book.

"Moses," the boy said, showing off.

"Yes."

He read a little, but the boy seemed more interested in the picture, content just to sit next to him and gaze. Egypt, exactly the way it still was, everyone's first imaginary landscape—the blue river, bullrushes, a boy on a donkey turning a waterwheel, date palms in a thin strip of green, then brown desert running to the top of the page. In the picture, women had come down to the water's edge to rescue the floating wicker basket, excited, in a huddle, just the way they had pulled Tully out in Potsdam. Drifting toward shore.

But Moses was supposed to be found, set into the current toward a better future. Tully had been flung in to disappear. How? Thrown from the bridge leading to town? Dragged in until the water took him? Dead weight, a grown man, much heavier than an emaciated child, a struggle for someone. Why bother at all? Why not just leave him where he'd fallen? What was another body in Berlin, where the rubble was still full of them?

Jake looked at the picture again, the excited women. Because Tully wasn't meant to be found. Jake tried to think what this meant. Not enough to get rid of him; he had to vanish. First simply AWOL, then missing, a deserter, then finally irretrievable, a file nobody would follow up. Nothing to investigate, permanently out of the way, every trace, even the dog tags, supposedly at the bottom of the Jungfernsee with him. But the riding boots had slipped off, not held by laces, and he'd floated, carried by the water and the wind until a Russian soldier had fished him out, like Pharaoh's daughter. Where he wasn't supposed to be found.

He looked up to find Lena watching him, her face drawn, so tired her eyes seemed weak, almost brimming. The boy had fallen asleep against his shoulder.

"We can go. Inge will stay with them."

Jake moved the boy gently onto the mattress and covered him.

Pastor Fleischman thanked him as he walked them to the door, a formal courtesy. "About the climate? It's hot there. So perhaps I should send the healthiest." He sighed. "How can I select?"

Jake looked back at the sleeping children, curled up in clumps under the blankets. "I don't know," he said.

"He's a good man," Lena said in the jeep. "You know, the Nazis arrested him. He was in Oranienberg. And the parishioners got him out. It was unusual, to do that."

What it was like, day to day. A waitress collecting a check, a thousand cruelties, then the odd act of grace.

"Did you know him before? I mean, was this your church?"

"No. Why?"

"I was wondering if anyone could trace you through him."

"Oh," she said quietly.

He glanced at her, her head nodding, not yet asleep but drowsy, as peaceful as one of the children. Not just bait but living with a man asking questions, vulnerable either way. There had to be another place, somewhere nobody knew. But who had flats? Generals' girls and whores.

"You passed the street," she mumbled as he sped up Tauentzienstrasse toward the Memorial Church.

"I have to make a stop. Just for a minute."

He double-parked in front of Ronny's in a row of jeeps.

"Here?" she said, puzzled.

"I won't be long." He turned to one of the waiting drivers. "Do me a favor, will you, and keep an eye on the lady?"

"Now I need a guard?" Lena said softly.

"Watch her yourself," the GI said, then took in Jake's uniform patch and stood up. "Sir," he said with a salute.

There was the usual blare of music as he went through the door, a trumpet leading "Let Me Off Uptown," loud even in the noisy room.

The club seemed more crowded than before, but Danny still had his own corner table, Noël Coward hair slicked back, drumming his fingers to the music, a permanent piece of the furniture. Only one girl tonight, and next to him Gunther, staring into a glass.

"Well, here's a treat," Danny said. "Come to cheer old Gunther up, have you?" He nudged Gunther, who barely managed an acknowledging glance before going back to his glass. "Bit down in the dumps, he is. *Not* the best advert for the girls. You remember Trude?" A hopeful smile from the blonde.

"Got a second?" Jake said. "I need a favor."

Danny stood up. "Such as?"

"Can you fix me up with a room? A flat, if you've got it."

"For yourself?"

"A lady," Jake said, leaning closer, not wanting to be overheard.

"How long do you need?" Danny said, glancing at his watch.

"No. A place to live."

"Oh, you don't want to be getting mixed up in that. Get their hooks in and then what? You want to spread the wealth. Cheaper in the end."

"Can you do it?"

Danny looked at him narrowly, ready for business. "It'll cost you."

"That's all right. But nobody's to know." He met Danny's eyes. "She has a husband. Can you fix it with the landlord?"

"Well, that'd be me, wouldn't it?"

"You own it?"

"I told you, nothing like property. You see how it comes in handy. Mind, I'll have to chuck somebody out—they won't like that a bit. They'll need a little something for relocation. That'd be extra."

"Done."

Danny glanced up, surprised not to have to bargain. "Right. Give me a day."

"And not with the other girls. I don't want people coming and going."

"Respectable, like."

"Yes."

"Well, it's your lookout. Smoke?" He opened a gold cigarette case, a prop from *Private Lives.* "Take my advice, don't do it. You don't want to settle in, makes it worse after. Me, I like a choice."

"I appreciate this," Jake said, ignoring him. He took out some money. "Do you want something down?"

Danny looked away, embarrassed again by actual cash. "You're good for it, aren't you? Friend of Gunther's." He turned and pulled out a chair. "Here, have a drink. Come on, Gunther, share and share alike. Pour out, pour out."

"That's all right," Jake said. "I've got somebody waiting." He nodded at the bottle. "Looks like I'd have a lot of catching up to do. You been here all day?" he said to Gunther.

"No," Gunther said calmly, "working for you." Looking at him steadily, so that Jake understood the trial that morning was to be put aside, something gone with the rest of the bottle. "I spoke to Willi."

"Let me guess," Jake said, sitting down for a minute. "A Russian's been paying him to watch the house."

"Yes."

"Find out about the one in the market? The sharpshooter?"

"I inquired, yes."

"One of Sikorsky's men?"

"He must have been. Vassily said he didn't know, and Vassily knows everyone. So." He looked up. "How did you know?"

"I talked to Shaeffer, the man who was shot. He and Sikorsky have been playing cat and mouse for a couple of weeks now. Sikorsky laid a trap and he walked right into it."

"But the mouse got away. So. You didn't need my services after all. What else do you know?"

"That Tully knew where Brandt was. He didn't just let him go, he sent him there. It was a setup. Then he collects some Russian money. They do connect. That's what he was selling—information about Brandt."

Gunther considered this for a moment, then picked up his drink. "Yes. It was the money that was confusing. So much. People are cheap in Berlin. You can sell them for less."

"Not this one. He's important. Your friend Sikorsky would be interested, for instance."

"My friend," he said, almost snorting. "A business acquaintance." He smiled slightly at Jake's expression. "Everybody does a little business."

"The Russians must have Emil. You thought so this morning."

A nod. "It's the logic. And you think Vassily would tell me? On these matters, I'm afraid, a man of principle. If he knows."

"Then maybe he'll tell you who drove Tully to Potsdam. I've been thinking about that. How did he get there?"

"The general is not a chauffeur, Herr Geismar."

"Somebody met Tully at the airport. Somebody drove him to Potsdam and killed him. It had to be a Russian."

"The same man?"

"What do you mean?"

"Would you spend all day with someone you intended to kill? What would you do with him all day? No, you would do it." He made a chopping motion with the side of his hand.

"He's got you there, mate," Danny said, surprising Jake, who'd forgotten he was at the table.

"But the driver, anyway," Jake said, annoyed at being interrupted, "he'd be Russian. Why not ask?"

"Because you would learn nothing," Gunther said, serious. "Nothing. And you would make yourself—conspicuous. Never be conspicuous with the Russians. Not a patient people. They strike." He lifted a finger for emphasis. "Keep your head down until you know. Be a policeman, follow the numbers."

"This is where they lead."

Gunther shrugged. "The airport, yes, that's interesting. The driver, what would that tell me? Unless it's the same man—but how could that be?" He shook his head. "It's the wrong question. Besides, you know, I have my interests to protect."

"Yeah. Everybody does a little business."

Gunther took a drink, looking down into the glass. "You forget, I'm a friend to the Soviet peoples." The accented German of the prosecutor, bitter, the trial still there after all. "Who knows?" he said, almost airy now, playing with it. "Maybe soon an employee. The general admires my work. There are not so many opportunities."

"You'd work for him?" Jake said, thrown by this. "You'd work for the Russians?"

"My friend, what difference does it make? When you leave, who will be here? We have to live. Calm yourself," he said, waving his hand, "for now it's not attractive. I'm working on a case." He raised his glass, a reassuring toast.

"You see?" Danny said. "That's what he likes. Old Sherlock. It's not the money with him."

"Then I'll try to keep you interested," Jake said, getting up. He looked down at Gunther, placidly draining his glass. "That's quite a future you have in mind, you and Vassily. You know, he was in the market when Shaeffer got hit. I guess that would make him the *greifer.*"

Gunther lowered the glass, drawn by the word. His face was slack, eyes lost and empty like one of the children on the platform. He looked at Jake for a moment, then grunted, slowly moving the glass aside, pushing it out of sight with everything else. "Be careful he doesn't become yours," he said, his voice composed, neutral.

"But—," Jake said, then stopped.

"But you have someone waiting," Gunther said. "The other matter we discussed—the living arrangements?"

"It's taken care of," Jake said, deliberately not looking at Danny.

"Good. Sometimes it's enough, just moving." He looked down. "Of course, not always."

Outside, the street was full of drivers, bored privates in khaki standing by while their officers danced. The GI on guard duty was talking to Lena, leaning casually against the jeep.

"He says he knows Texas," she said, smiling as Jake approached. "There are hills there, so that's good."

It took Jake a second, preoccupied, to realize she was back with the children.

"That's right, lots of hills," the soldier said in a cowpoke drawl. Any driver, maybe even him, pulled out of the pool to escort the visitor around.

"They'll like that," she said as Jake started the motor. "Like home." Rolling Silesian hills.

"Let's hope so."

"What were you doing?"

"Seeing a man about a place. We can have it tomorrow." He swung into the street.

"So soon."

"Why not? There's not much to pack."

"Oh, it's easy for you. That's how you live. A gypsy," she said, but smiling.

"Well, I'm used to it," he said. Tents and hotels and rented rooms.

"No, you like it."

He glanced over at her. "Will you?"

"Of course," she said, a forced brightness. "We'll be gypsies. One suitcase. You don't think I can do it?"

He smiled. "Well, maybe two cases."

There was no one in the street outside the flat, still safe, and no one inside either, Hannelore's party, as expected, running late.

"I have to wash," she said. "I won't be long. Look at the mess she's left. Well, I won't miss that."

"I'll clean it up."

"No, in the morning. It's so late. Am I standing up?"

But when the bathroom door closed, he went over to the sink anyway, thinking of when she'd been sick, washing the dishes to fill the time, waiting for the doctor, tidying up as a kind of medicine. Only three weeks ago. There wasn't much to do—cups, some scattered papers near the typewriter. Most of his clothes were at Gelferstrasse. Not even one suitcase. It would take only minutes to leave, another room. And yet it occurred to him that Frau Hinkel was wrong—he was home here, all the years before the war, then these last weeks when it seemed a kind of sanctuary, here longer than anywhere he'd ever been. His place. Nothing remarkable—the rumpled sofa where Hal used to pass out, the table where Lena had sat with coffee, sunlight pouring across her robe; his private piece of Berlin. But not a refuge anymore, a trap.

He heard the click of the door as Lena left the bathroom, and he walked over to the window, turning out the light behind him. Nothing. Wittenbergplatz was quiet. He looked up and down the street, eyes in two directions. Maybe Frau Hinkel was wrong about that too. But U-boats kept moving. His cards were lucky. Pariserstrasse was rubble, in a day this flat would be gone, but Lena was still here, brushing out her hair probably, sitting on the bed in her nightgown, waiting for him. He looked around in the dark. Just rooms.

In the bathroom he brushed his teeth, then washed off the day's layer of grime, coming alive with the water. She'd be wearing the prewar silk, a sentimental choice for their last night here, straps hanging loose on her shoulders. Maybe already packing, ready to go somewhere new. But when he opened the door, he saw her lying on the bed in the dim lamplight, curled up like one of the children, eyes closed. A long day. He stood for a moment looking at her face, damp from the heat, but not the fever of those days when he'd kept watch. A few of her things had been folded in a neat pile. Life in a suitcase, the last thing she wanted, but she'd said it. He turned off the light, undressed, and slipped quietly onto his side of the bed, trying not to wake her, thinking of that first night, when they hadn't made love either, just lay together. He turned on his side and she stirred.

"Jacob," she said, only half awake. "Oh, I'm sorry."

"It's all right. Go to sleep."

"No, I wanted—"

"Ssh." He smoothed her forehead, whispering. "Get some sleep. Tomorrow. We'll go to the lakes." Like a bedtime promise to a child.

"A boat," she murmured vaguely, not really following, still drowsy. "All right." A pause. "Thank you for everything," she said, oddly polite.

"Any time," he said, smiling at her words.

In the quiet he thought she had drifted off, but she moved closer, facing him, eyes now open. She put her hand on his cheek. "Do you know something? I've never loved you as much as I did tonight."

"When was that, exactly?" he said softly. "So I can do it again."

"Don't joke," she said, leaning her head into his. She stroked his cheek. "Never so much. When you read to him. I saw how it would have been. If nothing had happened."

He saw her eyes in the basement again, not tired, brimming with something else, a sadness out of reach, hanging in the air between them like rubble dust.

"Sleep," he said. He moved his hand up to close her eyes, but she took it in hers.

"Let me see it again," she said, tracing. "Yes, there." Satisfied, her eyes closing finally.

CHAPTER THIRTEEN

BRIAN HAD BEEN as good as his word. Jake's name was listed at the Grunewald yacht club and the boat was his for a signature.

"He said you'd be by," the British soldier said at the marina landing. "I'll have Roger bring it round for you. Know how to handle a sail?" Jake nodded. "'Course, she's only a sunny. Nothing to it. Still, we like to ask. Some of the lads—" He jerked his head toward the terrace café, where soldiers sat drinking beer under a row of flapping Union Jacks, one table in kilts, still in parade dress. "Wait here, I won't be a sec."

Lena was standing with her face to the sun, oblivious to everything but the day. There was a breeze off the lake, fresh, not even a trace of the city's smell.

The boat was a small single-masted sailboat scarcely big enough for two, with a toylike tiller and oars. It bobbed unsteadily when Jake stepped in, so that he planted his feet apart and held the dock piling before he reached for Lena's hand, but she grinned at his concern, slipping off her shoes and leaping in, surefooted, her skirt blowing up in the breeze. Half the terrace seemed to be watching, heads tilted to catch her legs.

"Sit first," she said to Jake, in control, then pushed the boat off.

"Watch the current," the soldier said. "It's not really a lake, you know. People forget."

Lena nodded, stretching the sail out along the jib, an old hand. They began moving on the water.

"I didn't know you were a sailor," Jake said, watching her tie the sail rope.

"I'm from Hamburg. Everyone knows boats there." She looked around, theatrically sniffing the air. "My father liked it. In the summer we used to go to the sea. Always, every summer. He would take me out with him because my brother was too small."

"You have a brother?"

"He was killed. In the army," she said, matter-of-fact.

"I didn't know."

"Yes, Peter. The same name."

"Were there others?"

"No, just him and my parents. There's no one left now from that life. Except Emil." She shrugged and lifted her head again. "Pull to your left, we have to bring it around. My god, what a day. So hot." Deliberately pushing them away from shore.

And in fact, the farther they went, the better it became, away from the war, the burned pockets of woods disappearing in the distance, only the standing pines visible. Not Berlin at all, little waves catching the sun in flashes, postcard blue. He looked across the water, shading his eyes from the glare. Not choked with bodies like the stagnant Landwehrkanal—all flushed to the North Sea with the current, except for what had settled to the bottom, bottles, scraps of shells, even riding boots. The surface, anyway, was bright and clear.

"A brother. I didn't know. What else? I want to know everything about you."

"So you can decide?" she said, smiling, determined to be cheerful. "Too late. You've already had the sample. It's like Wertheim's—no returns permitted, sales final."

"Wertheim's never said that."

"No? Well, I do." She flicked some water over the side at him.

"That's all right. I don't want to return anything."

She sat back against the prow, hiking her skirt up to her thighs, stretching her white legs in the sun.

"You look beautiful today."

"You think so? Then let's not go back. We'll live here, on the water."

"Careful you don't burn."

"I don't care. It's healthy."

The breeze had died down, the boat barely moving, as still as a beach. They lay on their backs like sunbathers, eyes closed, talking into the air.

"What will it be like, do you think?" she said, her voice lazy, like the quiet slap of water against the side of the boat.

"What?"

"Our life."

"Why do women always ask that? What happens next."

"So many have asked you that?"

"Every single one."

"Maybe we have to plan. What do you tell them?"

"That I don't know."

She trailed her hand in the water. "So that's your answer? 'I don't know'?"

"No. I know."

She said nothing for a minute, then sat up. "I'm going to swim."

"Not here you're not."

"Why not? It's so hot."

"You don't know what's in there."

"You think I'm afraid of fish?" She stood, holding on to the mast to steady the boat.

"Not fish," he said. Bodies. "It's not clean. You could get sick."

"Ouf," she said, waving it off, then reached under to slip off her pants. "You know, during the raids it was like that. Some nights you were afraid of everything. Then others, nothing. No reason, you just knew nothing would happen. And nothing did."

She took off her dress, pulling it over her head, then standing with her arms still up, stretched out, everything white but the patch of hair between her legs, brazen. "Your face," she said, laughing at him. "Don't worry, I won't swallow."

"Come on, Lena. It's not safe."

"Oh, safe." She tossed the dress aside. "You see, a gypsy," she said, flinging her arms out. She glanced back. "Hold the boat," she said, still pragmatic. "You don't want it to swamp." And then with a light bounce she was over, slicing into the water, her splash spraying the boat as it rocked in her wake.

He leaned over the side, watching her glide beneath the surface, long arms pushing back the water in smooth arcs, hair streaming behind her toward the round curve of her hips, a free streak of white flesh, so graceful that for a second he wondered if he had made her up, just an idea of a woman. But she bobbed up, spitting water and laughing, real.

"You look like a mermaid," he said.

"With fins," she said, rolling on her back in a fluid movement to point her toes upward, then slapping the water with them. "It's wonderful, like silk. Come."

"I'll watch."

She plunged down in a backward dive, making a circle underwater, performing. When she came back up she floated again, eyes closed to the sun, her skin glistening in the light. He looked across the water. They had drifted closer to the Grunewald shore, and he could make out the beach where they'd stood that day when the rain had caught them. Closed into herself, not even wanting to kiss, then shivering on the drive through the woods. Dancing to the records, wanting to come back to life. He thought of her moving down the stairs in Liz's shoes, tentative. Now splashing like a porpoise in the bright sun, somebody else, a girl who would jump off a boat. Lucky cards.

She swam over and held the side of the boat.

"Had enough?" he said.

"In a minute. It's so cool. When do we have to go back?"

"Whenever. I don't want to move till it's dark."

"Like thieves. Where is it?"

"I don't know yet."

"I have to tell Professor Brandt. He won't know where I am."

"I don't want him to. They're watching his house."

"For Emil?"

"For you."

"Oh," she said, then ducked her head in the water, still holding on to the side.

"I'll have somebody check on him, don't worry."

"It's just that he's alone. There's no one."

"Not Emil, that's for sure. He said he was dead."

"Dead? Why would he say that?"

Jake shrugged. "Dead to him, maybe. I don't know. That's what he said when they questioned him at Kransberg."

"So they wouldn't bother him. Arrest him. The Gestapo did that—took the families."

"The Allies aren't the Gestapo."

She looked up at him. "Well, it's different for you. When you think that way—" She turned back to the water. "Did he say I was dead too?"

"No, he wanted to find you. That was the trouble. That's how everything started."

"Then why not let him? And finish it? I don't want to hide."

"He's not the only one looking now."

She glanced up, a flicker of concern, then turned her face to the sun and pushed away from the boat.

"Lena—"

"I can't hear you," she said, swimming away in long strokes. He watched her head toward the club, just a speck in the distance, then turn over and float back toward the boat, lying suspended in the still water. Tully would have done the same, except it had been windy that night, enough to stir the waves, pushing the body along.

Getting back in the boat took longer than diving out, an awkward pull up, one leg flung over the side to prevent it from tipping. She shook herself, squeezing out her hair, then lay back again to dry in the sun.

After that they were content to drift in the gentle rocking motion, like Moses in his basket. The boat had turned again, facing down toward the Pfaueninsel, where Goebbels had given his Olympics party. No lights now, half the trees gone, the dreary look of a cemetery island. Bodies must have landed here with the other debris, bobbing sluggishly, like Tully's at the Cecilienhof, floating in circles until he'd ended up where he wasn't supposed to be found.

Jake felt a few drops on his face. Not rain, Lena sprinkling him awake.

"We'd better start back. There's not much wind—it'll take time." She was sitting up, having slipped on the dress while he was drifting.

"Let the current do it," he said lazily, his eyes still closed. "It'll take us right past the club."

"No, it's the wrong way."

He waved his fingers. "Simple geography. North of the Alps, the rivers flow north. South, south. We don't have to do a thing."

"In Berlin you do. The Havel flows south, then it curves up. Look at any map."

But the maps just showed a string of blue, off in the left-hand corner.

"Look where we are already," Lena said, "if you don't believe me."

He raised his head and looked over the side of the boat. The club was off in the distance; still no wind.

"You see? If you don't turn around, we'll end up in Potsdam."

He sat upright, almost knocking his head against the mast. "What did you say?"

"We'll end up in Potsdam," she repeated, puzzled. "That's where the river goes."

He looked around at the bright water, turning his head in a swivel, scanning the shore.

"But that's it. He wasn't put in there. He never *went* there."

"What?"

"He just ended up there. He didn't *go* there. The where was wrong." Turning his head again, scanning, as if the rest of it would come now in a rush, one piece unlocking all the others. But there was only the long Grunewald shore. So where did he go?

"What are you talking about?"

"Tully. He never went to Potsdam. Somewhere else. Do you have a map?"

"Nobody has maps except the army," she said, still puzzled, watching his face.

"Gunther has one. Come on, let's go back," he said, eager, pushing the tiller to make a circle. "The current. Why didn't I think of it before? Moses. Christ, it was right there. Thank you." He blew her a kiss.

A nod, but no smile, her face frowning, as if the day had turned cloudy.

"Who's Gunther?"

"A policeman. Friend of mine. He didn't think of it either, and he's supposed to know Berlin."

"Maybe not the water," she said, looking down at it.

"But you did," he said, smiling.

"So now we're all policemen," she said, then turned her face back up to the sun. "Well, not yet. Look how still it is. We can't go back yet."

But the idea seemed to produce its own momentum, refusing to wait, and in a few minutes brought a slight, steady breeze that blew them back to the club in no time.

Gunther was at home in Kreuzberg, sober and shaved. Even the room was tidied up.

"A new leaf?" Jake said, but Gunther ignored him, his eyes fixed on Lena.

"And this must be Lena," he said, taking her hand. "Now I see why Herr Brandt was so anxious to come to Berlin."

"But not to Potsdam. He never went there. Tully, I mean. Here, come look," Jake said, walking over to the map.

"American manners," Gunther said to Lena. "Some coffee, perhaps? It's fresh-made."

"Thank you," she said, both of them walking through a formal ritual.

"He lives on coffee," Jake said.

"I'm German. Sugar?" He poured out a cup and indicated his reading chair for her.

"The Havel flows south," Jake said. "The body floated to Potsdam. We were on the water today. It flows this way." He moved his hand down the map. "That's how he got there."

Gunther stood for a moment, taking this in, then walked over to the map, staring at the left-hand corner. "So, no Russian driver."

"No Russian driver. It solves the where."

Gunther raised an eyebrow. "And this makes you excited? Before, you had only Potsdam. Now you have all of Berlin."

"No, somewhere here," Jake said, making a circle around the lakes. "It has to be. You don't drive a body across town. You'd have to be near enough to think of it. Where to get rid of it, fast."

"Unless you planned it."

"Then you'd be *on* the water," Jake said, pointing to the shoreline. "To make it easy. I don't think it was planned. They never even took the time to go through his pockets, get his tags. They just wanted to get rid of him. In a hurry. Somewhere nearby—where nobody would find him." He pointed to the center of the blue patch.

Gunther nodded. "An answer for everything," he said, then turned to Lena. "An expert on crime, our Herr Geismar," he said pleasantly. "The coffee's all right?"

"Yes, an expert," Lena said.

"I have been looking forward to this meeting," he said, sitting down. "You don't mind if I ask you a question?"

"Somewhere here," Jake was saying at the map, his hand on the lake.

"Yes, but where?" Gunther said over his shoulder. "It's miles around those lakes."

"Not if you eliminate." He blocked off the western shore with his hand. "Not Kladow, the Russian zone." He moved his hand and covered the bottom. "Not Potsdam. Somewhere along here." He traced his finger from Spandau down to Wannsee, the long swatch of the Grunewald. "Where would he go?"

"A man who spoke only English? I would say to the Americans. In my experience, they prefer it."

Zehlendorf. Jake moved across the woods, the map alive in his hand. Kronprinzenallee, headquarters. The press camp. Gelferstrasse. The Kommandatura, across the street from the KWI, an Emil connection. But the KWI was closed, dark for months. The Grunewald itself?

"What question?" Lena said.

"Forgive me, I was distracted. Just a small point. I was curious about the time your husband came for you. That last week. You know, I was in Berlin then—the Volkssturm, even the police became soldiers at the end. A terrible time."

"Yes."

"Such confusion. Looting, even," he said, shaking his head, as if even now the behavior disturbed him. "How, I wondered, did you know he was here? You didn't see him?"

"The telephone. It was still working, even through that."

"I remember. No water, but still the telephone. So he called?"

"From his father's. He wanted to come for me, but the streets—"

"Yes, dangerous. The Russians were there?"

"Not yet. But near. Between us, I think, but what's the difference? It was impossible. The Germans were just as bad, shooting everybody. I was afraid to leave the hospital. I thought, at least I'll be safe here. Not even the Russians—"

"A terrible thing for him. So close. And after coming so far. The Zoo tower was still secure, I think, but perhaps he didn't know that. To get through that way."

Lena looked up. "You mustn't blame him. He's not a coward."

"My dear lady, I don't blame anyone. Not that week."

"I don't mean that. I told him not to come."

"Ah."

"I was the coward."

"Frau Brandt—"

"No, it's true." She lowered her head and took a sip of coffee. "I was afraid we'd both be killed if he waited. I didn't want another death. It was crazy to come then—there wasn't time. I told him to leave with his father before it was too late. I didn't want to go. I didn't care. It was foolish, but that's how it was. Why do you want to know this?"

"But his father didn't leave either," Gunther said, not answering. "Only the files. Did he mention them?"

"No. What files?"

"A pity. I'm curious about those files. It's how he got the car, I think. You remember there were no cars then. No gas either."

"His father said he came with SS."

"But even they had no cars for personal matters. Not then. So it must have been for the files. What files, do you think?"

"I don't know. You'll have to ask him."

"Or the Americans." He turned around to Jake. "What do the Americans say? Did you find out?"

"Admin files, Shaeffer said. Nothing special. No technical secrets, if that's what you mean."

"Maybe he doesn't know how to read them. Not like our Herr Teitel. A genius with files, that one. In his hands, a weapon." He raised his hand, uncannily like Bernie in the courtroom, the invisible file a kind of gun. "He knows."

"Well, if he does, he isn't saying, and he's been sitting under them for weeks now. It's his home away from home."

"What is?"

Jake stared at him, then turned to the map. "The Document Center," he said quietly, putting his finger down on Wasserkäfersteig, a short line, just a byway off the Grunewald. "The Document Center," he said again, moving his finger left. A straight line across the Grunewald, under the Avus, where they'd stopped in the rain, a straight line to the lake.

"You've thought of something?"

"Tully had an appointment with Bernie, right? The next day. But he came early. Why would anyone want to see Bernie?" He moved his finger back to the street. "Files. Nobody knows those files better than he does. He'd be the man to see." He thought of Bernie racing in to dinner, folders cascading over the startled serving man—the night, in fact, Tully was killed. He tapped his finger on the map. "That's where Tully went. The numbers connect here."

Gunther got up and looked where he was pointing, hand over chin in thought. "Bravo," he said finally. "If he went there. Unfortunately, only he can tell us."

"No, they keep records, a sign-in book. He'd be in there." He looked at Gunther. "Want to bet? Even money."

"No," Gunther said, shaking his head. "Today you have all the answers. But why?"

"To look at files," Jake said, improvising. "Tully was Public Safety too—he didn't need Bernie's permission to do that, just his help. But he came a day early. So he started on his own."

"On Herr Brandt's files," Gunther said. "I assume."

"That's where it connects."

"Where your friend found 'nothing special.' So what did Meister Toll hope to find?" He sighed. "Unfortunately, only he can tell us that too."

"But that's just it. It's still there. Nothing leaves the Document Center. It's like Fort Knox. Whatever he was after is still there."

"Then I suggest you start reading." Gunther touched Jake's shoulder, not quite patting it, and looked at the map again. "Nothing special. And yet Herr Brandt comes to Berlin for them."

"He came for me," Lena said.

"Yes, of course," Gunther said, nodding politely to her. "For you."

"But Tully didn't," Jake said.

"No," Gunther said, turning back to the map, thoughtful.

"Now what?" Jake said, reading his face.

"Nothing. I wonder, how did he know to look?"

"Emil must have said something. They did a lot of talking at Kransberg. They were friends."

"An expensive friend, perhaps."

"How do you mean?"

"Meister Toll—he wasn't the type to do anything for free."

Jake looked at him. "No, he never did anything for free."

It was late, but he had to know, so they made the long drive back to Zehlendorf. The same narrow street rising up from the dark woods, the wire fence spotted with floodlights. A guard chewing gum.

"We're closed, bub. Can't you read?" He jerked his thumb at a posted sign.

"I just want to see the night duty officer."

"No can do."

"For Captain Teitel," Jake said quickly. "He has a message for him."

A name that literally opened doors here, or at least the mesh gate, which instantly swung back.

"She stays here," the guard said. "Make it quick."

The hallway guard, half asleep with his feet propped up on the sign-in desk, seemed startled to see anyone at this hour. If Tully had been here, it hadn't been late.

"Captain Teitel asked me to check the sign-in book for him."

"What for?"

"Some report. How do I know? Can I see it, or what?"

The guard looked at him, dubious, but pushed the book around, a desk clerk with a hotel register.

"How far back does this go?" Jake said, beginning to leaf through it. "I need July sixteenth."

"What for?"

"Your needle stuck?"

The guard pulled out another book, opening it to the right page for him. Jake started scrolling down, running his finger under the names. A busy day. And suddenly there it was—Lt. Patrick Tully, a script to match the riding boots, showy. Signed in and out, no times. He looked at it for a second, the closest he'd been to him since the Cecilienhof, no longer elusive, caught where the numbers connected. He took the photograph from his breast pocket, an off chance.

"You ever see this guy?"

"What are you, an MP?"

"You see him?"

He glanced at the picture. "Not that I know of. You get people in and out here. After a while, they all look alike. What did he do?"

"Anybody takes a file, they sign it out, right?"

"Nobody takes files out of here. Can't."

"Teitel does."

"No, he brings them *in*. Nothing goes out unless you brought it in the first place. Not while I'm on duty, anyway."

"Okay, thanks. That's all I needed."

The guard began to pull the open book back.

"Wait a minute," Jake said, his eye caught by a florid signature. A few names down, Breimer, a rounded B. And underneath, Shaeffer. Where they'd gone that evening.

"Anything wrong?"

Jake shook his head, then closed the book. "I don't know."

Outside he stood for a moment, struck by the lights, just as he had when he'd walked into Liz's picture. Shaeffer had been here that day too. Two visits.

"Did you get what you wanted?" Lena said in the jeep.

"Yes, he was here. I was right."

"And the files?"

"Tomorrow. Come on, we'll go home. You got some sun."

She looked down at her skin, red under the floodlights.

"Yes, you were right about that too," she said with an edge.

"What's the matter?" Jake said as the jeep started down the hill.

"Nothing. They're so important, the files?"

"Tully thought so. He was here—I knew it."

"More numbers, for Emil's weapons. That's what's in them—numbers?"

"Not according to Shaeffer."

"But Emil came for them. That's what the policeman thinks. Not for me."

"Maybe he came for both."

"To make more weapons? The war was finished."

"To trade. That's what they have, the scientists—numbers to trade."

"For what?"

Jake shrugged. "Their future."

"To make weapons for someone else," Lena said.

Jake turned left at the bottom of the hill, then jogged right toward the woods.

"Where are you going?"

"I want to see how it worked. How long it took."

"What?"

"To dump the body."

She said nothing, hunching into herself the way she had the last time in the woods, shivering from the rain. The Grunewald was dark, nothing visible beyond the arc of their headlights and a small patch of moon reflecting on Krumme Lanke. No one in the road, the thick trees hiding whoever might be there, small bands of DPs looking for shelter. No one to see them either. The body could have been slumped over like a drunk. Easy. Anywhere along here, not the center with its guards and lights; here, in the dark. Or on the beach itself. In minutes they were there, the water rippling with moonlight. The last thing Tully might have seen.

Danny had a shrewd eye for real estate. His building, an art nouveau block on one of the side streets off Savignyplatz, had once been elegant and would always be well located. The flat was on the first floor, its door wedged open by a suitcase and some pillowcases stuffed with clothes, last minute packing.

"Don't worry, I'm leaving," the girl said when she saw them. Almost pretty, with ankle-strap heels and lipstick, an annoyed expression twisting her face. "He said by ten. Vultures." This to herself as she flung a skirt into the last bag.

"I'm sorry," Lena said, embarrassed.

"Ha."

Lena turned away and leaned against the wall to wait, not looking at Jake. Halfway down the hall a man carrying a rucksack was coming out of another flat. He squinted and then, recognizing them, walked over and took off his hat.

"Hello again. How are you feeling?"

"Oh, the doctor."

"Yes. Rosen. You're well?"

Lena nodded. "I never had the chance to thank you."

He waved this off, then turned to Jake, the same old eyes in the young face. He glanced down at the suitcases.

"She's living here?"

"Just for a while."

Rosen looked again at Lena. "No recurrences? The medicine worked? No fever?"

"No," she said with a polite smile, "just sunburn. What do I do for that?"

He lifted a scolding finger. "Wear a hat."

The girl was glaring at them from the doorway. "Here," she said, handing Jake the key.

"Take care. It's good to see you again," Rosen said to Lena, leaving. "Don't get too much sun." He nodded at the girl. "Marie," he said, then shuffled away.

"So you're the new girl. An American to pay—very nice for you. You already know Rosen?"

"He took care of me when I was ill."

The girl made a face. "That Jew? I won't let him touch me. Not there, with Jew hands."

"He saved my life," Lena said.

"Did he? Very nice for you." She grabbed up one of the bags. "Jews. If it wasn't for them—"

Jake carried their cases through the door to get away.

"I'm sorry to put you out," Lena said, following him.

"Go to hell."

The flat had the disarray of leave-taking, everything angled slightly out of place. In the next room he could see an unmade bed and a wardrobe with the door left open. A scarf had been draped over a lampshade, turning the light a dim red.

"Nice girl," he said.

Lena walked over to the lamp and lifted the scarf, then sank into the easy chair next to it, as if seeing the room had exhausted her.

"There were lots like her." She lighted a cigarette. "She thinks I'm a whore. Is that what this place is?"

"It's a flat. No one will bother you." He glanced out at the street, then drew the curtains.

She smiled wryly, staring at the cigarette. "My mother was right. She said if I came to Berlin I'd end up like that."

"I'll find someplace else if you don't like it."

She looked around the room. "No, it's a good size."

"It'll seem better after we clean it up. You won't even know she was here."

"Jew hands," she said moodily. "There was a girl like that at school. Not even a Nazi, a girl. How do you clean that away?" She drew on the cigarette again, her hand shaking a little. "You know, after the Russians came, they made us see films. Of the camps. Germans, they said, this is what was done in your name. Imagine, they did it for me. So now what? It's my fault too? All that business."

"Nobody says that."

"Yes. The Germans did it, everyone says that. And, you know, somebody did. Somebody did those things." She looked up. "Somebody made the weapons—maybe it's worse. German people. Even my brother. He came on leave, just before— You know what he said? That terrible things were being done there, in Russia, and no one must ever know. And I thought, what things would Peter do? A boy like that. Now I'm glad I don't know. I don't have to think about that. Whatever he did."

"Maybe he didn't do them," Jake said quietly. He sat down next to her. "Lena, what's this about?"

She put out the cigarette, still agitated, pushing it around the ashtray. "I don't want to know what Emil did either. To think of him that way. I don't want to know what's in the files. His numbers. Maybe it's terrible what they were doing, making weapons, but he was my husband. You know, when he came to Berlin, I thought I was saving *him*. Go, I told him, before it's too late. I said it for him. Now you're—"

"Now I'm what?"

"Making him a criminal. For working in the war. So did my brother. So did everybody, even your policeman. Who knows what they did? In my name. Sometimes I think I don't want to be German anymore. Isn't that terrible? Not wanting to be who you are. I don't want to know what they did."

"Lena," he said patiently, "the files are there. They've already been *seen*. Emil handed them over himself. They're not about him."

"Then why do you want to see them?"

"Because I think they can tell us something about the man who was killed. He was in the business of selling information, so what was there to sell? Now, doesn't that make sense?" he said calmly, coaxing a child.

"Yes."

"Then why does it worry you?"

She looked down. "I don't know."

"It's the flat. We'll move."

"It's not the flat," she said dully.

"Then what?"

She folded her hands in her lap. "He came to Berlin for me." She looked up, her voice faltering and dispirited. "He came for me."

He reached over and covered her hand. "So did I."

CHAPTER FOURTEEN

"THE PROBLEM IS the cross-referencing," Bernie said, walking past the rows of file cabinets. "They just threw everything in here and we're still sorting it out. Himmler's personal files are over there, the general SS ones here, but sometimes it pays to check one against the other if dates are missing. You know, what's personal? That's assuming Brandt's files haven't been *mis*filed. Which you can't assume. They got involved in the rocket program in 'forty-three, so you can skip all of these." He waved away half the room. "Program was designated A-four, so we try to keep it all together in an A-four section, but as I say, it pays to cross-check. Here," he said, pulling a drawer, "happy reading."

"And these would be what Brandt turned over?"

"Some of them. Sources aren't indicated, but if they're his, they'd be in here. Of course, the scientific documents were down in Nordhausen. Von Braun buried them for safekeeping—in some old mine, I think—so FIAT's got them, but you only wanted Brandt's, right?"

"Right."

"Then you're here," he said, tapping the cabinet.

"Christ," Jake said, looking at the long row of files.

"Yeah, I know. They were so busy covering ass you wonder when they got time to fight."

"Well, the army. They live on the stuff, don't they? I'd hate to see ours."

"These are a little different," Bernie said. "If you get bored, try the aeromedical files over there. Want to know how long it takes a man to freeze to death? It's all there—blood temp, pressure, right down to the last second. Everything but the screams. I'll be downstairs if you need any help."

But the first folders, at least, were ordinary—memos, staff directives, summary reports, the sort of thing he might have found in any office files, American Dye in Utica, except for the black SS letterheads. A paper trail of a bureaucratic takeover, with a Trojan horse of laborers. Peenemünde had been built with foreign conscripts, but by July '43 the program had needed more, the extra hands only the SS could supply—*häftlinge,* detainees, a memorandum word for prisoners in the death camps. After that first requisition, the fatal bargain, the real files began, thick with dates and events, a flurry of paper between department heads to seize opportunity while it lasted. July 7, an A-4 demonstration for Hitler, who is impressed. July 24, the great fire raid on Hamburg. July 25, A-4 gets a top priority go-ahead to produce its rockets, vengeance weapons. August 18, Peenemünde bombed. August 19, as night follows day, Hitler orders Himmler to provide camp labor to speed production. Three days later, August 21, Himmler takes charge of constructing a new production site at Nordhausen, far away from the bombs. August 23, the first workers arrive, the horse inside the gates.

The next folders followed the race to build Aladdin's cave, clawed out of the mountain to house the vast underground factory. File after file of numbing construction details, weekly progress reports, new camps for workers. Even as Jake's eyes glazed over at the day-to-day tallies, he was watching a whole city take shape, the sheer scale of the thing right there in the numbers. Ten thousand workers. Two giant tunnels reaching two miles back into the mountain; forty-seven cross tunnels, each two football fields long. Bigger every day, the way the pyramids must have been built. The same way, in fact. The ten thousand were slaves. No mention of how many were dying—you had to guess by the requisitions for replacements from Himmler's endless supply. The whole terrible business obscured by engineering estimates and monthly targets. In Berlin, the reports were dated, stamped, and filed away. Had Emil seen them back at Peenemünde, where the scientists gathered at night over coffee to discuss trajectories?

Meanwhile, page by page, the tunnels grow, rockets begin to be built, more camps, and finally the takeover is official—8 August 1944, Hans Kammler, SS lieutenant general, replaces Dornberger as head of the program. Now the scientists and their wonder rockets belong to Himmler. Medals are passed out. Jake looked for a minute at the memo describing the ceremony. Peenemünde, not Berlin; no families; a special luncheon. There had been champagne. Toasts were exchanged.

More folders. February '45, the rocket team finally abandons Peenemünde. A request for a special train, air travel too risky for scientific personnel, with the skies crowded with bombers. Everyone south now, scattered in villages near the great factory. The prison population reaches forty thousand—spillovers from the eastern camps as the Russians get closer. In spite of everything, V-2s are still streaming daily out of the mountain on their way to London. More files in March—demands, improbably, for increased production. And then the sudden end to the paper. But Jake could finish the story himself—he'd already written it. April 11, the Americans take Nordhausen. A-4 is over. He leaned back in his chair. But what did it mean? Drawers full of details not known to him but presumably known to someone. Nothing worth flying to Berlin for, getting killed for. What had he missed?

He left the last file open on the table and went outside for a smoke, sitting on the steps in the sun. A yellow afternoon light washed the trees of the Grunewald. Hours, to find nothing. Had Tully spent the day here?

"Need a break?" Bernie said from the doorway. "You lasted longer than most. Maybe you have a stronger stomach."

"They're not like that. Office politics, mostly. Production stats. Nothing."

Bernie lit a cigarette. "You don't know how to read them. That's not German, it's a new language. The words mean something else."

"Häftlinge," Jake said, an example.

Bernie nodded. "Poor bastards. I guess it made it easier for the secretaries to type. Instead of what they really were. See the 'disciplinary measures'? That's hanging. They strung them up on a crane at the tunnel entrance so everybody had to pass under when they went to work. They let them swing for a week, until the smell got bad."

"Discipline for what?"

"Sabotage. A loose bolt. Not working fast enough. Maybe they were the lucky ones—at least it was quick. The others, it took weeks before they dropped. But they did. The death rate was a hundred and sixty a day."

"That's some statistic."

"A guess. Somebody took a pencil and averaged it out. For what it's worth." He walked over to the steps. "I take it you didn't find what you wanted."

"Nothing. I'll go through them again. It has to be there somewhere. Whatever it is."

"Trouble is, you don't know what you're looking for and Tully did."

Jake thought for a minute. "But not where. He must have been fishing too. That's why he wanted your help."

"Then maybe he didn't find it either."

"But he came. His name's right there in the book. It has to be here."

"So now what?"

"Now I look again." He flicked the cigarette end into the dusty yard. "Every time I think I'm getting someplace, I'm back where I started. Tully getting off a plane." He stood up and brushed the seat of his pants. "Hey, Bernie, can I twist your arm for another favor? Talk to your pals in Frankfurt again—see if Tully's on a flight manifest for July sixteenth. On whose okay. I asked MG, but if I wait for them I'll be eighty. They have this way of getting lost in somebody's In box. And see if anybody knows where he went the weekend Brandt left."

"Frankfurt, they said."

"But where? Where do you spend the weekend in Frankfurt? See if he said anything."

"Does it matter?"

"I don't know. Just a loose end. At least it gives us something to do while I figure out these files."

Bernie looked up. "You know, it's possible he got it wrong—that there isn't anything here."

"There must be. Emil came to Berlin for them. Why would he do that if there's nothing in them?"

"Nothing you want, you mean."

"Nothing he'd want either. I just read them."

"That depends how you look at it. Want a theory?" Bernie paused, waiting for Jake to nod. "I think von Braun sent him."

"Why?"

"It took about two weeks to round up the scientists after we got to Nordhausen. They were all over the place down there. Von Braun himself didn't surrender until May second. So what were they doing?"

"I give up, what?"

"Putting their alibis in order."

"That's a DA talking. Alibis for what?"

"For being part of what you just read about," Bernie said, nodding toward the building. "'It wasn't us, it was the SS. Look, it's right here. They did everything. We're just the eggheads.' Might be a useful thing to have when people start asking questions. Which we did, after we got a look at their factory help. Von Braun was the team leader—he had the technical files, the real trump card. But these aren't bad as a bargaining chip. Clean hands." He held up his own. "'Let's shake and make a deal. Here are the specs and the drawings. Let's make some rockets together. The rest of it—you can see, we weren't responsible, it was SS.'"

"But it was SS—it's all there."

"Then he was right to want them, wasn't he? He's even convinced you."

"Come on, Bernie, they didn't string anybody up. They were in Peenemünde until February—it says so in the files. How much could they know?"

"Everybody knew," he said sharply, using his courtroom voice, making another case. "That's what no one wants to believe. Everybody knew. Renate Naumann knew. Gunther knew. Everybody in this goddamn country knew. You think somebody who could get an SS car those last weeks didn't know? They didn't stop hanging people after February—they had to have seen it. Not to mention all the others. They had forty camps for workers there, Jake, forty, and people were dying in all of them. They knew."

"That doesn't make them—"

"No, just accessories. You think they're any better because they knew how to work a slide rule? They knew." He stopped, dropping his prosecutor's voice. "And I can't touch them. Lucky for them the SS liked to take all the credit. So they're off a very big hook. Worth coming to Berlin for, wouldn't you say? Anyway, it's a theory. Got a better one?"

"Then why send Emil? Why not some flunky?"

"Maybe he was the only one willing to go. He had a wife here."

Jake looked away, then shook his head. "Except he didn't come alone. There were two men with him. Why risk sending him?"

"He knew what to look for."

Jake sighed. "So did Tully. He came *here*. There has to be something. And I'm missing it."

Bernie shrugged. "You read the files."

"Yes," he said, then looked up. "But I'm not the only one. Keep my seat warm, will you? I'll be back later."

"Where are you going?"

"To get a second opinion."

Shaeffer had moved from bed to chair, but the bandage was still in place, apparently itching now, because he was scratching himself when Jake walked in.

"Well, my new partner," he said, pleased to have a diversion. "Got something for me?"

"No, you've got something for me." Jake sat on the bed. "You went to the Document Center to read the A-four files. What did you find?"

Shaeffer looked at him, a boy surprised at being caught, then smiled. "Nothing."

"Nothing."

"That's right, nothing."

"That must have been disappointing. After looking twice."

"Real shamus, aren't you?"

"Your name's in the sign-in book. Tully's there too. Same day. But you knew that."

Shaeffer looked up. "No."

"But you're not surprised either."

Shaeffer scratched himself again, saying nothing.

Jake stared at him, then sat back, folding his arms over his chest. "We could do this all day. Want to tell me what you were looking for, or should we play twenty questions?"

"What? Something I didn't already know, that's what. I didn't find it."

Jake unfolded his arms. "Talk to me, Shaeffer. This isn't as much fun as you think. Man follows Tully to a place same day he's killed, looks at the same files, carries the same kind of gun that killed him—I've known people convicted on less."

"Now who's being funny. For ten cents I'd pop you one. I told you, I didn't *know* he was there."

"Let's try it a different way. Brandt said something to Tully. I assume you picked this up on one of your taps?"

Shaeffer nodded. "I didn't think anything of it at first. You know, the monitors jot down things that might be of interest—when they're listening. So you get these scraps. You have to figure out the rest yourself. Unless it's technical—then they take down everything."

"And this wasn't."

"One of their personal chats. This and that. And then he says, 'Everything we did, it's in the files.' Words to the effect, anyway. Nothing funny about that—it *was* all there in Nordhausen, they didn't hold anything back. Tons of the stuff. They want to use it themselves, right? So why hold anything back? And then he walks and I'm going through the transcripts and I thought, what if? Maybe he means the other files. It's worth a check. But nothing new there, unless you saw something I didn't. So I figured he did mean the Nordhausen files."

"But Tully didn't think so. And he knew something you didn't."

"What?"

"The rest of the conversation."

Shaeffer considered this for a moment, then shook his head. "But there's nothing there. I looked."

"Twice."

"So twice. Maybe my German's not as good as yours."

"How's Breimer's? He's in the book too. Is that why you asked him along? Or did he have reasons of his own?"

"He's out of this—"

"Tell me or I'll ask him myself. Partner."

Shaeffer glared at him, then dropped his shoulders and began picking at the adhesive tape. "Look, we're walking a fine line here. These guys are the best rocket team in the world—there's nobody else near them. We have to have them. But they're German. And some people are sensitive about that. It's one thing if they just followed orders—who the hell didn't?—but if there's anything else, well, we can't embarrass Breimer. We need his help. He can't—"

"Give jobs to Nazis."

"To bad ones, anyway."

"And you thought there might be something embarrassing in the files."

"No, I didn't think that." He looked away. "Anyway, there wasn't. I don't know what the hell Brandt meant, if he meant anything. The important thing is what *wasn't* there. These guys are clean."

"Teitel doesn't think they're so clean."

"He's a Jew. What do you expect?"

Jake looked over at him. "Maybe not to hear an American say that," he said quietly.

"You know what I mean. The guy's on a fucking crusade. Well, he's not getting these guys. There's nothing there."

Jake stood up. "There must be. Something Tully figured he could sell to the Russians."

"Well, not that they were Nazis. The Russians don't care."

"And neither do we."

Shaeffer raised his head, poster-boy chin out. "Not these guys."

Outside, the light had begun to fade, the lingering soft end of the day. In the billet they'd be getting ready for dinner, the old woman ladling soup. Jake left the jeep and walked down Gelferstrasse, thinking of that first evening when Liz had flirted with him in the bath. About the time Tully must have been reading files, waiting for someone. Or had he been surprised? Start the numbers over. Tully arriving at the airport. Somewhere in the blur of Liz's pictures, unless they were just another empty file too.

The old man was setting the table as he passed by the dining room, avoiding the drinks crowd in the lounge. Upstairs, his room had been dusted and aired, the pink chenille spread stretched tight. Maid service. Liz's photographs were stacked neatly on the vanity table, just as he'd left them, in no particular order. The wrecked plane in the Tiergarten, some DPs off in the corner. Churchill. The boys from Missouri. Another, but not a duplicate, the pose slightly shifted. Liz was like all the photographers he'd known—snap lots of pictures and pretend the good one was the only one you'd taken, a random art. One he'd missed before, him looking at the rubble in Pariserstrasse, shoulders slumped, his face slack with disappointment. In a magazine, without a caption, he might have been a returning soldier. He glanced up at his real face in the mirror. Somebody else.

The airport. He pulled the glossy out of the pile and studied it, moving his eyes slowly over the picture as if he were developing it, trying to sharpen figures in the blur. The effect, oddly, was like looking at the shot in Pariserstrasse, a scene out of context. Had he really been there? A second of time he'd missed. Ron standing at the center with his cocky grin, the Tempelhof crowd swirling behind him. The back of a head that might be Brian Stanley's, the bald spot catching the light. A French soldier with a pompom hat. Nothing. He picked up the next photograph, almost the same but angled, Liz having moved farther left. If you flipped from one to the other, the figures moved, like old posture pictures. Off to the right, a small gleam. Polished boots? He brought the photograph close to his face, fuzzier, then held it out again. Maybe boots, the right height, but the face was indistinct. He flipped them again, but the gleam didn't move. If it had been Tully, he'd been standing still, his side to the camera, looking left.

The knock was no more than a polite tap, scarcely audible. Jake swiveled to see the old man's head poking around the door.

"Excuse me, Herr Geismar. I don't mean to disturb you."

"What is it?"

For a second the old man just looked, blinking, and Jake wondered if he was seeing his daughter again in her usual seat, dusty with powder.

"Herr Erlich said to ask you about the basement room. The photographic equipment? It's not to hurry you, but you understand, we need the room. When it's convenient."

"I'm sorry. I forgot. I'll clean it out right away."

"When it's convenient," he said, backing out.

Jake followed him down the stairs and was almost at the basement door when Ron came out of the lounge, glass in hand. "I thought I saw you slinking around. Dining in tonight?" The same grin, as if he were still in the photograph.

"Can't. I'm just clearing out Liz's things. Where should I send them?"

"I don't know. Press camp, I guess. Listen, don't run away, I've got something for you." He took a folded paper from his pocket. "Don't ask me why, but they okayed it. She requested it, they said. There something between you two I don't know about? Anyway, you're in. Just show them this." He held out the paper. "Don't forget, you don't own this one. Everybody gets a piece of this."

"A piece of what?"

"The interview. Renate Naumann. The one you asked for, remember? Christ, here I'm turning cartwheels for the Soviets and you could care less. Typical."

"She asked to see me?"

"Maybe she thought you'd catch her good side. I wouldn't wait on this, by the way. The Russians change their minds every five minutes. Besides, you could use the story. The natives are getting restless." He pulled a telegram from the same pocket and held it up.

"You've read it?"

"Had to. Regulations."

"And?"

"'Great mail response hero story,'" he quoted without opening it. "'Send new copy ASAP. Friday latest.'" He tapped Jake's chest with both papers. "Saved by the bell, hero. You owe me one."

"Yeah," Jake said, taking them. "Put it on my bill."

Liz's darkroom was a small, musty enclosure near the coal bin, with deep wooden crates in one corner for root vegetables. A table with three trays for solutions under a dangling light fixed with her portable red bulb. A few tins of developer and some prints hanging from a string like laundry. A box of matte paper. Why not let the old couple have it all? It was bound to be worth something in the market. But who took photographs these days? Were there weddings anymore in Berlin?

Liz, at any rate, had taken a lot. The table was littered with contact sheets, the loose pile held down by a heavy magnifying glass, the kind librarians use to read small type. Jake looked through it, and the postage-stamp frames zoomed up to life size. Powerful enough to see if a gleam was coming off boots. He put it in his pocket, then stacked the rest of the equipment at one end of the table. Against the wall there was a side table with another set of prints. He flipped through. The same pictures he'd seen upstairs, but different shots, not quite as sharp—discards, the ones no editor would ever see. The Chancellery. The airport again, Ron still grinning, but the background even less clear. It was when he held it up to the dim light, looking for boots, that his eye caught the dull shine of the gun hanging on the wall.

He put down the print, reached for the holster, and brought it over to the light. A Colt 1911. But everyone had one—standard issue. He took it out, surprised at its weight. The gun she should have been wearing in Potsdam. Three of them in the market. He stared at it for a minute, reluctant even now to let his mind follow the thought through. Had it been fired? They could match the bullet, the carbon firing marks as distinctive as fingerprints. But this was crazy. He opened the gun. An empty chamber. He lifted it to his nose. Only a hint of old grease, but what had he been expecting? Did the smell of firing hang in the chamber like ash, or did it drift away? He turned the cylinder. No bullet there either. Then the next, until finally all of them turned up empty and he twirled the cylinder in a full circle, smiling to himself. Not even loaded, a showpiece to keep the wolves away. So much for Frau Hinkel, surrounding him with deception. He dropped the gun onto the prints, then scooped up the pile with both hands and carried it all back upstairs.

The magnifying glass was small, but it did the trick—the background still wasn't sharp, but at least the blurs took shape. Uniforms passing in front of other uniforms. Definitely boots. He followed the line up—an American uniform, a face that might have been Tully's, *had* to be, anchored by the boots. So Liz had caught him after all. But so what? There was nothing he hadn't known before. Tully had arrived and now stood looking left at something. Jake moved the glass across the picture. But there was only the back of Brian's head, the same uniforms as before, none of them looking toward Tully, and then the white edge.

He sat back and tossed the picture on the table, frustrated, Ron's grin a kind of taunt. When his face fell on its double in the pile, he even seemed to move his head in a laugh. One more, Liz would have been saying, moving around for a better angle, Ron the fixed point in a stereoscope. How many had she taken? Jake leaned forward, grabbing up the prints. Enough for a small panorama? He collected the airport shots from the discard pile and laid them out with the others in a fan shape, ignoring Ron, piecing together the overlapping bits of background—Brian's head on Brian's head, moving left, matching the exit doors, until the edges were covered and he could look across the crowd with Tully.

He picked up the magnifying glass and moved in a straight line left from Tully's face—soldiers going about their business, the annoying bulk of Ron's head blocking the view behind, but now more faces beyond the edge of the first picture, some sharper than others, a few looking back in Tully's direction. Somebody waiting with a jeep. Jake forced himself to move the glass slowly—in the crowd you could miss a face in a blink—so that when he neared the edge he caught it, a shape out of place, narrow straight board patches across the shoulders, the wrong uniform. Russian. He stopped the glass. Body turned toward Tully, as if he had sighted him, and then the face, almost clear among the blurs because it was so familiar, the broad cheeks and shrewd Slavic eyes. Sikorsky had met him.

Jake looked again, afraid the face would dissolve in the fuzzy crowd, something he only thought he saw. No mistake—Sikorsky. Who'd been interested in Nordhausen. Who'd had Willi watch Professor Brandt. It's a common name, I think, he'd said to Lena outside the Adlon. Connected to Emil, where the numbers met. And now connected to Tully. Sikorsky, who'd been the *greifer* at Potsdam, a different connection. Jake stopped, letting the glass go and reaching without thinking across the table for the gun, feeling the same prickling unease he'd felt behind the Alex. Not different, maybe the same connection after all, a direct line to him, blundering after Tully, the only one unwilling to let it go. Not Shaeffer. Not Liz. He looked up into the mirror at the man Sikorsky had pointed out, standing behind Liz in the market.

Now that he knew, what did he do with it? Call Karlshorst for an interview? He left the billet in an excited rush and then stood in the middle of Gelferstrasse, suddenly not sure which way to turn. A few lights had come on in the dusk, but he was alone in the street, as deserted as a western town before a shoot-out. He felt the gun, strapped to his hip. In one of Gunther's stories he'd be facing down the posse until the cavalry arrived. With an empty gun. He moved his hand away, feeling helpless. Who could he go to? Gunther, shopping for a new employer? Bernie, absorbed in a different crime? And then, oddly enough, he realized he was already where he needed to go. Don't forget whose uniform you have on. The cavalry was just down the street, scratching at a bandage.

Breimer had joined Shaeffer for dinner, the two of them sitting with trays on their laps. Jake stopped halfway through the door.

"What?" Shaeffer said, reading his face.

"I need to see you."

"Shoot. We don't have any secrets, do we, congressman?"

Breimer looked up expectantly, fork in hand.

"Sikorsky has him," Jake said.

"Has who?" Breimer said.

"Brandt," Shaeffer answered absently, without looking at him. "How do you know?"

"He met Tully at the airport. Liz took a picture—no mistake. Sikorsky's had him all along."

"Fuck," Shaeffer said, pushing away the tray.

"That's what you thought, isn't it?" Breimer said to him.

"I thought 'might.'"

"Well, now you know," Jake said. "Has."

"Great. Now what do we do?" Shaeffer said, not really a question.

"Get him back. That's your specialty, isn't it?"

Shaeffer looked up at him. "It would be nice to know where."

"Moscow," Breimer said. "The Russians don't have to go through the damn State Department to get things done—they just do it. Well, that's that," he said, leaning back. "And after all we—"

"No, he's in Berlin," Jake said.

"What makes you say that?"

"They're still looking for his wife. Brandt's no good to them if he won't cooperate—they want to keep him happy."

"Any suggestions?" Shaeffer said.

"That's your department. Put some men on Sikorsky. It's just a matter of time before he goes visiting."

Shaeffer shook his head, thinking. "That might be a little unfriendly."

"Since when did that stop you?"

"You boys don't want to go starting anything," Breimer said unexpectedly. "Now that we're in bed again." He picked up the *Stars and Stripes* on the windowsill. RUSSIA JOINS WAR ON JAPS. "Just in time for the kill, the bastards. Who asked them?" He put his fork down, as if the thought had ruined his appetite. "So now we play nicey-nicey and they'd just as soon slit your throat as look at you. If you ask me, we picked the wrong fight."

Jake looked at him, disturbed. "Not if you read the Nordhausen files," he said. "Anyway, maybe you'll get another chance."

"Oh, it's coming," Breimer said, ignoring Jake's tone. "Don't you worry about that. Godless bastards." He looked over at Shaeffer. "But meanwhile you'd better keep the cowboy stuff to a minimum, I guess. MG'll be bending over for the Russians now." He paused. "For a while."

"It's no good anyway," Shaeffer said, still thoughtful. "We can't tail Sikorsky. They'd pick it up in a minute."

"Not if you had the right tail," Jake said, leaning against the bookshelf, arms folded.

"Such as?"

"I know a German who knows him. Professional. He might be interested, for a price."

"How much?"

"A *persil.*"

"What's that?" Breimer said, but nobody answered. Instead, Shaeffer reached for a cigarette, staring at Jake.

"I can't promise that," he said, flicking his lighter. "My signature doesn't mean shit. He'd have to work on spec. Of course, if he actually located Brandt—"

"You'd find a better signature. I'll ask."

"You're talking about hiring a German?" Breimer said.

"Why not? You do," Jake said.

Breimer's head snapped back, as if he'd been slapped. "That's an entirely different matter."

"Yeah, I know, reparations."

"You don't want to get mixed up with Germans," Breimer said to Shaeffer. "FIAT's an American operation."

"Suit yourself," Jake said. "Somebody's got to get to Sikorsky—he's the only lead we've got."

Shaeffer looked at him through the smoke, not saying anything.

"Well, you guys think it over," Jake said, moving away from the shelf, impatient. "You wanted me to find Brandt. I found him. At least how to find him. Now the ball's in your court. Meanwhile, can I borrow some ammo?" He patted the gun. "Liz was fresh out. Same Colt, too," he said to Shaeffer.

"I thought press weren't allowed to carry arms," Breimer said, missing the look between them.

"That's before I started working for FIAT. Now I get nervous. I notice you carry one." He nodded toward the bulge in Breimer's pocket.

"For your information, this is going to a boy's father in my district."

Shaeffer opened the drawer to his nightstand, took out a box, and threw it to Jake.

"Careful you don't shoot yourself with it," Jake said to Breimer. "Hell of a way to lose an election." He sat on the bed and fit the bullets into the chambers of the gun, then snapped it closed. "There, that's better. Now all I have to do is learn how to use it."

Shaeffer, who'd been quiet, running the tip of his cigarette around the ashtray, now looked up. "Geismar, this isn't going to work, you know."

"I was kidding. I know how—"

"No, with Sikorsky. We're not going to get anywhere with a tail, yours or ours. I know him. If he's got Brandt stashed away, even his own men aren't going to know where. He's careful."

"They must have their own Kransberg. Start there."

Shaeffer looked down at the ashtray again, avoiding eye contact. "You have to bring her in."

"Bring who in?" Breimer said.

"Geismar's a friend of the wife's."

"Well, for Christ's sake—"

"No," Jake said. "She's not going anywhere."

"Yes, she is," Shaeffer said quietly, jaw set. "She's going to see her husband. And we'll be right behind her. It's the only way. We've been waiting for Brandt to come to her. Now the fun's over. We have to give Sikorsky what he wants. It's the only way to flush him out."

"Like hell it is. When did you get this bright idea?"

"I've been thinking it over. There's a way to work it, but we need her. You set it up with Sikorsky—or get your friend to do it, even better. That might be worth a *persil*. She goes to visit, we'll have a team on her the whole time. There's no danger to her, none. We get them both back. I guarantee it."

"You guarantee it. With bullets all over the place. Not a chance. Think again."

"No bullets. I said, there's a way to work it. All she has to do is get us there."

"She's not bait. Got it? Not bait. She won't do it."

"She'd do it if you asked her," Shaeffer said calmly.

Jake got up from the bed, looking from one to the other, both sets of eyes fixed on him. "I won't do that."

"Why not?"

"And risk her? I don't want him back that much."

"But I do," Shaeffer said. "Look, the best way to do this is nice—makes for a better team effort. But it's not the only way. If you won't bring her in, I'll do it myself."

"After you find her."

"I know where she is. Right across from KaDeWe. You think we didn't watch *you*?" he said, almost smug.

Jake looked at him, surprised. "You should have watched harder, then. I moved her. I wanted to keep her out of the Russians' hands. Now it looks like I'll have to keep her out of yours too. And I will. Nobody touches her, understand? One move and we're gone again. I can do it, too. I know Berlin."

"You used to. Now you're just a guy in uniform, like the rest of us. People do what they have to do."

"Well, she doesn't have to do this. Get another idea, Shaeffer." He started moving toward the door. "And by the way, I resign. I don't want to be a deputy anymore. Go watch someone else."

Breimer had been following this like a spectator, but now interrupted, his voice smoothing over, folksy. "Son, I think you forget whose side you're on. Kind of thing happens when you get your head up some kraut skirt. You need to think again. We're all Americans here."

"Some of us are more American than others."

"What's that supposed to mean?"

"It means you haven't got my vote. No."

"Your vote? This isn't a town meeting. There's a war going on here."

"You fight it."

"Well, I intend to. And so will you. What do you think we're doing here?"

"I know what you're doing here. The country's on its knees, and all you want to do is give favors to the people who put it there and kick everyone else in the balls. That your idea of our side?"

"Take it easy, Jake," Shaeffer said.

"I've seen a lot of men die. Years of them. They didn't do it to keep things fat for I. G. Farben."

Breimer flushed. "Just who the hell do you think you are, talking like that?"

"It's just his mouth," Shaeffer said.

"Who?" Jake said. "An American. I get to say no. That's what it means. I'm saying no to you, got it? No."

"Of all the piss-ant—"

"Drop it, Jake," Shaeffer said, his voice like a hand on Jake's shoulder, pulling him back.

Jake looked at him, suddenly embarrassed. "Enjoy your dinner," he said, turning to the door.

But Breimer was on his feet now, almost knocking over the tray as he got up. "You think I don't know how to deal with guys like you? You're a dime a dozen. You don't want to play ball, I'll get your ass fired right out of here. Bunch of pinks running around. All mouth, that's what you are. And they love it, the Russians. Aid and comfort to the enemy, that's what you're doing, and you don't even know it."

"Is that why they took a shot at me?" Jake said, turning back. "Funny thing about that, though. An American shot Tully, not Sikorsky. So why did Sikorsky want to kill me? Seems like he might have been doing a favor for someone on our side. The one we're all on. Who knows? Maybe you." Breimer gaped at him. "But somebody, one of ours. Makes you a little reluctant to take sides. All things considered."

"Geismar? See me tomorrow," Shaeffer said. "We'll talk."

"The answer's still no."

"You don't want to be alone out there too long. Think about it."

"That's it?" Breimer said. "Man thumbs his nose at the U.S. government and just goes back to his girlfriend and that's it?"

"He'll be back," Shaeffer said. "We're all a little hot under the collar here." He looked at Jake. "Sleep on it."

"I'm only thumbing my nose at you," Jake said to Breimer, ignoring Shaeffer. "Feels good, too—kind of a patriotic gesture."

"This is a waste of time," Breimer said abruptly to Shaeffer. "Go pick her up. She'll do what she's told."

Jake put his hand on the door, then turned back, his voice icy. "Maybe we should be clear about one thing. You lay a hand on her, one hand, and you won't know what hit you."

"You don't scare me."

"Try this. There's a big hole in a national magazine waiting for me to fill it. Maybe a father in Utica getting his boy's gun. There's a congressman not too busy to run an errand of mercy. Picture them together, it practically brings tears to your eyes. Or maybe the same congressman in Berlin. Not so nice. Lobbying for Nazi war criminals on your tax dollars. While our boys are still dying in the Pacific. Here's the picture layout. Farben ran a factory at Auschwitz. We get a shot of the Farben board, then right next to it one of the camp. One with a lot of bodies stacked up. I'll bet we can even find an old one, prewar, of the Farben boys shaking hands with their friends at American Dye. For all I know, you're in it too. Then a nice one of you—one of Liz's, she always wanted a credit in *Collier's*. I figure FIAT owes her."

"Jesus, Geismar," Shaeffer said.

"That's a lie," Breimer said.

"But I can write it. I know how to do it. I've written lots of lies—for our side. I can fucking write it. And you can spend the next two years denying it. Now leave her alone."

Breimer stood for a moment without breathing, his eyes fixed on Jake. When he spoke, his voice was hard, not even a trace of back home. "You just burned one hell of a bridge for some German pussy."

Jake opened the door, then looked back over his shoulder at Shaeffer. "Thanks for the ammo. Tell you what, if I do find him, I'll send up a flare."

Shaeffer was looking down at the floor as if someone had made a mess, but raised his head as Jake walked out.

"Geismar?" he said. "Bring her in."

Jake walked past the GI guard and the nurse coming down the hallway for the trays. Then he was out in Gelferstrasse again, even more alone than before.

CHAPTER FIFTEEN

GUNTHER REFUSED THE job, agreeing, ironically, with Shaeffer.

"It would never work. He's careful. And you know, this is not police work. This is—"

"I know what it is. I didn't realize you were so choosy."

"A question more of resources," Gunther said blandly.

"We *know* he met Tully," Jake said.

"So Vassily's the paymaster, but who else did Tully meet? Not Herr Brandt, I think. With an American bullet."

"The one leads to the other. And Sikorsky knows where Emil is."

"Evidently. But you keep confusing the cases. Who is it exactly you wish to find, Herr Brandt or the man who killed Tully?"

"Both."

Gunther looked at him. "Sikorsky won't lead us to Herr Brandt, but he may lead us to the other. If he doesn't suspect we know. You see, it's a question of resources."

"So what do you intend to do, just leave Emil with the Russians?"

Gunther shrugged. "My friend, I don't care who makes the rockets. We already made ours. You can see with what results." He got up from his chair to pour more coffee. "For now, let's just solve our case. Herr Brandt, I'm afraid, will have to wait."

"He can't wait," Jake said, frustrated.

Gunther looked over the edge of his cup. "Then read the files."

"I read the files."

"Read again. They're complete?"

"Everything he handed over."

"Then it must be there—what Vassily wants. You see, it's the interesting point. Why did Tully have to die at all? The deal was a *success*. Vassily got what he wanted, Tully got paid. A success. So why? Unless it wasn't finished. There must be something else Vassily wants."

"Besides Lena."

Gunther shook his head, dismissing this. "Herr Brandt wants her. Vassily is just the good host. No, something else. In the files. Why else would Tully read them? So go read." He wriggled his fingers, a schoolmaster shooing Jake away.

Jake checked his watch. "All right. Later. First I have to do some work."

"The journalist. More black market?"

Jake glanced up, sorry now that he had mentioned it. "No. Actually, Renate. An interview."

"Ah," Gunther said, walking back to the chair with his cup, avoiding it. "By the way," he said, sitting down, "did you check the motor pool?"

"No, I assumed Sikorsky drove—"

"All the way to Zehlendorf? Well, maybe so. But I like to be neat. Cross the *t*'s."

"Okay. Later."

Gunther picked up the cup, half hiding his face. "Herr Geismar? Ask her something for me." Jake waited. "Ask her how it felt."

At the detention center near the Alex he was shown into a small room as plain as the makeshift court—a single table, two chairs, a picture of Stalin. The escort, with elaborate courtesy, offered coffee and then left him alone to wait. Nothing to look at but the ceiling fixture, a frosted glass bowl that might once have been lighted with gas, a Wilhelmine leftover. Renate was led in through the opposite door by two guards, who left her at the table and positioned themselves against the wall, still as sconces.

"Hello, Jake," she said, her smile so tentative that her face seemed not to move at all. The same pale blue smock and roughly cut hair.

"Renate."

"Give me a cigarette—they'll think you have permission," she said in English, sitting down.

"You want to do this in English?"

"Some, so they won't suspect anything. One of them speaks German. Thank you," she said, switching now to German as she took the light and inhaled. "My god, it's better than food. You never lose your taste for it. I'm not allowed to smoke, back there. Where is your notebook?"

"I don't need one," Jake said, confused. Suspect what?

"No, please, I want you to write things down. You have it?"

He pulled the pad out of his pocket, noticing for the first time that her hand was trembling, nervous under the sure voice. The cigarette shook a little as she lowered it to the ashtray.

He busied himself with his pen, at a loss. Ask her how it felt, Gunther said, but what could she possibly say? A hundred nods, watching people being bundled into cars.

"It's so difficult to look at me?"

Reluctantly he raised his head and met her eyes, still familiar under the jagged hair.

"I don't know how to talk to you," he said simply.

She nodded. "The worst person in the world. I know—that's what you see. Worse than anybody."

"I didn't say that."

"But you don't look, either. Worse than anybody. How could she do those things? That's the first question?"

"If you like."

"Do you know the answer? She didn't—somebody else did. In here." She tapped her chest. "Two people. One is the monster. The other is the same person you used to know. The same. Look at that one. Can you do that? Just for now. They don't even know she exists," she said, tilting her head slightly toward the guards. "But you do."

Jake said nothing, waiting.

"Write something, please. We don't have much time." Another jerky pull on the cigarette, anxious.

"Why did you ask to see me?"

"Because you know me. Not this other person. You remember those days?" She looked up from the ashtray. "You wanted to sleep with me once. Yes, don't deny it. And you know, I would have said yes. In those days, the Americans, they were all glamorous to us. Like people in the films. Everyone wanted to go there. I would have said yes. Isn't it funny, how things turn out."

Jake looked at her, appalled; her voice was wavering like her hand, edgy and intimate at the same time, the desperate energy of a crazy person.

He glanced down at the notebook, anchoring himself. "Is that what you want? To talk about old times?"

"Yes, a little," she said in English. "Please. It's important for them." Her eyes moved to the guards again, then fixed back on him, steady, not crazy. A girl getting away with something. "So," she said in her German voice, "what happened to everybody? Do you know?"

When he didn't answer, still disconcerted, she reached over to touch his hand.

"Tell me."

"Hal went back to the States," he began, confused, watching her. "At least, he was on his way the last time I saw him." She nodded, encouraging him to go on. "Remember Hannelore? She's here, in Berlin. I saw her. Thinner. She kept his flat." The small talk of catching up. What did the guards make of it, standing under Stalin?

Renate nodded, taking another cigarette. "They were lovers."

"So she said. I never knew."

"Well, I was a better reporter."

"The best," he said, smiling a little, involuntarily drawn back with her. "Nothing escaped you." He stopped, embarrassed, in the room again.

"No. It's a talent," she said, looking away. "And you? What happened to you?"

"I write for magazines."

"No more radio. And your voice was so good."

"Renate, we need to—"

"And Lena?" she said, ignoring him. "She's alive?"

Jake nodded. "She's here. With me."

Her face softened. "I'm happy for you. So many years. She left the husband?"

"She will, when they find him. He's missing."

"When who finds him?"

"The Americans want him to work for them—a scientist. He's a valuable piece of property."

"Is he?" she said to herself, intrigued by this. "And always so quiet. How things turn out." She looked back at him. "So they're all still alive."

"Well, I haven't heard from Nanny Wendt."

"Nanny Wendt," she said, her voice distant, in a kind of reverie. "I used to think about all of you. From that time. You know, I was happy. I loved the work. You did that for me. No German would do that, not then. Even off the books. I wondered, sometimes, why you did. Not even Jewish. You could have been arrested."

"Maybe I was too dumb to know any better."

"When I saw you in the court—" She lowered her head, her voice trailing off. "Now he knows too, I thought. Now he'll only see her." She tapped the right side of her chest. "The *greifer*."

"But you still asked to see me."

"There's no one else. You helped me once. You remember who I was."

Jake shifted in his chair, awkward. "Renate, I can't help you. I have nothing to do with the court."

"Oh that," she said, waving her cigarette. "No, not that. They'll hang me, I know it. I'm going to die," she said easily.

"They're not going to hang you."

"It's so different? They'll send me east. No one comes back from the east. Always the east. First the Nazis, now them. No one comes back. I used to see them go. I know."

"You said you didn't know."

"I knew," she said, pointing again, then to the other side. "She didn't. She didn't want to know. How else to do it? Every week, more faces. How could you do it if you knew? After a while she could do anything. No tears. A job. It's all true, what they said in there. The shoes, the Café Heil, all of it. And the work camps, she thought that. How else could she do it? That's what happened to her."

Jake looked up, nodding to her real side. "And what happened to her?"

"Yes," she said wearily, "you came for that. Go ahead, write." She sat up, darting her eyes sideways to the guards. "Where shall we start? After you left? The visa never came. Twenty-six marks. A birth certificate, four passport pictures, and twenty-six marks. That's all. Except somebody had to take you, and there were too many Jews already. Even with my English. I can still speak it. You see?" she said, switching. "Not a bad accent. Speak for a while—they'll think I'm showing off for you. So they'll be used to it."

"The accent's fine," Jake said, still confused but meeting her gaze, "but I'm not sure I understand everything you're saying."

"Any change of expression from them?" she said.

"No."

"So I stayed in Berlin," she said in German. "And of course things got worse. The stars. The special benches in the park. You know all that. Then the Jews had to work in factories. I was in Siemenstadt. My mother too, an old woman. She could barely stand at the end of the day. Still, we were alive. Then the roundups started. Our names were there. I knew what it would mean—how could she live? So we went underground."

"U-boats?"

"Yes, that's how I knew, you see. How it was, what they would do. All their tricks. The shoes—no one else thought of that. So clever, they told me. But I knew. I had the same problem, so I knew they would go there. And of course they did."

"But you didn't stay underground."

"No, they caught me."

"How?"

She smiled to herself, a grimace. "A *greifer*. A boy I used to know. He always liked me. I wouldn't go with him—a Jew. I never thought of myself as Jewish, you see. I was—what? German. To think of that now. An idiot. But there he was, in the café, and I knew he must be underground, too, by that time. I hadn't spoken to anyone in days. Do you know what that's like, not to talk? You get hungry for it, like food. And I knew he liked me and I thought maybe he would help me. Anyone who could help—"

"And did he?"

She shrugged. "To the Gestapo car. They took me in and beat me. Not so bad, not like some of the others, but enough. So I knew I wasn't German anymore. And the next time would be worse. They wanted to know where my mother was. I didn't tell them, but I knew I would the next time. And then he did help. He had friends there—friends, the devils he worked for. He said he could make a bargain for me. I could work with him and they'd keep us off the list, my mother too. If I went with him. After this? I said. And you know what he said to me? 'It's never too late to make a bargain in this life. Only in the next.'" She paused. "So I went with him. That was the bargain. He got me and I kept my life. The first time I was sent out, we went together. His pupil. But I was the one who spotted the woman that day. I knew the look, you see. And after the first time—well, what does it matter how many, it's just the first one, over and over."

"What happened to him?"

"He was deported. When he was with me, it was all right for him. We were a team. But then they split us up, and on his own he was not so successful. I was the one, I had the eye. He had nothing to bargain anymore. So." She squashed out the cigarette.

"But you did," Jake said, watching her.

"Well, I was better at it. And Becker liked me. I kept my looks. You see here?" She pointed to her left cheek, folded up near the edge of her eye. "Only this. When they beat me, my face was swollen, but it went down. Only this. And Becker liked that. It reminded him, maybe. I don't know of what." She looked away, finally distressed. "Oh my god, how can we talk this way? How can I describe what it was like? What difference does it make? Write anything you want. It can't be worse. You think I'm making excuses. It was David, it was Becker. Yes, and it was me. I thought I could do this, that we could talk, but when I talk about it—look at your face—you see *her*. The one who killed her own. That's what they want for the magazines."

"I'm just trying to understand it."

"Understand it? You want to understand what happened in Germany? How can you understand a nightmare? How could I do it? How could they do it? You wake up, you still can't explain it. You begin to think maybe it never happened at all. How could it? That's why they have to get rid of me. No evidence, no *greifer,* it never happened."

She was shaking her head and looking away, her eyes beginning to fill.

"Now look. I thought I was finished with that, no tears. Not like my mother. She cried enough for both. 'How can you do this?' Well, it was easy for her. I had to do the work, not her. Every time I looked at her, tears. You know when they stopped? When she got in the truck. Absolutely dry. I thought, she's relieved not to have to live this way anymore. To see me."

Jake took a handkerchief from his back pocket and handed it to her. "She didn't think that."

Renate blew her nose, still shaking her head. "No, she did. But what could I do? Oh, stop," she said to herself, wiping her face. "I didn't want to do this, not in front of you. I wanted you to see the old Renate, so you would help."

Jake put down the pen. "Renate," he said quietly, "you know it won't make any difference what I write. It's a Soviet court. It doesn't matter to them."

"No, not that. I need your help. Please." She reached for his hand again. "You're the last chance. It's finished for me. Then I saw you in the court and I thought, not yet, not yet, there's one more chance. He'll do it."

"Do what?"

"Oh, look at this," she said, wiping her eyes again. "I knew if I started—" She turned to the guards, and for an instant it occurred to Jake that she was playing, the tears part of some larger performance.

"Do what?" he said again.

"Please," she said to the guard, "would you bring me some water?"

The guard on the right, the German speaker, nodded, said something in Russian to the other, and left the room.

"Write this down," she said to Jake in English, her voice low, as if it were coming from the back of a sob. "Wortherstrasse, in Prenzlauer, the third building down from the square. On the left, toward Schönhauserallee. An old Berliner building, the second courtyard. Frau Metzger."

"What is this, Renate?"

"Write it, please. There's not much time. You remember in court I told you I didn't do it for myself?"

"Yes, I know. Your mother."

"No." She looked at him, her eyes sharp and dry. "I have a child."

Jake's pen stopped. "A child?"

"Write it. Metzger. She doesn't know about me. She thinks I work in a factory. I pay her. But the money runs out this month. She won't keep him now."

"Renate—"

"Please. His name is Erich. A German name—he's a German child, you understand? I never had it done. You know, down there." She pointed to her groin, suddenly shy.

"Circumcised."

"Yes. He's a German child. No one knows. Only you. Not the magazines either, promise me? Only you."

"What do you want me to do?"

"Take him. Prenzlauer's in the east. She'll give him up to the Russians. You must take him—there's no one else. Jake, if you were ever fond of me at all—"

"Are you crazy?"

"Yes, crazy. Do you think after everything else I've done, I couldn't ask this? Do you have children?"

"No."

"Then you don't know. You can do anything for a child. Even this," she said, spreading her hand to the room, the *greifer*'s life. "Even this. Was I right to do it? Ask God, I don't know. But he's alive. I saved him, with their money. They gave me pocket money, you know, for the cafés, for—" She stopped. "Every pfennig was for him. I thought, you're paying to keep a Jew alive. At least one of us is going to live. That's why I had to stay alive, not for me. But now—"

"Renate, I can't take a child."

"Yes, please. Please. There's no one else. You were decent, always. Do this for him, if not the mother, what you think of her. Everything I did—one more day, one more day alive. How can I give up now? If you take him to America, they can hang me, at least I'll know I got him out. Safe. Out of this place." She grabbed his hand again. "He'd never know what his mother did. To live with that. He'd never know."

"Renate, how could I take a child to America?"

"The west, then, anywhere but here. You could find a place for him—I trust you, I know you'd make it all right, decent people. Not some Russian camp."

"What do I tell him?"

"That his mother died in the war. He's so young, he won't remember. Just some woman who used to come sometimes. You can tell him you used to know her when she was a girl, but she died in the war. She did," she said, looking down. "It's not a lie."

Jake looked at the blotchy face, the sharp eyes finally dulled by a sadness so oppressive that he felt his own shoulders sinking. Always something worse. He nodded his head toward the side she thought was real.

"She didn't," he said.

Her face was confused for a second, then cleared, almost in a smile. "That's only for today. So I could ask you. After this, there's only her," she said, putting her finger on the other side. "It's over."

"It doesn't have to be. At least let me talk to the lawyers."

"Oh, Jake, to say what? You were there, you saw them. What would mercy be—a Russian prison? Who survives that?"

"People do."

"To come back as what? An old woman, back to Germany? And meanwhile, what happens to Erich? No, it's over. If you want to help me, save my child. Ah, the water," she said, fluttering a little as the guard came through the door with a glass and handed it to her. "Thank you," she said in German, "it's very kind." As she drank, the guard looked at the other guard with an "anything happen?" expression, answered by a shrug.

"So you'll help?" Renate said.

"Renate, you can't ask me to do this. I'm sorry, but I don't—"

"In English now," she said, switching. "I'm not asking you, I'm begging you."

"What about his father?"

"Dead. When we were underground. One night he didn't come back, that's all. So I knew. I had the baby myself." She handed back the handkerchief. "You be the father."

"Stop. I can't do that."

"He'll die," she said, her eyes fixed on his. "Now, when it's over, after everything."

Jake turned his head, taking in the guards, Stalin's flat iconic gaze. "Look," he said finally, "I know a church. They work with children, orphans, try to place them. I can talk to the pastor, he's a good man, maybe there's something he—"

"They find homes? In the west? With Christians?"

"Well, yes, they would be. I'll ask. Maybe he knows a Jewish family."

"No. A German boy. So he'll be safe next time."

"You want him to be German?" Jake said, amazed. The endless, twisted cord.

"I want him to live. Americans—how can you know? How people are here. But promise me, a home, not some camp."

"I can't promise that, Renate. I don't know. I'll talk to the pastor. I'll do what I can. I'll try."

"But you'll move him from Frau Metzger? Before she gives him up?"

"Renate, I can't promise—"

"Yes, promise me. Lie to me. My god, can't you see I have to tell myself this? I have to think it's going to be all right."

"I won't lie to you. I'll do what I can. You'll have to be satisfied with that."

"Because I have nothing to bargain with, you mean. Finally, no more Jews."

Jake looked away. Every week a new list, trading yourself, until there was no other way to live. He had become one of her bosses.

"What do they say about the trial?" he said, moving somewhere else.

"My lawyers?" she said, a trace of scorn. "To be clever, play the innocent—that I couldn't help what I was doing. To be sorry."

"Well?"

"It's not enough to be sorry. It's not enough for me. I can't make it go away. I still see the faces, how they looked at me. I can't make them go away."

"One minute," the guard shouted out in German.

Renate drew a cigarette from the pack. "One more," she said in English, "for the road. That's right, isn't it? For the road?"

"Yes. I'll come back."

"No. They won't allow that. Only this once. But I'm so glad to see you. Someone from that world. In Berlin again, I never thought—"

She stopped, grabbing his hand. "Wait a minute. I can't bargain with it, but maybe it's something, if he's still there. Promise me."

"Renate, don't do this."

"You said they were looking for him, the Americans. So maybe it's something for you. Lena's husband—I know where he is. I saw him."

Jake looked up, stunned. "Where?"

"Promise me," she said steadily, still covering his hand. "One last bargain."

He nodded. "Where?"

"Can I believe you?"

"Where?"

"As if I have a choice," she said.

"Time," the guard called.

"One minute." She turned back to Jake, conspiratorial, talking quickly. "Burgstrasse, the old Gestapo building. Number Twenty-six. It was bombed, you know, but they still use part. They kept me there before here."

"And you saw him there?"

"Out the window, across the courtyard. He didn't see me. I thought, my god, that's Emil, why do they have him here? Is he on trial too? Is he?"

"No. What was he doing?"

"Just looking down into the courtyard. Then the lights went out. That's all. Is that something for you? Can you use that?"

"You're sure it was him?"

"Of course. My eyes are good, you know, always."

The guard approached the table.

"Give him some cigarettes," she said in English, standing. "They'll be nice to me."

Jake got up and offered the pack.

"So it's good?" she said. "One last job for you?"

Jake nodded. "Yes."

"Then promise me."

"All right."

She smiled, then her face twitched, the skin falling slack, as if she were about to weep again, finally drained of all composure. "Then it's over."

Before he could react, she moved around the table to Jake and, while the guard stuffed cigarettes into his pocket, put her arms around him, almost falling into him. He stood awkwardly, catching her, not really embracing her, feeling her bones sticking through the smock, brittle enough to snap. She hugged him once, then turned her mouth up to his ear, hidden from the guard. "Thank you. He's my life."

She stepped back and let the guard take her arm, but put her other hand on Jake's chest, pulling at the cloth. "But never tell him. Please."

When the guard tugged her arm, she went with him, looking over her shoulder at Jake, trying to smile, but the walk was clumsy, a half-hearted, forced shuffle, not even a trace of the lively steps he remembered on the platform.

Burgstrasse was only a few blocks west of the Alex, but he drove, feeling safer in the jeep. There'd be no point in stopping, but he had to see if it was there at all, not some lie, a last attempt to keep playing the angles. The street was across the open sewer of the Spree from the smashed-in cathedral, but part of Number 26 was still standing, just as she'd said, flying a red flag. He passed it slowly, pretending to be lost. Thick walls, stripped now of plaster, a heavy entrance door blocked by guards with Asiatic faces—the familiar Russian hierarchy, Mongols at the bottom. Behind it all, somewhere, Emil looking out a window. But how could Shaeffer get in? A raid in the middle of Berlin, bullets zinging over Lena's head? Impossible without some trick. But that was his specialty; let him plan it. At least now they knew. Renate's last catch, her part of the bargain. He stopped near the end of the street to check his wallet—enough money for Frau Metzger until he could get Fleischman to come. One final payment, off the books.

The Prenzlauer building was an old tenement block, three courtyards deep. He followed Renate's instructions to the second, strung with laundry, then up two flights of murky stairs lighted by a hole some shell had punched through the ceiling. He had to knock a few times before the door finally opened a suspicious crack.

"Frau Metzger? I've come about Erich."

"*You've* come? And what's the matter with her, too busy?" She opened the door. "It's about time. Does she think I'm made of money? Nothing since June, nothing on account. How am I supposed to feed anyone? A boy needs to eat."

"I'll pay for what she owes," Jake said, taking out his wallet.

"So now she's found an American. Well, it's not my affair. Better than a Russian, at least. Lots of chocolate for *you* now," she said, turning to a child standing near the table. About four, Jake guessed, skinny legs in short pants, with Renate's dark eyes, but larger, almost too large for the face, wide now in alarm. "Come on, let's get your things. Don't be afraid, he's your mother's friend," she said, not unkind but brusque, then turned back to Jake. "Her friend. She's a fine one. While the rest of us— No, it's too much," she said, looking at the money. "She only owes for two months. I'm not a thief. Only what's owed. I'll get his things."

"No, you don't understand. I'll send somebody for him. I can't take him today."

"What do you mean? She's not dead, is she?"

"No."

"Then he goes now. I'm going to my sister. You think I'm staying here, with the Russians? I'll give her one more week, I said, and then— But anyway, here you are, so it's all right. Come. I won't be a minute. There's not much. Get me clothing coupons, I told her, but did she? No, not her. She couldn't come herself? She has to send an Ami? You can see how he's frightened. Well, he never says much. Say hello, Erich. Ouf." She waved her hand. "Well, he's like that."

The boy stared at him silently. Not fear, a numb curiosity, an animal waiting to see what would happen to him.

"But I can't take him today."

"Yes, today. I waited and waited. You can't expect—" She began emptying a drawer, putting things in a string bag. "The war's over, you know. What does she expect? Here. I told you, there's not much."

She handed him the bag, past arguing.

Jake pulled out his wallet again. "But I can't—let me pay you something extra."

"A gift? Well, that's very nice," she said, taking it. "So maybe she's lucky now. You see, Erich, he's all right. You'll be fine. Come, give auntie a hug."

She bent down, barely clasping him, an indifferent sendoff. How long had they been together? The boy stood, not moving. "Go on," she said, giving him a little push. "Go to your mother."

The boy jerked forward. Jake looked at her hand on the boy's shoulder, stung, his heart dulled by every terrible thing he'd heard in Berlin and now moved finally by this, a single moment of casual cruelty. What had happened to everybody?

The boy took a step, looking down. Frau Metzger flicked through Jake's bills, then shoved them in her apron pocket.

"That's all you can say to him?" Jake said. "Just like that? He's a child."

"What do you know about it?" she said, eyes flashing. "I took care of him, didn't I? While she had her good times. I earned every mark. And how long will you last, I wonder. Well, tell her not to come back when it's over—the hotel is closed." She had reached the door and held it open, then looked down at Erich with a twinge of embarrassment. "I did the best I could. You, you be a good boy, don't forget. Don't forget your auntie."

And then they were in the hall, the door closing behind them, a soft click, maybe the only thing the boy wouldn't forget, a click of the door. They stood motionless for a second, and then the boy lifted his hand, still not speaking, just waiting to be led away.

It was no better in the jeep. He sat quietly, utterly passive, watching the streets go by, like the children from Silesia. Down the gentle slope of Schönhauserallee, then out past the pockmarked walls of the *schloss* to the Linden. Bicycles and soldiers. The plane wreckage in the Tiergarten. Registering everything without a word. He took Jake's hand again on the walk from Savignyplatz.

"My god, who's this?" Lena said.

"Another one for Fleischman. Erich."

"But where did you—"

"He's Renate's child. You remember, from the office?"

"Renate? But I thought all the Jews—"

He stopped her. "It's a long story. I'll tell you later. First let's get him to the church."

"First some food, I think," she said, kneeling down. "Look how thin. You're hungry? Don't be afraid, it's safe here. Do you like cheese?"

She led him over to the table and brought out a small block of rubbery PX cheese. The boy looked at it warily.

"It's real," Lena said. "That's the color it is in America. Here, there's still some bread. It's all right—eat."

He picked up the bread dutifully and took a nibble.

"So Erich, it's a good name. I knew an Erich once. Dark hair, like yours." She reached over and touched it. "It's good, the bread? Here, try some more." She broke off a piece and offered it to him by hand, gently, the way you would feed a stray. "See, I told you. Now some cheese."

She fed him for a few minutes, until he began to eat on his own, taking in the food as quietly as the sights on the drive. She looked up at Jake. "Where is she?"

Jake shook his head, a not-in-front-of-the-child gesture. "He's been living with a woman in Prenzlauer. I think he's had a rough time. He doesn't say much."

"Well, it's not so important, is it, to talk?" she said to the boy. "Sometimes I'm quiet too, when things are new. We'll have something to eat, then maybe a little rest. You must be tired. All the way from Prenzlauer."

The boy was nodding at her, reassured, Jake saw, by her German, familiar, without Jake's accent.

"We should get him to Fleischman," Jake said. "It's getting late."

"There's plenty of time," she said easily, then turned. "But if she's alive— You're taking him from his mother? To Fleischman?"

"I promised her I'd find a place. I'll explain later," he said, feeling the boy's eyes on him.

Lena offered him another piece of cheese. "It's good, yes? There's more—take as much as you like. Then we'll sleep, what do you say?" Her voice soft, lulling.

"Lena," Jake said, "he can't stay here. We can't—"

"Yes, I know," she said, not really hearing it. "But for one night. That basement. You can see how tired he is. It's all strange for him. You know my name?" she said to the boy. "It's Lena." She yawned, an exaggerated gesture, raising her hand to her mouth. "Oh, I'm so tired too."

"Lena," Jake said. "You know what I mean."

She looked at him. "Yes, I know. It's just for tonight. What's the matter with you? You can't send him away like this. Look at his eyes. Men."

But the eyes were still wide, not drooping, moving from one to the other as if he were making a decision. Finally he fixed them on Jake, got up, and came over to him, lifting his hand again. For a second, confused, Jake thought he was asking to leave, but then he spoke, surprisingly clear after the long silence.

"I have to go to the bathroom," he said, holding out his hand.

Lena smiled, laughing softly to herself. "Well, you're good for that," she said as Jake led him, two men, to the toilet.

After that there was nothing to do but let her take charge, whatever he'd planned slipping away like a card move turned by an unexpected joker in the deck. From the table, he could see her settle the boy on the bed, running her hand over his forehead and talking softly, a low, steady stream of words. He lit a cigarette, restless, then glanced at his notebook. Renate being picked up in the café, an idle flirtation, the *greifer*'s *greifer*. The story Ron wanted him to share. He looked again into the bedroom, where Lena was still talking the boy to sleep, and, not knowing what else to do, started putting the notes in order to block out the story, wondering how to tell it without the one thing that had really mattered. But when he took a sheet of paper, it seemed to frame itself, opening with Marthe Behn, then dissolving to the first café and working its way back, one sinking twist after another, to the moment of the nod. Not an apologia; something more complicated, a crime story where everyone was guilty. He wrote in a rush, wanting to get it done, as if it would all go away once it was on paper, just words. The shoes, the mother, Hans Becker, trading favors. Still beyond belief. What had happened to everybody? A city where he used to drink beer under trees. How many had even looked up in the café when the men arrived? Not accomplices, people looking the other way. Except Renate, who still saw the faces.

He'd been writing for a while, lost in it, before he realized that the murmuring in the bedroom had stopped, the only sound in the flat the faint scratch of his pen. Lena was standing in the doorway watching him, a tired smile on her face.

"He's asleep," she said. "You're working?"

"I wanted to get it done while it's fresh."

"Sewing with a hot needle," she said, a German expression. She sat down across from him, taking one of the cigarettes. "I don't think he's well. I want Rosen to look at him, just in case. I saw him again today—he's always here, it seems."

"He takes care of the girls."

"Oh," she said, a little flustered. "I didn't realize. Still, a doctor—"

"Lena, we can't keep him. You don't want to get attached."

"Yes, I know. But for one night—" She stopped, looking at him. "That's the terrible part, isn't it? Nobody's attached to him. Nobody. I thought, standing over there, it's a little like a family. You working like this, him sleeping."

"We're not his family," he said, but gently.

"No," she said, letting it go. "So tell me about Renate. What happened? He won't hear now."

"Here," he said, moving the papers across the table. "It's all there."

He got up and went over to the brandy bottle and poured two glasses. He set hers down, but she ignored it, her eyes fixed on the page.

"She told you this?" she said, reading.

"Yes."

"My god." A slow turn of the page.

When she finished, she pushed the papers back, then took a sip from the glass.

"You don't mention the child."

"She doesn't want anybody to know. Especially the child."

"But nobody will know why she did it."

"Does it matter, what people think? The fact is, she did it."

"For the child. You do anything for your child."

"That's what she said," he said, slightly jarred. "Lena, this is what she wanted. She doesn't want him to know."

"Who he is."

"That would be a hell of a thing to carry around with you, wouldn't it? All this," he said, touching the paper. "He's better off this way. He'll never have to know any of it."

"Not to know your parents—" she said, brooding.

"Sometimes it can't be helped."

She looked up at him, then put her hands on the table to get up. "Yes, sometimes," she said, turning away. "Do you want something to eat? I can fix—"

"No. Sit. I have some news." He paused. "Renate saw Emil. She told me where he is."

She stopped, halfway out of her chair. "You waited to tell me this?"

"There wasn't time, with the boy."

She sat down. "So it's come. Where?"

"The Russians are holding him in a building in Burgstrasse."

"Burgstrasse," she said, trying to place it.

"In the east. It's guarded. I went to see it."

"And?"

"And it's guarded. You don't just walk in."

"So what do we do?"

"We don't do anything. We let Shaeffer's team handle it—they're experts at this."

"Experts at what?"

"Kidnapping. That's what it will mean. The Russians aren't going to hand him over—they probably won't even admit they have him. So Shaeffer needs to figure out a way. He wanted to use you. Kind of a decoy."

She looked down at the table, taking this in, then picked up the glass and finished her brandy.

"Yes, all right," she said.

"All right what?"

"I'll do it."

"No, you won't. People go to the Russians, they don't always come back. I'm not taking that risk. This is a military operation, Lena."

"We can't leave him there. He *came* for me—he risked his life. I owe him this much."

"You don't owe him this."

"But Russians—"

"I told you, I'll talk to Shaeffer. If anybody can get him, he can. He wants him. He's been waiting for this."

"And you don't, is that it? You don't want him?"

"It's not that simple."

She reached over. "You can't leave him there. Not with the Russians. I won't."

"A few weeks ago you thought he was dead."

"But he's not. So now it's this. You were the detective, looking everywhere. So you found him. I thought that's what you wanted."

"It was."

"But not now?"

"Not if it's dangerous for you."

"I'm not afraid of that. I want it to be over. What kind of life do you think it will be for us, knowing he's there? With them. I want it to be over. Not this prison—you don't even want me to leave the flat. Talk to your friend. Tell him I want to do it. I want to get him out."

"So you can leave him? He won't thank you for that."

She lowered her head. "No, he won't thank me for that. But he'll be free."

"And that's the only reason?"

She looked over at him, then reached across, touching his face with her finger. "What a little boy you are. After everything that's happened, to be jealous. Emil's my family—it's different, not the way it is with you. Don't you know that?"

"I thought I did."

"Thought. And then, like that, a schoolboy again. You remember Frau Hinkel?"

"Yes, two lines."

"She said I had to choose. But I did. Even before the war. I chose you. How silly you are, not to know that."

"I still don't want you taking chances with Shaeffer."

"Maybe that's my choice too. Mine."

He met her stare, then looked away. "Let me talk to him. Maybe he doesn't need you anyway, now that we know where Emil is."

"Then what?"

"Then we wait. We don't go into the east. We don't go to Burgstrasse. They'll move him for sure if they think we know. And we don't volunteer. Understand?"

"But you'll tell me if they do want—"

He nodded, cutting her off, then snatched her hand. "I don't want anything to happen to you."

"Well, do you know something? Neither do I," she said, making light of it, then rubbed his hand. "Not now." She tilted her head, alert. "Was that him? Let me check." She slid her hand away and hurried to the bedroom.

Jake sat watching her go, uneasy. Another bargain he shouldn't have made. But nothing risky, whatever Shaeffer said. And then what? Three of them.

She came back into the room with her finger to her lips, half closing the door.

"He's asleep, but restless. We'll have to be quiet."

"He's going to stay in there?"

"We'll move him later, when he's really asleep."

She came over to him and kissed his forehead, then began unbuttoning his shirt.

"What are you doing?"

"I want to see you. Not the uniform."

"Lena, we have to talk about this."

"No, we've already talked. It's decided. Now we're going to pretend—the children are asleep, but there's the couch, if we're quiet. Let's see how quiet we can be."

"You're just trying to change the subject."

"Ssh." She kissed him. "Not a sound."

He smiled at her. "Wait till you hear the couch."

"Then we'll go slowly. It's nice slow."

She was right. The quiet itself became exciting, each touch furtive, as if the creak of a spring would give them away. When he slipped inside her, he moved so slowly that it seemed something only they knew, a secret between them, betrayed by the gasp of breath in his ear. Then the gentle rocking, an endless, sweet tease, until finally it ended as it began, the same rhythm, so that not even the shuddering disturbed the room around them. She kept him in her afterward, stroking his back, and for a few minutes he felt no difference between making love and simply being there, the one drifting into the other.

But the couch was cramped and awkward, its lumps poking into the usual forgetting, the unconsciousness of sex, and instead of drifting, his mind began to dart away. Had it been like this with them? Another couple using the couch so they wouldn't wake their boy? Uncannily, as if he'd spoken, she reached up to touch his face.

"I chose you," she said.

"Yes," he said, kissing her, then withdrew and sat up next to her, restless. "Do you think he heard?"

She shook her head, dreamy. "Cover me. I just want to lie here for a minute. How can you get up?"

"I don't know. Do you want a drink?" he said, going over to pour one.

"Look at you," she said, watching him, then stirred, lifting herself up. "Jake? The boy—I noticed. I thought all the Jews—you know," she said, nodding at his penis, as self-conscious as Renate had been, even lying there still wet with him.

"She didn't have it done. She wanted him to be German."

Lena sat up, troubled, holding the dress to cover herself. "She wanted that? Even after—"

He took a drink. "To protect him, Lena."

"Yes," she said dully, shaking her head. "My god, what it must have been like for her."

He looked down at the story on the table with its missing piece. "You said it yourself—you do anything for your child." He took the glass again, then stopped it halfway to his lips and put it down in a rush. "Of course."

"Of course what?"

"Nothing," he said, moving over to his clothes. "Something I just thought of."

"Where are you going?" she said, watching him dress.

"I don't know why I didn't see it. A reporter's supposed to know when something's missing. You read the story and you can *feel* it's not there." He looked up, finally aware of her. "Just a hunch. I'll be back."

"At this hour?"

"Don't wait up." He bent over and kissed her forehead. "And don't open the door."

"But what—"

"Ssh, not now." He held his finger to his lips. "You'll wake Erich. I'll be back."

He raced out of the building, then up the side street where he'd stashed the jeep, fumbling in the dark with the ignition. There was only a glimmer of moon in the narrow streets off the square, but when he got up to the broad Charlottenburger Chausee there was an open field of light, pale white and unexpectedly beautiful. Now, when he had no time to look at it, the blunt, unlovely city had turned graceful, making him stop in surprise, its secret self, maybe there all the time, when everything else was dark. It occurred to him, fancifully, that it was finally lighting the way for him, like Hansel's white pebbles, down the wide, empty street, then up Schloss Strasse, making good time, and still there when he needed it most, picking his way through the trail in the rubble, all easy going, so that he knew he must be right. Not even a shadow at young Willi's lookout post, just the pointing, friendly light. When Professor Brandt opened the door, he no longer had any doubts at all.

"I've come for the files," he said.

"How did you know?" Professor Brandt said as Jake started to read.

They were sitting at a table with a single lamp, a pool of light just wide enough for the pages but not their faces, so that his voice seemed disembodied.

"He told them at Kransberg you were dead," Jake said absently, trying to concentrate. "What possible reason could he have, unless he didn't want them to find you? Didn't want to take the chance—"

"That I would tell them," he said. "I see. He thought that."

"Maybe he thought they'd search." He turned a page, a report from Mittelwerks in Nordhausen, another piece missing from the Document Center. Not cross-referenced, never handed over—the missing part of the story, like Renate's child. "Why did he leave them with you?"

"He didn't know how bad it was in Berlin, how far the Russians had come. Not just the east, almost a circle. Only Spandau was open, but for how long? A rumor, that's all. Who knew? It was possible he wouldn't get out—I thought so myself. If they were captured—"

"So he hid them with you. In case. Did you read them?"

"Later, yes. I thought he had died, you see. I wanted to know."

"But you didn't destroy them?"

"No. I thought, someday it's important. They'll lie, all of them. 'We had nothing to do with it.' Even now they— I thought, someone has to answer for this. It's important to know."

"But you didn't turn them over, either."

"Then you told me he was living. I couldn't. He's my son, you understand. Still."

He paused, causing Jake to look up. In his dressing gown he seemed frail, no longer held together by the formal suit, but the scrawny neck was erect, as if the old high collar were still in place. "Was it wrong? I don't know, Herr Geismar. Maybe I kept them for you. Maybe they answer to you." He turned away. "And now it's done—you have them. So take them, please. I don't want them in my house anymore. You'll excuse me, I'm tired."

"Wait. I need your help. My German isn't good enough."

"For that? Your German is adequate. The problem, maybe, is believing what you read. It's just what it says. Simple German." He made a small grimace. "The language of Schiller."

"Not the abbreviations. They're all technical. Here's von Braun, requesting special workers. French, is that right?"

"Yes, French prisoners. The SS supplied the list from the camps—engineering students, machinists. Von Braun made his selection from that. The construction workers, it didn't matter, one shovel's as good as another. But the precision work—" He looked over to the word Jake was pointing at. "Die cutter."

"So he was there."

"Of course he was there. They all went there, to inspect, to supervise. It was their factory, you understand, the scientists. They saw it, Herr Geismar. Not space, all those dreams. They saw this. You see the other letter, from Lechter, where he says the disciplinary measures are having an unfortunate effect? The workers don't like to see men hanging—it slows production. Exact words. His solution? Hang them off-site. Yes, and Lechter complains that on the last visit some of his colleagues were taken to an area where cholera had broken out. Couldn't this be prevented in the future? Visitors should be taken to safe areas only. To risk the health—" He stopped, clearing his throat. "Would you like some water?" he said, getting up, an obvious excuse to leave the table.

Jake turned another page, hearing the water run behind him. A memo requesting a transfer back to Peenemünde for a Dr. Jaeger, proof that he'd been there, a carbon for the files, evidence for Bernie. Just paper. Was anyone not compromised? Drinking brandy at Kransberg, waiting for visas. But how much had Tully known? He realized for the first time, a Gunther point, that no one had actually seen the files but Professor Brandt. Tully must have left the center as frustrated as Jake had been, all the way to Berlin for an incomplete story.

"Here's Emil," he said, turning to a page filled with figures.

"Yes," Professor Brandt said over his shoulder, "the estimates. The estimates." He shuffled back to his chair.

"But of what? What's this?" Jake pointed to one of the sets of numbers.

"Calories," Professor Brandt said quietly, not looking, clearly familiar with the paper.

"Eleven hundred," Jake said, stuck on the math. "That's calories?" He looked over at the old man. "Tell me."

Professor Brandt took a sip of water. "Per day. At eleven hundred calories per day, how long would a man survive? Depending on the original body weight. You see the series on the left. If it fell—to nine hundred, say—the factors average out to sixty. Sixty days—two months. But of course it's not exact. The variables are not in the numbers. In the men. Some more, some less. They die at their own speed. But it's useful, the average. You can calculate how many calories it would take to extend it, say, for another month. But they never extended it. The work in the first month, before they weakened, was actually more productive than any extension. The table near the bottom demonstrates that. There was no point in keeping them alive unless they were specialists. The numbers prove it." He looked up. "He was right. I checked the math. The second page shows how much to increase rations for skilled workers. I think, you know, that he was using this to persuade them to allow more food, but I can't be sure. The others died to the formula. An average only, but accurate. He based them on actual numbers from the previous month. Not a difficult exercise."

He interrupted himself for another sip, then continued, a teacher working through a long blackboard proof. "The others also. Simple. Time of assembly, units per twenty-four-hour period. You don't have to look, I remember them all. Optimum number of workers per line. Sometimes they had too many. The assembly was complicated—better to have one skilled set of hands than three men who didn't know what they were doing. He proves this somewhere. You would think, common sense, but evidently they liked to see this. In numbers. These were the kinds of problems they had him working on."

Jake looked at the paper, not saying anything, letting Professor Brandt collect himself as he drank the last of the water.

"He must have done other work, not just this."

"Yes, of course. It's a great achievement, technically. You can see that. The mathematics involved, the engineering. Every German can be proud." He shook his head. "Dreams of space. This is what they were worth. Eleven hundred calories a day."

Jake flicked through the remaining pages, then closed the folder and stared at it. Not just Emil, most of the team.

"You're surprised?" Professor Brandt said quietly. "Your old friend?"

Jake said nothing. Just numbers on paper. Finally he looked up at Professor Brandt, the simple, inadequate question. "What happened to everybody?"

"You want to know that?" Professor Brandt said, nodding, then paused. "I don't know. I asked too. Who were these children? Our children? And what's my answer? I don't know." He glanced away, toward the stuffed bookshelves. "My whole life I thought it was something apart, science. Everything else is lies, but not that. So beautiful, numbers. Always true. If you understand them, they explain the world. I thought that." He looked back at Jake. "I don't know," he said, exhaling it, a gasp. "Even the numbers they ruined. Now they don't explain anything."

He reached over and picked up the folder. "You said you were his friend. What will you do with this?"

"You're his father. What would you do?"

Professor Brandt brought it closer to his chest, so that involuntarily Jake started to reach out his hand. A few pieces of paper, the only proof Bernie would ever have.

"Don't be alarmed," Professor Brandt said. "It's just that—I want you to take it. If I see him again, I don't want to say I gave it up. You took it."

Jake gripped the file and pulled it firmly out of the old man's hands. "Does it really make any difference?"

"I don't know. But I can say it, I didn't give them away, him and his friends. I can say that."

"All right." Jake hesitated. "It's the right thing, you know."

"Yes, the right thing," Professor Brandt said faintly.

He drew himself up, erect, then moved away from the light, just a voice again.

"And you'll tell Lena? That it wasn't me?" He paused. "If she stops coming, you see, there's no one."

He didn't have to tell her anything. She was asleep on the bed, clothed, the boy next to her. He closed the door and sank down on the lumpy couch to read through the file again, even more dismayed than before, time enough now to see the picture fill up with its grisly details, each one a kind of indictment. Valuable to Bernie, but to who else? Is that what Tully intended to sell? But why would Sikorsky want it? The simple answer was that he didn't—he wanted the scientists, busily making their deals with Breimer, each page in the file a pointing finger that they thought had gone away. Valuable to them.

He lay back with his arm over his eyes, thinking about Tully, a business in *persilscheins* before Kransberg, selling releases at Bensheim, sometimes selling them twice. Crooks followed a pattern—what worked once worked again. And these were better than *persilscheins*, as valuable as a ticket out. Deplorable things might have happened, but there was nothing to involve them but pieces of paper, something worth paying for.

When he awoke, it was light and Lena was at the table, staring straight ahead, the closed file in front of her.

"Did you read it?" he said, sitting up.

"Yes." She pushed the file aside. "You made notes. Are you going to write about this?"

"They're points to verify at the Document Center. To prove it all fits."

"Prove to whom?" she said vacantly, then stood up. "Do you want some coffee?"

He watched her light the gas ring and measure out the coffee, going through the ordinary motions of the morning ritual as if nothing had happened.

"Did you understand them? I can explain."

"No, don't explain anything. I don't want to know."

"You have to know."

She turned away to face the stove. "Go wash. The coffee will be ready in a minute."

He got up and went over to the table, glancing down at the folder, caught off balance by her reaction.

"Lena, we need to talk about this. What's in here—"

"Yes, I know. Terrible things. You're just like the Russians. 'Look at the film. See how terrible you are, all you people. What you did in the war.' I don't want to look anymore. The war's over."

"This isn't the war. Read it. They starved people to death, watched them die. That's not the war, that's something else."

"Stop it," she said, raising her hands to her ears. "I don't want to hear it. Emil didn't do those things."

"Yes, he did, Lena," he said quietly. "He did."

"How do you know? Because of that paper? How do you know what they ordered him to do? What he had to do? Look at Renate."

"You think it's the same? A Jew in hiding? They would've murdered—"

"I don't know. Neither do you. He had to protect his family too—it could be. They took families. Maybe to protect me and Peter—"

"You don't really believe that, do you? Read it." He flung open the folder. "Read it. He wasn't protecting you."

She looked down. "You want me to hate him. It's not enough for you that I'm with you? You want me to hate him too? I won't. He's my family, what's left of it. He's all that's left."

"Read it," Jake said evenly. "This isn't about us."

"No?"

"No. It's about some guy in Burgstrasse with blood all over his hands. I don't even know who he is anymore. Not anyone I know."

"Then let him tell you. Let him explain. You owe him that."

"Owe him? As far as I'm concerned, he can rot in Burgstrasse. They're welcome to him."

He looked at her stricken expression and then, angry at himself for being angry, left the room, closing the bathroom door with a thud. He splashed water on his face and rinsed his mouth, as sour as his mood. Not about them, except for her unexpected defense, guilty with an explanation, what everyone in Berlin said, now even her. Two lines in the cards. Still here, even after the file.

He came back to find her standing where he had left her, staring at the floor.

"I'm sorry," he said.

She nodded, not saying anything, then turned, poured out the coffee, and brought it to the table. "Sit," she said, "it'll get cold." A *hausfrau* gesture, to signal it was over.

But when he sat down, she stood next to the table, her face still troubled. "We can't leave him there," she said softly.

"You think he'll be better off in an Allied prison? That's what this means, you know. They try people for this." He put his hand on the folder.

"I won't leave him there. You don't have to do it. I will. Tell your friend Shaeffer," she said, her voice flat.

He looked up at her. "I just want to know one thing."

She met his gaze. "I chose you," she said.

"Not that. Not us. Just so I know. Do you believe what's in here? What he did?"

"Yes," she said, nodding, barely audible.

He flipped open the cover and turned the pages, then pointed to one of the tables.

"This is how long it takes—"

"Don't."

"Sixty days, more or less," he said, unable to stop. "These are the death rates. Still want to get him out?"

He looked up to find that her eyes had filled, turning to him with a kind of mute pleading.

"We can't leave him there. With them," she said.

He went back to the page with its spiky typed numbers and pushed it away. Two lines.

They avoided each other most of the morning, afraid to start in again, while she tended to Erich and he worked up the rest of his notes about Renate for Ron. The story they all had to have, but at least his would be first, ready to send. At noon Rosen turned up and examined the boy. "It's a question of food only," he said. "Otherwise he's healthy." Jake, relieved at the interruption, gathered up his papers, eager to get away, but to his surprise Lena insisted on coming along, leaving Erich with one of Danny's girls.

"I have to go to the press camp first," he said. "Then we can see Fleischman."

"No, not Fleischman," she said, "something else," and then didn't say anything more, so they drove without talking, drained of speech.

The press camp, depleted after Potsdam, was quiet except for the poker game. Jake took only a minute to drop off the notes, grabbing two beers from the bar on his way out.

"Here," he said at the jeep, handing her one.

"No, I don't want it," she said, not sullen but melancholy, like the overcast skies. She directed him toward Tempelhof, and as they got nearer, her mood grew even darker, nothing in her face but a grim determination.

"What's at the airport?"

"No, beyond. The *kirchhof*. Keep going."

They entered one of the cemeteries that sprawled north of Tempelhof.

"Where are we going?"

"I want to visit. Stop over there. No flowers, do you notice? No one has flowers now."

What he saw instead were two GIs with a POW work party, digging a long row of graves.

"What gives?" he said to one of the GIs. "Expecting an epidemic?"

"Winter. Major says they're going to drop like flies once the cold sets in. Get it done before the ground freezes."

Jake looked beyond a cluster of tombstones to another set of fresh graves, then another, the whole cemetery pockmarked with waiting holes.

Peter's was a small marker, no bigger than a piece of rubble, set in a scraggly patch of ground.

"They don't keep it up," Lena said. "I used to take care of it. And then I stopped coming."

"But you wanted to come today," Jake said, uneasy. "This is about Emil, isn't it?"

"You think you know everything he did," she said, looking at the marker. "Before you judge him, maybe you should know this too."

"Lena, why are we doing this?" he said gently. "It doesn't change anything. I know he had a child."

She kept looking at the marker, quiet, then turned to him. "Yours. He had yours. It was your child."

"Mine?" he said, an involuntary word to fill the space, taken up now by a kind of dizziness, an absurd rush of elated surprise, almost goofy, caught off guard in some cartoon of waiting rooms and cigars. In a graveyard. He looked away. "Mine," he said, guarded again. "Why didn't you tell me?"

"Why? To make you sad? If he had lived—I don't know. But he didn't."

"But how—you're sure?"

A disappointed half-smile. "Yes. I can count. You don't have to be a mathematician for that."

"Emil didn't know?"

"No. How could I tell him that? It never occurred to him." She turned back to the marker. "To count."

Jake ran his hand through his hair, at a loss, not sure what to say next. Their child. He thought of her face in the church basement while he read. The way it would have been.

"What did he look like?"

"You don't believe me? You want proof? A photograph?"

"I didn't mean that." He took her arm. "I want it to be. I'm glad we—" He stopped, aware of the marker, and dropped his hand. "I was just curious. Did he look like me?"

"Your eyes. He had your eyes."

"And Emil never—"

"He didn't know your eyes so well." She turned. "No, never. He looked like me. German. He was German, your child."

"A son," he said numbly, his mind flooded with it.

"You left. I thought for good. And here it was inside me, this piece of you. No one would know, just me. So. You remember at the station, when you went away? I knew then."

"And you never said."

"What could I say? 'Stay'? No one needed to know, not even Emil. He was happy, you know. He always wanted a child, and it didn't happen, and then there it was. You don't look at the eyes—you see your own child. So he did that. He was the father of your child. He paid for him. He loved him. And then, when we lost him, it broke his heart. That's what he was doing—while he did all those other things. The same man. Do you understand now? You want to let him 'rot'? There is a debt here. You owe him this much, for your child."

"Lena—"

"And me. What did I do? I lied to him about you. I lied to him about Peter. Now you want me to turn my back on him? I can't do it. You know, when Peter died—American bombs—I thought, it's a punishment. For all the lies. Oh, I know, don't say it, it was crazy, I know. But not this. I have to put it right."

"By telling him now?"

"No, never. It would kill him to know that. But to help him—it's a chance to make it right. A debt."

He took a step back. "Not mine."

"Yes, yours too. That's why I brought you here." She pointed to the marker. "That's you too. Here, in Berlin. One of us. His child—your child. You come in your uniform—so easy to judge when it's not you. All these terrible people, look what they did. Walk away. Let's go to bed—everything will be like before." She turned to him. "Nothing's like before. This is the way it is now—all mixed up. Nothing's like before."

He looked at her, disconcerted. "Maybe one thing. You must still love him, to do this."

"Oh my god, love." She moved forward and put her hands on his chest, almost pounding it. "Stubborn. Stubborn. If I didn't love you, do you think I would have kept it? It would have been so easy to get rid of it. A mistake. These things happen. I couldn't do it. I wanted to keep you. I looked at him, I could see you. So I made Emil his father. Love him? I used Emil to keep you."

He said nothing, then took her hands off his chest. "And this would make it right."

"No, not right. But it's something."

"He'll go to prison."

"It's for certain? Who decides that?"

"It's the law."

"American law. For Germans."

"I am an American."

She looked up at him. "Then you decide," she said, moving away to start back. "You decide."

He stood for a moment, looking from the row of graves down to the marker, the part of him that was here now, then turned slowly and followed her down the hill.

III

Reparations

CHAPTER SIXTEEN

THE FIRST PART of Shaeffer's plan was to get the location moved.

"They've got too many men at Burgstrasse."

"You mean you can't do it?"

"We can do it. It might get messy, that's all. Then we've got an incident. Hell of a lot easier if you get him moved." He scratched his bandage through his shirt, dressed now. "An apartment, maybe."

"They'd have guards there too."

"But not as many. Burgstrasse's a trap. There's only one entrance. To think he's been there all along— How did you find out, by the way? You never said."

"A tip. Don't worry, he's there. Somebody saw him."

"Somebody who?" Schaeffer said, then looked at Jake's face and let it go. "A tip. What did that cost you?"

One small boy. "Enough. Anyway, you wanted to know. Now all you have to do is get him out."

"We'll get him. But let's do it right. I don't like her at Burgstrasse. That's cutting it close, even for us."

"I still don't see why you need her at all. You know where he is. Just go in and get him."

Shaeffer shook his head. "We need the diversion, if we want to do it right."

"That's what she is, a diversion?"

"You said she agreed to do it."

"I haven't."

"You're here, aren't you? Come on, stop wasting time. I've got things to work out. But first, see if you can get him moved."

"Why would Sikorsky do that?"

Shaeffer shrugged. "The lady's got delicate feelings. She won't want to start her new life in a cell—gives a bad taste to it. Might make her think twice. I don't know, figure something out. You're the one with the smart mouth—use it on them for a change. Maybe *you* don't like it, since you're making the delivery. That still the way you want it?"

"I go with her or she doesn't go."

"Suit yourself. Just cover your own ass. I can't worry about you too—just Brandt. Understand?"

"If anything happens to her—"

"I know, I know. You'll hunt me down like a dog." Shaeffer picked up his hat, eager to go. "Nothing's going to happen if we do it right. Now, how about it? First have your little talk with Sikorsky. You're in luck, too," he said, glancing at his watch. "He's in the zone. Control Council meets today, so you won't even have to go out to Karlshorst. You can see him at the banquet. There's always a banquet. Nobody'll even know it's a meeting—you just happened to run into him. With something to offer. How much are you going to ask, have you decided?"

"How much?"

"It plays better if you're selling her. Just don't go overboard—she's not the husband. You want this to happen. The point is to set it up, not make a score."

Jake looked away, disgusted. "Fuck you."

"Try to get him moved," Shaeffer said, ignoring him. "But either way, give me a day or two. I still have to lay my hands on some Russian uniforms."

"What for?"

"Well, we can't go in with American uniforms, can we? Might look a little conspicuous in the Russian zone."

Cowboy stuff. Improbable. "I don't like this. Any of it."

"Let's just get it done, okay?" Shaeffer said. "You can grouse later. Right now you just sweet-talk the Russian and get the door open. We'll do the rest." He grinned at Jake. "I told you we'd make a good team. Takes all kinds, doesn't it?"

Guards had been posted at the driveway entrance to the Control Council building, but Muller's name got him through. He swung around to the gravel forecourt facing the park, then had to find a place in the crowd of jeeps and official cars. The work party had done its job—the park had been cleaned up, everything neat and polished, like the white-scarved sentries. Officers with briefcases rushed through the heavy doors, late or just self-important, a blur of motion. Jake followed one group into the chandeliered hall without drawing a glance. The meeting room, off-limits to press, would be another matter, but Muller's name had worked once and might work again, so he headed down the corridor to his office. His secretary, nails still bright red, was just on her way to lunch.

"He won't be out for hours. The Russians don't start till late, then they go on all afternoon. Want to leave a name? I remember you—the reporter, right? How did you get *in* here?"

"Could you take a message in?"

"Not if I want to keep my job. No press on meeting days. He'd kill me."

"Not him. One of the Russians. Sikorsky. He's—"

"I know who he is. You want to see him? Why not ask the Russians?"

"I'd like to see him today," he said, smiling. "You know what they're like. If you could take in a note? It's official business."

"Whose official business?" she said dryly.

"One note?"

She sighed and handed him a piece of paper. "Make it quick. On my lunch hour, yet." As if she were on her way to Schrafft's.

"I appreciate it," he said, writing. "Jeanie, right?"

"Corporal," she said, but smiled back, pleased.

"By the way, you ever find that dispatcher?"

She put her hand on her hip. "Is that a line, or is it supposed to mean something?"

"Airport dispatcher in Frankfurt. Muller was going to find him for me. Ring a bell?"

He looked up at her face, still puzzled, then saw it clear.

"Oh, the transfer. Right," she said. "We just got the paperwork. Was I supposed to let you know?"

"He was transferred? What name?"

"Who remembers? You know how much comes through here?" she said, cocking her head toward the filing cabinets. "Just another one going home. I only noticed because of Oakland."

"Oakland?"

"Where he was from. Me too. I thought, well, at least one of us is going home. Who is he?"

"Friend of a friend. I said I'd look him up and then I forgot his name."

"Well, he's on his way now, so what's the diff? Wait a minute, maybe it's still in pending." She opened a file drawer, a quick riffle through. "No, it's filed," she said, closing it, another dead end. "Oh well. Does it matter?"

"Not anymore." A transport ship somewhere in the Atlantic. "I'll ask Muller—maybe he remembers."

"Him? Half the time he doesn't know what comes in. It's just paper to him. The army. And they said it would be a great way to meet people."

"Did you?" Jake said, smiling.

"Hundreds. You writing a book there or what? It *is* my lunch hour."

She led him down the corridor to the old court chamber, breezing past the guards by holding up the note. Through the open door Jake could see the four meeting tables pushed together to form a square, smoke rising from the ashtrays like steam escaping from vents. Muller was sitting next to General Clay, sharp-featured and grim, whose face had the tight forbearance of someone listening to a sermon. The Russian speaking seemed to be hectoring everyone, even those at his own table, who sat stonily, heads down, as if they too were waiting for the translation. Jake watched Jeanie walk over to the Russian side of the room, surprising Muller, then followed the pantomime of gestures as she leaned over to hand Sikorsky the note—a quick glance up, a finger pointing to the corridor, a nod, a careful sliding back of his chair as the Russian delegate droned on.

"Mr. Geismar," he said in the hall, his eyebrows raised, intrigued.

"I'm sorry to interrupt."

"No matter. Coal deliveries." He nodded his head toward the closed door, then looked at Jake expectantly. "You wanted something?"

"A meeting."

"A meeting. This is not perhaps the best time—"

"You pick. We need to talk. I have something for you."

"And what is that?"

"Emil Brandt's wife."

Sikorsky said nothing, his hard eyes moving over Jake's face.

"You surprise me," he said finally.

"I don't see why. You made a deal for Emil. Now you can make one for her."

"You're mistaken," he said evenly. "Emil Brandt is in the west."

"Is he? Try Burgstrasse. He'd probably appreciate hearing from you. Especially if you told him his wife was coming to visit. That ought to cheer him up."

Sikorsky turned away, marking time by lighting a cigarette. "You know, it sometimes happens that people come to us. For political reasons. The Soviet future. They see things as we do. That would not, I take it, be the case with her?"

"That's up to her. Maybe you can talk her into it—tell her how much everybody likes it on the collective farm. Maybe Emil can. He's her husband."

"And who exactly are you?"

"I'm an old friend of the family. Think of it as a kind of coal delivery."

"From such an unexpected source. May I ask what prompts you to make this offer? Not, I think, Allied cooperation."

"Not quite. I said a deal."

"Ah."

"Don't worry. I'm not as expensive as Tully."

"You're talking in riddles, Mr. Geismar."

"No, I'm trying to solve one. I'll deliver the wife, you deliver some information. Not so expensive, just some information."

"Information," Sikorsky repeated, noncommittal.

"Little things that have been on my mind. Why you met Tully at the airport. Where you took him. What you were doing in the Potsdam market. A few questions like that."

"A press interview."

"No, private. Just me and you. A good friend of mine got killed that day in Potsdam. Nice girl, no harm to anybody. I want to know why. It's worth it to me."

"Sometimes—it's regrettable—there are accidents."

"Sometimes. Tully wasn't. I want to know who killed him. That's my price."

"And for that you would deliver Frau Brandt? For this family reunion."

"I said I'd deliver her. I didn't say you could keep her. There are conditions."

"More negotiations," Sikorsky said, glancing behind him at the door. "In my experience, these are never satisfactory. We don't get what we want, you don't get what you want. A tiresome process."

"You'll get her."

"What makes you think I'm interested in Frau Brandt?"

"You've been looking for her. You had a man watching Emil's father in case she showed up."

"With you," he said pointedly.

"And if I know Emil, he's been mooning over her. Hard to debrief a man who wants to see his wife. Awkward."

"You think that's the case."

"He did the same thing to us when we had him. Won't go anywhere without her. Otherwise, you'd have shipped him east weeks ago."

"If we had him."

"Are you interested or not?"

Behind them the door opened, a summoning burst of Russian. Sikorsky turned and nodded to an aide.

"The British are responding. Now it's grain. Our grain. Everybody, it seems, wants something."

"Even you," Jake said.

Sikorsky looked at him, then dropped his cigarette on the marble floor and ground it out with his boot, an unnervingly crude gesture, a peasant under the shellac of manners.

"Come to the Adlon. Around eight. We'll talk. Privately," he said, pointing to Jeanie's pen, still in Jake's hand. "Without notes. Perhaps something can be arranged."

"I thought you'd say that."

"Yes? Then let me surprise you. A riddle for you this time. I can't meet your price. I want to know who killed Lieutenant Tully too." He smiled at Jake's expression, as if he had just won the round. "So, at eight."

Jake backtracked down the hall, nervously turning Jeanie's pen over in his hand. None of it would work, not Shaeffer with his borrowed Soviet cap, not even this meeting, another negotiation in which the pieces never moved. I can't meet your price. Then why had he agreed? A sly Slavic smile, squashing a cigarette as easily as a bug.

The office door was closed but not locked, the desk just as Jeanie had left it, tidied up for lunch. He put the pen back in its holder, then looked over at the files. Where did she eat lunch? A mess somewhere in the basement? He pulled open the drawer where the pending folder had been to find a thick wad of carbons, the rest a row of alphabetical tabs. Frankfurt to Oakland. Even without the name to help, it must be here somewhere. And then what? A message through channels, a cable to Hal Reidy to track him down? Weeks either way. Whoever he was sailed nameless on the Atlantic, another *t* uncrossed. Jake slid the drawer shut.

He put his hand on the next cabinet, where Jeanie had filed the police report weeks ago, and, curious, flicked the drawer open to see if it was still there. Tully had a thin folder to himself. The CID report, all of it, with ballistics; an official condolence letter to the mother; a shipping receipt for the coffin and special effects; nothing else, as if he really had been swallowed up in the Havel, out of sight. He looked at the report again, but it was the same one he'd seen, service record, previous assignments, promotions. Why is Sikorsky still interested in you? he wondered, flipping the pages and getting the usual blank reply.

He opened the drawer below, rummaging now. Something cross-referenced, perhaps, like the files at the Document Center. Kommandatura minutes, food supply estimates, all the real business of the occupation, drawers of it. He worked his way back up to the transfer file and opened it again, automatically reaching for the T's, idly thumbing through and then stopping, surprised, when the name leaped out at him. Maybe another Patrick Tully, luckier. But the serial number was the same.

He took the sheet out. Traveling orders, Bremen to Boston, a July 21 sail date. Home to Natick at the end of that week. A new wrinkle, but what kind? Why come to Berlin? Not to fly on to Bremen, with no luggage. The obvious answer was payday, to collect the traveling money for the trip home. Then why go to the Document Center? Jake stared at the flimsy. There hadn't been any orders in his effects. Was it possible that Tully hadn't known? Still up to business as usual while his ticket home floated through the paper channels that crisscrossed Germany?

"Find what you're looking for?"

He turned to see Jeanie standing in the door with a sandwich and a Coke.

"You've got a nerve."

"Sorry. It's just that I did remember his name, after you left. So I thought I'd get the address. I didn't think you'd mind—"

"Next time you want something, ask. Now how about getting out of here before I find out what you're really up to."

He shrugged, a schoolboy with his hand in the principal's file. "Well, I said I was sorry," he said, putting the paper back and closing the drawer. "It's not exactly a state secret."

"I mean it, blow. He finds you in here, he'll have both our heads. You're nice, but you're not that nice."

Jake held up his hands in defeat. "Okay, okay." He went to the door, then stopped, his fingers on the knob. "Can you tell me something, though?"

"Such as?"

"How long does it usually take for orders to come through? Copies, I mean."

"Why?" she said, suspicious, then put the Coke on the desk and leaned against the edge. "Look, things get here when they get here. Depends where they started. Your friend was in Frankfurt? Any time. Frankfurt's a mess. Munich comes right away, but Frankfurt, who knows?"

"And if they were canceled?"

"Same answer. What is this, anyway?"

"I'm not sure," he said, then smiled. "Just wondering. Thanks for the help. You've been a peach. Maybe we can have that drink sometime."

"I'll hold my breath," she said.

He left the office and started down the sweep of opera house stairs. Any time from Frankfurt. But the dispatcher's orders were already here—why not Tully's cancellation, which must have been earlier? Unless no one had bothered, letting death cancel itself out, a no-show on the manifest, one less paper to send.

Outside he took in the line of jeeps stretched across the forecourt like one of the old taxi ranks at Zoo Station or the Kaiserhof. Now they parked here, or at headquarters in Dahlem, motor pool branches, waiting for different fares. If you wanted a ride, this would be the place to come. Unless you already had a Russian driver.

He got back to Savignyplatz to find Erich playing with some of the girls from down the hall, their new pet. More attention, Jake thought, than he'd probably had in his life. Rosen was there with his medical bag, drinking tea, the whole room oddly domestic. Lena followed him into the bedroom.

"What happened?"

"Nothing yet. Sikorsky wants to have dinner at the Adlon."

"Well, the Adlon," she said ironically, patting her hair. "Like old times."

"Not for you. Dinner for two."

"You're going alone? What about Shaeffer?"

"First I have to set things up."

"And then I go?"

"Let's see what he has to say first."

He took Liz's gun from the bureau and opened the cylinder, checking it.

"You mean he won't do it?"

"Well, at the moment he says Emil's in the west."

"The west?"

"He says," Jake said, catching her anxious expression in the mirror. "Don't worry, he'll do it. He just wants to do a little fencing."

"He doesn't believe you," she said, still agitated.

He turned to her. "He believes me. It's his game, that's all, so we play by his rules." He took her shoulder. "Now stop. I said I'd get Emil out and I will. This is the way we do it. He's the kind of guy who likes a little dinner first, to break the ice."

She turned away. "It's true? That's all, dinner?"

"That's all."

"They why are you taking the gun?"

"Seen the Adlon lately?" She looked at him blankly. "Lots of rats."

CHAPTER SEVENTEEN

IT WENT WRONG from the start. The Russians, for no apparent reason, had set up a checkpoint at the Brandenburg Gate, and by the time Jake had shown his ID and was waved through he was late. He lost more time trying to find his way through the deserted shell of the Adlon, rescued finally by a man in a formal cutaway who appeared out of the dark like a ghost from the old days, a desk clerk without a desk. Given the damage, it seemed a miracle that anyone still lived here at all. The lobby and main block facing the Linden were smashed, but a rough path had been cleared through the rubble to a wing in the back. The clerk led him with a flashlight past small heaps of brick, stepping over them as if they were just something the hall maid hadn't got around to yet, then up a flight of service stairs to a dim corridor. At the end, as surreal as the rest of it, was a brightly lit dining room, buzzing with Soviet uniforms and waiters in white jackets carrying serving dishes. The open windows looked down on the gaping hole of the garden where Goebbels' house had been, and Sikorsky sat near one of them, blowing smoke out into the night air. Jake had barely started toward him when a hand caught his sleeve.

"Whatever are you doing here?"

Jake jumped, more nervous than he'd realized. "Brian," he said numbly, the florid face somehow surreal too, out of place. He was sitting at a table for four, with two Russian soldiers and a pale civilian.

"Not the food, I hope. Although Dieter here swears by the kohlrabi. Have a drink?"

"Can't. I'm meeting someone. Interview."

"You couldn't do better than this lot. Took the Reichstag. This chap here actually planted the flag."

"He did."

"Well, he says he did, which comes to the same thing." He glanced across the room. "Not Sikorsky, is it?"

"Mind your own business," Jake said.

"You won't get anything there. Blood out of a stone. You'll be at the camp later? Ought to be quite a blowout."

"Why?"

"Haven't you heard? The Rising Sun's about to set. They're just waiting for the cable. Be all over then but the shouting, won't it? Six bloody years."

"Yeah, all over."

"Cheers," Brian said, lifting his eyes toward Sikorsky as he raised his glass. "Watch your back. Killed his own men, that one did."

"Says who?"

"Everybody. Ask him." He drained the glass. "Actually, better not. Just watch the back."

Jake clamped him on the shoulder and moved away. Sikorsky was standing now, waiting for him. He didn't offer to shake hands, just nodded as Jake took off his hat and placed it on the table facing his, brim to brim, as if even the hats expected a standoff.

"A colleague?" Sikorsky said, sitting down.

"Yes."

"He drinks too much."

"He just pretends to. It's an old newspaperman's trick."

"The British," Sikorsky said, flicking an ash. "Russians drink for real." He poured a glass from the vodka bottle and pushed it toward Jake, his own eyes clear and sober. "Well, Mr. Geismar, you have your meeting. But you don't speak." He took a puff from his brown cigarette, holding Jake's eyes. "Something is wrong?"

"I've never looked at a man who wanted to kill me before. It's a strange feeling."

"You weren't in the war, then. I've looked at hundreds. Of course, they also looked at me."

"Including Russians?" Jake said, poking for a reaction. "I heard you killed your own men."

"Not Russians. Saboteurs," he said easily, unaffected.

"Deserters, you mean."

"There were no deserters at Stalingrad. Only saboteurs. It was not an option. Is this what you want to discuss? The war? You know nothing about it. We held the line. Guns in front, guns at your back. A powerful inducement to fight. It was necessary to win. And we did win."

"Some of you did."

"Let me tell you a story, since you are interested. We had to supply the line from across the Volga, and the Germans had the shore covered from the cliffs. We unload the boats, they shoot at us. But we had to unload. So we used boys. Not soldiers. We used the children."

"And?"

"They shot them."

Jake looked away. "What's your point?"

"That you cannot possibly know what it was like. You cannot know what we had to do. We had to make ourselves steel. A few saboteurs? That was nothing. Nothing."

"I wonder if they thought so."

"You're being sentimental. We didn't have that luxury. Ah," he said to the waiter, handing him some coupons. "Two. There is no menu, I'm afraid. You like cabbage soup?"

"It's one of my favorites."

Sikorsky raised his eyebrows, then waved the waiter away. "It's as Gunther says. Fond of jokes. A cynic, like all sentimentalists."

"You've discussed me with him."

"Of course. Such a curious mix. Persistent. What did you want? That, I still don't know."

"Did you pay him too?"

"To discuss you?" A thin smile. "Don't concern yourself. He is not corrupt. A thief, but not corrupt. Another sentimentalist."

"Maybe we don't want to be steel."

"Then you will not win," Sikorsky said simply. "You'll break."

Jake sat back, staring at the hard soldier's face, the shine of sweat literally metallic in the bright light. "Tell me something," he said, almost to himself. "What happens when it's over?" The old question, turned around. "The Japanese are going to surrender. What happens to it all then? All the steel?"

Sikorsky looked at him, intrigued. "Does it feel over to you?"

Before he could say anything, the waiter came with the food, his frayed white sleeve too long for him, almost dipping into the soup. Sikorsky began to eat noisily, not bothering to put out his cigarette.

"So, shall we begin?" he said, dropping a chunk of bread into the soup. "You want to make conditions, you say, but you really have no intention of bringing Frau Brandt to us. So what are you playing at?"

"What makes you say that?" Jake said, thrown off-balance.

"She's the woman I met in the Linden? Not just a friend, I think." He shook his head. "No, no intention."

"You're wrong," Jake said, trying to keep his voice firm.

"Please. But it's of no importance. I'm not interested in whether Herr Brandt has his wife. Pleasant for him, perhaps; of no importance to me. You see, you have brought the wrong thing to the table. Next time, try coal, something that's wanted. You can't negotiate with this."

"Then why haven't you moved him?"

"I have moved him. The minute you told me where he was. If you knew, perhaps others know too. A precaution. Of course, perhaps not. You work on your own, Gunther says. He admires that in you. A man like himself, maybe. But he's a fool." He looked up from the soup. "We are not fools. So many make that mistake. The Germans, until we destroyed them." He took the soaked piece of bread into his mouth and sucked it.

"But you kept him in Berlin," Jake said, not letting it go.

"Yes. Too long. That was your Lieutenant Tully. Keep him, I may need his help, he said. A mistake."

"Help in doing what?"

"Get the others," Sikorsky said simply.

"Emil would never—"

"You think not? Don't be too sure what a man will do. But as it happens, I agree with you. Not like Tully. Now there was a man who would do anything."

"Like use Lena. To make Emil help."

"I thought this too—that it was his plan. So, as you say, I looked for her—the bargaining chip. But now I see it was a mistake. Tully didn't know."

"Know what?"

"About you. What use is a wife with another man? No use. The unfaithful Frau Brandt. You see, Mr. Geismar, you have come on a fool's errand. You offer her—you pretend to offer her—but I want his colleagues, not his wife. She's of no use to me anymore. She never was, it seems. Thank you for clarifying this matter. It's time Brandt left Berlin. There's no reason to keep him here now. Not at Burgstrasse. You knew that how?"

"He was seen," Jake said.

"By the Americans? Well, as I thought—better to move him. And he has work to do. A mistake, this waiting. Eat your soup, it's getting cold."

"I don't want it."

"You don't mind, then?" Sikorsky reached over to switch the plates. "To waste food—"

"Help yourself," Jake said, his mind still wandering, trying to sort things out. The bargaining chip. But Tully hadn't looked for her. He'd gone to the Document Center. Had Sikorsky known? Still giving away nothing, eating soup. Behind them, Brian's table had got louder, glasses clinking in a toast, a spurt of laughter reaching him like an echo as he stared at the soup plate. You've brought the wrong thing to the table.

"Why did you ask me here, then?"

"It was you who asked me," Sikorsky said blandly, tipping his plate to spoon the soup.

"And you thought it would be amusing to tell me to go fly a kite."

"Amusing, no. I'm not so fond of jokes as you. An idea of mine. A different negotiation. Something we both want. Shall I surprise you?"

"Try me."

"I'm going to take you to Emil Brandt."

Jake looked down quickly, not trusting his own reaction. A white tablecloth, stained, Sikorsky's blunt fingers resting against the spoon.

"Really. And why would you want to do that?"

"It would be useful. He is—what did you call it? Mooning. It's true, he speaks of her. 'When is she coming?'" he said, raising his voice in a falsetto. "It would be better for his work not to have these false hopes now. Would he believe me? But you, her sweetheart," he said, twisting his mouth over the word. "You can say goodbye for her, and he can leave in peace. A small service." He wiped the corner of his mouth, then crumpled the napkin on the table.

"You're a real prick, aren't you?"

"Mr. Geismar," Sikorsky said, his eyes almost twinkling. "I'm not the one sleeping with his wife."

"And when does all this happen?" Jake said, pretending to be calm.

"Now. He leaves tomorrow. It's better, if the Americans know Burgstrasse. They will excite themselves. You can put their minds at rest too. He's not coming back."

"They'll protest."

"Yes, they like that. But he'll be gone. Another who has chosen the Soviet future. Shall we go?" He reached for his hat.

"You're going too fast."

Sikorsky smiled. "The element of surprise. Very effective."

"I mean we're not finished. I still don't have what I want."

Sikorsky looked at him blankly.

"Information. That was the deal."

"Mr. Geismar," he said, sighing. "At such a moment." He dropped the hat and took out another brown cigarette instead, checking his watch. "Five minutes. Your friend at the market? I've told you, an unfortunate—"

"You were there to point me out. Why?"

"Because you were a nuisance," he said quickly, bored, waving some smoke away. "You're still a nuisance."

"To whom? Not to you."

Sikorsky looked at him, not answering, then turned to the open window. "What else?"

"You said you wanted to know who killed Tully. Why?"

"Isn't that obvious to you? My partner in crime, as you would say. Now we'll have to arrange another source of supply. An inconvenient death." He turned back. "What else?"

"You met him at Tempelhof. Where did you take him?"

"This matters to you?"

"It's my story. I want to know the details. Where?"

Sikorsky shrugged. "To get a jeep. He wanted a jeep."

"At the Control Council?" Jake said, taking a shot.

"Yes. Kleist Park. There are jeeps there."

"And after?"

"After? It's your idea that we should make a tour of Berlin? Be seen together?"

"You were seen at Tempelhof."

"By whom?" he said, suddenly alert.

"By the woman you killed at Potsdam."

"Ah," he said, frowning, not quite knowing what to make of this, then brushed it away with some ash on the table. "Well, she's dead."

"But you were seen. So why meet him in the first place?"

"You can guess that, I think."

"To give him money."

Sikorsky nodded. "Of course. With him it was always money. Such a love of money. An American failing."

"That's easy for you to say when you print it with our plates."

"Paid for with blood. You envy us that bookkeeping? We paid for every mark."

"All right. So you paid him off for Brandt."

"As a matter of fact, no. It's important to you, these details? He was paid for Brandt when they arrived at the border. Cash on delivery."

"Tully drove him to the Russian zone?" Not a weekend in Frankfurt after all.

Sikorsky leaned back, almost smug, a veteran telling war stories. "It was safer. To fly Brandt out would have been risky—easier to trace. He had to disappear, no trail. So Tully drove him. Not such a great distance. Even so, you know he demanded gasoline for the return trip? Always a little something extra. He was that kind of man. Another detail for you. He went back on Russian gas."

"So why pay him at Tempelhof?"

"For future deliveries."

"In advance? You trusted him?"

Sikorsky smiled. "You didn't know him. Give him a little, he'd be back for more. You could trust him to do that. A safe investment."

"Which you lost."

"Regrettably. But it's not important. As you say, we can print more. Now, you're satisfied? Come, you can see the end of the story."

"Just one more thing. Why do you care who killed him? That's why you asked me here, isn't it? To see what I could tell you."

"And you have. You've told me what I want to know. You don't know."

"But why should it matter at all? You've got Brandt. You didn't care about the money. Revenge? You didn't give a damn about Tully."

"About him, no. About his death, yes. A man drives off and is killed. A victim of bad company? In this case, I must say, nothing could be more likely—a man like him, not a surprising end. But the money is still there. Not so likely. Unless, instead, it's something else. The Americans. If they know about our arrangement. In that case, some action would need to be taken before—well, before anything else happened. So what does our Mr. Geismar want? I wonder. Is he working for them? Then I watch your face as you move your pieces up, your questions, and I know. It's only you. When you play chess with a Russian, keep something in reserve, Mr. Geismar, a piece in the back row. Now, enough foolishness."

He reached again for his hat. Jake gripped the edge of the cloth, as if the table itself, like everything else, was slipping away. Do something.

"Sit down," Jake said.

Sikorsky glanced up sharply, bristling, not used to taking orders, then slowly moved his hand back.

"That's better. I don't play chess. And you're not as good at reading faces as you think you are. What makes you think I'd go anywhere with you? A man who tried to kill me?"

"Is that all? If I wanted to kill you, I could do it here. I still could."

"I doubt it. Not with witnesses." He jerked his head toward Brian's table. "An accident in the market, that's more your line. Too bad you didn't do it yourself. I'll bet you're a good shot."

"Excellent," Sikorsky said, exhaling smoke.

"But a lousy judge of character. Let's watch your face now and see what comes up. Tully wasn't going to deliver anything, he was playing you for a sap. He was going home at the end of the week—don't bother, it's true, I've seen his orders. He was just collecting a little something extra before he ran out on you."

Sikorsky stared at him stonily, his face showing no reaction at all.

"Mm. I thought so. Want more? He also had an appointment with a Public Safety officer. That interest you? It should. He liked to collect twice. Maybe you weren't the highest bidder."

"For what?" Sikorsky said quietly.

"What he was going to use to get to the others at Kransberg. A little going-out-of-business sale. And you can take my word for it, it wasn't Emil or his wife."

"Why should I take your word for anything?"

"Because I know where he went that day and you don't. You just told me so yourself."

"Where?"

"Well, if I told you, then both of us would know. What would be the sense in that? This way, I can buy a little insurance—something to keep your finger off the trigger. I'm too valuable to shoot."

Sikorsky stubbed out his cigarette, rubbing it back and forth. "What do you want?" he said finally.

Jake shook his head. "Your information isn't good enough. You see, *you* brought the wrong thing to the table. I don't want to see Emil. You can tell him goodbye yourself."

"You don't want to see him," he said skeptically.

"Not especially. But his wife does. All I wanted was to make an arrangement, as a favor to her. No skin off your nose, as far as I could see. But no. You just want to prove what a tough guy you are. Steel. So nobody gets what he wants." He paused, then looked up. "She wants to see him. That's still the deal. If I were you, I wouldn't be in such a hurry to move him—if you want us to have another little talk."

There was a roar behind them as Brian, in his cups now, laughed at one of his own jokes.

"An old newspaperman's trick," Sikorsky said sarcastically. "This too, I think."

"Suit yourself. I'd give it some thought. You know, suspicion's a funny thing—it eats everything up. Even steel can rust. A Russian failing." Now it was his turn to reach for his hat. "Anyway, thanks for the soup. When you change your mind, let me know."

He stood up, so that Sikorsky was forced to rise as well, eyes still locked on his.

"It seems we've wasted our time, Mr. Geismar."

"Not exactly. There was only one thing I wanted to know, and now I do."

"One thing. Yet so many questions."

"A newspaperman's trick. Get people talking and they'll usually tell you what you're looking for."

"Is that so?" Sikorsky said dryly. "And what have you learned?"

Jake leaned forward, resting his hands on the table. "That it's still going on. It didn't end with Tully—you just want us to think so. That's why you want me to see Emil—so I can tell everybody I saw him go and I know who his delivery boy was. Case closed. But it isn't. You just told me so. Future deliveries. Emil had to disappear, no trace. Why? Tully gets killed. Game over? No, an inconvenience, just a hitch in the operation. Was he going home? Not the end of the world either. Why? Because he wasn't working alone." Jake leaned back. "It's like Stalingrad, isn't it? You're still protecting your supply line. Tully wasn't your partner, he was just one of those kids the Germans could pick off. Expendable. As long as the boats kept running. You don't care who killed him, just whether we know how it all worked. And now here's Geismar, sticking his nose in. He makes the connection to Tully, half the story. So let's let him think he's got it all, let's even give him a goodbye interview. I told you you were a lousy judge of character. Do you think I'm going to stop? When this started, I thought I had a bad apple in the black market. Then it kept getting bigger and bigger. Not just Tully, not just Brandt. Not even just you. Now it's a whole rotten barrel. With your supplier still in place, selling us out. That's the story I want."

Sikorsky stood still, expressionless. "If you live to write it."

"Well, that's up to you, isn't it?" Jake said, nodding toward Sikorsky's holster. "If you're sure I'm the only one who knows. Are you?"

They stood facing each other for another second, not moving.

Jake put on his hat. "Checkmate."

Sikorsky stared at him, then slowly raised his hand palm out in a stop sign. Then, resigned, he turned it down toward the table, gesturing to Jake to take his seat. "You are attracting attention."

Sikorsky sat down, but even after Jake followed he said nothing, looking away toward the room, as if he were sifting through his options. Jake waited him out. How would he start? But Sikorsky stayed silent, apparently at a loss, his gaze stuck over Jake's shoulder. Then, unexpectedly, he raised his eyebrows and smiled oddly, no more than a tremor of his closed mouth.

"You're a poor chess player, Mr. Geismar," he said, still looking past Jake.

"Am I?"

"Very. Even a poor player knows not to move up the queen."

Now the smile broadened, almost a smirk, so that Jake turned to follow it, feeling some new disturbance in the room.

She was standing near Brian's table, letting him take her hand, hair pinned up, the palm of sequins glittering on the front of her dress, the whole room quiet, looking at her. In the startled second that followed, Jake saw everything in a rush, a jerky loop of film—Brian kissing her hand, offering a drink, the Russians getting up, Lena shaking her head politely, then finally her face coming toward him, bold and determined, flushed with its own daring, the same face that had jumped off the sailboat into the Havel. He felt himself rise, the room skidding around him, but in the panic of everything going wrong what struck him, and wouldn't let go, was the sequins, that she had dressed for Emil.

"Frau Brandt," Sikorsky said, moving a chair. "An opportune visit. You've come to see your husband?"

"Yes."

"Good. He'll be pleased. Mr. Geismar here has refused our invitation. But you, I think, may feel differently."

"Refused?" she said to Jake.

"The general isn't interested in a meeting. They're taking Emil east tomorrow," Jake said evenly.

"East? But then—" She halted, stopped by his glance.

"Yes," Sikorsky said. "So you see, opportune. Of course, you would be welcome too. An honored guest of the state."

"You mean he's leaving?" She turned to Jake, glaring. "Did you know this?"

"A little surprise from the general. We were just discussing a different arrangement. A later departure date."

"Oh," she said, looking down, finally aware. "A later date."

"Unnecessary now," Sikorsky said.

"I thought he wouldn't believe you," she said weakly, still looking down at the table.

"You were correct. My apologies," Sikorsky said to Jake. He poured some vodka and moved the glass to Lena. "A drink?"

She shook her head, biting her lower lip. "Leaving. So I won't see him."

"No, no. Dear lady, you can see him now. That's what I'm telling you." He turned to Jake, enjoying himself. "That is what you wanted, isn't it?" he said smoothly.

Lena answered for him. "Yes. I want to see him. You can arrange that?"

Sikorsky nodded. "Come with me."

"Nobody's going anywhere," Jake said, moving his hand to cover hers. "You think I'm going to let her walk out of here with you?"

Sikorsky rolled his eyes. "Your friend is suspicious. Like a Russian," he said, playing. "Calm yourself. We don't go far. Upstairs. Then I'll bring Frau Brandt back to you and we can finish our talk. An interesting conversation," he said to Lena. "Mr. Geismar still has things to tell me." He looked at Jake. "You'll be the guarantee for her return."

"Upstairs?" Jake said. "You mean he's here?"

"I thought it better to keep him close. For his safety. And you see how convenient."

"Had it all figured out, didn't you?"

"Well, I did not expect Frau Brandt. Sometimes—"

"Then figure again. She doesn't go. Not like this."

Sikorsky sighed. "A pity. But it's of no importance."

Lena looked at Jake, then slipped her hand out from under his. "Yes, I'll do it."

"No, you won't."

"It's my choice," she said to him.

"As you say, Frau Brandt," Sikorsky said. "Your choice. Have a drink, Mr. Geismar. We won't be long."

Jake looked from one to the other, cornered. Sikorsky moved his chair back.

"If she goes, I go with her."

"You don't think your presence would be intrusive?" Sikorsky said, amused.

"I won't be watching them, just you. Try one move—"

Sikorsky waved his hand, brushing this away.

"All right," Jake said, "then sit here nice and quiet while I tell Brian where we're going. If we're not back down in fifteen minutes, he'll—"

"What? Bring in reinforcements? But you came alone."

"You sure?" Jake said, standing.

"Oh yes," Sikorsky said easily. "My men had instructions to inform me if you were followed. At the checkpoint."

Jake stopped for a minute, taking this in. All figured out. And what else?

Sikorsky nodded toward the other table, where Brian was laughing. "A poor choice of hero."

"Good enough to pull an alarm. I don't intend to disappear without a trace. And you don't want to make that kind of noise. Not you."

"As you wish. And give him your gun." He smiled. "Or did you intend to use it upstairs?" He wagged his forefinger. "A little trust, Mr. Geismar. Please." He pointed to the gun, holding his gaze until Jake took it out and put it on the table.

Lena sat up, rigid, as if it were something alive, waiting to strike, there all along under the words. Jake watched her as he moved to the other table to speak to Brian. Her shoulders were straight and tense, and he saw that she was finally frightened, but as he came back, leaving an open-mouthed Brian, she got up without a word. When Sikorsky led them out of the room, even the waiters stopped to watch, caught by the flash of sequins.

The walk down the hall felt like a forced march, quiet and plodding. When they started up the stairs, Lena grabbed his arm, as if she were about to trip.

"I didn't know," she said, almost whispering. "I'm sorry. I didn't know. I've ruined everything."

"No, I'll think of something," he said in English. "He still wants to talk to me. Just see Emil and get out. Don't wait."

"But what about—"

"There's enough light?" Sikorsky said from above.

"I'll think of something," he said, hushing her.

But what? The checkpoint, arranged. Emil ready to go. All the pieces moved into place. But Sikorsky wanted to talk, not sure what Jake knew. Ready for a bargaining chip, if Jake could think of one, something that might threaten the supply line. Where Tully had gone in his jeep that day, maybe, anything to play it out a little further, until Lena was safely away. Just one more move. Except Sikorsky always seemed one ahead.

There was no mistaking where they were going—a door with two guards in front carrying machine guns, menacing in an ordinary hotel corridor. The guards came to attention as Sikorsky approached, looking straight ahead as he swept past, ignoring them, and reached for the handle.

"Wait a minute," Lena said, hesitating, flustered. "It's just—so silly. I don't know what to say."

"Frau Brandt," Sikorsky said, with almost comic exasperation, as if she were rummaging through her purse.

Lena took a breath. "Yes, all right."

Sikorsky opened the door, letting her go first.

Emil was reading at a table near the window, jacketless, looking exactly the same, the only person Jake had seen in Germany who seemed not to have lost weight. The same dark hair and wire glasses, the same pale skin and drooping shoulders, all the same. When he turned and started to get up, too astonished to smile, his face turned soft. He gripped the back of the chair.

"Lena."

For an instant, Jake could see him take in the good dress, the pile of blond hair, like the ghost of some old Adlon evening, his eyes moist, not yet ready to believe his happiness.

"Visitors, Herr Brandt," Sikorsky said, but Emil seemed not to have heard him, moving toward her, still dazzled.

"They found you. I thought—" Then he was there, his face against her hair, his hand scarcely touching the back of her neck, as if a stronger physical contact would make her disappear. "How you look," he said, his voice low and familiar. Jake felt a tiny nick, like a paper cut.

Lena moved back, with his arm still around her, and reached up to brush a lock of hair away from his forehead. "You're well?"

He nodded. "And now you're here."

She dropped her hand to his shoulder. "It's just for a little while. I can't stay." She saw his confused face and took another step back, out of the embrace, then turned to Sikorsky. "Oh, I don't know what to say. What have you told him?"

Emil finally looked at the others, stopping, dumbfounded, when he saw Jake, a different kind of ghost.

"Hello, Emil," Jake said.

"Jacob?" he said, uncertain, almost sputtering.

Jake stepped closer so that they were literally head to head, the same height, and now he saw that Emil had changed after all, the eyes no longer just shortsighted and vague but hollow, the life behind them scraped away.

"I don't understand," Emil said.

"Mr. Geismar has brought Frau Brandt to visit," Sikorsky said. "He was concerned that she be returned safely."

"Returned?"

"She has decided to remain in Germany. A patriot," he said dryly.

"Remain? But she's my wife." Emil turned back to Lena. "What does it mean?"

"You will have things to say to each other," Sikorsky said, glancing at his watch. "So little time. Sit." He indicated a frayed couch. "Mr. Geismar, come with me. These are private matters, you agree? It's safe—the same room." He nodded to an open connecting door.

"He's staying with you?" Jake said.

"A suite. Convenient for guests."

For the first time, Jake looked around the small sitting room, shabby from the war, a crack running up the wall, the couch covered with Emil's rumpled sheet. Guards outside.

"I don't understand," Emil said again.

"They're sending you east," Lena said. "It was a chance to see you. Before it was too late. There—how else to say it?"

"East?"

She nodded. "And it's because of me, I know it. You were safe there. And now—all this," she said, her voice catching. "Oh, why did you leave? Why did you believe that man?"

Emil looked at her, shaken. "I wanted to believe him."

"Yes, for me. Like before. That last week, to come to Berlin—I thought you were dead. My fault. All these things, for me." She stopped, lowering her head. "Emil, I can't."

"You're my wife," he said numbly.

"No." She put her hand gently on his arm. "No. We have to make an end."

"An end?"

"Come," Sikorsky said to Jake, suddenly embarrassed. "We have other matters."

"Later."

Sikorsky narrowed his eyes, then shrugged. "As you wish. In fact, it's better. You can stay until he's away. No one to pull the alarm. You can have the couch. You don't mind? He says it's not bad. Then we can talk as long as you like."

"You said he was leaving tomorrow."

"I lied. Tonight." One step ahead.

"Talk about what?" Emil said, distracted. "Why is he here?"

"Why are you here, Mr. Geismar?" Sikorsky said playfully. "Would you like to explain?"

"Yes, why do you come with her?" Emil said.

But Jake didn't hear him, his mind fixed instead on the hard eyes above Sikorsky's smile. As long as you like. All night, waiting to hear something Jake didn't know. Locked up here until he did. Worse than cornered—caught.

"But she leaves," Jake said, looking directly at Sikorsky.

"Of course. That was the agreement."

But why believe this either? He saw Lena being bundled onto a train with Emil, while he sat, helpless, in his Adlon cell, making up stories. I lied. They'd never let her go now.

Sikorsky put his finger on Jake's chest, almost poking it. "A little trust, Mr. Geismar. We'll give her to your friend. Then we'll have a brandy. It loosens the tongue. You can tell me all about Lieutenant Tully."

"Tully? You know Tully?" Emil said.

Before he could answer, there was an abrupt knock on the door, so unexpected that he jumped. Two Russians, chests half covered with medals, started talking to Sikorsky even before they were in the room. For a second Jake thought they'd come for Emil, but their attention was elsewhere, some crisis that involved quick spurts of Russian back and forth, a blur of hands, until Sikorsky, annoyed, waved them to the bedroom door. He glanced at his watch again.

"Excuse me. I'm sorry to miss your explanation," he said to Jake. "An interesting moment. Frau Brandt, there isn't much time. I suggest you save the details for later." He looked at Jake. "Send your husband a letter. Perhaps Mr. Geismar will help you with it." He raised his head and barked out something in Russian to the other room, evidently answering a question only he had understood. "Of course, it's better like this. The personal touch. But hurry, please. I'll only be a moment—a small office matter, not so dramatic as yours." He turned to go.

"Why should he help you with a letter?" Emil said. "Lena?"

Sikorsky smiled at Jake. "A good starting point," he said, then crossed over to the bedroom with another burst of Russian, leaving the door open so that the sound of him was still in the room.

Jake looked away from the door, his eyes stopping at the crack in the wall, another collapsing house, suddenly back there again, the creak of joists whistling inside his head. No newsreel cameras waiting outside this time, machine guns, but the same calm panic. Get her out before it comes down. Don't think, do it.

"Why do you bring her?" Emil said. "What do you have to do with all this?"

"Stop it," Lena said. "He came to help you. Oh god, and now look. Jake, what are we going to do? They're going to take him. There isn't time—"

He could hear the sound of Russian through the open door, low, like the rumbling of the settling wall in Gelferstrasse. He'd just walked out the door. A hero. People saw what they wanted to see. I'll only be a moment.

"Time for what?" Emil said. "You come here together and—"

"Stop it, stop it," Lena said, tugging at his sleeve. "You don't understand. It was for *you*."

He did stop, surprised by the force of her hand, so that in the sudden quiet the sound of Russian in the next room seemed louder. Jake glanced again at the crack. One more move. The element of surprise.

"No, keep talking," Jake said quickly. "Just say anything. It doesn't matter what, as long as they think we're talking." He took off his hat and put it on Emil's head, lowering the brim, testing it.

"What are you doing? Are you crazy?"

"Maybe. Keep *talking*. Lena, say something. They need to know you're here." He started tearing off his tie. "Come on," he said to Emil, "strip. Hurry."

"Oh, Jake—"

"He's crazy," Emil said.

"Do you want to get out of here or not?"

"Get out? It's not possible."

"Take off the goddamn shirt. What have you got to lose? They're giving you a one-way ticket to Nordhausen, except this time you're one of the guys in the tunnel."

Emil looked at him, amazed. "No. They promised—"

"The Soviets? Don't be an ass. Lena, help. And say something."

She looked at him for an instant, too frightened to move, then Jake nudged her toward Emil and she started unbuttoning his shirt. Pale white skin. "Do what he says. Please," she said. Then, raising her public voice, "You know, Emil, it's so difficult, all this." The words dribbled out, a kind of nervous gibberish.

Jake dropped the holster belt on the couch and unzipped his pants. "We're the same size. Just keep the brim down on the hat. They don't know me. All they'll see is the uniform."

Lena was keeping up a patter, but flagging. Jake stepped out of the trousers. This would be the moment. Caught literally with his pants down.

"Quick, for Christ's sake."

"You know about Nordhausen?" Emil said.

"I was there." He flung the pants at him. "I saw your work."

Emil said nothing, staring.

"Jake, I can't do it," Lena said, struggling with the buckle.

Wordlessly, almost in a trance, Emil unhitched it and dropped his pants.

"Right. Now it's your turn," Jake said to Emil. "Put these on and say something. Loud, but not too loud. Just a little spat. Lena, come here." He nodded at Emil to start talking and took her by the shoulders. "Now listen to me."

"Jake—"

"Ssh. You walk out of here with the uniform." He jerked his head toward Emil, putting on Jake's pants. "Like nothing happened. The guards don't care about us, just him. We're the visitors. Don't say anything, just go. Casual, see. Then you go downstairs to Brian and get out fast. Tell him it's an emergency, *now,* understand? But keep him with you. If Brian doesn't have a car, take the jeep. It's on the Linden, keys in the pants there, got that? Then go like hell. They'll follow.

Don't go through the Brandenburg, they've got a checkpoint. Okay? But fast. Pull Brian away if you have to. Go to the flat and stay there and keep him out of sight." He pointed his thumb to Emil, dressed now. "Ready?" he said to him, straightening the army tie. "See, a real American."

"What about you?" Lena said.

"Let's get him out first. I told you I would, didn't I? Now get going."

"Jake," she said, reaching for him.

"Later. Come on, say something," he said to Emil. "And keep the hat down."

"And if they stop us?" Emil said.

"They stop you."

"You'll get us all killed."

"No, I'm saving your life." Jake looked up at him. "Now we're quits."

"Quits," Emil said.

"That's right. For everything." He reached up and took off Emil's glasses.

"I can't see," Emil said feebly.

"Then take her arm. Move." He reached for the door handle.

"If you do this, they'll kill you," Lena said quietly, a pleading.

"No, they won't. I'm famous," he said, trying for a smile but meeting her eyes instead. "Now, quick." He turned the handle, careful not to make noise. "Don't say goodbye. Just go."

He stood behind the door, opening it for them, waving them out with a frantic shooing motion. A second of hesitation, more dangerous even than going; then she looked at him once more, biting her lip, and slipped her arm under Emil's and led him out. Jake closed the door and started talking, so that his voice would reach the other room, reassuring everyone, even the guards, with the sound of conversation. Use your smart mouth. But how long would the Russians keep talking? In the hall by now, approaching the stairs. Just a few minutes, a little luck. Until Sikorsky came out and reached for his gun. Because of course Lena was right—they'd kill him. No more moves left.

He started buttoning Emil's shirt, trying to think and talk at the same time. A holster belt on the couch. Why hadn't he told them to pick up the gun downstairs, or would Brian be sober enough to grab it on his way out? Making his excuses at the table, following them across the field of rubble to the street, not running, stumbling in the dark. They'd need time. He looked around the room. Nothing. Not even a closet, a Wilhelmine armoire. The bathroom was next door, off the bedroom. Nothing but a door to the machine guns and a window to Goebbels' garden. A soft landing, but not from two stories up. No, three, a hopeless drop. In prison movies they tied sheets together, a white braid, like Rapunzel's hair. Fairy tales. He glanced again at the couch—one sheet, nothing to anchor it but the radiator under the windowsill, visible to the Russians through the open door. Even the simplest knot would take too long. They'd shoot before he made the first hitch.

He reached for the belt to Emil's pants, wondering why he was bothering to dress at all. There had to be something, some way to talk himself past the guards. They all wanted watches, like the Russian behind the Alex. But he was Emil now, not a GI with something to trade. He looked toward the window again. An old radiator that probably hadn't felt heat in a year, even with the control handle all the way open. Old-fashioned, shaped to match the door handle. From the next room there was a sudden burst of laughter. They'd be breaking up soon. How long had it been? Enough time for Brian to get them to the Linden? He talked again to the empty room, the scene Sikorsky had been sorry to miss.

He started threading the belt through the pants loops then stopped, looking up again at the window. Why not? At least it was something to minimize the drop. He picked up the holster belt. Thicker, not the same size. Still. He pushed the end into Emil's buckle, squeezing it to fit, forcing the metal prong through the thick leather, then pulling it tight. If it held, the double length would give him—what? six feet? "Do you have any better ideas?" he said aloud, as if Emil were still there arguing with him. And the holster buckle was an open square, big enough to slip over the radiator handle, if he was lucky. I'm saving your life.

More laughter. He moved silently toward the doorway, sweating. He wiped his palm dry, wrapped the end of the belt around it, gripping it, and held out the buckle, fixing his eye on the radiator. If it took more than a second, he'd be dead. A short intake of breath for good luck, then he darted forward, slipped the buckle on the handle, and scrambled over the sill. A small clink of metal as it hooked on, evidently unheard over the Russian talk, then a strained grunt as he dropped, catching the belt with his other hand, holding on, trying not to fall, his feet dangling in open air. He held tight for an instant, not trusting the belt yet, then felt himself slipping, a raw burning as the leather slid through his hand until it reached the other buckle, something to grip. Both hands now, his entire weight hanging by a single brass prong, his arms beginning to cramp.

He looked below. Rubble, not a flower bed. He'd need all of the belt, every foot a hedge against a broken ankle. The windows in the back were holes in a smooth façade, no lintels, nothing to break his fall but a pipe that branched off from the corner and snaked across the wall. Europe, where they put the pipes outside. He tried to guess the distance. Maybe just close enough if he let the belt out, something to hold his feet until his arms came back. Then a close slide down, grabbing the pipe in time, a drop in stages. A cat burglar could do it.

He moved his hands carefully off the buckle, just an inch, to the thinner leather of Emil's belt. One over the other, clutching his hands stinging from the leather burn, as if he were gripping nettles. Still no sound from above, just his own ragged panting and the scrape of his shoes against the plaster. Almost at the pipe.

And then it gave. Either the radiator handle or the other buckle, impossible to tell which, broke off, and he plunged with the belt, his feet hitting the pipe and bouncing off, his hands reaching out for anything on the wall until they met the pipe and clutched, stopping his body with a wrench of his shoulders. He held on, his body jerking, trying to stop his legs from flailing, and then he was going lower again, the pipe bending, weakened, too light for his weight, a groan at the joint near the corner and then a crack, like a shot, as it snapped and a loud crash as he went down with it, metal clanging against the rubble and his own cry as his body smashed against the ground. For a moment he seemed to black out, an absolute stillness between breaths, then another piece of pipe clattered down and he heard shouts from the window, the air filled with noisy alarm, as if dogs had started barking.

Move. He raised his head, wet at the back, a flash of nausea, and rolled slightly on his shoulder, wincing from a sharp pain. His feet, however, seemed all right—just a dull ache in one of the ankles, throbbing with the shock of the fall but not broken. A white shirt anyone could pick out in the darkness. He rolled toward the wall and pulled himself up, bracing against it so that if he fainted he'd be falling backward, not into firing range. Louder shouts now, probably the guards. He sidled toward the recess of a doorway, still in shadow, then jumped, startled at the sound of the blasts, a machine gun firing at random down into the yard. The first thing he'd learned about combat—how the sound exploded in your ears, loud enough to reach inside you, right into the blood.

He pressed into the doorway, away from the bullets. Was it open? But the hotel was a trap, the last place he'd be safe. And what if they weren't out yet? Head away from the Linden, a few more seconds of diversion. He looked around the yard, trying to fix its layout. An unbroken wall to the corner, then another, seamless. No, a gap where it had been damaged by shelling. Which might not lead anywhere, a rat hole. But the yard itself was impossible—one streak of his white shirt and the bullets would have him. And now there was more light, slim shafts from flashlights, darting in confusion, then raking steadily across the rubble, strong enough to poke into corners, picking up piles of debris and the dull gleam of the pipe, coming toward him. In a minute he'd be in the beam, trapped, like one of the boys huddling against the Volga cliffs, easy target practice.

He bent down, picked up a piece of brick, and hurled it right toward the broken pipe, a desperate ring toss. It hit. A sharp clang, with the flashlight beams jerking back, another burst of shots. Without even testing his ankle, he bolted left toward the gap, hearing the crunch of broken plaster under his feet, more shouts in Russian. Just a few more steps. Endless. Then the light was back, shining against the wall and the shelling hole, drawing fire again. He crouched down in a feint, making the light follow him, then leaped away from it and dived into the gap, rolling downward on his bad shoulder and covering his head as the bullets ripped into the plaster at the opening, a furious ricochet whistling, just a foot or so too high. His whole body shaking now, finally in the war.

He rolled again, away from the opening, on a floor covered with glass and scattered papers, office litter. Bullets still tore into the room, one of them hitting metal with an echoing zing. He took his hand away from the back of his head, sticky with blood, opened when he'd hit the ground in the fall, and thought of Liz's throat, gushing. Just one bullet. All it would take.

And then suddenly the bullets stopped, replaced by more shouting. He kept rolling until he reached a hulk of metal, a filing cabinet, and crawled behind it, raising his head to look out. There were heads at all the windows now, looking at the yard, yelling to each other, but none at Sikorsky's, the machine guns redeployed, no doubt racing down the stairs, already after him.

He felt his way through the dark room to another, heading toward what he thought must be Wilhelmstrasse, a diagonal from the Adlon wing. Keep going away from the Linden. The next room was lighter, open to the sky, and he saw that he had left the standing part of the building behind. Now there was just a small hill of rubble, then an open patch to the ruined shell of the front. He started running toward the street. They'd come through the courtyard behind. He'd have a few seconds to get out, melt into the ruins while they searched the back of the Adlon. But when he came to an opening, ready to spring, he could hear the boots clomping in the street, more Russians. Front and behind.

He headed right, snaking his way around another mound of bricks, still parallel to the street. They'd go first to the room with the filing cabinet, hoping to find him dead, not down Wilhelmstrasse. He took in the street again through the building shell. Just keep going. Another room, big, with twisted girders sticking up like teepee frames. Behind him, he could hear the boots entering the building. All of them? One more room, quietly. He stopped. Not just rubble; a small mountain, even the shell collapsed in, a dead end in the maze. He'd have to go back. But the boots were there again, crunching, fanning out through the building. He looked up toward the dark sky. The only way out was over.

He started up the pile, terrified that a slip would dislodge the bricks, send them tumbling down like alarms. If he could make the top, he could get to the next building, breathing space while they searched this one. He reached up, shoulder aching, scrambling on all fours. Bricks moved, settling and falling away as he found one foothold after another, but no louder than small clinks, not as loud as the Russians, still yelling from room to room. But what if the mound dropped sheer on the other side, propped up by a standing wall?

It didn't. When he reached the top, lying down, he saw that it became one of those aprons of rubble that spilled into the street, without a connection to the next building. He also saw, ducking his head, lights sweep into the street, an open Soviet military car, Sikorsky jumping out, gun in hand, then pointing the car down the street, away from the Linden. Sikorsky stood for a minute, looking everywhere but up, and it occurred to Jake that he could just lie here, perched on his mountain, the one place they'd never look. Until when? The morning sun caught his white shirt and they surrounded him with guns? Another car came down the street, idled while Sikorsky gave a direction, and moved on to Behrenstrasse, the next cross street down, blocking that route. Now the only way out was the unbroken western side of Wilhelmstrasse, if he could get there before the headlights lit up the street. He watched Sikorsky take one of the soldiers and head into the building. Now, while the car was still turning into Behrenstrasse.

He inched down the rubble on his back, as if he were sliding down a sand dune, but the bricks rolled with him, a small avalanche, not sand. In a few seconds they'd hear the clattering over their engine. He crouched, then took a breath and started running down the slope, pitched forward by gravity, flying, so that he thought he'd reach the pavement face first. He staggered from the jolt of hitting flat ground, then hurled himself down the street. How long before they turned? His shoes smacking the pavement now, in shadow and racing south, putting space between him and the wrecked ministry. Getting away with it. Until the air exploded again with a spray of bullets. The Behrenstrasse car, catching his shirt in its lights. He ducked but kept running, looking frantically for another open space in the wall of rubble. Shouts behind him, more boots—probably Sikorsky and his men responding to the gunfire, back in the street.

One long dark stretch, the other Soviet car visible now at the end, standing in the middle of the Voss Strasse intersection, by the Chancellery. Head right somewhere, behind the buildings, the wasteland near Hitler's bunker. But the rubble ran in an unbroken line here. Shouts in the dark. There would be guards at the bunker, even at night, watching for looters. Who would they think he was, running away from guns? The street would end any second now, with the roadblock, and someone had started firing again, maybe at random, maybe at the pale glow of his shirt.

He swerved right off the pavement into a dark space in the rubble. A cul-de-sac, like a moon crater, one of its rims backing onto the Chancellery itself. He thought of Liz snapping pictures. The long gallery and then the smashed office opening out to the back. No one would be collecting souvenirs now. He clambered up another apron of rubble to the ground-floor window and vaulted through, finally out of the street. He stayed down for a minute, his eyes adjusting to the dark, and started across the room, hitting his shin against an overturned chair, then retreated back to the wall, feeling his way toward the next window. More light here, just faint enough to see that the long gallery was still a mess, a minefield of broken furniture and fallen chandeliers. He moved farther along the wall, avoiding the booby traps of debris in the center. Shouts outside again. They would have reached the roadblock, would be doubling back now to pick their way through the ruins, a rat hunt. Get to the end of the room somehow, toward the bunker. Maybe the guards hadn't been alerted yet. The element of surprise.

He had reached another chair, with stuffing spilling out of the ripped upholstery, when the tall doors banged open, flung back in a hurry. He dived behind the chair, holding his breath, as if even a slight rasp would give him away. Sikorsky with a few men, one of them a Mongol guard from outside. Machine guns and flashlights waving around the still hall. Sikorsky motioned with his hands for them to spread out. For another second no one moved, letting the noisy echo of their entrance die down, then Sikorsky took a step toward the wall with the chair and Jake froze, the back of his neck tingling. Not fear; a trickle of blood running down, soaking into the shirt. How much had he lost?

"Geismar!" Sikorsky shouted into the air, another echo, looking now toward the end of the gallery, where the office and garden windows were. "You cannot leave here." Not through the garden anyway, and not back into the street either. "No more shooting. You have my word." All the while motioning to the others to begin their sweep, guns ready. In Stalingrad they'd fought building by building, a war of snipers. "We have Brandt," he said, cocking his head to hear a reply. Jake let out a breath, half expecting it to echo. But did they? No, they'd raced around the Adlon too fast, not stopping for anything. A poor chess player.

Sikorsky nodded and his men began to move with their flashlights, only one of them left stationed by the door. But armed. Jake followed the lights. They'd sweep to the end, then back, until they were sure. No way to get to the garden. He raised his head a little, glancing out the window. Distract the Mongol, make a break for it across Voss Strasse. But the open car was there at the corner, ready to fire, maybe a second Mongol still posted on the steps. Back the way he had come, to the moon crater? Every step echoing in the giant room, no weapon except a splintered armrest. Endgame.

The Russians were nearing the end of the hall, shining lights into the office where GIs had chipped off pieces of Hitler's desk. Two of them dispatched to check the room, then back, returning now toward Jake's end. How many? Four, plus Sikorsky. He heard the crunch of glass, a chandelier globe caught underfoot. Minutes. Then they stopped, heads swiveling, alert to a sound. Had Jake moved, paralyzed behind his chair? No, a different sound, not in the room, getting louder—a pop, a grind of motors, raucous whoops. Jake strained a little closer to the window, looking out. Rumbling down Wilhelmstrasse, almost in the headlights. "It's over!" he heard in English. "It's over!" Football game yelling. Then he could see the jeep, soldiers standing with beer bottles, fingers raised in Churchill *V*'s. In the light now. Americans, like some phantom rescue party out of Gunther's westerns. If he could get through the window, he'd be almost there. The Russians at the roadblock, too stunned to react, looked around in bewilderment, not knowing what to do. Then, before Jake could move, the GIs, still whooping, started firing into the air, victory fireworks. "It's over!"

But all the Russians heard was gunfire. Startled, they started firing back, a machine gun strafing the jeep, one GI flung back, then whirling, falling forward over the windshield.

"What the fuck are you doing?" a GI screamed, the reply lost under another barrage of shots.

Then the GIs were crouching, firing too, into the roadblock, and Jake saw, horrified, that it was the Potsdam market again, a confusion of screams and bullets, real combat, men actually going down in the crossfire.

Inside the Chancellery, Sikorsky's men raced toward the doors, stumbling over pieces of debris, shouting to each other. Gunfire must mean that Jake was out there. They ran out onto the steps, saw the American jeep at the roadblock, and started firing. The Russians in the street, caught by surprise shots from the side, automatically swerved and fired back. Open stairs, nowhere to hide. The Mongol was hit first, falling headlong, the others ducking. Sikorsky yelled out something in Russian, then clutched his stomach. Jake watched, amazed, as he sank to his knees, bullets still raking the columns behind him. "Fuck! Ed's hit!" somebody yelled. Another round into the blockade from the jeep. Then a hoarse scream in Russian from the steps, and all at once it stopped, the soldiers in the roadblock looking, dazed, at the Chancellery, Sikorsky still kneeling there, his uniform finally visible to them as he rolled over.

"Are you fucking crazy?" the GI yelled, bent over his friend. "You shot him!"

The Russians, crouching for cover, held their guns out, waiting to see what would happen, not ready to believe they weren't under attack.

"You shoot!" one yelled in broken English.

"You idiot! We're not shooting. *You're* shooting. It's over!" The soldier took out a handkerchief and waved it, then stepped tentatively out of the jeep. "What the hell's the matter with you?"

A Russian stood up beside the car and took a step toward him, both holding their guns. Then no one said anything, a stillness you could touch, the others beginning to move from their places in slow motion, staring at the bodies in the street, appalled. The Russian looked toward the steps, terrified, as if he expected to be punished, still not sure what had happened. The Mongol, not dead, called out something, and the Russian just kept looking, stupefied, not even moving when Jake limped out of the building, went over to Sikorsky, and picked up the revolver near his hand.

"Who the fuck are you?" the GI called, spotting him. A man in civilian clothes.

Jake looked down at Sikorsky. His eyes were glazed but he was still alive, breathing hard, struggling for air, his front coated with blood. Jake knelt down next to him, holding the revolver. The other Russians still didn't move, confused, as if Jake were another inexplicable phantom.

Sikorsky twisted his mouth in a sneer. "You."

Jake shook his head. "Your own men. It was your own men."

Sikorsky looked toward the street. "Shaeffer?"

"No. Nobody. The war's over, that's all. The war's over."

Sikorsky grunted.

Jake looked at the stomach wound, welling blood. Not long. "Tell me who he was working with. The other American."

Sikorsky said nothing. Jake moved the revolver in front of his face. The Russian in the street stirred but made no move, still waiting. What would they do if he fired? Start killing each other again?

"Who?" Jake said. "Tell me. It can't matter now."

Sikorsky opened his mouth and spit at him, but weakly, without force, so that the strand of saliva fell back on his own lips.

Jake put the gun closer to his chin. "Who?"

Sikorsky glared at him, still sneering, then looked directly into the gun. "Finish it," he said, closing his eyes.

The only one who could tell him, slipping away, the last thing that would go wrong. Jake looked at the closed eyes for another second, then took the gun away from Sikorsky's face, drained.

"Finish it yourself. It took my friend about a minute to die. The one you killed. I hope it takes you two. One to think about her. I hope you see her face."

Sikorsky opened his eyes wide, as if in fact he were looking at something.

"That's right, like that. Scared." Jake stood up. "Now take another for the kids in the boat. See them?" He stared for another second, Sikorsky's eyes locked on his, even wider. "Steel," he said, then walked down the stairs, not turning even when he heard the strangled gasp behind him. He handed the gun to the stunned Russian.

"Will somebody tell me what the *fuck* is going on here?" the GI said.

"Speak German?" Jake said to the Russian. "Get your men out of here."

"Why did they shoot?"

"The Japs surrendered." The Russian looked at him, dumbfounded. "These men are wounded," Jake said, suddenly dizzy. "So are yours. We have to get them out. Move the car."

"But what do I say? To explain?"

Jake looked down at a Russian in the street, spattered with blood. As stupid and pointless as it always was.

"I don't know," he said, then turned to the GI, feeling the back of his head. He brought his hand back down, bloody. "I'm hurt. I need a ride."

"Jesus." The GI turned to the Russian. "Move, you fuck."

The Russians looked at them both, uncertain, then waved his hand at the driver to start the car.

In the party jeep, the men moved to make a place, one of them still holding a beer bottle.

"So the war's over?" Jake said to the GI.

"It was."

CHAPTER EIGHTEEN

HE AWOKE TO find Lena's face floating over his.

"What time is it?"

A faint smile. "After noon." She reached up and felt his forehead. "A good sleep. Erich, go get Dr. Rosen. Tell him he's awake."

There was a scampering in the corner, then a blur as the boy darted out of the room.

"How did you do it?" she said. "Can you talk?"

How? A bumpy ride in the jeep, getting off in a Ku'damm swarming with headlights and blaring horns, packs of rowdy GIs with girls, dancing out of the clubs into the street, then a blank.

"Where's Emil?" Jake said.

"Here. It's all right. No, don't get up. Rosen says—" She smoothed his forehead again. "Can I get you something?"

He shook his head. "You got out."

Rosen came through the door with Erich by his side and sat down on the bed, taking a pinpoint light out of his bag and shining it into each of Jake's eyes.

"How do you feel?"

"Peachy."

He reached behind, checking the bandage on the back of Jake's head. "The stitches are good. But you should see an American doctor. An injury to the head, there's always a risk. Sit up. Any dizziness?" He felt below the bandage, freeing his other hand by passing the light to Erich, who put it carefully into the bag. "My new assistant," Rosen said fondly. "An excellent medical man."

Jake bent forward as Rosen prodded with his fingers.

"A little swelling, not bad. Still. The Americans have an X ray? For the shoulder too."

Jake glanced down and saw an ugly splotch of bruise, and moved the shoulder, testing. Not dislocated.

"You got this how?" Rosen said.

"I fell."

Rosen looked at him, dubious. "A long fall."

"About two stories." He squinted at the bright afternoon light. "How long have I been out? Did you give me something?"

"No. The body is a good doctor. Sometimes, when it's too much, it shuts down to rest. Erich, would you check for fever?"

The boy reached up and rested his dry palm on Jake's forehead, looking at him solemnly. "Normal," he said finally, his voice as small as his hand.

"You see? An excellent medical man."

"Yes, and now sleepy," Lena said, her hands on his shoulders. "He stayed up all night, watching you. To make sure."

"You mean you did," Jake said, imagining him slumped next to her in the easy chair.

"Both. He likes you," she said pointedly.

"Thank you," Jake said to him.

The boy nodded gravely, pleased.

"So you'll live," Rosen said, gathering his bag. "A day in bed, please. In case."

"You too," Lena said, moving the boy. "Time to rest. Come, I have coffee for you," she said to Rosen, busy, organizing them, so that they followed without protest. "And you," she said to Jake. "I'll be right back."

But it was Emil who brought the coffee, closing the door behind him. Back in his own clothes again, a frayed shirt and thin cardigan.

He handed Jake the mug stiffly, averting his eyes, his movements shy and prickly at the same time.

"She's putting the boy to sleep," he said. "It's a Jewish child?"

"It's a child," Jake said over the mug.

Emil raised his head, bristling a little, then took off his glasses and wiped them.

"You look different."

"Four years. People change," Jake said, raising his hand to touch his receding hair, then wincing in surprise.

"Broken?" Emil said, looking at the bruised shoulder.

"No."

"It's a terrible color. It hurts?"

"And you call yourself a scientist," Jake said lightly. "Yes, it hurts."

Emil nodded. "So I should thank you."

"I didn't do it for you. They would have taken her too."

"And that's why you changed the clothes," he said skeptically. "So thank you." He looked down, still wiping. "It's awkward, to thank a man who—" He stopped, putting away the handkerchief. "How things turn out. You find your wife, then she's not your wife. I have you to thank for this too."

"Listen, Emil—"

"Don't explain. Lena has told me. This is what happens now in Germany, I think. You hear it many times. A woman alone, the husband dead maybe. An old friend. Food. There's no one to blame for this. Just to live—"

Was this what she'd told him, or simply what he wanted to believe?

"She's not here for the rations," Jake said.

Emil looked at him steadily, then turned away, moving over to sit on the arm of the chair, still toying with the glasses. "And now? What are you going to do?"

"About you? I don't know yet."

"You're not sending me back to Kransberg?"

"Not until I know who took you out in the first place. They might try again."

"So I'm a prisoner here?"

"It could be worse. You could be in Moscow."

"With you? With Lena? I can't stay here."

"They'd grab you the minute you hit the streets."

"Not if I'm with the Americans. You don't trust your own people?"

"Not with you. You trusted them, look where it got you."

"Yes, I trusted them. How could I know? He was—sympathetic. He was going to take me to her. To Berlin."

"Where you could pick up some files while you were at it. Von Braun send you this time too?"

Emil looked at him, uncertain, then shook his head. "He thought they were destroyed."

"But you didn't."

"I thought so. But my father—I couldn't be sure, not with him. And of course I was right. He gave them to you."

"No. He never gave me anything. I took them. He protected you right to the end. God knows why."

Emil looked at the floor, embarrassed. "Well, no difference."

"It is to him."

Emil took this in for a moment, then let it go. "Anyway, you have them."

"But Tully didn't. Now why is that? You tell him about the files and then you don't tell him where they are."

The first hint of a smile, oddly superior. "I didn't have to. He thought he knew. He said, I know where they are, all the files. Where the Americans have them. He was going to *help,* if you can imagine such a thing. He said only an American could get them. So I let him think that. He was going to get them for me," he said, shaking his head.

"Out of the kindness of his heart?" Collecting twice.

"Of course for money. I said yes. I knew they weren't there—I would never have to pay. And if he could take me out— So I was the clever one. Then he delivered me to the Russians."

"Quite a pair. Why the hell did you tell him in the first place?"

"I never had a head for drink. It was—a despair. How can I explain it? All those weeks, waiting, why didn't they send us to America? Then we heard about the trials, how the Americans were looking for Nazis everywhere, and I thought, we'll never get out, they won't send us. And maybe I said something like that, that the Americans would call us Nazis, *us,* because in the war we had to do things, and how would it look now? There were files, everything we did. What files? SS, I said, they kept everything. I don't know, I was a little drunk maybe, to say that much. And he said it was only the Jews who were doing that, hunting Nazis—the Americans wanted us. To continue our work. He understood how important that was." His voice firmer now, sure of something at last. "And it's right, you know. To stop now, for this—"

Jake put down the mug and reached for a cigarette. "And the next thing you knew, you were off to Berlin. Tell me how that worked."

"It's another debriefing?" Emil said, annoyed.

"You've got the time. Have a seat. Don't leave anything out."

Emil sank back onto the armrest, rubbing his temples as if he were trying to arrange his memory. But the story he had to tell was the one Jake already knew, without surprises. No other Americans, the secret of Tully's partner still safe with Sikorsky. Only a few new details of the border crossing. The guards, apparently, had been courteous. "Even then, I didn't know," Emil said. "Not until Berlin. Then I knew it was finished for me."

"But not for Tully," Jake said, thinking aloud. "Now he had some other fish to fry, thanks to your little talk. Lots of possibilities there. Did the others at Kransberg know about this, by the way?"

"My group? Of course not. They wouldn't—" He stopped, nervous.

"What? Be as understanding as Tully was? They'd have a mess on their hands, wouldn't they? Explaining things."

"I didn't know he would have this idea. I thought the files were destroyed. I would never betray them. Never," he said, louder, aroused. "You understand, we are a team. It's how we work. Von Braun did everything to keep us together, everything. You can't know what it was like. Once they even arrested him—a man like that. But together, all through the war. When you share that—no one else knows what it was like. What we had to do."

"What you had to do. Christ, Emil. I read the file."

"Yes, what we had to do. What do you think? I'm SS too? Me?"

"I don't know. People change."

Emil stood up. "I don't have to answer to you. You, of all people."

"You'll have to answer to someone," Jake said calmly. "You might as well start with me."

"So it's a trial now. Ha, in this whorehouse."

"The girls weren't at Nordhausen. You were."

"Nordhausen. You read something in a file—"

"I was there. In the camps. I saw your workers."

"My workers? You want us to answer for that? That was SS, not us. We had nothing to do with that."

"Except to let it happen."

"And what should we do? File a complaint? You don't know what it was like."

"Then tell me."

"Tell you what? What is it you want to know? What?"

Jake looked at him, suddenly at a loss. The same glasses and soft eyes, now wide and defiant, besieged. What, finally?

"I guess, what happened to you," he said quietly. "I used to know you."

Emil's face trembled, as if he'd been stung. "Yes, we used to know each other. It seems, both wrong. Lena's friend." He held Jake's eyes for a second, then retreated to the chair, subdued. "What happened. You ask that? You were here. You know what it was like in Germany. Do you think I wanted that?"

"No."

"No. But then what? Turn my back, like my father, until it was over? When was that? Maybe never. My life was then, not when it was over. All my training. You don't wait until the politics are convenient. We were just at the beginning. How could we wait?"

"So you worked for them."

"No, we survived them. Their stupid interference. The demands, always crazy. Reports. All of it. They took away Dornberger, our leader, and we survived that too. So the work would survive, even after the war. Do you understand what it means? To leave the earth? To make something new. But difficult, expensive. How else could we do it? They gave us the money, not enough, but enough to keep going, to survive *them*."

"By building their weapons."

"Yes, weapons. It was the war by then. Do you think I'm ashamed of that?" He looked down. "It's my homeland. What I am. Lena too," he said, glancing up. "The same blood. You do things in wartime—" He trailed off.

"I saw it, Emil," Jake said. "That wasn't war, not in Nordhausen. That was something else. You saw it."

"They said it was the only way. There was a schedule. They needed the workers."

"And killed them. To meet your schedule."

"Ours, no. Their schedule. Impossible, crazy, like everything else. Was it crazy to mistreat the workers? Yes, everything was crazy. When I saw it, I couldn't believe it, what they were doing. In Germany. But by then we were living in a madhouse. You become crazy yourself, living like that. How can it be, one sane person in the asylum? No, all crazy. All normal. They ask for estimates, crazy estimates, but you are crazy if you refuse. And they do terrible things to you, your family, so you become crazy too. We knew it was hopeless, all of us in the program. Even their numbers. Even *numbers* they made crazy. You don't believe me? Listen to this. A little mathematical exercise," he said, getting up to pace, the boy who could do numbers in his head.

"The original plan, you know, was for nine hundred rockets a month, thirty tons of explosives per day for England. This was 1943. Hitler wanted two thousand rockets per month, an impossible target, we could never come close. But that was the target, so we needed more workers, more workers for this crazy number. Never close. And if we had done it? That would mean sixty-six tons per day. Sixty-six. In 1944, the Allies were dropping *three thousand* tons a day on Germany. Sixty-six against three thousand, that is the mathematics they were working with. And to do this, forty thousand prisoners finally. More and more for this number. You want me to explain what happened? They were crazy. They made us crazy. I don't know what else to tell you. How can I answer this?" He stopped pacing, turning his hands up in question.

"I wish somebody could. Everybody in Germany has an explanation. And no answer."

"To what?"

"Eleven hundred calories a day. Another number."

Emil looked away. "And you think I did that?"

"No, you just did the numbers."

Emil was still for a moment, then came over to the bedside table and picked up the cup. "You've finished your coffee?" He stood near the bed, staring down at the cup. "So now I'm to blame. That makes it easy for you? To take my wife."

"I'm not blaming you for anything," Jake said, looking up into his glasses. "You do it."

Emil nodded to himself. "Our new judges. You blame us, then you go home, so we can accuse each other. That's what you want. So it's never over."

"Except for you. You go to the States with the rest of your group and go on with your fine work. That's the idea, isn't it? You and von Braun and the rest of them. No questions there. All forgotten. No files."

Emil peered over his glasses. "You're so sure the Americans want these files?"

"Some of them do."

"And the others at Kransberg? You would do this to them too? It's not enough to accuse me?"

"This isn't just about you."

"No? I think so, yes. For Lena."

"You're wrong. About that, too."

"You think it would make her happy? To send me to jail?"

Jake said nothing.

Emil raised his head, letting out a breath. "Then do it. I can't stay here. They're looking for me, she told me this. So send me. What difference where I'm a prisoner?"

"Don't be too anxious to go. You're a liability now, undelivered goods. He'll have to do something."

"Who?"

"Tully's partner."

"I told you, there was no one else."

"Yes, there was." Jake looked up, a new idea. "You talk to anyone else at Kransberg?"

"Americans? No. Just Tully," Emil said absently, not interested.

"And Shaeffer. The debriefing," Jake said, explaining. "Ever meet his friend Breimer?"

"I don't know the name. They were all the same to us."

"Big man, government, not a soldier?"

"That one? Yes, he was there. To meet the group. He was interested in the program."

"I'll bet. He talk to you?"

"No, only von Braun. The Americans, they like a von," he said, shrugging a little.

Jake sat back for a moment, thinking. But how could it be? Another column that wouldn't add up.

Emil took his silence for an answer and moved toward the door, carrying the mug. "You'll at least send word to Kransberg? My colleagues will worry—"

"They'll keep. I want you missing a little while longer. A little bait."

"Bait?"

"That's right. Like Lena was for you. Now you can be the bait. We'll see who bites."

Emil turned at the door, blinking behind his glasses. "It's no good, talking. The way you are now. What is it, some idea of justice? For whom, I wonder. Not for Lena. You think I ask for myself—for her too. Think what it means for her."

"I see. For her."

"Yes, for her. You think she wants this trouble for me?" He opened his hand, taking in not just the room but the files, the whole clouded future.

"No, she thinks she owes you something."

"Maybe it's you who owes something."

Jake looked up at him. "Maybe," he said. "But she doesn't."

Emil shook his head. "How things turn out. To think I left Kransberg for her. And now this—all our work. So you can prove something to her. Wave these files in my face. 'You see what kind of man he is. Leave him.'"

"She has left you," Jake said.

"For you," Emil said, shaking his head at the implausibility of it, drawing his round shoulders back, upright, the way they must have looked in uniform. "But how different you are. Not the same man. I thought you would understand how it was here—leave me my work, that much. No, you want that too. Your pound of flesh. Make all of us Nazis. She won't thank you for this. Does she even know, how different you are?"

Jake stared at him for a minute, the same man on the station platform, no longer blurry, as if the train had slowed so he could really see.

"But you're not," he said, suddenly weary, the dull ache in his shoulder spreading to his voice. "I just didn't know you. Your father did. Some missing piece, he called it."

"My father—"

"You never had anything in your head but numbers. Not her. She was your excuse. Even Tully bought it. Maybe you believe it yourself. The way you think Nordhausen just happened. All by itself. But that doesn't make it true. Owes you something? You didn't come to Berlin for her—you came to get the files again."

"No."

"Just like the first time. She thinks you risked your life to get her. It wasn't for her. Von Braun sent you. It was his car, his assignment. To keep the work going. No embarrassing pieces of paper. You never even tried to get her, just save your own sorry skin."

"You weren't there," Emil said angrily. "Get through that hell? How could I do that? I had the other men to think of. There was only one bridge left—"

"And you drove right out with them. I don't blame you. But you don't blame yourself either. Why not? You were in *charge*. It was your party. How long did it take you to get the files? That was your priority. Passengers? Well, if there was time. And then there wasn't."

"She was at the hospital," Emil said, raising his voice. "Safe."

"She was raped. She almost died. She tell you that?"

"No," he said, looking down.

"But you got what you really came for. You left her and saved the team. And now you want to do it again, even make her help this time, because she thinks she owes you something. She's lucky she got the phone call."

"It's a lie," Emil said.

"Is it? Then why didn't you tell von Braun you were leaving Kransberg with Tully? You couldn't, could you? Not the real reason. He thought you'd already taken care of the files. But you had to be sure. That's why you came. It's always been about the files. Not her."

Emil kept staring at the floor. "You'd do anything to turn her against me," he said, his tone aggrieved, closed off. He looked up. "You've told her this?"

"You tell her," Jake said steadily. "I wasn't there, remember? You were. Tell her how it was." He watched Emil stand there, shaking his head numbly in the sudden stillness, and sank back against the pillow. "Then maybe she'll figure it out for herself."

Brian turned up after dinner, bringing a newspaper and a bottle of NAAFI scotch.

"Well, safe and sound. That looks nasty," he said, pointing to the shoulder. "You ought to see to that." He opened the bottle and poured two drinks. "Quite a hidey-hole, I must say. I saw a lovely thing in the hall. Nothing under the wrapper, by the looks of it. I don't suppose they give out samples. Cheers." He tossed back the shot. "How'd you find it?"

"It's British owned."

"Really? That's the stuff."

"Anybody see you come here?"

"Well, what's to that? At my age I'm expected to pay for it." He glanced over. "No, no one. Jeep's in the courtyard behind, by the way. I thought you might like it off the street. Tempting."

"Thanks."

"I take it that's the husband," he said, nodding toward the living room. "The one moping on the couch. What are the sleeping arrangements, or am I being prurient?"

"Thanks for that too. I owe you."

"Don't worry, I'll collect. Your stunt, my exclusive. Fair?"

Jake smiled.

"You made the papers," Brian said, handing it to him. "At least, I assume it's you. No names. Not much sense either."

Jake opened it up. PEACE headlined in bold across the top, with the picture of Marines raising the flag on Iwo Jima. At the bottom right, in smaller type, WWIII BEGINS? WHO FIRED FIRST?, an account of the Chancellery shoot-out as confusing as the crossfire, with the implication that everyone had been drunk.

"You can't imagine the hullabaloo. Well, maybe you can. Russians have been stamping their feet, cross as anything. Formal notes, want a special Council session, the lot. Say they won't march in the victory parade—there's a loss. Want to tell me what really happened?"

"Believe it or not, this is what happened. A mess. Except the Russians weren't drunk."

"That would be a first."

"And I'm not in it," Jake said, finishing the piece.

"Strictly speaking, boyo, you weren't. You were with me."

"Is that what you told them?"

"Had to. No end of questions otherwise. You're the most popular man in Berlin these days. Absolutely belle of the ball—everybody wants to dance with you. If they knew where you were. Damned if I do. Came down to the dining room with a lady, offered me a lift—I might have been a little the worse for wear—dropped me on the

Ku'damm for a nightcap, and that's the last I saw you. As for this," he said, pointing to the paper, "what I *hear* is there was a civilian in the middle of it. Nobody knows who. German, would be my guess. Of course, the Russians aren't saying, but they're not supposed to be missing anybody in the first place."

"But I spoke English."

"Americans think everyone does. You tell them who you were?"

"No. And I spoke German to the Russians. Sikorsky wouldn't have had time to—"

"You see? Believe me, nobody's thinking about anything except covering their behinds. Damned silly, when you think of it, going to the bunker for a drink. Wanted to dance on Hitler's grave, I suppose. *Very* unwise, all things considered. The point is, you were seen leaving the Adlon with me. Witnesses. And if I don't know you, who would? That *is* the way you wanted it, isn't it?"

Jake smiled at him. "You don't miss a trick."

"Not when the story's mine. Exclusive, remember? It doesn't do to share with your gang. So fair's fair? What's it all about?"

"It's yours, I promise. Just wait a little."

"Not even a taste? What in god's name were you and the general wagging about? The late general, I should say. There's a service tomorrow, by the way—all the Allies. That awful band of theirs, no doubt. I suppose you won't be sending a wreath."

"That's right," Jake said, not really listening. "You don't know."

"No, I don't know," he said, imitating Jake's voice. "Until you tell me."

"No, I mean nobody knows. What he said to me. Nobody knows. It could have been anything."

"But what did he say?"

"Let me think for a minute. It's important. I need to work this out."

"You don't mind, then?" Brian said, pouring another drink. "Always so gripping to watch someone think."

"Anything. I mean, suppose he had told me?"

"Told you what?"

Jake was quiet for a minute, sipping his scotch.

"Hey, Brian," he said finally, still brooding. "I want you to do something for me."

"What?"

"Have a drink at the press camp. My treat."

"And?"

"Talk loose. Have a few. You saw me and I've got hold of a story and wouldn't cut you in on it so you're annoyed."

"So I would be. And the point is?"

"I want everybody to know that I've got something. It's like the village post office there—it won't take long to get around. Wait, even better. Got some paper?"

Brian took out a notebook and handed it to him, then watched as he wrote.

"Send this to *Collier's* for me—here's the cable address."

Brian took it and read aloud. "'Save space next issue big story scandal.' And when you don't send one? They won't like that."

"Well, I might. So will you. But chances are this won't go out anyway. They censor the cables. Young Ron'll take one look and start playing Chicken Little. He'll be all over the place with it."

"All over me, you mean."

"Ask him what the fuss is all about—he'll go shy on you. Then ask him who Tully was."

"Someone you mentioned in passing when I saw you."

"That's right. I called it my Tully story."

"And this is going to get you what, exactly?"

"The man who killed him. The other American."

"The bird in the bush. You're sure there is one."

"Somebody tried to have me killed in Potsdam. It wasn't Tully—he was already dead. Yes, I'm sure."

"Steady. You don't want any more excitement, not like this," Brian said, indicating Jake's shoulder. "Twice lucky. Third time—"

"Third time he comes to me. He'll have to. Ever hear of a squeeze play?"

"And this will squeeze him out?" he said, holding the paper.

"Part of the way. The way it works is to get the Russians to do the rest. They think Emil's loose. He is still loose. What if they had the chance to get him back? Sikorsky's dead. Tully's dead. Who else do they send to get him?"

"Especially if he can get you as well? I don't like that. And how do you intend to manage this, may I ask?"

"Just go have the drink, okay? We're almost there."

"With loose talk. Which he'll hear."

"He's heard everything else."

"One of ours, then."

"I don't know. The only one I know it isn't is you."

"Very trusting of you."

"No. It was an American bullet. You buy British," Jake said, pointing to the bottle.

Brian folded the paper and pocketed it. "Speaking of which, you'll want this back." He brought a gun out of the pocket. "If you're determined to keep asking for trouble."

"Liz's gun," Jake said, taking it.

"Something of a rush at the Adlon, but I managed to pick it up. Just in case."

"He killed her, you know. Sikorsky."

"So that's it?" Brian said. He got up to go. "It's a fool's game, getting even. It never turns out the way you expect."

"It's not about that."

"Then it's a lot to do for a story."

"How about getting away with murder? Is that enough?"

"Dear boy, people get away with murder all the time. You've only to look around you. Especially here. Years of it."

"Then let's stop it."

"Now I do feel old. Nothing like the young for putting things right. Well, I'll leave you to it. And this lovely scotch. Second thought, perhaps I won't," he said, picking up the bottle. "Never know how many rounds I'll have to buy before the old tongue loosens up properly. On my expenses, too."

"Thanks, Brian."

"Well, Africa together—it has to count for something. No point in telling you to be careful, I suppose. You never were. Still, Russians. I should have thought you'd have your hands full sorting out your ménage." He nodded to the next room.

"It'll sort itself out."

"The young," Brian said, sighing. "Not in my experience."

It took Jake ten minutes to dress, his stiff arms fumbling with the buttons, even tying his shoes a small agony.

"You're going out?" Lena said, looking up from the table where she and Erich were leafing through a magazine rescued from one of the girls. *Life,* pictures from another world. Emil sat on the couch, his face vacant, lost in himself.

"I won't be long," Jake said, starting toward her to kiss her goodbye, then stopping, even the most ordinary gesture somehow awkward now. Instead he rubbed Erich's head.

"Rosen said to rest," Lena said.

"I'm all right," Jake said, feeling Emil watching him so that, like an intruder, he wanted to hurry out, away from them. "Don't wait up," he said to Erich, but taking them all in. Only Erich moved, giving him a little wave.

The street was a relief, the comforting anonymity of the dark. A soldier in a jeep. He drove out toward Kreuzberg, not even noticing the ruins. Even Berlin could become normal, a question of what you were used to.

He found Gunther playing solitaire, a half-full bottle on the table beside him, methodically laying out rows of cards like his columns of obvious points.

"A surprise visit," Gunther said, not sounding surprised at all, barely looking up from the cards.

"I thought I'd bring you up to date," Jake said, sitting down.

Gunther grunted, continuing to lay out cards as Jake told him about the Adlon, not even pausing when bullets hit the Chancellery steps.

"So once again you're lucky," he said when Jake finished. "And we still don't know."

"That's why I've come. I have an assignment for you."

"Leave me alone," he said, turning over a card. Then he looked up. "What?"

"I want you to go to a funeral tomorrow."

"Sikorsky's?"

"A friend. Naturally you'd want to go."

"Don't be ridiculous."

"And pay your respects to his successor. I assume his number two—they haven't had time to bring anyone in yet. Maybe his boss. Either way, whoever's Sikorsky now. It's good business, for one thing." He glanced at the stacks of black market boxes.

"And the other?"

"New business."

"With me," Gunther said, raising an eyebrow.

"You have to think of it from his point of view—what he knows or what he's been told. They must have grilled the Russians at the Adlon. What he knows is that Sikorsky saw us there—Lena and me—and let us pay a visit. He knows Brandt escaped and Sikorsky was killed chasing him. He knows the Americans don't have him—Tully's partner would have told him. So where is he? The logical place?"

Gunther made a questioning sound, still playing.

"Where he's always wanted to be—with his wife. Who came with me. And I'm a friend of yours. And you—you kept tabs on me for Sikorsky," Jake said, slapping the words down in order, jack, ten, nine. "His source."

Gunther stopped. "I told him nothing. Nothing important."

"So he said. The point is, they know he got it from you. They know you know me. They might even think you know where I am. Which means—"

"An interesting situation, I agree," Gunther said, turning a card slowly. "But I don't know where you are. I have never wanted to know that, if you remember. To be in this position."

"If they believe that. Maybe they don't think you're so high-minded. Maybe they just think you're a rat."

Gunther glanced up, then went back to his cards. "Are you trying to provoke me? Don't bother."

"I'm trying to show you how he'll see things. When you talk to him tomorrow."

"And what do you want me to say?"

"I want you to betray me."

Gunther put down the cards, reached for his glass, and sat back, looking at Jake over the rim. "Go on."

"It's time to move up in the world. Cigarettes, watches, a little bar gossip—there's no real money in that. But even a small-time crook gets a chance once in a while. Something big to sell. Sometimes it falls right into your lap."

"I take it Herr Brandt is that opportunity."

Jake nodded. "I came to you to get some travel permits. To get the happy couple out of town."

"And I would have these?"

"They're on the market. You're *in* the market. They'll think you could. But now you've got a situation. You want to keep your options open. Your friend Sikorsky is gone—why not make some new friends, and a bundle on the side? Hard to resist."

"Very."

"So you arrange to meet us, with the permits. If someone else shows up instead—"

"Where?" Gunther said, oddly precise.

"I don't know yet," Jake said, brushing it aside. "But in the American zone. That's important. They need to send an American. If they're Russians, I'll smell a setup right away. It has to be an American, so I won't suspect until it's too late."

"And they'll send him, your American."

"He's the obvious person. He knows who I am. And he'll want to come. I've put the word out that I'm on to something. He can't take that chance. He'll come."

"And then he will have you."

"I'll have him. All you have to do is lead him to me."

"Be your *greifer,*" Gunther said, his voice low.

"It can work."

Gunther moved his eyes back to the cards and began to play again. "A pity you weren't on the force, before the war. Sometimes the bold move—"

"It can work," Jake said again.

Gunther nodded. "Except for one thing. I have no quarrel with the Russians. As you say, I want to keep my options open. If you succeed, where am I? With no options. The Russians will know I betrayed them. Get someone else."

"There isn't anyone else. They'll believe you. It's your case too."

"No, yours. It was interesting to help you, a way to pass the time. Now it's something else. I don't stick my neck out. Not now."

Jake looked at him. "That's right. You never did."

"That's right," Gunther said, refusing to be drawn.

Jake reached over and placed his hand on the cards, stopping the play. "Then stick it out now."

"Move your hand."

Jake held it there for another minute, staring at him.

"Leave me alone."

Jake lifted his hand. "How long do you intend to stay dead? Years? That's a lot of time to pass with your head down. You're still a cop. We're talking about murder."

"No, survival."

"Like this? You tried that once. A good German cop. So you kept your head down and people died. Now you want to stick it down a bottle. For what? A chance to snitch for the Russians? You'd be working for the same people. You think it'll be any different?" He pushed his chair away, frustrated, and walked over to the wall map. Berlin as it used to be.

Gunther sat stonily for a second, then laid down another card, almost a reflex.

"And the Americans are so much better?"

"Maybe not by much," Jake said, his eyes moving left, toward Dahlem. "But that's who's here. That's the choice." He turned from the map. "You have a choice."

"To work for the Americans."

"No, to be a cop again. A real one."

Neither of them said anything for a minute, so when the door rattled with a sharp knock, it seemed even louder in the thick silence. Jake looked up, alarmed, expecting Russians, but it was Bernie, pushing through the door with folders under his arm just as he had that first night at Gelferstrasse, running into a plate. Now it was the sight of Jake that stopped him in mid-dash.

"Where have *you* been? People are looking for you, you know."

"I heard."

"Well, it's good you're here. Saves a trip," he said, not explaining and moving toward the table. "*Wie gehts,* Gunther?" He looked down at the cards. "Seven on the eight. Things a little blurry?" He picked up the bottle, gave it a quick glancing measurement, and put it aside.

"Clear enough."

"I brought the Bensheim copies you asked for. I'll need them back, though. We're not supposed to—"

"According to Herr Geismar, unnecessary now."

"What's Bensheim?" Jake said.

"Where Tully was before Kransberg," Bernie said.

"To cross the *t*'s," Gunther said, opening one of the folders, then looking at Jake. "Not bold, methodical. So often there's a pattern.

I thought, to whom was he selling these *persilscheins*? Which Germans? Perhaps someone I would recognize. An idea only."

"So that's what they look like," Jake said, coming over and picking one up.

The usual buff-colored paper and ragged type wedged into boxes, ink scrawled across the bottom. The name on top was Bernhardt, no one he knew. A different page layout, yet still familiar, like all the occupation forms. He scanned down the sheet, then handed it back. Innocuous paper, but worth a reputation to Bernhardt.

"But as I say, no longer necessary," Gunther said.

"Why's that?" Bernie said.

"Gunther's retiring from the case," Jake said. "He wants to do his drinking elsewhere."

"Still, you don't mind if I look? Since you went to the trouble?" Gunther said, taking the folders.

"Be my guest," Bernie said, pouring himself a drink. "Did I walk into the middle of something?"

"No, we're done," Jake said. "I'm off."

"Don't go. I have some news." He tossed back the drink and swallowed it with a small shudder, a gesture so uncharacteristic that it drew Jake's attention.

"I thought you didn't drink."

"Now I see why," Bernie said, still grimacing. He put down the glass. "Renate's dead."

"The Russians—"

"No, she hanged herself."

No one spoke, the room still as death.

"When?" Jake said involuntarily, a sound to fill the space.

"They found her this morning. I never expected—"

Jake turned away from them to the map, his eyes smarting, as if they had caught a cinder. "No," he said, not an answer, just another sound.

"Nobody thought she'd—" Bernie stopped, then looked over at Jake. "She say anything to you when you talked to her?"

Jake shook his head. "If she did, I didn't hear it." His eyes moved over the map—the Alex and its impossible trial, Prenzlauer where she'd hidden the child, Anhalter Station, cadging a cigarette on the platform. You could trace a life on a map, like streets. The old Columbia office, delivering items with her sharp eye.

"So now it's an end," Gunther said, his voice neutral, emotionless.

"It didn't start this way," Jake said. "You didn't know her. How she was. So—pretty," he said inadequately, meaning alive. He turned to them. "She was pretty."

"Everybody dies," Gunther said flatly.

"I don't know why I should mind," Bernie said. "Everything she did. And a Jew. Still." He paused. "I didn't come here for this. To see another one die."

"She was part of that," Gunther said, still flat.

"So were a lot of people," Jake said. "They just kept their heads down. Maybe they couldn't help it either, the way it was."

"Well, maybe she's found her peace," Bernie said. "A hell of a way to do it, though."

"Is there another?" Gunther said.

"I guess that depends on what you can live with," Bernie said, picking up his hat.

Gunther glanced up at this, then looked away.

"Anyway, I thought you'd want to know. You coming?" he said to Jake. "I still have things to do. Two days with these, okay, Gunther?" He touched the folders. "I have to send them back. You all right?"

Gunther didn't answer, reaching instead for a folder and opening it, avoiding them by reading the page. Jake stood, waiting, but Gunther's only response was to turn the page, like a policeman going through mug shots. They were at the door before Gunther raised his head.

"Herr Geismar?" he said, getting up slowly and walking over to the map, his back to them. He stood for a second, studying it. "Pick the place. Let me know before the funeral."

Lena was in the big chair, legs tucked beneath her, wreathed in smoke rising from the ashtray perched on the wide arm, the room shadowy with a faint glow from the scarf-draped lamp. She looked as if she'd been sitting for hours, coiled into herself, too fixed now to move even when he walked over and touched her hair.

"Where's Emil?"

"Bed," she said. "Not so loud, you'll wake Erich." She nodded at the couch, where the boy lay curled up under a sheet. Brian's sleeping arrangements answered, in shifts.

"What about you?"

"You want me to share the bed?" she said, unexpectedly short, lighting a new cigarette from the stub of the other. "Maybe I should go to Hannelore. To live this way—" She looked up. "He says you won't let him leave. He wants to go to Kransberg."

"He will. I just need him for one more day." He brought one of the table chairs over and sat next to her so they could talk in murmurs. "One more day. Then it'll be over."

She tapped the cigarette in the tray, moving the ash around. "He thinks you took advantage of me."

"Well, I did," he said, trying to break her mood.

"But he forgives me," she said. "He wants to forgive me."

"What did you tell him?"

"It doesn't matter. He doesn't listen. I was weak, but he forgives me—that's how it is for him. So you see, I'm forgiven. All that time, before the war, when I thought— And in the end, so easy."

"Does he know that? Before the war?"

"No. If he thought that Peter— You didn't tell him, did you? You must leave him that."

"No, I didn't tell him."

"We must leave him that," she said, brooding again. "What a mess we've made for ourselves. And now he forgives me."

"Let him. It's easier for him this way. Nobody's fault."

"No, yours. It's you he doesn't forgive. He thinks you want to ruin him. That's the word he uses. And poison me against him. Anything crazy he can think of. So that's the thanks you get for saving him." She leaned her head back against the chair and closed her eyes, blowing smoke up into the air. "He wants me to go to America."

"With him?"

"They can take the wives. It's a chance for me—to leave all this."

"If they go."

"We can start over. That's his idea. Start over. So that's what you saved him for. Maybe you're sorry now."

"No. It was in my cards, remember?"

She smiled, her eyes still closed. "The rescuer. And now here we are, all your strays. What are you going to do with us?"

"Put you to bed, for a start. You're talking in your sleep. Come on, we'll move Erich, he won't mind."

"No, leave him. I'm too tired to sleep." She turned and looked at the boy. "I sent one of the girls to see Fleischman. He asks, can we keep him a little longer? The camps are so crowded. You don't mind? He's no trouble. And you know, Emil doesn't like to talk in front of him, so it's good that way. It gives me some peace."

"What about Texas?"

"They want babies only. Before they become too German, maybe," she said, more dispirited than angry. She rubbed out the cigarette. "All your strays. You take us in, then you're responsible. You know, he thinks you're going to take him to his mother. What do I say to that? After prison, maybe?"

"Not even then," Jake said quietly. "She killed herself last night."

"Oh." A wounded sound, like a faint yelp. "Oh, she did that?" She glanced again at the couch, then down into her lap, her eyes filling. Jake reached for her, but she waved him away, covering her eyes with her hand. "So stupid. I didn't even know her. Someone from the office. Don't look. I don't know what's wrong with me."

"You're tired, that's all."

"But to do that. Oh, how much longer like this? Boiling water, just to drink. The children, living like animals. Now another one dead. And this is the peace. It was better during the war."

"No, it wasn't," Jake said softly, pulling out a handkerchief and handing it to her.

"No," she said, blowing her nose. "I'm just feeling sorry for myself. Boiling water, my god. What does that matter?" Another sniffle, then she wiped her face, the shaking subsiding. She leaned back, drawing a breath. "You know, after the Russians there were many—like her. I never cried then. You saw the bodies in the street. Who knew how they died? My friend Annelise? I found her. Poison. Like Eva Braun. Her mouth was burned from it. And what had she done? Hide until some Russian got her. Maybe more than one. There was blood there." She pointed to her lap. "You didn't cry then, there were so many. So why now? Maybe I thought it was over, that time." She gave her face another wipe, then handed back the handkerchief. "What are you going to tell him?"

"Nothing. His mother died in the war, that's all."

"In the war," she said vaguely, looking at the sleeping boy. "How can you leave a child alone?"

"She didn't. She left him to me."

Lena turned to him. "You can't send him to the DPs."

"I know," he said, touching her hand. "I'll think of something. Just give me a little time."

"While you arrange things," she said, leaning back again. "All our lives. Emil's too?"

"Emil can arrange his own life. I'm not worried about Emil."

"No, I am," she said slowly. "He's still something to me. I don't know what, not my husband, but something. Maybe it's because I don't love him, isn't that strange? To worry about someone you don't love anymore? He even looks different. It happens that way, I think—people look different when they don't love each other anymore."

"Is that what he said?"

"No, I told you, he forgives me. It's easy, isn't it, when you don't love somebody?" she said, her voice drifting, back in an earlier thought. "Maybe he never did. Only the work. Even when he talks about you, it's that. Not me. I thought he'd be jealous, I was ready for that, but no, it's how he can't go back if you use those files. The others won't work with him, not after that. Those stupid files. If only his father—" She stopped, looking away and drawing herself up. "You know what he talks to me about? Space. I'm trying to feed a child on food you steal for us and he talks to me about rocket ships. His father was right—he lives in his head, not here. I don't know, maybe after Peter died there wasn't anything else for him." She turned to him. "But to take that away now—I don't want to do that."

"What do you want?"

"What do I want?" she said to herself. "I want it to be over, for all of us. Let him go to America. They want him there, he says."

"They don't know what they're getting yet."

She lowered her head. "Then don't tell them. Leave him that too."

Jake sat back, disturbed. "Did he ask you to say this?"

"No. He doesn't ask for himself. It's the others—it's like a family for him."

"I'll bet."

She took out another cigarette, shaking her head. "You don't listen either. Both my men. They already know. Maybe he's right a little, that it's personal with you."

"Is that what you think?"

"I don't know—no. But you know what will happen. They think everybody was a Nazi."

"Maybe he'll talk them out of it. He's already convinced himself."

"But not you."

"No, not me."

"He's not a criminal," she said flatly.

"Isn't he?"

"And who decides? The ones who win."

"Listen to me, Lena," Jake said, covering the matches with his hand so that she was forced to look at him. "Nobody expected this. They don't even know where to begin. They're just soldiers. It's got mixed up with the war, but it wasn't the war. It was a crime. Not the war, a crime. It didn't just happen."

"I know what happened. I've heard it, over and over. You want him to answer for that?"

"What if nobody answers for it?"

"So Emil answers? He's the guilty one?"

"He was part of it. All of them were—his 'family.' How guilty does that make them? I don't know. All I know is we can't ignore it—we can't be guilty of that too."

"Numbers, that's all he did."

"You didn't see the camp."

"I know what you saw."

"And what I didn't see? At first I didn't even notice, you don't take things in, it's so—I didn't notice."

"What?"

"There were no children. None. The children couldn't work, so they were the first to go. They were killed right away. That one." He pointed to Erich. "That child. They would have killed him. That's what the numbers were. Erich."

She looked at the couch, then put down the cigarette without lighting it, folding her arms across her chest, drawing in again.

"Lena—" he started.

"All right," she said, moving her legs out from underneath and getting up, finished with it.

She went over to the couch and bent down, rearranging the sheet on the boy, a gentle tucking-in motion, then stood watching him sleep.

"I'm like all the others now, aren't I?" she said finally, keeping her voice low. "Frau Dzuris. Nobody suffered but her. I'm no different. I sit here feeling sorry for my own troubles." She turned to him. "When they made us see the films, you know what I did? I turned my head."

Jake looked up. His own first reaction, a bony hand pulling him back to make him see.

"And after, people were quiet, and then it began. 'How could the Russians make us look at that? They're no better. Think of the bombing, how we suffered.' Anything to put it out of their minds. I was no different. I didn't want to look either. And then it's on your couch."

Jake said nothing, watching her move toward the easy chair, running her hand along the back.

"You expect too much from us," she said. "To live with this. All murderers."

"I never said—"

"No, just some of us. Which ones? You want me to look at my husband. 'Was it you?' Frau Dzuris' son? My brother, maybe. 'Were you one of them?' How can I ask? Maybe he *was*. So I'm like the others. I know and I don't know."

"Except, this once, you do."

She looked down. "He's still something to me."

Jake stood and went over to the table, rifled through his papers, and pulled out a file. "Read it again," he said, holding it out to her. "Then tell me how much. I'm going for a walk."

"Don't leave." Her eyes moved down to the folder. "See how he comes between us."

"Then don't put him there."

"You expect too much," she said again. "We owe him something."

"And paid it off at the Adlon. We owe *him* something," he said, nodding his head at the couch.

She sank onto the broad arm of the chair. "Yes, and how do you pay? What are you going to arrange for him? Imagine his life in Germany. Renate's child."

"No one will know."

"Someone will. You can't save him from that." She had slumped forward, staring at her bare feet.

"You want to keep him," he said.

She shook her head. "A German mother? And one day he looks at me—'Were you one of them?' No, he should have a Jewish home. She paid for that."

"Then we'll find one."

"Just like that. You think there are so many left?"

"I'll talk to Bernie. Maybe he knows someone."

"An answer for everything," she said, breathing out in a half-sigh. She got up and began to pace, caged, arms folded across her chest. "Everything's so easy for you."

"You're not. Not tonight. What is it, Lena?" he said, watching her back as she crossed the room, as if he could follow her mood, slippery as mercury.

"I don't know." She took another step, then stopped, facing the bedroom door. "And I'm the one who wanted him here. Anything but the Russians, that's all I could think. And now he's here—now what? I'm angry at him. Then angry at you. I listen to you and I think, he's right—and I don't want you to be right. Maybe it's personal with me too. So it's a fine mess." She paused. "I don't want you to be right about him."

"I can't make the files go away," Jake said quietly.

"I know," she said, rubbing her sleeve. "I know. But don't let it be you. Let someone else—"

She bit her lower lip.

"Is that what you want?"

She looked up at the ceiling, head back, reading the plaster for an answer.

"Me? What do I want? I was thinking before, how it would be if none of it had ever happened." She lowered her head, looking past him, her voice slowly drifting again. "What I want. Shall I tell you? I want to stay in Berlin. It's my home, even like this. Work with Fleischman, maybe—he needs me, someone to help. Then after, I'll come home and cook. Did you know I could? My mother said it's something a man will always appreciate." She raised her eyes to his, taking him in now. "So we'll eat dinner and be together. And once in a while we'll go out, get dressed up and go out together. And we'll be at a party, it'll be nice, and I'll turn around and you'll be looking at me, the way you did at the Press Club. And nobody will know, just me. That's all. Millions of people live like that. A normal life. Can you arrange that?"

He reached out his hand, but she ignored it, still wrapped up in herself.

"Not in Berlin, I think. Not even an American can arrange that now."

CHAPTER NINETEEN

IT WAS GUNTHER who chose the place.

"Not the station. It's too exposed. And there's Herr Brandt to consider."

"Emil? I'm not taking Emil."

"You must. It's Brandt he wants. He won't show himself for you." He got up with his coffee, cold sober, and walked to the map. "Imagine what he's thinking. He can't lose him again. If you're alone, what has he accomplished, even if he kills you? Still no Brandt. No, he wants a simple pickup. You don't suspect anything, so he surprises you, and he takes Brandt away. Or both of you. You for later. But the meeting must happen somewhere he can't risk drawing attention. If he kills you there, he'll lose everything. You need that protection."

"I can take care of myself," Jake said, touching the gun on his hip.

Gunther turned, the beginning of a smile on his face. "So it's true. Americans say such things. I thought only in Karl May." He glanced at the bookshelf. "But in real life, foolish, I think. In real life, you get protection."

"Where? I still have to do it alone. There's no one I can trust."

"Do you trust me?" He caught Jake's eye and, almost embarrassed, turned back to the map. "Then you won't be alone."

"You're going to cover me? I thought you didn't stick your neck out."

"Someone has to. In a police operation, always use a partner. Two set the trap. One, the cheese. The other, the spring. *Snap.*" He clicked his fingers. "He thinks he surprises you, but I surprise him. Otherwise—" He paused, thinking. "But we need protection."

"There's nowhere in Berlin with that much protection."

"Except tomorrow," Gunther said. "What occurred to me was to use the American army."

"What?"

"You know they parade tomorrow, all the Allies. So we meet here," he said, putting his finger on Unter den Linden.

"In the Russian zone?"

"Herr Geismar, even the Russians won't shoot you in front of the American army." He shrugged. "Very well." He moved his finger left, past the Brandenburg Gate. "The reviewing stand will be here, inside the British zone."

"Just."

"It doesn't matter, as long as the army is there. So, opposite the reviewing stand. Stay in the crowd."

"If I'm that protected, why would I go away with him?"

"Well, he might have a gun in your back. Discreet, but persuasive. That's what I would do. 'Come quietly,'" he said in a policeman's voice. "They usually do."

"If that's the way the Russians play it."

"They will. I'm going to suggest it to them." He turned from the map. "The problem is, we don't know. I would feel better if we knew who to expect. Now we wait until the last minute—his surprise. You can set the trap, but a surprise is never safe. Logic is safe."

"I know, follow the points. Find anything in the *persilschein*s?" Jake said, glancing at the table.

"No, nothing," Gunther said glumly. "But there must be some point we're missing. There is always a logic to a crime."

"If we had the time to look for it. I'm out of leads. My last one died with Sikorsky."

Gunther shook his head. "No, something else. There must be. I was thinking, you know, about Potsdam, that day in the market."

"We know that was him."

"Yes, but why then? It must be a point, the when. Something happened to make him strike then. Why not before? If we knew that—"

"You don't give up, do you?" Jake said, impatient.

"That's the way you solve a case, logic, not like this. Traps. Guns." He waved his hand toward the bookshelf. "Wild West in Berlin. You know, we can still—"

"What? Wait for him to pick me off while you work it out? It's too late for that now. We have to finish it before he tries again."

"That's the logic of war, Herr Geismar, not a police case." Gunther moved away from the map.

"Well, I didn't start it. Christ, all I wanted was a story."

"Still, it's as you say," Gunther said, picking up his funeral tie from the table. "Once you begin, nothing matters but the finish." He began threading it under his shirt collar, not bothering with a mirror. "Let's hope you win it."

"I've got a good deputy and the U.S. Army behind me. We'll win. And after—"

Gunther grunted. "Yes, after." He looked down at the tie, straightening the ends. "Then you have the peace."

The afternoon at the flat was claustrophobic, and dinner worse. Lena had found some cabbage to go with the B-ration corned beef, and it sat on the plate, sodden, while they picked around it. Only Erich ate with any enthusiasm, his sharp Renate eyes moving from one sullen face to another, but even he was quiet, used perhaps to wordless meals. Emil had brightened earlier at the news that he'd be turned over tomorrow, then lapsed into an aggrieved sulk, spending most of the day lying on the couch with his arm over his eyes, like a prisoner with no yard privileges. The ersatz coffee was weak and bitter, merely an excuse to linger at the table, not worth drinking. They were all relieved when Rosen turned up, grateful for any sound louder than a tense clinking spoon.

"Look what Dorothee found for you," he said to Erich, handing him a half-eaten bar of chocolate and smiling as the boy tore off the foil. "Not all at once."

"You're good to him," Lena said. "Is she better?"

"Her mouth is still swollen," he said. A slap two nights before from a drunken soldier. "Too swollen for chocolate, anyway."

"Can I see her?" Erich said.

"It's all right?" Rosen said to Lena and then, when she nodded, "Well, but remember, you must pretend she looks the same. Thank her for the chocolate and just say, 'I'm sorry you have a toothache.'"

"I know, don't notice the bruise."

"That's right," Rosen said softly. "Don't notice the bruise."

"Can I do anything?" Lena said.

"She's all right, just swollen. My assistant will fix her up," he said, handing Erich the bag. "We won't be long."

"And that's the life you give her," Emil said to Jake when they'd gone. "Whores and Jews."

"Be quiet," Lena said. "You've no right to say such things."

"No right? You're my wife. Rosen," he said dismissively. "How they stick together."

"Stop it. Such talk. He doesn't know about the boy."

"They always know each other."

Lena glanced at him, dismayed, then stood up and began to clear. "Our last evening," she said, stacking the plates. "And how pleasant you make it. I wanted to have a nice dinner."

"With my wife and her lover. Very nice."

She held a plate for a second, stung, then dropped it on the stack. "You're right," she said. "It's no place for a child here. I'll take him to Hannelore's tonight."

"You can't get back before the curfew," Jake said.

"I'll stay there. It's no place for me either. You can listen to this nonsense. I'm tired."

"You're leaving?" Emil said, caught off-guard.

"Why not? With you like this. I'll say goodbye here. I'm sorry for you. So hurt and angry—there's no need to end this way. We should be happy for each other. You'll go to the Americans. That's the life you want. And I'll—"

"You'll stay with the whores."

"Yes, I stay with the whores," she said.

"You've got a nerve," Jake said.

"It's all right," Lena said, shaking her head. "He doesn't mean it. I know him." She moved toward him. "Don't I?" She lifted her hand to place it on his head, then looked at him and dropped it. "So angry. Look at your glasses, smeared again." She took them off and wiped them on her skirt, familiar. "There, now you can see."

"I see very well. How it is. What you've done," he said to Jake.

"Yes, what he's done," she said, her voice resigned, almost wistful. "Saved your life. Now he's giving you a chance for a new one. Do you see that?" She lifted her hand again, this time resting it on his shoulder. "Don't be like this. You remember in the war—how many times?—we wondered if we would survive. That's all that mattered then. And we have. So maybe we survived for this—a new life for both."

"Not all of us survived."

She moved her hand away. "No, not all."

"It's convenient for you, maybe, that Peter's gone. In your new life."

Only her eyes reacted, a quick wince.

Jake glared at him. "Listen, you bastard—"

Lena waved her hand, stopping him. "We've said enough." She looked down at Emil. "My god, to say that to me."

Emil said nothing, staring at the table.

Lena went over to the bureau, opened a drawer, and pulled out a snapshot.

"I have something for you," she said, carrying it over. "I found it with my things."

Emil held the picture in front of him, blinking, his shoulders sinking as he studied it, everything softening, even his eyes.

"Look at you," he said quietly.

"And you," Lena said over his shoulder, so intimate that for a second Jake felt he was no longer in the room. "Would you like it?"

Emil looked up at her, then pushed the photograph away and stood, holding her eyes for another minute before he turned and without a word crossed the floor and closed the bedroom door behind him.

Jake picked up the picture. A young couple, arms around each other on a ski slope, goggles pushed up over their knit caps, smiles as broad and white as the snow behind them, so young they must be someone else.

"When was this?" he said.

"When we were happy." She took the picture from him and glanced at it again. "So that's your murderer." She put it down. "I'll get Erich. You can do the dishes."

“Don’t look for me. I will see you,” Gunther had said, and in fact when Jake and Emil arrived at the parade he was nowhere in sight, hidden somewhere in the crowd of uniforms that bunched around the Brandenburg Gate and then straggled out through the wasteland of the Tiergarten on the Charlottenburger Chausee. The Allies had won even the weather—the humid, overcast sky had turned bright and cloudless for the parade, with a breeze strong enough to flap the marching rows of flags. Posters of Stalin, Churchill, and Truman hung from the arch, and through the columns Jake could see the troops and armored vehicles beginning to flow toward them down the Linden, thousands of them, with more crammed along the pavement to cheer. There were only a handful of civilians—grim-faced curiosity seekers, small bands of apathetic DPs with nowhere else to go, and the usual packs of children, for whom any event was a distraction. The rest of Berlin had stayed home. Along the gray avenue of charred tree stumps and ruins, the Allies were celebrating themselves.

When Jake got to the reviewing stand the first bands had already passed, an overture of blaring horns. He thought of the other parades here, five years ago, the trees of the Linden shaking from the heavy thud of boots back from Poland. This was looser and more colorful, the French almost playful in their red pompoms, the British marching so casually they seemed already demobilized, shuffling home. The spit and polish had been left to the 82nd Airborne, wearing shiny helmets and white gloves under shoulder straps, but with the music and scattered applause the effect was more theatrical than military, show soldiers. Even the reviewing stand, with bunting and microphones for speeches later, rose up from the street like a stage, filled with generals in uniforms so elaborate they looked like bassos ready to burst into song.

Zhukov was the gaudiest, both sides of his chest lined with medals that ran all the way to his hips. Next to him, Patton’s plain battle jacket and few ribbons had a kind of defiant simplicity. But the drama was in the positioning. Zhukov, front and center, would take a step forward only to find Patton moving up with him, so that by the time he reached the railing, finally upstaged, they had become a bobbing vaudeville turn of generals. The press responded, snapping pictures from their own viewing stand, and Jake saw that even General Clay, usually somber, was trying to suppress a smile, almost winking at Muller, who answered with a tolerant roll of his eyes, silver-haired Judge Hardy still, suffering fools. For a second Jake wished he were just covering it all for *Collier's*— the noisy air, the absurd jockeying, the backdrop curtain of the burned-out Reichstag in the distance. An interview with Patton maybe, who would remember him and was always good copy. Instead, anxious, he was searching the crowd for a face. What he thought, as more troops marched by, was that he had never seen so many guns in his life and that Gunther had been wrong, he didn't feel protected at all. Any one of them, milling around, waiting to make a move.

"We're going to watch the parade?" Emil said, puzzled.

"We're meeting somebody," Jake said, glancing at his watch. "It won't be long."

"Who?"

"The man who got you out of Kransberg."

"Tully? You said he was dead."

"His partner."

"So it's another trick. No Americans."

"I told you, I need you as bait. Then we'll go see your pals."

"And the files?"

"It's a package deal. They get you both."

"You won't do that."

"You're sure."

"You can't. Think what it will mean for Lena, a trial."

"Wonderful how you're always thinking of her. Listen, you're getting out with your life. That's more than you can say for the workers at Camp Dora."

Emil's eyes narrowed behind his glasses. "Then go to hell," he said, turning to go.

Jake grabbed his arm. "Try it and I'll shoot you in the foot. I'd enjoy it, but you wouldn't." They looked at each other for a moment, stalemated, then Jake dropped his hand. "Now watch the parade."

Jake scanned the crowd. Not a single familiar face. But why would it be someone he knew? On the stand Zhukov had leaned farther against the railing, ready to take the salute from his lancer unit. More stage uniforms, a pounding thud of jackboots, swords actually drawn and raised, flashing in the light, but no longer comic, Goebbels' old warning, the scourge from the east. A small huddle of DPs turned and started away from the crowd, looking back at the swords, and Jake saw in the cowed hunch of their shoulders that it was really a Russian show, all of it, the rest of the Allies harmless extras. The message wasn't victory but the crushing boots. No one can stop us. It was a parade out of the next war. Smiles faded on the stand. What happens when it's over, he'd wondered. Another.

It was then, watching the Russians, that he felt the poke in the small of his back.

"Quite a show."

He whirled around, hand on his holster.

"Steady," Brian said, surprised by the abrupt movement. "Hello again," he said to Emil. "No uniform this time, eh?"

"What are you doing here?" Jake said. Brian? But he'd already had Emil once.

"What do you mean? Everybody's here. Nothing like a parade. Just look at old Zhukov. Bloody Gilbert and Sullivan. Coming to the press stand?"

"Not now, Brian. Scram."

But Brian's eyes were fixed over Jake's shoulder at the lancers. "Be in Hamburg before Christmas by the looks of them."

"I mean it. I'll see you later." He glanced to either side of him, expecting Gunther to arrive, everything happening too soon.

"You might let me wait out the swords. You don't want to get in the way of that." He turned, peering at Jake. "What is it? What are you doing now?"

"Nothing. Just scram," Jake said, still looking nervously to the side.

Brian stared at him, then Emil. "Three's a crowd? Right. I'm off. Save you a place?"

"Yeah, save me a place."

"If young Ron lets the rope down. I've known headwaiters with better manners. Christ, here come the pipers." He looked again at Jake. "Watch yourself."

He pushed his way through to the front, hesitating as the last of the Russians passed, then sprinted across the sudden gap to the viewing stands. Jake lost him as he picked his way through the crowd to the back stairs of the press stand, then saw him reappear on top, talking to Ron. Why not Ron? Who'd left the dinner table at Gelferstrasse that night to play poker but could have gone to the Grunewald. Who now had the perfect vantage point to spot Jake in the crowd, waiting for the right moment, a nod of the head to close the trap. But neither he nor Brian was looking in Jake's direction, busy with themselves. Jake checked his watch. Where was Gunther? Only a few minutes to the agreed time—he had to be in place somewhere nearby. Then why hadn't he come forward when Brian approached them? What if it had been him, smoothly leading them away without even a snap of the spring?

He almost jumped when the bagpipes started wailing, cutting right to the nerves. On the stand, the British now stepped forward, rearranging the line so that the visiting dignitaries with the generals came into view. Breimer, just behind Clay, in a double-breasted suit, who stayed and stayed, with unfinished business in Berlin. Jake imagined how it might happen—the sighting from the stand, the quick excuse to the others, the unsuspected walk across to Emil, a waiting car. Jake looked behind. No car. And Breimer would never risk anything himself. He was where he belonged, on a speakers' platform, out of combat. Even Ron was more likely. He glanced back at the press stand. Huddled now with a cameraman, lining up shots of the parade. No one, in fact, was looking toward Jake. But someone must be.

Unexpectedly, the pipers stopped for a demonstration, a blast of jangling air, forcing the unit behind them to mark time. Jake moved his head slowly from left to right, as if he were looking through binoculars, tracking across a field. What combat always came down to: a hunt for prey, every sense on edge, watching for a sudden movement. But everything here seemed to be in motion. People came and went along the parade line, the generals shuffled in the stand, even the stationary pipers were working their bags. Heads bobbed in the crowd, straining to see or falling back for a smoke. A field full of deer, moving at will, none of them stopping long enough to stay in a rifle sight. He turned in a complete circle, away from the parade, taking in the Tiergarten. Already past time and still no Gunther. I can take care of myself. But could he? As he turned back to the parade, sweeping the stands again for a face, it occurred to him that he had got it backward—he was one of the deer, alert but not knowing what to look for. The hunter, lying still, would be watching him.

He was following the pipers as they started up again when he caught it, a flicker near the corner of his eye, the only thing in the swirl before him that was not moving. Absolutely still. A row of pipers passed. If it turned away, he'd be wrong, but another row of heads went by and the dark glasses were still fixed on him. Maybe just watching the parade. Then Shaeffer raised his hand, as if he were going to salute, and took off the glasses, folding them with one hand and slipping them into his pocket without even blinking, his eyes steady on Jake, hard as steel. Not even a nod, just the eyes. Only the mouth moved, more a grim tic than a smile. *Snap.* Shaeffer. Another row and now they were locked on each other, that split second in a hunt when no one else was in the field. Not surprised to see him, knowing he'd be there, waiting for the crosshairs to clear. Jake held his breath, caught by the eyes. We won't know who, Gunther had said, but now he did, there was no mistaking the look. Not surprised. The man who'd come for him.

The bagpipes were almost gone and Shaeffer took a step forward, but the waiting unit behind moved up into place, blocking him with a new row of heads. How long before he could cross? Near the Brandenburg Gate there was a clunking roar, like thunder, and involuntarily Jake darted his eyes toward the line of march. Soviet tanks, heavy and massive, crunching the already torn pavement and coming fast, refusing to be idled. Shaeffer hadn't even bothered to look, his eyes still frozen where they had been, on Jake. Sikorsky's face in Liz's picture, ignoring the crowd at Tempelhof. Shaeffer. Follow the points. Who had the right gun. Who'd debriefed at Kransberg—the perfect opportunity, the perfect cover. Above suspicion for netting the Zeiss engineers—worthless?—while he was cherry-picking the rocket team instead. Who could have tipped off Sikorsky before the Adlon meeting. Who looked for the files. And finally, all that really mattered, who was here, knowing Jake would be here. And who was now waiting to cross the street.

Jake looked quickly behind. No Gunther, just an exposed swatch of park. Two to spring a trap. But why bother at all? All he'd wanted was to know. The point now was to get Emil away before Shaeffer could get to him. The jeep was farther down the chausee, close but too far to reach if someone chased them. Another look to the side, the only place Gunther could be. No civilians, only uniforms. I want you to betray me, he'd said, and maybe Gunther had, keeping his options open after all. Or had Shaeffer got to him already, keeping him somewhere, making sure? Jake took Emil's arm and saw Shaeffer lift his head and step forward again, ready to spring.

"What is it?" Emil said, annoyed.

If they moved, he'd bolt across, right through the marchers. Jake scanned the crowd again, all oblivious except Shaeffer, no protection at all. Wait for the tanks. Even Shaeffer wouldn't make a dash through rolling tanks. Hold his eye, make him think they'd wait, stuck.

"Listen to me," Jake said in a monotone, barely moving his lips, not wanting Shaeffer to read any expression in his face. "We need to get over to the press stand. After the tanks. When I say go, just follow me. Fast."

"What's wrong?"

"Never mind. Just do it."

"Another trick," Emil said.

"Not mine. The Russians'. They've sent someone for you."

Emil looked at him, skittish. "For me?"

"Just do what I say. Get ready."

A clanking of heavy metal as the tanks ground into place before the stand. Zhukov raised his arm, puffed up and solemn. Below him, Shaeffer stood rigid, eyes still looking across, as if he could see through the steel plates as well as the gaps in between. When half the unit had passed, the tanks slowed to a halt, motors still throbbing as they began revolving their gun turrets in a display salute. For an instant, as the row of guns turned in place, Shaeffer disappeared behind the long barrels. Now.

Jake started moving left, toward the front of the unit, but the guns kept swinging around and Shaeffer spotted them through the suddenly empty space. His head jerked up, alarmed, and he left the curb, darting across between two rows of tanks. How long would it take? Seconds. Jake glanced behind. Still no Gunther. No one, in fact. An exposed back. The gun turrets had almost finished circling, the tanks ready to start up again, an impenetrable moving wall soon, with Shaeffer on their side of the parade.

Jake grabbed Emil's arm and dragged him in front of the nearest row of tanks, his protest drowned out by the deafening motors. Run. Could anyone in the high turrets see them, ignore the command to start moving? A crunch as the gears shifted. Jake yanked at Emil's arm, sprinting as the creaking tread belts began to roll forward. Jog to the left, ahead of the row. One slip to fall underneath. They were almost at the last tank when he saw it was coming too fast to outrun. He stopped short, steadying himself as Emil bumped into his suddenly still body, and stood wedged sideways between two tanks, waiting for the column to pass. Just enough space after this one if he timed it right. He stared at the treads, almost counting them, then lurched forward the moment the tank passed. "Go!" he shouted, tugging at Emil's sleeve and pulling him toward the amazed spectator line, barely missing the next set of treads, but there, finally across.

"Where's the fire?" a soldier said to him, but he kept going, pushing through bodies until they were surrounded, just part of the crowd. They were behind the press stand before he stopped, taking in a gulp of air.

"Are you crazy?" Emil said, panting, his face white.

"Go up there and stay with Brian—the man from the Adlon. He knows you. Try to keep out of sight. And don't go anywhere, with anyone. Got it?"

"Where are you going?"

"To make a diversion."

"It's still not safe?" Emil said, worried.

Wasn't it? Who would snatch them in front of the press corps, safer in the end than the army itself? But who knew what Shaeffer would do? His last chance.

"He's still out there. He may not be alone." A man who could get Russian uniforms for a raiding party. Jake turned.

"You're going to leave me here?" Emil said, glancing around for an opening, ready to bolt.

"Don't even think about it. Believe it or not, I'm the best chance you've got. So we're stuck with each other. Now go on up. I'll be back."

"And if you're not?"

"Then all your problems will be over, won't they?"

"Yes," Emil said, looking at him. "They will."

"But you'll be on a train to Moscow. Plenty of time to think things over then. Right now, just do what I say if you want to get out of here. Come on. Now."

Emil hesitated for an instant, then placed his hand on the wooden rail of the stairs and began to climb. Jake squeezed his way back to the front of the spectators. Get Shaeffer's attention before he looked toward the stand. But the eyes were already there, frantically searching through the crowd on Jake's side, then stopping, a surprised glowering, when they caught his face. Another Russian unit was passing in tight formation. Head away from the stand. Jake started to move left, just behind the front row, still visible but surrounding himself with other heads, so that Emil's might be one of them. Across the street, Shaeffer followed, his tall frame stretching up over the crowd to keep Jake in sight. Jake pushed toward the thicker crowds at the gate, brushing past clumps of indifferent GIs. Away from the stand. He glanced over the columns of marchers. Still there, head turned toward Jake as he moved, the same determined eyes, exasperated, waiting for a break in the line. He must have seen by now that only Jake's head was moving down the street, Emil left somewhere behind. Why keep coming? Not a diversion anymore, a running to ground. First Jake, then go back for Emil. Who would believe him, relieved to see the friendly debriefer, and close his own trap.

Up ahead, Jake could see the Big Three draped on the Brandenburg. After that the street widened out into Pariserplatz, a bulge of crowd where it would be easier to get lost. More Russian troops, rifles shouldered, the tall blond head keeping up with Jake across the rows of gray tunics. Beyond them, past the gate, a halt in the march, a gap big enough to use. Shaeffer would cross there. Jake went faster, trying to put more distance between them. He edged past the gate into the crowded square. A band was playing "The Stars and Stripes Forever." He glanced behind. Shaeffer, just as he'd thought, was running across the open space before the band could fill it. On his side now. Jake looked up the Linden, the sidewalks lined with Russians. He'd have to melt into the crowd, backtrack toward the Reichstag. But the crowd was denser here, a cover but also an obstacle, slowing him down. Behind, over the marching band, he heard Shaeffer shout his name. Lose him now. He pitched forward as if he were wading through mud, his body ahead of his feet.

The Russians were less good-natured than the GIs, grumbling as he passed through them, and he knew, stuck in a wall of bodies, that he wasn't going to make it. Did it matter? Shaeffer wouldn't shoot in this crowd. But he wouldn't have to. The Russian zone, where people disappeared. A formal inquiry, a shrug of shoulders over toasts. Why had he left the stand? Shaeffer couldn't risk exposure in the west. But here Jake could be swallowed up without anyone ever knowing. Even if he made a scene, he'd lose. Russian MPs, a quick call to Sikorsky's successor, and only Shaeffer would go back. Nothing would have happened. Missing, like Tully.

"*Amerikanski*," the Russian said as Jake bumped into him.

"Sorry. Excuse me."

But the Russian was looking ahead, not at him, where some American troops were following the band. He stepped back to let Jake pass, apparently thinking he was trying to join his unit. Don't forget whose uniform you've got on. He looked at the parade. Not the showy 82nd; ordinary uniforms like his own, Gunther's protection. He ducked his head, crouching down out of Shaeffer's line of sight, and wormed his way through to the curb, keeping low as he darted into the march. A few Russians on the edge laughed—hungover, a familiar scrambling, sure to catch hell later. He sidestepped ahead of the moving ranks and near the middle of the row nudged a soldier aside to make a place, joining the line.

"Who the fuck are you?"

"I've got an MP after me."

The soldier grinned. "Get in step then."

Jake skipped, a fumbling dance move, until his left foot matched the others, then straightened his shoulders and began swinging his arms in time, invisible now just by being the same. Don't look back. They were passing the point where Shaeffer would be, head swiveling, furious, plowing through the Russians, looking everywhere but at the parade itself.

"What did you do?" the soldier mumbled.

"It was a mistake."

"Yeah."

He waited to hear his name shouted again, but there was only Sousa, tinkling bells and drums. As they tramped through the gate into the west, he smiled to himself, marching in his own victory parade. Not the Japanese, a private war, left behind now in the east. They were approaching the stand, moving faster than anyone could through the crowd. Even if Shaeffer had given up and started heading back, it would be minutes before he'd reach the press stand, long enough to hustle Emil into the jeep and get away. He looked to the side, a quick check. Patton saluting. Enough time, but still only minutes. At least now he knew. Except what had happened to Gunther.

It was easier getting out of the parade than getting in. After the reviewing stand there was a brief halt, and while they marched in place Jake skipped over to the side and back through the curbside crowd to the press stand. Only minutes. What if Emil had bolted after all? But there they were, not even up in the stand, huddled by the stairs having a smoke.

"There, what did I tell you? He always does come back," Brian said. "Catch your breath."

"You're down here? Did he try to run?"

"Naw, good as gold. But you know Ron. Curiosity killed the cat. So I thought—"

"Thanks, Brian," Jake said in a rush. "I owe you another one." He looked back over his shoulder. No one yet. Brian, watching him, motioned his head away from the stand.

"Better go if you're going. Safe home."

Jake nodded. "If I'm not—just in case—go see Bernie Teitel. Tell him who you've been babysitting and he'll send up a flare." He took Emil's arm and began to lead him away.

"Try newspaper work next time," Brian said. "Easier all around."

"Only the way you do it," Jake said, touching his shoulder, then moving off.

They crossed with a few GIs who'd had enough and were taking advantage of another break in the line to drift away through the park.

"Who's Teitel?" Emil said. "An American?"

"One of your new friends," Jake said, still slightly out of breath. Just a little farther to the jeep.

"A friend like you? A jailer? My god, all this for Lena? She's free to do as she likes."

"So were you. Keep walking."

"No, not free." He stopped, making Jake turn. "To survive. You go along to survive. You think it's different for you? What would you do to survive?"

"Right now, I'm getting us out of here. Come on, you can make your excuses in the jeep."

"The war's *over,*" Emil said, almost shrill, a pleading.

Jake looked at him. "Not all of it."

Behind Emil, something moved on the landscape, a blur faster than the marchers and the idling crowd, coming closer through the park. Not on a road, where it should be, out of place, bumping over the torn-up ground.

"Christ," Jake said. Coming toward them.

"What is it?"

A black Horch, the car at Potsdam. No, two, the second obscured in the dust churned up by the first.

"Get to the jeep. Now. Run."

He pushed Emil, who staggered, then caught his arm, both of them dashing for the jeep. Of course he wouldn't have come alone. The jeep wasn't far, parked behind the crowd with a few others, but the Horch was close enough to hear now, the noise of the motor like a hand on his back. He pulled out his gun as he ran. To do what? But if it came to it, a shot in the air would draw attention, give them at least the protection of the crowd.

They were almost at the jeep when the Horch pulled ahead, blocking them with a squeal of brakes. A Russian in uniform jumped out and stood by the door with the motor still running.

"Herr Brandt," he said to Emil.

"Get out of the way or I'll shoot," Jake said, pointing the gun upward.

The Russian glanced at him, almost a smirk, then nodded at the other car pulling up behind. Two men, civilian clothes. "By that time you will be dead. Put the gun down." Sure of himself, not even waiting for Jake to lower his hand. "Herr Brandt, come with us, please." He opened the back door.

"He's not going anywhere."

"Not with travel permits, no," the Russian said blandly. "No need, you see. A different arrangement. Please." He nodded to Emil.

"You're in the British zone now," Jake said.

"Make a protest," the Russian said. He looked at the other car. "Shall I ask my men to assist?"

Emil turned to Jake. "Now see what a mess you've made for us."

The Russian blinked, confused by this dissension in the ranks, then opened his hand toward the back seat. "Please."

"I said I'd shoot and I will," Jake said.

The Russian waited, but the only movement was the opening of the passenger door. Gunther got out and walked toward them, gun drawn.

"Get in the car, Herr Brandt."

For a moment, as Jake stared at the man with the pointed gun, his lungs seemed to deflate, his whole body going limp with disappointment. I want you to betray me. Emil shuffled reluctantly to the car. The Russian closed the rear door. *Snap.*

"A good German cop," Jake said quietly, looking at Gunther.

"Now you," Gunther said to Jake, waving his gun toward the car. "In the front."

The Russian looked up, surprised. "No. Brandt only. Leave him."

"Get in," Gunther said.

Jake crossed over to the passenger side and stood by the open door. There was a high-pitched whistle. He looked over the roof of the car. Down the road, Shaeffer had stopped running, two fingers in his mouth, then lunged forward again. A soldier detached himself from the crowd, running behind him. The rest of the trap, closing up the rear.

"What are you doing?" the Russian said to Gunther.

"I will drive."

"What do you mean?" he said, alarmed now.

Gunther swung his gun toward the Russian. "Over with the others."

"Fascist swine," the Russian shouted. He jerked his gun out, his hand stopping midway as Gunther's bullet hit him, an explosion so sudden it seemed for a second he hadn't fired at all. There was a rush of movement around them, like the startled flight of birds in a field. Spectators nearby ducked without looking, a reflex. On the reviewing stand a delayed reaction, aides shoving the generals down. Yells. The men in the other car jumped out and raced over to the fallen Russian, dazed. Jake saw Shaeffer stop, just a beat, then start running in a crouch. Everything at once, so that Gunther was already in the car before Jake realized it had started moving. He leaped in, holding on to the open door as he pulled his other leg inside. They spun left, back onto the broken ground of the park, bouncing violently, heading west toward the Victory Column, racing ahead of the parade at their side. Gunther swerved away from a shallow bomb crater and hit a deep rut instead, jolting the car, smashing Jake's sore shoulder against the door.

"Are you crazy?" Emil shouted from the back, his hand on the top of his head where it had bumped the roof.

"Stay down," Gunther said calmly, twisting the wheel to avoid a stump.

Jake looked back through the dust. The other Horch had started after them, jouncing over the same rough ground. Farther behind, a jeep, presumably Shaeffer, was tearing away from the crowd that had formed around the dead Russian. Through the open window, bizarrely, came trumpets and the steady thump of drums, the world of five minutes ago.

"I tried to delay them," Gunther said. "The wrong time. I thought you would be gone, know something was wrong."

"Why you?"

"You were expecting me. I would lead you to the car, for the permits. But he saw Brandt. Running. So. An impulsive people," he said tersely, holding the wheel as they bounced over another hole in the pitted field.

"You were pretty impulsive yourself. Why you and not the American?"

"He couldn't come."

Jake glanced back. Gaining a little. "He did, though. In fact, he's coming now."

Gunther grunted, trying to work this out. "A test maybe, then. Can they trust a German?"

"They got their answer." Jake looked over at him. "But I should have. I should have known."

Gunther shrugged, focused on driving. "Who knows anyone in Berlin?" He jerked the wheel, skirting a Hohenzollern statue that had somehow survived, only the face chipped away by blast. "Are they still there?" he said, not trusting himself to look away to the rearview mirror. Jake turned.

"Yes."

"We need a road. We can't go faster like this." The traffic circle at the Grosser Stern was now in sight, a bottleneck jammed with marchers. "If we can cut across—hold on." Another swerve to the left, jolting the car away from the parade, deeper into the battered park. In the back Emil groaned.

Jake knew that Gunther was taking them south, toward the American zone, but all the landmarks he had known were gone, the stretch ahead of them desolate, broken by stumps and twisted scraps of lampposts. Ron's lunar landscape. The ground was even rougher, not as cleared as the border of the chausee, the earth thrown up here and there in mounds.

"Not far," Gunther said, rising out of his seat over a bump, even the solid Horch springs pounded flat, and for a moment, looking behind at the dust, the cars coming after them, Jake realized, an unexpected thought, that Gunther finally had his Wild West, stagecoach bucking across the badlands at a gallop. And then, eerily, the other Horch entered the Karl May dream too, firing at them from behind. A firecracker sound of shots, then a shattering pop at the back window.

"My god, they're shooting at us," Emil yelled, his voice jagged with fear. "Stop. It's madness. What are you doing? They'll kill us."

"Keep flat," Gunther said, hunching a little farther over the wheel.

Jake crouched and peered back over the edge of the seat. Both vehicles firing now, an aimless volley of stray shots.

"Come on, Gunther," Jake said, a jockey to a horse.

"It's there, it's there." A clear space of asphalt in the distance. He steered right, as if he were heading back to the Grosser Stern, then sharply left, dodging a fallen limb not yet scavenged for firewood, confusing the two cars behind. More shots, one grazing the back fender.

"Please stop," Emil said, almost hysterical on the back floor. "You'll kill us."

But they were there, crashing over a mound of broken pavement piled up at the edge of Hofjägerallee and landing with a loud *thunk* on the cleared avenue. Improbably, there was traffic—two convoy trucks, grinding toward them on their way to the traffic circle. Gunther shot out in front of them and wrenched the wheel left, tires squealing, so close there was an angry blast of horn.

"Christ, Gunther," Jake said, breathless.

"Police driving," he said, the car still shuddering from the skid.

"Let's not have a police death."

"No. That's a bullet."

Jake looked back. The others weren't as lucky, stuck at the side of the road until the trucks lumbered past. Gunther opened up the engine, speeding toward the bridge into Lützowplatz. If they could make it to the bridge, they'd be back in town, a maze of streets and pedestrians where at least the shooting would stop. But why had the Russians fired in the first place, risking Emil? A desperate logic—better dead than with the Americans? Which meant they thought they might lose after all.

But not yet. The Horch behind them had picked up speed too on the smooth road. Now the route was straight—get past the diplomatic quarter at the bottom of the park, then over the Landwehrkanal. Gunther honked the horn. A group of civilians was trudging down the side of the road with a handcart. They scattered in both directions away from the car but still on the road, so that Gunther had to slow down, pumping the brake and the horn at the same time. It was the chance the Russians were looking for, racing to close the gap between the cars. Another shot, the civilians darting in terror. Still coming. Jake swiveled to his open window and fired at the Horch behind, aiming low, a warning shot, two, to make them slow down. Not even a pause. And then, as Gunther slammed the horn again, the Russians' car began to smoke—no, steam, a teakettle steam that poured out of the grille, then blew back over the hood. A lucky shot ripping into the radiator, or just the old motor finally giving up? What did it matter? The car kept hurtling toward them, driving into its own cloud, then began to slow. Not the brake, a running down.

"Go," Jake said, the road finally clear of civilians. Behind them, the Horch had stopped. One of the men jumped out and rested his arm on the door to take aim. A target gallery shot. Gunther pressed the accelerator. The car jumped forward again.

This time Jake didn't even hear the bullet, the splintering pop through the window lost under the noise of the engine and the shouts behind. A small thud into flesh, like a grunt, not even loud enough to notice, until the spurt of blood splashed onto the dashboard. Gunther fell forward, still clutching the wheel.

"Gunther!"

"I can drive," he said, a hoarse gargle. More blood leaping out, spattering the wheel.

"My god. Pull over."

"Not far." His voice fainter. The car began to veer left.

Jake grabbed the wheel, steadying it, looking around. Only the jeep was chasing them now, the Horch stranded behind it. They were still moving fast, Gunther's foot on the pedal heavy as dead weight. Jake threw himself closer, putting both hands on the wheel, trying to kick Gunther's foot off the pedal. "The brake!" he shouted. Gunther had slumped forward again, a bulky, unmovable wall. Jake held on to the wheel, his hands now slippery with blood. "Move your leg!"

But Gunther seemed not to have heard him, his eyes fixed on the blood still spilling out onto the wheel. He gave a faint nod, as if he were making sense of it, then a small twitch of his mouth, the way he used to smile.

"A police death," he mumbled, almost inaudible, his mouth seeping blood, then slumped even farther, gone, his body falling on the wheel, pressing against the horn, so that they were racing toward the bridge with the horn blaring, driven by a dead man.

Jake tried to shove him aside, one hand still on the wheel, but only managed to push his upper body against the window. He'd have to dive underneath to move Gunther's feet, get to the brake, but that would mean letting go.

"Emil! Lean over, take the wheel."

"Maniacs!" Emil said, his voice shrill. "Stop the car."

"I can't. Grab the wheel."

Emil started up from the floor, then heard another shot and fell back again. Jake looked through the shattered window. Shaeffer, blowing his horn now, signaling them to stop.

"Grab the fucking wheel!" Jake yelled. Another truck appeared in the oncoming lane. Now there wasn't even the option of spinning in circles, hands slipping around the bloody wheel, trying to keep a grip. The bridge ahead, then people. Get the brake. With one hand he pushed hard against Gunther's leg, a cement weight, but moving, sliding back from the gas pedal, wedged now at the bottom. A little more and the car would slow. Only a matter of seconds before something gave.

It was the tire. A stopping shot from Shaeffer, more effective than a horn blast. The Horch careened wildly, as if Jake's hands had left the wheel. Heading straight for the truck. Jake wrenched the wheel back hard, swerving right, missing the truck, heading off the road in the other direction, but after that lost all control, plunging past some piles of rubble, bouncing furiously, the wheel meaningless. He shoved at Gunther's leg again, dislodging it from the pedal. But the car was moving on its own now, a last surge of momentum that carried it away from the bridge, over the embankment, only choking to a stop in midair. Nothing beneath them, a giddy suspension. Not even a full second at the top of a roller coaster, an impossible floating through nothing. Then the car pitched down.

Jake crouched lower, bracing himself against Gunther, so that he didn't see the water as they plunged into the canal, just felt the shock of the crash, throwing him forward against the dash with a crunch, a sick snapping sound at his shoulder, his head bumping hard against the wheel, a sharp pain that blotted out everything but the last instinct, to take a deep gulp of air as the water rushed in to flood around him.

He opened his eyes. Murky, almost viscous water, too cloudy to see far. Not a canal anymore, a sewer. Absurdly, he thought of infection. But there wasn't time to think about anything. He lifted himself, shoulder throbbing in a spasm, and reached over the seat with his good hand, grabbing Emil's shirt and pulling at it. Emil was moving, not dead, squirming up off the floor. Jake yanked the shirt, lifting him over the seat and pushing him toward the window. Buoyant, floating weight, just a matter of steering him out, but the front was crowded, Gunther taking up precious space.

Jake leaned back, twisting Emil's body so that he could shove it head first, watching Emil's feet flailing as he kicked his way out. Hurry. The canal wasn't deep; enough time to get to the surface if his air held. He began to follow through the window, bumping his head again on the frame, pulling himself with one arm, the other useless. Halfway out, Emil's shoe caught his shoulder, kicking, the pain so startling he thought he might black out and sink, the way rescuers were accidentally taken down by the thrashing of the people they were trying to save. His legs were now through the frame. He began to stroke up to the surface but the shoe struck him again, a strong kick, catching him now at the side of the head, a solid running pain to his shoulder. Don't gasp. For Christ's sake, Emil, move away. Then another kick, downward, not flailing this time, deliberate, intended to connect. Another. One more and he might be knocked out, bubbles rising to the surface, not a weapon in sight. No more air. He swam sideways with his good arm, only one effort left, and pushed up. Gentle Emil. What would you do to survive?

As he broke the surface, he barely got a gulp of air before the hand caught his throat and started to push his head back under. A squeal of tires and shouts from the bank. The hand came away. Jake pulled his head up, sputtering.

"Emil."

Emil had turned to look at the bank, once a solid wall, now bombed in places to slopes of rubble. Shaeffer and his man were picking their way down, their attention on the awkward footing, away from the water. A minute, maybe. Emil looked back at Jake, still gasping, his shoulder now an agony.

"It's over," Jake said.

"No." Barely a whisper, his eyes on Jake. Not like Shaeffer's, a hunter's, but something more desperate. What would you do? Emil reached for him and caught his throat again, and as Jake's head went under, he saw, with a sinking feeling worse than drowning, that he was losing the wrong war—not Shaeffer's, the one he hadn't even known he was fighting. A kick to the stomach now, forcing out air, as the hand gripped his hair, holding him under. Losing. Another kick. He'd die, the kick marks no more suspicious than crash bruises. Emil getting away with it again.

He yanked his head down, pulling Emil with him, scratching at his fingers. No good punching through water. He'd have to claw the fingers off. Another kick, below his stomach, but the hand was letting go, afraid perhaps of being dragged under with his victim. Do what he expects. Die. Jake sank lower. Emil couldn't see through the thick water. Would he follow? Let him think it had worked. He felt a final kick, the shoulder again, and for a moment he was no longer pretending, sinking deeper, without the strength to pull himself back up, the dizziness before a blackout. His feet hit the roof of the car. Below, he could see Gunther's head lolling out of the car window, floating like kelp. The way he'd look. Bastards. He dropped, bending his knees, no breath left at all, then pushed away with a last heave, away from Emil, toward the bank.

"Here he is!" Shaeffer shouted as his head bobbed up. He sucked in air, choking, spitting the water that came with it.

The other soldier had waded in to get Emil, who gazed at Jake in shock, then dropped his head, looking down at his hand, where the scratches were welling with blood.

"You all right?" Shaeffer was saying. "Why the hell didn't you stop?"

Jake kept gasping, drifting toward the bank. Nowhere else to go now. Then he felt Shaeffer's hand on his collar, dragging him onto the bank, struggling, then gripping his belt and yanking, like Tully being fished out of the Jungfernsee. He fell back against the broken concrete, looking up at Shaeffer. A splash, the sound of water dripping as Emil came out a few yards away.

He closed his eyes, fighting a wave of nausea from the pain, then opened them again to Shaeffer. "You going to finish me off here?"

Shaeffer looked at him, confused. "Don't be an asshole. Here, let me give you a hand," he said, reaching for him.

But he grabbed the wrong arm. As Shaeffer pulled him up, Jake's shoulder went hot with pain and he couldn't stop the scream, the last thing he heard before everything finally, almost a relief, did go black.

CHAPTER TWENTY

THEY SET HIS shoulder at the officers' infirmary near Onkel Tom's Hütte, or at least he was told they did, a day later, when he lay with a morphine hangover under the pink chenille spread at Gelferstrasse. People had drifted in and out, Ron to check, the old woman from downstairs playing nurse, none of them quite real, just figures in a haze, like his arm, white with gauze and adhesive, hanging in a sling, not his at all, someone else's. Who were they all? When the old woman came back, recognizable now, the billet's owner, he realized, embarrassed, that he didn't even know her name. Then the stranger with her, an American uniform, gave him a shot, and they disappeared too. What he saw instead was Gunther's face, floating in the water. No more points. And later, awake, the face still in his mind, he knew the haze was not just the drugs but a deeper exhaustion, a giving up, because he had done everything wrong.

He was sitting by the window, looking down on the garden where the old woman had snipped parsley, when Lena finally came.

"I've been so worried. They wouldn't let me go to the hospital." Military only. What if he had died?

"You look nice," he said as she kissed his forehead. Hair pinned up, the dress he had bought in the market.

"Well, for Gelferstrasse," she said, a look between them, blushing a little, pleased that he'd noticed. "And look, here's Erich. They say it's not so bad, the shoulder only. And ribs. Do the drugs make you sleepy? My god, this room." She went over to the bed, busy, and straightened the spread. "There," she said, and for an instant he saw her as a younger version of the old woman, a Berliner, going on. "See what Erich brought. It was his idea."

The boy handed over half a Hershey bar, eyes on the sling.

Jake took the bar, the haze lifting a little, unexpectedly touched. "So much," he said. "I'll save it for later, okay?"

Erich nodded. "Can I feel?" he said, pointing to the arm.

"Sure."

He ran his hand over the tape, working out the mechanics of the sling, interested.

"You have a light touch," Jake said. "You'll make a good doctor."

The boy shook his head. *"Alles ist kaput."*

"Someday," Jake said, still hazy, then looked at Lena again, trying to focus, clear his head. What, in fact, were they doing here? Was Shaeffer keeping him here? Had they told Lena? He turned to her. Get it over with. "They got Emil."

"Yes, he came to the flat. With the American. Such a scene, you can't imagine."

"To the flat?" Jake said. "Why?" Nothing clear.

"He was looking for something," Erich said.

The files, even now. "Did he find it?"

"No," Lena said, looking away.

"He was angry," the boy said.

"Well, now he's happy," Lena said to him quickly. "So never mind. He's going away, so he's lucky too." She looked at Jake. "He said you saved his life."

"No. That's not what happened."

"Yes. The American said so too. Oh, you're always so modest. It's like the newsreel."

"That didn't happen either."

"Ouf," she said, brushing this away. "Well, now it's over. Do you want something? Can you eat?" Busy again, picking up a shirt from the floor.

"I didn't save him. He tried to kill me."

Lena stopped, still half bent over, the shirt in hand. "Such talk. It's the drugs."

"No, that's what happened," he said, trying to keep his voice level and clear. "He tried to kill me."

She turned slowly. "Why?"

"The files, I guess. Maybe because he thought he could. No one would know."

"It's not true," she said quietly.

"No? Ask him how he got the scratches on his hand."

For a moment, silence, broken finally by someone clearing his throat.

"Well, suppose we put all that behind us now, shall we?" Shaeffer came through the door, Ron trailing behind him.

Lena turned to him. "So it's true?"

"Anybody in a car crash gets a few scratches, you know. Look at you," he said to Jake.

"You saw it," Jake said.

"Confusing situation like that? A lot of splashing, that's what I saw."

"So it is true," Lena said, sinking onto the bed.

"Sometimes the truth's a little overrated," Shaeffer said. "Doesn't always fit."

"Where have you got him?" Jake said.

"Don't worry, he's safe. No thanks to you. Hell of a place to pick to go swimming. God knows what's in there. Doc says we'd better get some sulfa drugs into him before we take him to Kransberg. Might spread."

"You're taking him to Kransberg?"

"Where'd you think I was taking him—to the Russians?" Said genially, without guile, his smile pushing the rest of Jake's haze away. Not Shaeffer after all. Someone else.

"Tell me the truth," Lena said. "Did Emil do that?"

Shaeffer hesitated. "He might have got a little agitated is all. Now let's forget about all that. We'll get Geismar fixed up here and everybody'll be just fine."

"Yes, fine," Lena said, distracted.

"We have a few things to go over," Ron said.

Lena looked at the boy, who'd been following their conversation like a tennis match.

"Erich, do you know what's downstairs? A gramophone. American records. You go listen and I'll be down soon."

"Take him down and get him set up," Shaeffer said to Ron, giving orders now. "Your kid?" he said to Lena.

Lena shook her head, staring at the floor.

"All right," Shaeffer said, turning to Jake, back to business. "Why the hell did you keep running away from me?"

"I thought you were someone else," Jake said, still trying to work it out. "He knew I'd be there." He looked up. "But you knew I'd be there too. How did you?"

"Boys over in intelligence got a tip."

"From whom?"

"I don't know. Really," Shaeffer said, suddenly earnest. "You know how those things work. You get a tip, you don't have time to chase around to see where it comes from—you find out if it's true. You ran out on us once. Why the fuck wouldn't I believe it?" He glanced over at Lena. "I thought you were doing the lady another favor."

"No, I was doing you a favor."

"Yeah? And look what happened. Who'd you think I was?"

"The man who shot Tully."

"Tully? I told you once, I don't give a shit about Tully." He looked over. "Who was it?"

"I don't know. Now I'm not going to."

"Well, who cares?"

"You should. The man who shot him got Brandt out of Kransberg."

"Well, I'm putting him back. That's all that matters now. The rest, that's all forgotten." Another American smile, last week's game.

"You've still got some bodies to account for. You going to forget about them too?"

"I didn't shoot them."

"Just the tire."

"Yeah, well, the tire. I figure I owe you for that one. Not that I fucking owe you anything. But it fits. Ron says we can play it this way."

"What are you talking about? You've got people shot in public. Witnesses. How do you play that?"

"Well, that's a question of what was seen, isn't it? A German guns down a Russian officer, hightails it away, gets followed, gets killed. Kind of thing happens in Berlin."

"In front of the whole press corps."

Shaeffer smiled. "But the only one they recognize in the whole mess is you. Isn't that right, Ron?"

"Afraid so," Ron said, coming back in. "Hard to keep track of what's what when things are—hectic."

"So?"

"So they know you were there. You were seen, so we had to explain you."

"Explain me how?"

"Damned fool thing going after him like that," Shaeffer said. "But that's the kind of damned fool thing you do. Got a reputation for it. And the press—you can't blame them—they always like it when the hero's one of their own."

"Fuck you. That's not the way I'm going to write it."

Ron looked at him. "That's the way it's gone out. From everybody. While you've been on the critical list. 'Hanging by a thread,' as they say. They did, too."

"I said I owed you for the tire. So now you're a fucking hero. Not that you deserve it. But it fits."

"Maybe the Russians won't agree. They were there too."

"Only the one who's dead."

"You shoot the guys in the Horch?"

"What Horch?" Shaeffer said, looking up. "Next question."

"Who shot Gunther then? He didn't die in a car crash. There's a bullet in him. So who put it there?"

"You did," Shaeffer said calmly.

Ron leaped in before Jake could say anything. "See, Kalach—that's the Russian he shot—saw him aim for the stands. Lucky Kalach got to him before he could take out Zhukov—that's who we think he was after. Of course, not so lucky for Kalach. But hell, it might have been Patton. On Victory Day. That kind of thing brings them out, makes a statement. Apparently there were personal problems—a drunk, never really got over the war. Cop who went bad—you know, when they do that, there's nothing worse. Do anything. Not that I blame him for having a grudge against the Russians."

"You can't do that to him," Jake said quietly. "He was a good man."

"He's dead," Shaeffer said. "It fits."

"Not for me. And it won't fit for the Russians."

"Yes, it will. A Russian saved Zhukov. He'll get the thanks of a grateful nation. And you get ours. Allied cooperation."

"And how do you explain Emil?"

"We don't. Emil wasn't there. He's been in Kransberg. We can't say we lost him. The Russians can't say they ever had him. There was no incident. That's the way this one works." Shaeffer stopped, meeting Jake's eyes. "Nobody wants an incident."

"I won't let you do this. Not to Gunther."

"What are you beefing about? You're sitting pretty. You'll get a fat contract, we get Brandt back, and the Russians can't do a damn thing. That's what I call a happy ending. See? I always said we'd make a good team."

"It's not true," Jake said stubbornly.

"It is, though," Ron said. "I mean, you've got a whole press corps that's just filed the story, so it must be."

"Not after I file mine."

"I hate to say it, but people are going to be awfully annoyed if you do that. They make you a hero and you throw egg on their faces? No, you don't want to do that. In fact, you can't."

"Because you'd spike it? Is that the way we do our reporting now? Like Dr. Goebbels."

"Don't get carried away. We make certain accommodations, that's all," Ron said, indicating Shaeffer. "For the good of the MG. So will you."

"Real sweethearts, aren't you?" Jake said, his voice low, scraping bottom.

"You want to cry over some dead kraut, do it on your own time," Shaeffer said, impatient now. "We've had enough trouble as it is getting our man back. We understand each other?"

Jake looked out the window again. After all, did it matter? Gunther was gone and so was the lead to the other man, the case as hopeless now as the scraggly garden below.

"Go away," he said.

"Which means yes, I suppose. Well, fine." Shaeffer picked up his hat. "I gather the lady's staying with you?"

"Yes," Lena said.

"Then I guess you got what you wanted too. That the reason for the little water fight?"

So he still didn't know. But did that matter either? Emil would search again and find the overlooked file, solve that problem too. His happy ending. Innocent, the way Shaeffer would want it anyway.

"Why don't you ask him?" Jake said.

"Never mind," Shaeffer said, glancing at Lena. "Can't say I blame him." An easy compliment. He turned to go. "Oh, one more thing. Brandt says you have some papers that belong to him."

Lena looked up. "Did he say what they were?"

"Notes of his. Something he needs for von Braun. Seems to think they're pretty important. Kind of tore the place apart, didn't he?" he said to Lena. "I'm sorry about that."

"More lies," she said, shaking her head.

"Ma'am?"

"And you're taking him to America."

"We're going to try."

"Do you know what kind of a man he is?" she said, looking directly at him, so that he shifted on his feet, uncomfortable.

"All I know is Uncle Sam wants him to build some rockets. That's all I care about."

"He lies to you. And you lie for him. You told me he saved Jake's life. My god, and I believed you. And now you believe him. Notes. What a pair you are."

"I'm only doing my job."

Lena nodded, smiling faintly. "Yes, that's what Emil said too. What a pair you are."

Shaeffer held up his hand, flustered. "Now, don't get me involved in domestic arguments. What happens between a man and his wife—" He dropped it and turned to Jake. "Anyway, whatever they are, do you have them?"

"No, he doesn't," Lena said.

Shaeffer peered at her, unsure where to take this, then looked back at Jake. "Do you?"

But Jake was looking at Lena, everything clear now, not even a wisp of haze. "I don't know what Emil's talking about."

Shaeffer stood for a second, fingering his hat, then let it go. "Well, no matter. They're bound to turn up somewhere. Hell, I thought he could do everything in his head."

Afterward, the room was quiet enough to hear his footsteps on the stairs.

"Did you destroy them?" Jake said finally.

"No, I have them."

"Why didn't you?"

"I don't know. I thought I would. And then they came to the flat. He was like a crazy man. Where are they? Where are they? You're on *his* side. The way he looked at me then. And I thought, yes, his side." She stopped, looking at him.

"Where were they?"

"In my bag." She walked over to the bed and pulled the papers out of her bag. "Of course, he never thought to look there. My things. Everywhere else. I stood there watching him—like a crazy man—and I knew. He never came to Berlin for me, did he?"

"Maybe both."

"No, only these. Here." She carried them over to his chair. "You know and you don't know—that's how everything was. Just now, when you told me what happened, there was a click in my head. Do you know why? I wasn't surprised. It was like before—you know and you don't know. I don't want to live like that anymore. Here."

But Jake didn't move, just looked at the buff sheets held out between them.

"What do you want me to do with them?"

"Give them to the Americans. Not that one," she said, gesturing toward the door. "He's the same. Another Emil. Any lie." Then she pulled the papers back to her so that for a second Jake thought she couldn't go through with it after all. "No. I'll take them. Tell me where. There's a name?"

"Bernie Teitel. I can't ask you to do that."

"Oh, it's not for you," she said. "For me. Maybe for Germany, does that sound crazy? To start somewhere. So there's still something left. Not just Emils. Anyway, look at you. Where can you go like that?"

"As it happens, he lives downstairs."

"Yes? So it's not so far."

"For you it is." He reached up for the papers. "He's still something to you."

She shook her head. "No," she said slowly. "Just a boy in a picture."

They looked at each other for a minute, then Jake leaned forward, ignoring the papers and covering her hand instead.

She smiled and turned his hand over, tracing the palm with her finger. "Such a line. In a man."

"You make a nice couple." Shaeffer, standing in the doorway with Erich. "I brought the kid back." He crossed over to them, Erich in tow. "Aren't you the sly one?" he said to Lena, holding out his hand. "I'll take them."

"They don't belong to you. Or Emil," Lena said.

"No, the United States government." He wiggled the fingers of his open hand in a give-me gesture. "Thanks for saving me another look-see. I figured." He took the end of the papers. "That's an order." He stared at her until she released them.

"What do you think you're doing?" Jake said.

"What do you think *you're* doing? This is government property. You're going to get yourself in trouble if you're not careful."

"They go to Teitel."

"I'll save you the trip." He started riffling through, glancing at the pages. "Not rocket notes, I take it. Want to tell me?"

"Reports from Nordhausen," Jake said. "Facts and figures from the camps. Slave labor details. What the scientists knew. Lots of interesting stuff. Keep looking—you'll find a lot of your friends there."

"Is that a fact. And you think this might make things a little embarrassing for them."

"It might make them war criminals."

Shaeffer looked up from the files. "You know, your trouble is you're in the wrong war. You're still fighting the last one."

"They were involved," Jake said, insistent.

"Geismar, how many times do I have to tell you? I don't care."

"You should care," Lena said. "They killed people."

"That's good, coming from a German. Who do you think killed them? Or do you just want your husband to take the rap? Convenient."

"You can't talk to her that way," Jake said, starting to get up, wincing as Shaeffer pushed him back.

"Watch your shoulder. Well, now we've got a situation. What a pain in the ass you are."

"I'll be a bigger pain in the ass if Teitel doesn't get those files. Not even Ron's going to spike this story."

"Which one is that?"

"Try a congressman bringing Nazis into the States."

"He wouldn't like that."

"Or a tech team playing hide-and-seek with the Russians. Lots of ways to go, if I want to. Or we could do it the right way. You helping the Military Government do what it says it's trying to do, bring these fucks to trial. A trial story. This time, you're the hero."

"Let me explain something to you," Shaeffer said. "Plain and simple. Look at this country. These scientists are the only reparations we're likely to get. And we're going to get them. We need them."

"To fight the Russians."

"Yes, to fight the Russians. You ought to figure out whose side you're on."

"And it doesn't matter about the camps."

"I don't care if they banged Mrs. Roosevelt. We need them. Got it?"

"If Teitel doesn't get those files, I'll do the story. Don't think I won't."

"I think you won't."

Shaeffer turned the papers sideways, and before Jake could move, tore them across.

"Don't," Jake said, starting to rise, the sound of tearing jolting across him like the pain shooting through his shoulder. Another tear, Jake only half out of his seat, then falling back, watching helplessly as the paper became pieces. "You bastard." A final rip.

Shaeffer took a step toward the window and flung them out, large bits of paper, suspended, then caught by the wind, flying over the garden—not small; about the same size, Jake saw, staring hypnotically, as the bills that had danced and blown over the Cecilienhof lawn.

"Like I said," Shaeffer said, turning back, "you're in the wrong war. That one's over."

Jake watched him go, brushing past Lena and wide-eyed Erich, who had already known everything was *kaput*.

"I feel I've let you down too," Jake said to Bernie. "You more than anybody, I guess."

They had come to Gunther's to pick up the *persilscheins* and found the room ransacked, stacks pulled apart, torn boxes littering the floor.

"Join the crowd. Everybody lets me down," Bernie said, a light growl, not really angry. "Christ, look at this. Word gets around fast. Ever notice how the liquor's the first thing to go? Then the coffee." He picked up the folders from the floor and stacked them. "Don't beat yourself up too much, okay? At least I know what to look for. That's more than I had before. There's lots of evidence floating around Germany—some of it could still land on my desk."

"You'll never get them," Jake said, gloomy.

"Then we'll get someone else," Bernie said, going through a bureau drawer. "Not exactly a shortage."

"But doesn't it bother you?"

"Bother me?" He turned to Jake, shoulders sagging. "Let me tell you something. I came over here, I thought I was really going to do something. Justice. And where did I end up? At the back of the line. Everybody's got a hand out. 'We can't do it all.' Feed the people—they're starving. Get Krupp up and running again, get the mines open. The Jews? Well, that was terrible, sure, but what are we supposed to do this winter if we don't get some coal out of the Russians? Freeze? Everybody's got a priority. Except the Jews aren't on anybody's list. We'll deal with that later. If anybody has the time. So I lose a few scientists? I'm still trying to get the camp guards."

"Small fry."

"Not to the people they killed." He paused. "Look, I don't like it either. But that's the way it is. You think you're going to set the world on fire and you come here—all you do is pick through the damage. Without a priority. So you do what you can."

"Yeah, I know, one at a time. An eye for an eye."

Bernie looked up. "That's a little Old Testament for me. There isn't any punishment, you know. How do you punish this?"

"Then why bother?"

"So we know. Every trial. This is what happened. Now we know. Then another trial. I'm a DA, that's all. I bring things to trial."

Jake looked down, fingering the *persilschein*s on the table. "I still wish I had the files. They weren't guards—they should have known better."

"Geismar," Bernie said softly, "everybody should have known better."

"Would it help if I wrote something? Got you some press?"

Bernie smiled and went back to the drawer. "Save your ink. Go home. Look at you, all banged up. Haven't you had enough?"

"I'd like to know."

"What?"

"Who the other man is."

"That? You're still on that? What's the point?"

"Well, for one thing, he could still be working for the Russians." Jake dropped the folder on the table. "Anyway, I'd like to know for Gunther, finish the case for him."

"I doubt he cares anymore. Or do you have ways of getting messages up there?"

Jake walked over to the map, left in place by the scavengers. The Brandenburg. The wide chausee, where the reviewing stand had been.

"Why would someone working for the Russians tip off the Americans where Emil was going to be? Why would he do that?"

"You got me."

"Now, see, Gunther would have figured it out. That's the kind of thing he was good at—things that didn't add up."

"Not anymore," Bernie said. "Hey, look at this."

He had pulled an old square box from the back of the drawer, velvet or felt, like a jewel case, opened now to a medal. Jake thought of the hundreds lying on the Chancellery floor, not put away like this, treasured.

"Iron Cross, first class," Bernie said. "Nineteen seventeen. A veteran. He never said."

Jake looked at the medal, then handed it back. "He was a good German."

"I wish I knew what that meant."

"It used to mean this," Jake said. "Almost done?"

"Yeah, grab the files. You think there's anything in the bedroom? Not many effects, are there?"

"Just the books." He took a Karl May from the shelf, a souvenir, then moved to the table and picked up one of the folders and flipped it open. A Herr Krieger, said to have been in a concentration camp, now Category IV, no evidence of Nazi activity, release advised. He glanced idly down the page, then stopped, staring at it.

Of course. No, not of course. Impossible.

"My god," he said.

"What?" Bernie said, coming in from the bedroom.

"You know how you said evidence lands on your desk? Some just landed on mine. I think." Jake scooped up the files. "I need the jeep."

"The jeep?"

"I have to check something. Another file. It won't take long."

"You can't drive like that. One hand?"

"I've done it before." Bumping through the Tiergarten. "Come on, quick," he said, his hand out for the keys.

"It's getting dark," Bernie said, but tossed them over. "What am I supposed to do here?"

"Read that." He nodded at the Karl May. "He tells a hell of a story."

He headed west to Potsdamerstrasse, then south toward Kleist Park. In the dusk only the bulky Council headquarters had shape, lit up by a few offices working late, the car park nearly deserted. Up the opera house staircase, down the hall, the translucent door to Muller's office dark but not locked. Only the Germans huddled behind locks now.

He flicked on the light. Jeanie's usual neat desk, every pencil put away. He went over to the filing cabinet and flipped the tabs until he found the right folder, then carried it back to the desk with the *persilscheins*. It was only after he'd looked through it, then at the *persilscheins* once more, that he sat down, sinking back against the chair, thinking. Follow the points. But he saw, even before he reached the bottom of the column, that Gunther had found it without even knowing. Sitting there all along.

And now what? Could he prove it? He could already see, with the inevitable sinking feeling, that Ron would take care of this too, another story to protect the guilty, in the interests of the Military

Government. Maybe a little quiet justice later, when no one was looking. And why should anyone look? Emil back safe, the Russians foiled—everyone satisfied except Tully, who hadn't mattered in the first place. The wrong war again. Jake would win and get nothing. Not even reparations. He sat up, staring at Tully's transfer sheet, the block capitals in fuzzy carbon. Not this time. Not an eye for an eye, but something, a different reparation, one for the innocent.

He leaned over, opened the desk drawers to his side, and rummaged through. Stacks of government forms, printed, second sheets gummed for carbons, arranged in marked piles. He mentally tipped his hat to Jeanie. Everything in its place. He pulled one out, then looked for another, a different pile, and swung around to the typewriter, removing the cover with his good hand and rolling in the first form, aligning it so that the letters would fill the box without hitting the line, official. When he started to type, a one-finger peck, the sound of the keys filled the room and drifted out to the lonely corridor. A guard came by, suspicious, but only nodded when he saw Jake's uniform.

"Working late? You ought to give it a rest, with the sling and all."

"Almost done."

But in fact it seemed to take hours, one keystroke at a time, his shoulder hurting. Then he realized he'd need a supporting document and had to search the desk again. He found it in the bottom drawer, next to a stash of nail polish from the States. So Jeanie had a friend. He rolled the new form into place and started typing, still careful, nothing messy. He was almost finished when a shadow from the doorway fell over the page.

"What are you doing?" Muller said. "The guard said—"

"Filling out some forms for you."

"Jeanie can do that," he said, wary.

"Not these. Have a seat. I'm almost done."

"Have a seat?" he said, drawing his shoulders back in surprise. Old army.

"There," Jake said, rolling the form out. "All ready. All you have to do is sign."

"What the hell are you doing?"

"You know how to do that. That's what you do. Lots of signatures. Like these." He pushed over the Bensheim releases from Gunther's.

Muller picked them up, a quick glance. "Where did you get these?"

"I looked. I like to know things."

"Then you know these are forged."

"Are they? Maybe. This isn't." He held up the other folder.

"What isn't?" Muller said, not even bothering to look.

"Tully's transfer home. You transferred him. Tully was attached to Frankfurt. There was never any reason for a copy of his orders to end up here, except a copy would go to the authorizing officer. Regulations. So one did. Maybe you didn't even know it was here—Jeanie just filed it away with everything else that came in. She's an efficient girl. Never occurred to her to—" He dropped the folder. "Of course, it never occurred to me either. Why there'd be a copy here. But then, a lot of things didn't occur to me. Why you'd hold out on me with the CID report. Why you'd lead me on that wild goose chase with the black market. I thought I was dragging it out of you—that must have been fun to watch, me asking all the wrong questions. Let's not embarrass the MG." He paused, looking up at the lean Judge Hardy face, older than he remembered. "You know the funny thing? I still don't want it to be you. Maybe it's the hair. You don't fit the part. You were one of the good guys. I thought at least there had to be one."

"Don't want what to be me?"

"You killed him."

"You can't be serious."

"And it almost worked, too. If he'd just stayed down there in the Havel. Just—disappeared. The way Emil did. But he didn't."

"You enjoy this? Making up stories?"

"Mm. This is a good one. Let me try it on you. Have a seat."

But Muller remained standing, shoulders erect, his tall frame looming over the desk, waiting, like a weapon held in reserve.

"Let's start with the transfer. That's what should have tipped me if I'd been paying attention. Gunther would have seen it—that's the kind of thing he noticed. Transfer a man you didn't know. Except you did. Your old partner." Jake nodded at the *persilschein*s. "Just why you wanted to get him home I'm not sure, but I can guess. Of course, he wasn't the most reliable guy to do business with in the first place, but my guess is that you got nervous. Everything worked the way it was supposed to. Brandt's trail was cold before they even knew there was one. But then Shaeffer started sniffing around. He's a guy who likes to make noise. Set off some bells and whistles—I think that's the expression he used. Which means he went to MG. Which means they started going off *here*. With a congressman behind him. Nothing to connect you yet. But now it wasn't going to go away either. And there's Tully—talk about a weak link. Who knew what he'd say? How long before Shaeffer found out you'd done business before?" Another nod at the Bensheim file.

"You with me so far? So the easiest thing was to send him home—all you had to do was sign a form. That's what everybody wants, isn't it? Except this time it didn't take. Tully didn't want to go home—he had plans here. You call him to Berlin, in a hurry, not even time to pack, get him on the first plane. You might have waited, by the way. Did you know he was coming anyway? A Tuesday appointment. But no matter. The point was to get it done fast. Here's your hat, what's your hurry. Sikorsky meets him at the airport and drops him at the Control Council."

Muller raised his head to speak.

"Don't bother," Jake said. "He told me so himself. So Tully comes to pick up a jeep. But nobody just waltzes in and takes a jeep. It's not a taxi stand out there. Motor pool assigns them. To you, for instance. I could check how many you had signed out that day, but why bother now? One of yours.

"Where you were, I don't know—probably at a meeting, defending the free and the brave. Which is why you couldn't meet him in the first place. The plane was late, which must have cut into your schedule. Anyway, busy. Which was too bad, because Tully got busy too, down at the Document Center, so that when you met him there later, he had a new racket going. Not to mention a new payment from Sikorsky. Which he didn't, I guess—mention, that is."

He watched Muller's face. "No, he wouldn't. But all the more reason now to hang around—more money where that came from. You tell me how it played from there. Did he tell you where to stick your transfer? Or did he threaten to expose you if you didn't play ball? In for a penny, in for a pound. Plenty of money to be made on those SS files. Shaeffer? You could take care of him. You'd taken care of Bensheim, hadn't you? And if you couldn't—well, you'd have to, or he'd take you down with him. Anyway, he sure as hell wasn't going to Natick, Mass., when there was a fortune to be made here. Of course, it's possible you got rid of him to keep the files all to yourself, but he didn't *have* the files yet, the Doc Center had come up dry so far, so I think it's just that he boxed you in so tight, you didn't think you had much choice. The transfer would have been so easy. But you still had to get rid of him somehow. Is that more the way it was?"

Muller said nothing, his face blank.

"So you did. A little ride out to the lake to talk things over—you don't want to be seen together. And Tully's stubborn. He's got a belt full of money and god knows what dancing in his head, and he tells *you* the way it's going to be. Not just Brandt. More. And you know it's not going to work. Brandt was one thing—he even helped. But now you've got Shaeffer around. Do the smart thing—take the money and run, before it's too late. The last thing Tully wants to hear. Maybe the last thing he did hear. I'll give you this much—I don't think you planned it. Too sloppy, for one thing—you didn't even take his tags after you shot him, just threw him in. No weights. Maybe you thought the boots would do it. Probably you weren't thinking at all, just panicked. That kind of crime. Anyway, it's done and he's gone. And then—here's the best part, even I couldn't make it up—you went home and had dinner with me. And I liked you. I thought you were what we were here for. To make the peace. Christ, Muller."

"Everything okay here?" The guard, surprising them from the door.

Muller swiveled, moving his hand to his hip, then stopped.

"We're almost done," Jake said steadily, staring at Muller's hand.

"Getting late," the guard said.

Muller blinked. "Yes, fine," he said, his MG voice, dropping his hand. He turned back and waited, his eyes locked on Jake, until the steps in the hall grew faint.

"Jumpy?" Jake said. He nodded at Muller's hip. "Watch yourself with that."

Muller leaned forward, placing his hands on the desk. "You take some chances."

"What? That you'll plug me? I doubt it." He waved his hand. "Anyway, not here. Think of the mess. What would Jeanie say?

Besides, you already tried that once." He looked at him until Muller took his hands away from the desk, as if he'd literally been pushed back by Jake's stare.

"I don't know what you're talking about."

"In Potsdam. That's when everything started falling apart. Now you had real blood on your hands. Not just a small-time chiseler. Liz. How'd that make you feel when you heard?"

"Heard what?"

"You killed her too. Same as if you pulled the trigger."

"You can't prove this," Muller said, almost a whisper.

"Want to bet? What do you think I've been doing all this time? You know, I might not even have tried if it had just been Tully. I guess you could say he got what was coming to him. But Liz didn't. Gunther was right about that too. The when. Why try to kill me then? Another thing that didn't occur to me until now, when I started putting things together. Why do it at all? Tully's dead, and so's Shaeffer's trail. No way to connect you. Even after he washes up—quick report, body's shipped out before anybody can take a good look. Not that anybody wanted to—all they were looking at was the money. What other explanation could there be? It's sure as hell the only one you wanted me to have. Talk about a lucky break for you. Money you didn't even know he had. What did you think when it turned up, by the way? I'd be curious to know."

Muller said nothing.

"Just a little gift from the gods, I guess. So you're safe. Shaeffer's stuck and I'm off looking at watches in the black market. And then something happens. I start asking questions about Brandt at Kransberg—for personal reasons, but you don't know that, you think I must know something, made the connection no one else did. And if I'm asking, maybe somebody else is going to put two and two together too. But you can't get me out of Berlin, that would just make things worse—I'd make a stink and people would wonder. And then, at Tommy's going-away party, what do I do? I ask you to check the dispatcher at Frankfurt, the one *you* called—or did you get Jeanie to do it? No, you'd do it yourself—to get Tully on the plane. Personal authorization, not on the manifest. Which he'd remember. Not just close anymore, a real connection. So you panic again. You transfer his ass out of there like *that,* but even that's not safe enough. You get somebody to get rid of me in Potsdam. The *next day*. But that didn't occur to me either, not then. I was just lying there with an innocent woman's blood all over me."

Muller lowered his head. "That wasn't supposed to happen."

Jake sat still. Finally there, the confession, so easily said.

"That girl. That wasn't supposed to happen," Muller said again. "I never meant her to—"

"No, just me. Christ, Muller."

"It wasn't me. Sikorsky. I told him I'd transfer Mahoney, that would do it. I never told him to kill you. Never. Believe me."

Jake looked up at him. "I do believe you. But Liz is still dead."

Now Muller did sit down, his body sagging slowly into the chair, head still low, so that only his silver hair caught the light of the desk lamp. "None of this was supposed to happen."

"You start something, people get in the way. I suppose Shaeffer would have been a bonus."

"I didn't even know he was there. I didn't know. It was all Sikorsky. He was worse than Tully. Once they start—" His voice trailed off.

"Yeah, it's hard to get away. I know." Jake paused, toying with the folder. "Tell me something, though. Why'd you tip Shaeffer that I'd be at the parade with Brandt? It had to be you—I'll bet you know just how to get something to Intelligence like it came out of the air. But why do it? Gunther sets it up with Kalach, who tells you, but you can't go. The one person who couldn't. You're brass, General Clay's man—you had to be at the parade. Another thing that didn't occur to me. So, our mistake. But Kalach's going to make the snatch anyway. You could have watched the whole thing without anyone's being the wiser. Right up there with Patton. Why tip Shaeffer?"

"To put an end to it. If Shaeffer got him back, he'd stop. I wanted it to stop."

"And if he didn't get him? It didn't really matter who got him, did it? Maybe Kalach would after all and take Shaeffer out doing it, and it would stop that way. While you were watching."

"No. I wanted Shaeffer to have him. I thought it would work. Sikorsky would have been suspicious if something went wrong, but the new man—"

"Would have taken the blame himself. And you'd be home free."

Muller looked over. "I wanted out. Of all of it. I'm not a traitor. When this started, I didn't know what Brandt meant to us."

"You mean how much Shaeffer would want him back. Just another one of these," Jake said, picking up the Bensheim file. "For ten thousand dollars."

"I didn't know—"

"Let's do us both a favor and skip the explanations. Everybody in Berlin wants to give me an explanation, and it never changes anything." He dropped the folder. "But just give me one. The one thing I still can't figure. Why'd you do it? The money?"

Muller said nothing, then looked away, oddly embarrassed. "It was just sitting there. So easy." He turned back to Jake. "Everybody else was getting theirs. I've been in the service twenty-three years, and what's it going to get me? A lousy pension? And here's a little snot like Tully with plenty of change in his pockets. Why not?" He pointed to the *persilschein*s. "The first few, at Bensheim, I didn't even know what I was signing. Just more paper. There was always something—he knew how to slip them through. Then I finally realized what he was doing—"

"And could have court-martialed him. But you didn't. He make you a deal?"

Muller nodded. "I'd already signed. Why not a few more?" he said, his voice vague, talking to himself. "Nobody cared about the Germans, whether they got out or not. He said if it went wrong later, I could say he'd forged them. Meanwhile, the money was there—all you had to do was pick it up. Who would know? He could be persuasive when he wanted to be—you didn't know that about him."

"Maybe he had a willing audience," Jake said. "Then things got tricky at Bensheim, so you got him out of there—another one of your quick transfers—and the next thing you know, he turns up with another idea. Still persuasive. Not just a little *persilschein* this time. Real money."

"Real money," Muller said quietly. "Not some lousy pension. You know what that's like, waiting for a check every month? You spend your whole life just to get the rank and these new guys come in—"

"Spare me," Jake said.

"That's right," Muller said, his mouth twisted. "You don't need an explanation. You already know everything you want to know."

Jake nodded. "That's right. Everything."

"You couldn't leave it alone, could you?" Muller said. "Now what are you going to do? Call the MPs? You don't really think I can let you do that, do you? Not now."

"Ordinarily, no. But don't get trigger-happy yet," Jake said, glancing toward Muller's hip again. "I'm a friend to the army, remember?"

Muller looked up. "Meaning?"

"Meaning nobody's going to call anybody."

"Then what? What are you going to do?"

"I'm going to let you get away with murder." Neither of them said anything for a moment, staring. Then Jake sat back. "That seems to be the general policy around here. If it's useful to us. So now you're going to be useful to me."

"What do you want?" Muller said, still staring, not quite sure how to take this.

Jake tossed one of the forms over to him. "Your signature. First this one."

Muller picked it up and looked it over, a bureaucrat's reflex. Read before you sign, Tully's inadvertent lesson. "Who's Rosen?"

"A doctor. You're giving him a visa for the States."

"A German? I can't do that."

"Yes you can. In the national interest. Like the other scientists. This one's even clean—no Nazi affiliations at all. He was in a camp. You fill in the classification code." He handed over a pen. "Sign it."

Muller took the pen. "I don't understand," he said, but when Jake didn't answer, he leaned forward and scribbled in one of the boxes, then signed the bottom.

"Now this one."

"Erich Geismar?"

"He's my son."

"Since when?"

"Since you signed this. U.S. citizen. Rosen's taking him home."

"A child? He'll need proof of citizenship."

"He has it," Jake said, tossing him the last form. "Right here. Sign that too."

"The law says—"

"You're the law. You asked for proof and I gave it to you. It says so right here. Now sign off on it and it's official. Sign it."

Muller began writing. "What about the mother?" A clerk's question in a consulate.

"She's dead."

"German?"

"But he's American. MG just said so."

When Muller was finished, Jake took the forms back and tore off the bottom carbons. "Thank you. You just did something decent for a change. Your copies where?"

Muller nodded to a box on Jeanie's desk.

"Careful you don't lose them. You'll need the particulars, in case anybody wants to verify them with you. And you will verify them. Personally. If there's any problem at all. Understood?"

Muller nodded. Jake stood up, folding the papers into his breast pocket. "Fine. Then that does it. Always useful to have a friend in the MG."

"That's all?"

"You mean am I going to put the bite on you for something else? No. I'm not Tully." He patted his pocket. "You're giving them a life. That seems a fair trade to me. I don't particularly care what you do with yours."

"But you know—"

"Well, that's just it. You were right about one thing, you see. I can't prove it."

"Can't prove it," Muller said faintly.

"Oh, don't get excited," Jake said, catching Muller's expression. "Don't get any ideas either. I can't prove it, but I can come close. CID must still have the bullet they took out of Tully. They could make a match. But maybe not. Guns have a way of disappearing. And I suppose I could track down the dispatcher you sent home. But you know something? I don't care anymore. I have all the reparations I want. And you—well, I guess you'll have some worried nights, and that's fine with me too. So let's just leave it there. But if anything goes wrong with these," he said, touching his pocket again, "your luck runs out, understand? I can't prove it in court, but I can come close enough for the army. I'd do it, too. Lots of mud, the kind of thing they don't like at all. Maybe a dishonorable. The pension for sure. So just play ball and everybody walks away."

"And that's all?"

"Well, one more thing, now that you mention it. You can't transfer yourself home, but make the request to Clay. Health reasons. You can't stay here. The Russians don't know you tipped Shaeffer. They think you're still in business. And they can be persuasive too. That's the last thing the MG needs—a worm in the barrel. They've got their hands full just trying to figure out what they're doing here. Maybe they'll even bring in somebody who can do the place some good. I doubt it, but maybe." He stopped, looking down at the silver hair. "I thought that was you. But I guess something got in your way."

"How do I know you'll—"

"Well, strictly speaking, you don't. Like I said, some worried nights. But don't have them here. Not in Berlin. Then I might just change my mind." Jake picked up the Bensheim folders and stacked them. "I'll keep these." He went around the desk, starting for the door. "Go home. You need a job, go see American Dye. I hear they're hiring. I'll bet they'd go for somebody just like you, with your experience. Just stay out of Berlin. Anyway, you don't want to run into me again—that'd just make you nervous. And you know what? I don't want to run into you either."

"You're staying here?"

"Why not? Lots of stories in Berlin."

Muller shook his head. "Your press pass expires," he said dully, an official.

Jake smiled, surprised. "I'll bet you know the exact hour too. All right, one more thing then. Have Jeanie do up a residence permit tomorrow. Indefinite stay. Special from the MG. Sign that and we're done."

"Are we?" Muller said, looking up.

"I am. You have some nights to get through, but you will. People do. It's something you learn here—after a while nobody remembers anything." He walked to the door.

"Geismar?" Muller said, stopping him. He rose from the chair, his face even older, slack. "It was just the money. I'm a soldier. I'm not a— Honest to god, I never meant this to happen. Any of it."

Jake turned. "That should make them easier, then. The nights." He looked over at him. "It's not much, though, is it?"

CHAPTER TWENTY-ONE

AT THIS HOUR, Tempelhof was almost deserted. Later, when the afternoon flights came in, the high marble hall would fill up with uniforms, just as it had that first day, but now there were only a few GIs sitting on duffel bags, waiting. The doors were still closed to the stairs that led down to the runways.

"Now remember what I told you," Lena was saying, crouched down in front of Erich, fussing, brushing his hair back. "Stay close to Dr. Rosen when you change for Bremen. So many people. Hold his hand, yes? You remember?"

Erich nodded. "Can I sit by the window?" he said, already on his way.

"Yes, the window. You can wave. I'll be right there." She pointed to the observation deck. "But I'll see you. You won't be afraid, will you?"

"He's excited," Rosen said to Jake, smiling. "A first airplane. And a ship. Well, mine too. This kindness—I can never repay you."

"Just be a good father to him. He's never had one. His mother—I don't know what he remembers. A few visits."

"What happened to her?"

"She died. In the camps."

"You knew her?"

"A long time ago." He touched Rosen's arm. "Raise him as a Jew."

"Well, how else?" Rosen said mildly. "That's what you want?"

"Yes. She died for that. Tell him, if he asks, that he should be proud of her." He paused, for a moment at the Alex again, watching the shuffling walk back to the cell. "Now, you've got Frank's number at *Collier's*?"

"Yes, yes."

"I told him to meet the boat. But just in case, that's where to reach him. He'll have money for you. He'll fix you up with anything you need. Till you get on your feet."

"In New York. It's like a dream."

"It won't seem like a dream after you've been there a while."

"Do you want to go to the bathroom?" Lena said to Erich. "On the plane, I don't know. There's still time. Come."

"To the women's?" Erich said.

"Oh, so big all of a sudden. Come." She led him away.

"I wonder, does he know what you do for him?" Rosen said. "How lucky he is."

Jake glanced at him. What passed for luck in Berlin. But Rosen was looking over his shoulder.

"Who is the old man? He knows you."

Professor Brandt was coming toward them in his old dark suit, the high Weimar collar as stiff as his walk.

"Good morning," he said. "So you've come to see Emil off too?"

"Someone else," Jake said. "I didn't know he was on the plane."

"I thought, perhaps it's the last time," Professor Brandt said hesitantly, explaining himself. He looked at Jake. "So you were a friend to him after all."

"No. He didn't need me. He arranged things himself."

"Ah," Professor Brandt said, mystified but reluctant to pursue it. He checked his pocket watch. "They'll be late."

"No, there they are."

Coming through the waiting hall like the front wedge of a military unit, heels loud against the floor, Emil and Shaeffer, Breimer with them, trailed by GIs carrying bags. An airport GI, as if alerted by the heels, appeared from the side and opened the door, standing at the head of the stairs with a clipboard. When they reached the gate, they stopped short, surprised to find visitors.

"What the hell are you doing here?" Shaeffer said to Jake.

Jake said nothing, watching Emil walk up to his father.

"Well, Papa," Emil said, disconcerted, a young voice.

"Come to see the boys off, huh?" Breimer said. "Nice of you, Geismar."

Professor Brandt stood still for a moment, looking at Emil, then extended his hand. "So it's goodbye," he said, his voice shaky behind the formal gesture.

"Well, not for good," Emil said pleasantly, caught by the hand but trying to sidestep any sentiment. "I'll come back sometime. You know, it's my home, after all."

"No," Professor Brandt said faintly, touching his arm. "You have done enough for Germany. Go." He dropped the hand, looking at him. "Maybe things will be different for you now, in America."

"Different?" Emil said, flushing, aware that the others were looking. But their eyes were on Professor Brandt, whose shoulders had started to shake, a raw, uncontrolled blubbering, catching everyone off-guard, an emotion no one expected. Before Emil could react, the old man reached out and clutched him, wrapping his arms around him, holding on, a death grip. Jake wanted to look away but instead kept staring at them, dismayed. Maybe the only story that really mattered, the endless ties of life's cat's cradle, tangled like yarn.

"Well, Papa," Emil said, leaning back.

"You made me so happy," Professor Brandt said. "When you were a boy. So happy." Still shaking, his face wet, so that now the others did turn away, awkward, as if he had somehow become incontinent.

"Papa," Emil said, still helpless in the grasp.

Then Professor Brandt pulled away, collecting himself, patting Emil's upper arm. "Well, but here are your friends too." He turned to Jake. "Forgive me. An old man's foolishness." He stepped aside, ceding place, not bothering to wipe his face.

Emil looked at Jake, oddly relieved, grateful for any interruption but now uncertain what to do. He started to offer his hand.

"So," he said, "all ends for the best."

"Does it?" Jake said, ignoring the hand.

He nodded at Jake's sling. "The shoulder. It's all right?"

Jake said nothing.

"It's a misunderstanding about that. Shaeffer told me."

"No misunderstanding." Jake opened his mouth to speak again, then glanced at Professor Brandt and instead just turned away.

"We certainly don't want that," Breimer said, genial. "Not after what you two have been through."

"No, we certainly don't want that," Shaeffer said pointedly to Jake, a signal to take Emil's hand.

But the moment had passed, because now Emil had turned too, toward the edge of the gate area, where Lena was coming around the corner with Erich. She was bent over, talking to him. When she glanced up and saw the waiting party, she stopped, slowly raising her head. Another second and then she began walking again, shoulders back, determined, the way she'd come into the Adlon dining room. Not in her good dress this time, a cheap print with tiny flowers, but beautiful, catching the light just by walking in it.

"What's she doing here?" Shaeffer said as she approached.

"That the wife?" Breimer said. "Well, why the hell not? Say goodbye to her husband."

Within earshot now, standing in front of Emil.

"No, you're mistaken," she said to Breimer, but looking at Emil. "My husband died. In the war."

She moved past him, leaving a silence. Jake looked at Emil. The same flustered expression he'd given Professor Brandt, a confused despair, as if he had finally glimpsed the missing piece, then seen it float away before he could tell what it was.

"In the war?" Breimer said.

Lena took Jake's arm. "They're boarding. Come, Erich."

Rosen put a hand on the boy's shoulder and they moved toward the stairs behind the GIs with duffel bags.

"Now, remember to hold hands, yes?" Lena turned to Rosen. "You have the lunch?"

Rosen held up the bag with a tolerant smile.

Lena knelt in front of Erich. "Like the mother hen, that's what he thinks. Is that what you think?" Erich grinned. "Well, then give me a hug. A hug from my chick. Always so good. I'll write to you. Shall I do that in English? Dr. Rosen can read, then you. You can practice, how's that for a plan? Jake too. Come," she said to Jake, standing up, "say goodbye."

Jake hunched down, one arm on Erich's shoulder. "Be good and listen to Dr. Rosen, okay? You'll have lots of good times. And I'll come visit someday."

"You're not my father?" the boy said, curious.

"No. Your father's dead, you know that. Now Dr. Rosen is going to take care of you."

"You gave me your name."

"Oh, that. Well, everybody gets a new name in America. That's how they do it there. So I gave you mine. Is that all right?"

Erich nodded.

"And I'll come to see you. I promise."

"Okay," the boy said, then reached up and put one arm around Jake's neck, a quick hug, but careful of the sling so that the thin arm was almost weightless, light as a loose strand of yarn. "Geismar," he said. "That's English? It's not German?"

"Well, it used to be, before. Now it's American."

"Like me."

"That's right, like you. Come on, you'd better hurry if you want a window," he said, shooing him to Rosen.

"Don't forget to wave," Lena said as they started down the stairs. "I'll be watching."

She turned, acknowledging Professor Brandt for the first time by touching his sleeve. "So it's good you came. We can see over there," she said, turning from the group toward the big window.

"You watch. I said goodbye. Now to you too, it seems," he said, glancing toward Emil. He raised his hand, stopping her before she could say anything, then leaned over and kissed her lightly on the forehead. He looked at her for a second, then nodded, a mute goodbye, and started back toward the amber hall.

Shaeffer had checked their names on the list and was now waiting for Emil, who still stood motionless, his eyes on Lena. "Come on, Emil," he said, impatient, then turned to Breimer. "I'll see you in Frankfurt. Thanks for everything."

"Died in the war?" Emil called to Lena. "That's how we leave each other?"

She turned back, looking at him angrily. "No, I'm leaving you with Peter. Now go."

"With Peter? What does that mean? What do you mean by that?" Frustrated, his voice louder.

Jake looked over at Lena, her face still hard, and for an instant he thought she might do it, as easily as Gunther's waitress asking for a check. Then she glanced at Professor Brandt and lowered her head.

"Nothing. Like the rest of it. It means nothing. Go away." She walked over to the window, not looking back.

"Come on, Emil," Shaeffer said, leading him down the stairs.

"Well, that's a hell of a thing," Breimer said to Jake. "You ought to talk to her. Acting like that. Who the hell does she think—"

"One more word and I'll flatten you. I won't even wait for the next election to vote you out."

Breimer looked at him, startled. "Now, don't get all hot. No disrespect meant. I suppose under the circumstances— Still, that's no way to act. After everything he's been through. Hell, after everything you've been through. Joe told me what you did for us. I know, you like to think you're a wise-ass—you are, too," he said, glancing up. "You're a hard man to like, you know that? But then we get down to the short hairs and you came through. I take my hat off to you for that one." He stopped, the words sounding hollow even to him. "Anyway, we got him, that's the main thing. But these people—" He looked toward Lena. "I'll never understand them if I live to be a hundred. You do everything for them—"

"What are we doing for them?" Jake said quietly. "I'd like to know."

"Why, we're helping them, that's what," Breimer said easily. "Got to, now. Who else is going to do it, the Russians? Look at this place. You can see what they've been through."

Jake looked down at the runway. A faint clunk of propellers, Emil and Shaeffer hurrying past the ground crew to the plane. Across the field the light had come up, pale and dusty, hanging over the miles of broken houses.

"Do you have any idea what happened here?" he said, half to himself. "I mean, any idea?"

"I suppose you're going to tell me. Well, I know all about that, so let me tell you something. I like to look ahead. What's past is past. All these people want to do is forget. You can't blame them for that."

"So that's what we're going to do," Jake said, suddenly tired, his shoulder starting to ache again. "Help them forget."

"You want to put it that way, yes, I guess we are. The good Germans, anyway."

"Like Brandt," Jake said, watching him board the plane.

"Certainly like Brandt. Who else?"

"One of the good ones," Jake said, moving away from the window and glancing over toward Lena, standing with her hand half raised, ready to wave. He turned to Breimer. "Is that what you think?"

Breimer looked at him, eyes steady. "He has to be, doesn't he?" he said smoothly. "He's one of ours."

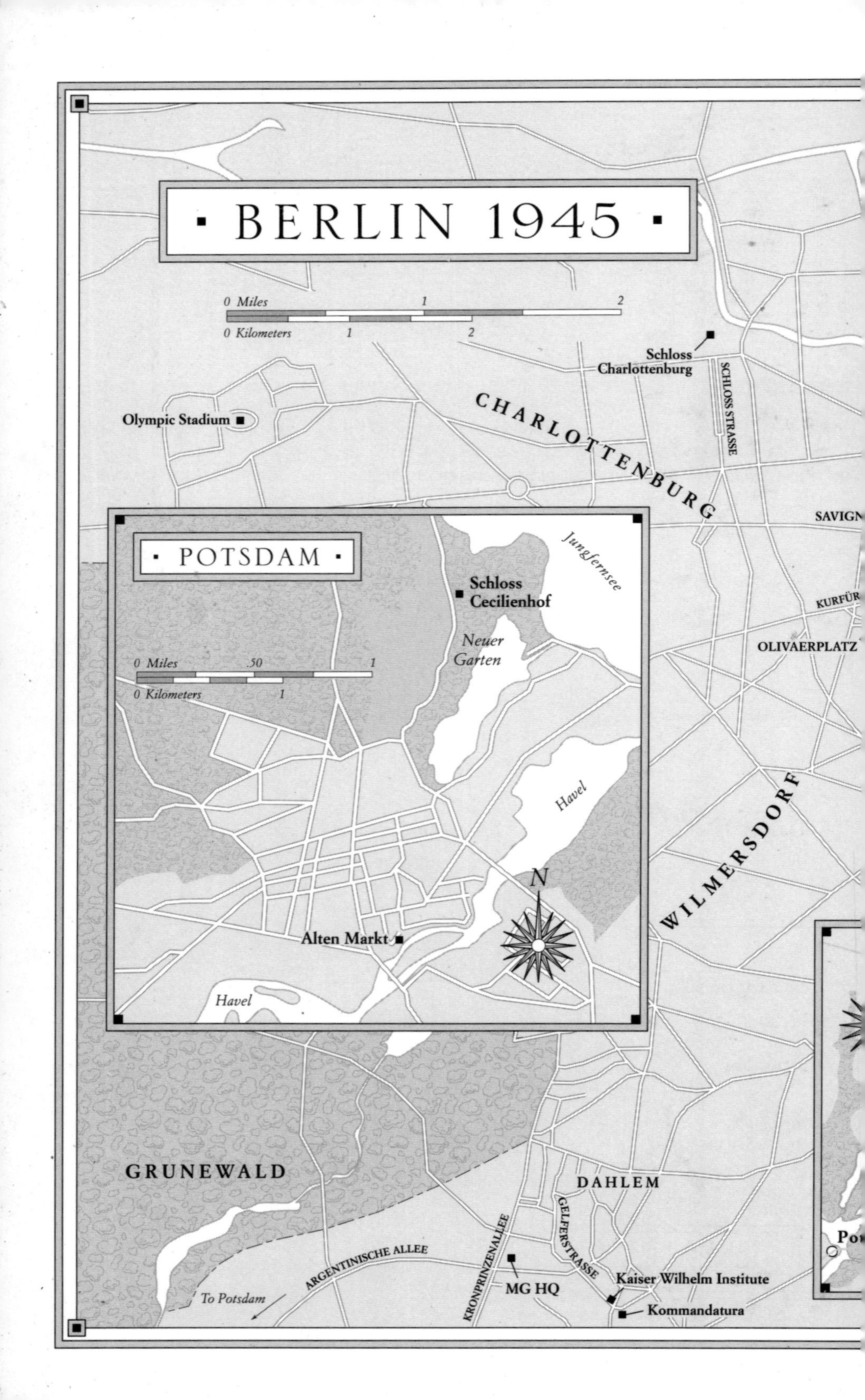

BERLIN 1945
0 Miles 1 2
0 Kilometers 1 2
Schloss Charlottenburg
SCHLOSS STRASSE
Olympic Stadium
CHARLOTTENBURG
SAVIGN
KURFÜR
OLIVAERPLATZ
WILMERSDORF
POTSDAM
Jungfernsee
Schloss Cecilienhof
Neuer Garten
0 Miles .50 1
0 Kilometers 1
Havel
N
Alten Markt
Havel
GRUNEWALD
DAHLEM
GELFERSTRASSE
KRONPRINZENALLEE
ARGENTINISCHE ALLEE
MG HQ
Kaiser Wilhelm Institute
Kommandatura
To Potsdam